ENGULFING DARKNESS . . .
MURDEROUS RAGE . . .
A BLIND INSTINCT TO SURVIVE . . .

"They twisted and shoved, desperate gasps jerking from their mouths. The attacker flexed his shoulder to break Bogart's manic grip and took another vicious swipe. . . . Confused, fearful, Bogart stepped back, colliding against a hand-carved coffee table. All arms and legs, he landed agonizingly on his back. He rolled, knowing he had only one chance . . . one chance before the dark figure bludgeoned him to death. . . ."

BOGART '48

John Stanley and Kenn Davis

A DELL BOOK

Published by
Dell Publishing Co., Inc.
1 Dag Hammarskjold Plaza
New York, New York 10017

Acknowledgments
Lyrics from "Lullabye of Broadway" (Lyric by Al Dubin;
Music by Harry Warren): © 1935 Warner Bros. Inc.
Copyright renewed. All rights reserved.

Lyrics from "And Her Tears Flowed Like Wine" (Words
—Joe Greene; Music— Stan Kenton & Charles Lawrence):
© 1944. Renewed 1973 by Knollwood Music Corp. Used
by permission. All rights reserved. © 1944 Robbins Music
Corporation N.Y. Used by permission.

Dell ® TM 681510, Dell Publishing Co., Inc.

ISBN: 0-440-10853-5

Printed in the United States of America

First printing—February 1980

**Dedicated
To all the Bogart fans
in the world**

"I don't care what anybody says about me as long as it isn't true."
—HUMPHREY BOGART

PROLOGUE

With the forward thrust of 1,720,253 registered motor vehicles along 5,464.63 miles of streets, expressways, alleys and trails, the City of Angels had become a breeding ground for devils-on-wheels.

At 8 A.M. the crossroads of Sunset and Figueroa were a nightmare of congestion, where roughly 117 cars per minute squeezed past the ever-changing stoplights.

The sullen, gray-faced man at the wheel of the black 1946 Cadillac coupe was an excellent driver, yet even he miscalculated as he slid up behind a green 1934 Chevrolet parked at the intersection and accidentally nudged its rear bumper.

But it might have been a head-on collision, judging from the way the owner of the Chevy leaped out and stormed toward the Cadillac. The muscles of his thickset arms bulged. His face was swollen and flushed when he reached the Cadillac's window and accused its driver with glaring eyes.

The driver refused to acknowledge the glare—just continued to scrutinize the Chevy as though admiring its peeling paint job and well-worn tires. His window was rolled down so he had no trouble hearing the thickset man over the idling engines.

"You blind, Mac?" raged the Chevy owner. "You trying to—" He couldn't continue because his mouth had dropped open. For several moments he stood stock still.

Finally, heavily apologetic, "I didn't know . . ." The bluster went out of him, like air rushing from a

punctured balloon. His face flushed with embarrassment. "I'm sorry. Hey, listen, I wonder if . . ." He
fumbled through his pockets and produced a ragged
scrap of paper. He unfolded the crumbling sheet,
thrusting it and a stub of pencil toward the Cadillac
driver. "Do you mind . . . the kids would love it . . .
just say 'To Eddie.' "

The Cadillac driver finally shifted his blank stare to
the Chevy owner. He said nothing, but morosely accepted the paper and scribbled words, almost savagely, as the thickset man rattled on: "Nothing to
worry about. Couldn't have been any serious damage.
We'll just forget the whole thing."

The red arm of the stop signal dropped, to be replaced by a green arm with Go written across it. Some
wise guy had written TO HELL beneath it in block letters.

The driver thrust the paper back to the Chevy
owner, gave him one final, irascible stare, then shot
the Cadillac around the idling Chevy.

The thickset man's mouth was still hanging open as
he unfolded the battered paper and read the inscrip-
tion:

To Eddie —

Kiss my Ass!

Humphrey Bogart

DAY ONE

Tuesday, March 16, 1948

BOMB HIDDEN ABOARD SCHOOL BUS KILLS 12 ISRAELI CHILDREN AND WOUNDS SIX ON THE OUTSKIRTS OF TEL AVIV . . .

PRESIDENT TRUMAN ORDERS FEDERAL AGENCIES TO TURN DOWN REQUESTS FROM CONGRESS ON LOYALTY INVESTIGATIONS OF GOVERNMENT EMPLOYEES . . .

TWENTIETH CENTURY-FOX THEATER CHAIN ACCUSES COMMUNIST PARTY FOR FEBRUARY 20TH BOMB BLAST IN THE LOBBY OF THE SAN FRANCISCO FOX THEATER. SPOKESMEN CLAIM BLAST IS RETALIATORY ACT TO RELEASE OF NEW FOX MOTION PICTURE *The Iron Curtain.*

LEO F. FORBSTEIN, 56, MUSICAL DIRECTOR AT WARNER BROTHERS FOR TWENTY-TWO YEARS, SUFFERS SEVERE HEART ATTACK AND IS ADMITTED TO CEDARS OF LEBANON HOSPITAL.

HUMPHREY BOGART MAKES PLANS TO RACE IN THIS YEAR'S HONOLULU YACHT RACE. LAST YEAR HE SPENT $10,000 ON NEW SAILS AND EQUIPMENT FOR HIS YAWL, THE *Santana.*

ONE

Standing in the shadow of a sandstone rock formation that angled almost vertically into the sky, two men faced each other, oblivious to the film production crew milling around them.

Johnny Hawks, the younger and taller of the two, planted his feet firmly in the sun-scorched soil and clenched his fists. He hated to pull his punches. Especially with a man he despised as much as Ernie Leach.

"Anytime you're ready, big shot," rasped Leach, a ramrod of muscle and gunmetal-gray eyes.

Hawks led with his right, crossing an inch in front of Leach's jawbone. Leach automatically snapped his head back and stumbled away, slamming realistically against the base of the pocked boulder that formed part of Vasquez Rocks.

Hawks threw himself onto the balls of his feet and feigned another right cross, then a flurry of punches . . . just as they had choreographed it, only now each swing missed by less than an inch and Hawks could see new defiance in Leach's eyes, his face locked in its perpetual sneer and his body rigidly tense. Hawks pretended one final powerhouse punch and Leach sprawled to the ground, growling, "And that's when I take the dive. Right, big shot?"

Hawks lowered his fists. He dusted his hands on his leather chaps and corduroy jeans and adjusted the cartridge belt tied to his lean hips, making certain the tie-down thongs were tight around his thighs. He checked the single-action 1872 Colt, dropping it into the holster. That the action of *Raiders of the Badlands* took place in 1867 bothered no one, least of all the firearms technical advisor.

Hawks was a rawboned actor of twenty-seven who seldom allowed personal problems to interfere with his work. Yet his mind kept returning to early that morning. He had been getting ready to leave the apartment when he heard something heavy dropping in the garage below. He had found the sliding door ajar, the lock cut open. The hood of the Oldsmobile was unlatched. A check of the engine revealed the generator wires cut, their insulation stripped away to shiny copper ends. Next to the engine block, under the generator, he found strips of black electrical tape.

It was obvious someone had been interrupted in the act of wiring a bomb.

Fear had clung to Hawks as he drove the fifty miles from Malibu to the Vasquez Rocks location site. Halfway there, his hands had begun to tremble. He was certain his unknown caller was somehow linked to the screenplay.

It had to be the screenplay.

He was sorry now he had ever read *Hollywood Armageddon*. He wished he had never carried the copy away and then snooped around in dangerous places . . .

Now somebody wanted him dead!

Hawks and Leach paused to drink lemonade from a cooler while the movie cast and crew moved in lazy rhythm around them.

A steady parade of actors went to and from the portable dressing rooms and honey wagon. Bored extras played pinochle or read *Variety*. Wranglers in faded jeans and denims unloaded skitterish horses from trailers while electricians and grips maneuvered to avoid fresh piles of manure. A man in buckskin chatted with another man in buffalo wraps and war bonnet. Makeup artists powdered shiny noses and turned lips into sun-blistered puffs of flesh.

Lew Landers, a prolific B-picture director, strode up to Hawks and Leach. "Okay, boys, you know the routine. We've only got enough film to shoot it once, so let's get it right the first time. Now remember, Leach, when you go over the cliff, give us that graceful, realistic look."

"Graceful," repeated Hawks, "but don't flap your arms."

Leach's reply was cut short by Landers. "For Chrissake get it right, boys, or Sam'll blow his top."

"Goddamn right I will." The booming voice belonged to Sam Katzman, a dapper, rotund man wearing a vulgar sports shirt, white pants with matching loafers and a two-tone fedora. As he strutted toward Landers, the producer supported himself on a cane with a handle in the shape of a fist with forefingers extended. A cigar was thrust into Katzman's mouth. "It's almost eight o'clock and we ain't got but one shot in the can so far."

Hawks bent over to wipe the dust from his squared-toed cowboy boots. He had worked often enough for Katzman to know that the producer prided himself on "big little productions" that were brought in on budget—and on time. All that finally mattered to Katzman and his boss, Harry Cohn, was the almighty box-office dollar.

Leach scrambled up the rock and Landers returned to the camera crew, which was huddled around the Mitchell camera like a team of doctors probing a wealthy patient.

"Look, Sam," said Hawks, his voice hardening, "it's

been nearly a month since we last talked about my idea. I think it's time—"

Katzman scowled. "You talking about that 'Purloined Letter' idea you want to produce for Basil Rathbone? Forget it, Johnny. Your problem is, you've got the bug. Every guy who makes a little dent in Hollywood wants to produce pictures."

"This idea could elevate you into class pictures, Sam."

"Show me a class picture," growled Katzman, "and I'll show you an empty theater. Johnny, forget this artsy-craftsy crap. Hell, I've yet to see an Oscar that didn't have an ulcer. Besides, Poe's been dead too long. What you need is a topical story. Keep 'em topical and you'll keep their glands happy. Send your pal Rathbone around to see me; maybe I can give him a part in my next picture."

Landers returned to say the camera was ready. Hawks smoothed his sandy hair and adjusted his stained Stetson as Sam prodded him with the handle of the cane. "Don't forget, Johnny, one take."

"Yeah," said Landers, "once Ernie drops, turn in profile to the camera and draw your thunderstick."

"Hot damn," interjected Katzman, "that'll put you against that clear blue sky. That'll look great in Cinecolor."

"When you turn," continued Landers, "that's when Edmundsen hits the special charges."

"Don't flinch, Johnny," warned Katzman. "Hell, bullets don't faze Luke Ankers. You're determined to stop the feud and help the dirt farmers." Katzman flicked the dangling ash from his cigar. "You keep going like you ain't scared of nothing, kid. There's no bullet made that can stop Luke Ankers."

Fighting back his frustration, Hawks followed

Leach's trail toward the highest peak of Vasquez Rocks, a freakish formation thrown up by the San Andreas Fault millions of years ago. The namesake of a Mexican bandido who once used it as his hideout, Vasquez now served as a picturesque background for countless Westerns, sword-and-sandal epics and Khyber Pass action films.

As he climbed, Hawks brooded. *Raiders of the Badlands,* he told himself, was hardly destined to become a classic. His role as Luke Ankers, wandering cowboy caught up in a bloody range war, was stereotyped and would do nothing to promote him into better pictures. Still, he had to consider this a part of his learning process if he was ever to become a producer.

Then there were the words of Humphrey Bogart, often repeated to him during their weekend cruises on the *Santana*: "Take all the parts they offer you, kid. If you're good, you'll stand out. You'll be noticed. If you're bad . . . well, hell, you've had some fun and made some dough."

Hawks paused on the slanting face of the rock to watch Edmundsen, the special-effects man, drill two holes in the sandstone and then insert shiny copper wiring into small explosive charges. The detonating wires trailed off to a large outcropping where Edmundsen would remain out of camera range.

Hawks turned to watch the cast and crew surrounding Vasquez. Grips manning large silver reflectors shifted position to watch the ever-shifting sun and train light on the actors. Beyond the furthest reflector, a stagecoach driver practiced cracking his bullwhip. Johnny had to shield his eyes from the glare of the half-dozen reflectors.

For a moment Hawks felt a sense of pleasure at being detached from the frenzied activity below . . .

but then he recalled the unlatched hood of his Oldsmobile and a new chilliness, not entirely due to the Santa Ana wind at this height, washed over him.

Far off to the side of the camera crew, where he had parked the Oldsmobile, Johnny's eye was caught by a brief flash.

A small reflector?

Landers waved that the camera team was ready.

Leach hurried from the tip of the rock and took a position near Hawks. Below Leach, out of camera range, were a heap of broken cardboard boxes and several sagging mattresses.

Hawks signaled to Landers that they were ready.

Once again the two men faced each other.

Leach's face became a snarl. "You punk big-shot actors give me a royal pain. You all think you're great fucking producers."

"Shut up, Leach," snapped Hawks. "I'm sick of you."

"You're no producer, big shot. Never will be—"

It wasn't Landers's cry for action that set Hawks into motion. He darted in angrily, stepping surefootedly and lashing out for Leach's face.

This time he didn't pull his punches.

But Leach was too experienced a stuntman. Instinctively he snapped his head away to avoid Johnny's fist. Leach's return swing landed clumsily on Hawks's cheek. Hawks slid on the irregular sandstone but kept his balance. He delivered a left to Leach's stomach, then whipped a right into his chest.

Leach's bullish face was red with bewilderment. He lashed out again, aiming for Hawks's nose. The actor bobbed and drove pistonlike jabs into Leach's midriff. The next swing felt even better to Hawks as it ground into Leach's jaw.

Leach's backward momentum was too great. He

plunged over the ledge, arms flailing, and thudded into the mattresses with a grunt, the air knocked from his body by the imperfect landing.

His anger satisfied, Hawks reached for the Colt handgun, turning away from the ledge to silhouette himself in profile. Two steps, sliding on the pitted surface, and he had placed himself between the explosive charges.

KRAK.

A geyser of sandstone and dust shot up to his right. Hawks ducked instinctively.

The small reflector glinted again.

KRAK.

The second charge exploded near his left boot. He slipped on loose stone and scrambled for footing. It was a minor miscalculation, but one which he knew would look good on film.

KA-POW.

The Colt was blown from his grasp.

Hawks felt a searing pain across the back of his right hand and he heard something richocheting from the sandstone. As he dropped, his only thought was that he had ruined the scene.

He clung to the sandstone, flat on his stomach, numb with shock. He watched blankly as blood flowed from his hand. Trembling, he squirmed to a protective outcropping. From beneath the ledge came Leach's accusing voice: "That bastard hit me. He really hit me."

Katzman was only halfway up the rock, his short legs pumping crazily, when Landers reached Hawks. "Damn it," he swore, "we had it perfect until you flipped away the pistol— What the hell . . . is that blood, Johnny?"

"I've been shot, Lew."

Katzman arrived, red-faced and blustering. "You knew we needed that take, Johnny. Now Leach has to fall again. Know how much a fall costs these days?" Then Katzman saw the blood. "Sonofabitch."

Hawks tore the red-checkered bandana from around his neck and wrapped the injured hand. "I been shot, Sam."

"Maybe it was a richochet from the charges," said Katzman.

"Richochet, shit. There was a third shot. I heard it."

Landers turned angrily on Edmundsen. "How many charges did you plant? If you overloaded those—"

"Christ, Lew, I know my job. Two charges, as tiny as you can make 'em."

Hawks scurried off the rock, ignoring Katzman's startled face. Katzman's mouth was still hanging open, his cigar at his feet, as Hawks knocked over a reflector and leaped into the yellow Oldsmobile. And sped away.

"Where the hell's he going?" asked Landers.

"On the unemployment list," said Katzman, picking up the cigar, wiping flakes of dust from it, and replacing it in his mouth.

Nothing ever went to waste on a Sam Katzman picture.

"I'm sorry, Mr. Hawks, but Mr. Cohn is in a meeting with Mr. Rossen and doesn't—"

"Break in, Liz, for God's sake. I'm bleeding all over the floor."

"Just a moment . . ."

". . . Johnny? You're gonna be bleeding a lot worse if I get my hands on you. Where the hell are you?".

"In a store. Near Vasquez."

"You're not on the set? Goddamn it, I'm spending millions and you're—"

"Fuck *Raiders of the Badlands*, Harry. Someone just tried to kill me. Took a shot at me at Vasquez Rocks."

"Christ, you're serious."

"Harry, do you remember a screenplay called *Hollywood Armageddon?*"

"Hollywood . . . Do I! But what the hell's that got to do with you?"

"Harry, I've got proof that the guy who wrote it intends to carry out the script, step by bloody step."

"Wait a minute. What guy?"

"The author. Blake Richards."

"Jesus H. Christ, Johnny. Have you lost your mind?"

"I'm gonna lose my life if you don't give me protection."

"Calm down, Johnny, just calm down . . . Richards . . . I'm trying to remember the guy. Hell, Johnny, I never met Richards. Bogart dropped the script on my desk . . ."

"Bogart did what?"

"Yeah, he asked me to read the thing as a personal fucking favor. Back in—when the hell was it? . . . yeah, '44."

"Harry, I've got proof to back up my story and I'm coming in. Maybe Bogart can help us straighten out this mess. But I'm not going back to Vasquez and get shot at again. Harry, you gotta protect me."

"All right, Johnny, all right. Calm the fuck down. We'll diaper your ass. I don't leave my contract players in the lurch—no matter how bad the dailies look. Get your young ass back to L.A. and come right up to my office. We'll work this thing out. Fucking right we will."

"Thanks, Harry, I won't forget this. You'll smooth things out with Katzman?"

"Katzman can go fuck himself . . ."

Johnny Hawks felt a new surge of vitality as the cold air rushed past his face. He felt in control again.

The road east was empty; the speedometer held steadily at sixty miles per hour. His hands were gripping the steering wheel calmly as he eased into a horseshoe turn two miles from the Vasquez General Store.

To his left, on a low hillside, sunlight flashed off metal.

The icy touch of fear which had stricken him at Vasquez pricked at his scalp.

Impulsively he stomped the accelerator, then realized he was traveling too fast around the bend. The edge of the road came up under his front wheel and the car bounced violently. Slid. A yard beyond the shoulder the ground sloped sharply into a drainage ditch. Hawks pumped the brakes, fighting down a new surge of panic.

The Oldsmobile slowed and once again he was gaining control of the wheel. The front tires bounced over stones and slithered along the edge of the shoulder, spewing gravel and dust. The front fender slammed against a diamond-shaped road sign and the upper half spun into the ditch.

Hawks had the car completely under control when the first bullet hit dead center in the windshield, shattering the glass in spidery trails that obscured his view. He was aware of a "plop" as the slug buried itself in the upholstery.

He spun the wheel crazily. The car fishtailed.

The second bullet richocheted off the door interior and grazed Hawks's rib cage.

He told himself none of this was happening. It was all an illusion, a movie.

And then he released the steering wheel, clutched at his side and blacked out.

The Oldsmobile ran against the embankment, leaped over the shoulder at twenty miles an hour and careened into the drainage ditch. Metal screeched against unyielding hardpan and glass shattered as the car settled over onto its right side.

Hawks had no way of knowing how long he had been unconscious but he assumed it had been only a minute or less, for dust was still drifting in a large cloud from the point of impact; he could hear the lazy spinning of wheels. He pulled his hand away from his ribs. His fingers felt sticky. He saw they were smeared with blood. The slight gnawing pain in his side was beginning to intensify. His labored breath seemed louder than the eerie sound of the Olds's engine sickishly turning over.

He groped for the handle of the door, shoving it open with a grunt of pain. He kept it open with his foot. With each labored movement, new waves of pain shot to his brain.

Finally he was out and sprawled at the foot of the ditch. From there the Oldsmobile looked like some giant yellow beetle that had been flipped on its side.

None of this is real, Hawks repeated to himself as though that would make it all go away. I'm at the movies . . . I'm dreaming or I'm . . .

Footsteps crunched in gravel at road level. Hawks twisted in their direction, clutching his wounded ribs.

Someone was coming over the lip of the embankment.

He carried a rifle in his arms.

He cradled it affectionately.

The rifle swung toward Hawks.

That movement was the last thing Johnny Hawks ever saw.

TWO

The City of Angels gagged on its own offal. Oil refineries, foundries and open-hearth steel plants spewed 800 tons of gaseous waste into the atmosphere.

As he wheeled his Cadillac along Hollywood Boulevard, Humphrey DeForest Bogart felt nauseous. He also felt the urgent need for a cigarette and fumbled in his coat pocket. It was a habitual, and ritualistic, procedure: He slid a Chesterfield between his lips, cupped four fingers of his left hand against the wind and lit up. He drew in the smoke and savored it, the smog and erratic drivers momentarily forgotten.

"... *weekend storm brought point seventy-one inches in rain, breaking a drought that has plagued southern California for several months* ..."

The radio blared on but his mind remained fixed on the lines of dialogue from *Key Largo* he would have to recite later that morning.

"... *meanwhile we can expect additional light showers later this afternoon, with a low of 44 and a high of 62.*"

Bogart's face was forty-eight years long. It had the look of a battlefield after the debris has been washed away by rain. The slightly damaged right corner of his upper lip gave his mouth a certain unnaturalness that had become a permanent part of his saturnine face. The penetrating brown eyes were bloodshot; his hair was clipped short and well combed.

Bogart brushed ashes away from his gray-striped slacks that were neither tailored nor stylish. He also wore a plain white shirt without a tie, unbuttoned at the throat, a threadbare tweed jacket and his *Casablanca* brown shoes that he had pressed into the wet cement outside Grauman's Chinese Theatre in 1946.

He barely heard the fanfare for a commercial on the forthcoming Tucker automobile, nor the voice of Art Mooney as he began a rendition of "I'm Looking Over a Four-Leaf Clover."

Hollywood seemed a smog-shrouded phantom as he approached "the boulevard"—a business district in central Hollywood carelessly composed of expensive shops, cheap novelty stores and overpriced restaurants.

It was enough to make him feel sick again.

Near Hollywood and Vine, Bogart turned onto Ivar and parked in front of the Knickerbocker Hotel. With its clientele of rich entertainers, the Knickerbocker was one of movieland's poshest residences; yet Bogart still referred to it as a joint. To him it symbolized the phony opulence and all-too-real decadence of that part of Hollywood he most despised.

Bogart crossed the ornate oval lobby stuffed with Provincial furniture and early American antiques. An aging elevator operator with sunken cheeks held the door, shooting off his stool as though a commanding officer, not an actor, had just entered.

"Another nice Tuesday morning, Mr. Bogart."

"Only if you happen to be wearing a gas mask." Bogart flipped open his wallet and pressed a twenty into the old man's palm. "Simpson, make sure my pal Griff gets something to drink with the meals he never eats."

"It'll be 'tended to, Mr. Bogart."

Bogart found himself alone in a lengthy, carpeted corridor. He knocked lightly on 301 and waited.

No response. He knocked again.

The sound of stockinged feet . . . the door opened

a fraction, hesitantly. A face appeared, scrutinized Bogart with suspicion, then disappeared as a chain was unslid. The door yawned just wide enough for Bogart to slide through.

The smell of cheap gin turned Bogart's stomach as he hurried to a window and threw it open. He worked his way back through the clutter, angling past stacks of yellowing *Times*es, heaps of unwashed clothes, ashtrays brimming with cigarette butts and a table littered with empty gin bottles. The refuse almost concealed the Old English furniture and bountiful fixtures.

Bogart tried to put the smell of gin out of his mind and focus on the seventy-three-year-old man before him. "You look rotten, Griff," he said accusingly. A far cry from the father of Hollywood film directors, he thought.

David Wark Griffith wore wrinkled blue-striped pajamas, deteriorating leather slippers and a scowl aimed at Bogart. Griffith's face was hollow and sunken, his thin white hair uncombed, his chin grizzled with beard. His breath, Bogart noted sadly, reeked.

Griffith was also very drunk.

He scratched crudely at his long nose and staggered toward Bogart, muttering that Bogart needed a drink.

"You know how I feel about getting bagged when I'm working."

Griffith's upper lip pulled into a tighter grimace. "Since when were films work?"

"Someone thinks so. I get paid money."

"You're one of the few who's worth it. You've learned your art. You're the best of the present generation. Me, I belong to the silent era. And you know how dead that is."

"You haven't done so badly," said Bogart, smiling.

"You started out as an impatient, impetuous, brash young man. Now you're an impatient, impetuous, brash old fart."

"An old fart who made 443 pictures in his time. Those were the days when five hundred feet of film was a big deal. Ten exciting minutes of moving objects. We didn't waste in my day. Now they shoot scenes they never use. Hundreds of thousands of dollars for a storm at sea in *Green Dolphin Street,* completely cut from the final print. I read it in *Life.*"

"Any mail?" asked Bogart. "Any phone calls?"

Griffith shook his head, then negotiated a perilous path through the room's debris to a stack of 16-millimeter film cans. "I suppose you want something for next weekend."

"*Birth of a Nation.*"

"You've borrowed it twice already."

"And I'll borrow it again. It's a classic."

"To you and the rest of the world who don't know any better."

"You trying to tell me that picture didn't help your career?" It was a question in the form of a challenge—a Bogart trait.

"Helped my career." Griffith laughed ironically in short bursts. "Oh yes, indeed. It's what a picture does to your insides—that's what determines whether it's worth a damn or not. The investors kicked me out when the picture lost money. That's all you feel after a while—the kick."

"All right," acquiesced Bogart, "forget *Birth of a Nation.* I'll take a print of *Intolerance.*"

"Now there was an epic, Bogie. Three yarns unraveling simultaneously. Full-scale battles. The Palace of Belshazzar, King of Babylon, biggest set ever designed . . ." Griffith fell back into the chair, settling into a stack of *Life* magazines. "But it was a disaster from the outset. Cost one point seven million and that was in 1916. You shoulda heard 'em holler when the box office grosses didn't start to roll in . . . That's how you remember a picture, Bogie, by what it does to your stomach. Movies? Hah."

Bogart sensed a drowsiness settling over Griffith and realized the director had already downed most of a fifth since his arrival.

". . . all ass backward. Should be a form of expression, the movies. As powerful as the printed word, but more alert and agile. Power for good and evil never denied . . ."

Griffith's head sank onto his chest and the glass rolled out of his fingers and thumped gently on the carpet. He was snoring by the time Bogart reached the stack of movie tins. It took only a minute to find *Birth of a Nation,* then he hurried to the door, unfastened the chain, stepped outside and pulled the door tightly shut. He was turning when he heard the phone ring.

It rang twice before he realized it was coming from Griffith's apartment. "Griff," he shouted, pounding the door. "Hey, Griff, your phone."

It continued to ring and Bogart continued to pound frenetically, but all he aroused was an irate neighbor who threatened to call the management until he recognized Bogart and let the matter drop.

The phone stopped ringing.

"Damn," muttered Bogart. This is the Hollywood jungle, he told himself. If you don't fight the bastards, Griff, you can't win. Nobody in this town is his brother's keeper. Nobody owes anybody anything. What the hell is Hollywood but an abstraction.

But he didn't believe a syllable of it.

THREE

"I've said it before, I'll say it again: I'm no Communist—but if I were, it's nobody's business but my own. I owe the public nothing but a good performance." Bogart leaned back in his canvas chair, listening with a part of his mind to the muted sound-stage sounds outside the open doorway of his bungalow dressing room.

"Now, Bogie," said Hedda Hopper in her unctuous tone, "you took that trip to Washington last year to protest the House Un-American Activities Committee hearings leveled against Hollywood."

"So what? I've admitted it was probably a foolish thing to do. I went there because I honestly felt good Americans were being deprived of their constitutional rights. And that's a damn good reason for sticking your neck out."

Bogart watched as Hopper wrote rapidly in her note pad with a pencil sharpened to a needle point.

An accurate reflection of her own personality, Bogart thought.

Hedda Hopper was about fifty-seven, slightly over five foot seven, a trim 125 pounds. She sat opposite Bogart wearing a silk moire dress, bangly jewelry at her wrists and gaudy pearls around her neck. Topping off her ensemble was her trademark: a ludicrous wide-brimmed hat of woven linen, covered in grapes and red cherries and crowned with a shiny, baroque-tied scarlet ribbon.

She looked at Bogart. "Then you don't believe that the Communists are a threat to the American way of life?"

"There is no *one* American way." Bogart lit a cigarette, four fingers cupping it. "When people believe that any foreign ideology can overcome their heritage, then their own system has failed. *I* don't think our system has failed, Hedda. Is that why you think the Communists are going to take over?"

Inwardly, Bogart smiled. Hopper's phony condescension couldn't hide her lack of original thought. He also knew she employed a staff of eight to do her legwork and write her columns. Her gossip-mongering was a vacuous career at best. It was inconceivable to Bogart that millions of newspaper readers pored each morning over her tidbits, innuendoes and bitchy comments.

Hopper straightened her hat, as if this would steer the conversation in another direction. "What about this year's crop of nominated films, Bogie? Many people consider them un-American."

Bogart leaned forward. "Hedda, I'm in favor of controversial films. I think that a movie like *Gentleman's Agreement* should be seen by every thinking American. The other liberal films, too. *Crossfire*, for one."

The phone on the end table rang.

"Yeah?" asked Bogart.

"Mr. Bogart, this is the studio switchboard . . . we have an urgent call for you from Mr. Harry Cohn."

"I'm not in, sweetheart. Not to Cohn. That guy would slice his mother's heart out for the right deal." He hung up.

Her pencil had become slightly dull, so Hopper changed to another needle-sharp point. "I'm surprised. I thought you and Harry Cohn were on good terms since making *Sahara*."

"We were on good terms until last year. John Lawson, the man who wrote *Sahara*, came under fire during the HUAC hearings. When Cohn refused to speak in John's behalf, I blew my stack."

"Lawson? Wasn't he indicted? One of the Hollywood Ten?"

"Thank Cohn for that. Another career down the drain. It could happen to any of us. Even you, Hedda."

Hopper scribbled. "That's an impossible thought." She laughed, tossing her brown hair and flashing her green eyes.

She adjusted the brim of her outrageous hat over one eye. "Now, what about your life with Betty?"

Bogart relaxed; Hopper had dropped to safe and easy ground. "Betty's in New York with her mother. She needed a break after working on *Key Largo*. Betty hasn't seen her mother for a while, and this gives me some free time."

"How does it feel to be Hollywood's highest paid actor?"

"I've survived in a very tough, very competitive business. I keep working, people keep coming to see me. I'm a Scaramouche, remember, getting everyone else in trouble. I like sticking pins in balloons. In Hollywood there are more overinflated, phony, self-important balloons than anywhere."

"You're going into independent production for yourself. I'm certain my readers would want to know how that's working out."

"Santana Productions. Morgan Maree, my business manager, put the company together. I was planning to go into partnership with Mark Hellinger, but as you know, he died suddenly."

"What's your first picture?" she asked keenly.

"Willard Motley's *Knock On Any Door*. Hellinger had some terrific casting suggestions: Me as the defense attorney, Jennifer Jones as my wife, and that young actor from New York . . . the one with the odd name—Marlon Brando—as the kid on trial."

The phone rang again.

"Mr. Bogart, this is the switchboard again—"

"Yeah, what is it this—"

"Bogie," a harsh voice interrupted, *"this is Cohn. Goddamn it, don't you hang up on me!"*

"Go to hell, Harry, and if you phone again—"

"Johnny Hawks is dead!"

A cold chill swept over Bogart.

"What was that again, Harry?"

"He was shot. Murdered."

Bogart looked blankly at the phone. "I'll talk . . . I'll talk to you later . . ." He dropped the phone into its cradle.

Hedda Hopper looked curiously at Bogart, but he barely acknowledged her.

"Bad news, Bogie?"

Bogart didn't reply, just stared down at the receiver.

Hopper shrugged and collected her note pad. "I've got a deadline to beat. I'd better be going."

He was distantly aware of her leaving, distantly aware of her walking across the sound stage and passing through the large doors to the outside.

Johnny . . . It didn't seem possible. It had only been two weekends ago that Johnny and Dewey Martin had crewed for him aboard the *Santana*.

A production assistant popped a smiling face through the doorway. "Five minutes, Mr. Bogart. The set's about ready."

Bogart didn't answer. He stood, hooked his thumbs along the top of the narrow belt of his slacks and made his way toward the set.

Bogart was barely aware of the familiar territory.

The sounds of carpenters and electricians came through a hazy mind. Unconsciously he stepped around cables and light stands. He had been on countless sound stages, countless sets where he had memorized thousands of lines.

How many times had the word *murder* been used?

"Hi, Bogie." A carpenter.

"Looks like rain today, Bogie." A makeup assistant.

"Retakes are no fun, are they, Bogie?" A camera assistant.

Bogart stood at the edge of a rim of light bathing the set, a bathroom in a Florida Keys hotel. The fascination, the awareness of illusion crept into Bogart's mind. Slowly the men and women functioning on the set lost their shadowland quality and became living beings.

"A half-scrim on that key, Lee!" The voice echoed through the vast, hangarlike cavern of the sound stage. Bogart watched as Lee Wilson, the head electrician, signaled his men high in the rafters. One of them dropped an open-wire mesh screen in front of a ten-thousand-watt light.

Karl Freund checked the light level with his Norwood meter, glancing at the quality and quantity of light splashed over the walls and furniture. It was to Freund's satisfaction: 150 footcandles covering most of the set.

Bogart walked to the edge of darkness and tried to shake off the feeling of intense melancholia without success.

His memory continued to prick him with scenes of Johnny on board the *Santana*, along with the undigestible fact of his death. Bogart unconsciously rolled and rubbed the ruby ring on the third finger of his right hand.

Death. It was certainly no stranger to Bogart. He twisted the ring as he remembered his father, who had given him the ring on his deathbed, fourteen years ago.

Beyond the immediate shadows, beyond the Mole-Richardson lamps, were fifty or more electricians, carpenters, set decorators, painters, plasterers and property masters.

Hawks would have loved it.

Nearby was the camera crew, bustling with the heavy Mitchell, wheeling it closer onto the set. It was strange to realize that Bogart's career had been made by the camera, a single piece of man-made machinery. Without it, he would have none of the things he had come to appreciate. Money. Recognition. Prestige.

The camera was his lifeline.

Just as it had been Hawks's lifeline.

Bogart watched distractedly as craggy, horse-faced John Huston scrubbed at a shock of dark hair that fell over one brow and conferred with Freund, who accepted a chilled martini from his assistant.

Bogart and Hawks had discussed the relationship, almost a love affair, between actors and the camera.

Each little frame of film a piece of reality set aside for preservation. Bits of time. Frozen motion.

Who would want to kill Johnny Hawks?

Suddenly the assistant cameraman closed the blimp door. The thumping sound broke Bogart's chain of thought; he was back on the sound stage, ready to work.

Bogart walked to his canvas chair with *Tiller of the Ship* stenciled on the backrest sling. Nearby sat Edward G. Robinson, idly leafing through the February issue of *Art News*.

"Hey, Bogie, ready for more?" he asked in his gravelly voice.

"What? Oh, yeah, Eddie. How did the shooting go?"

"Huston decided to come in tight on the fan, then pull the camera back to show me sitting in the bathtub fulla suds, reading the racing news. That's a much better introduction to the Rocco character than just coming down the stairs."

Bogart turned as Huston walked up.

"Listen, boys," Huston said in his slow drawl, rolling the rs. "We think scene fifty-one needs more intimacy. Just between you two, McCloud and Rocco. Rudy Fehr agrees with me. It'll cut with more impact."

"Sure," Robinson said. "Anything you say, John."

The two actors went to their respective marks. The camera crew maneuvered in the McAllister dolly. Freund sipped his martini, keeping a critical eye on the key lights.

"Sound," Huston called.

"Speed," replied the sound recordist.

The microphone-boom man lowered the mike close to the clapper man standing in front of the lens. The clapper man raised the lid of the marking slate: "*Key Largo*. Scene fifty-one, take six." He dropped the bar, which made a loud clacking sound on the slate, then dodged out of camera range. The boom man swung the microphone above Robinson and Bogart.

"Camera," called Huston.

"Rolling," replied the camera operator.

"Action!"

Bogart and Robinson held their respective poses, getting back into the roles of the disillusioned returning war veteran and the fascistic gangster, Johnny Rocco.

"Do you know what you want, Rocco?" asked McCloud/Bogart.

There was a pause. "Sure. I want . . . I want . . ."

"You want more, isn't that it, Ricco?"

"Cut," called Huston. "That's Rocco, Bogie. Let's try it again."

The clapper and scene routine were repeated. Bogart fluffed his line. Huston stepped up to Bogart, who stared out into the darkness beyond the lights.

"What's the matter, Bogie?"

Bogart lifted his eyes and saw puzzled looks on many of the crew. *Damn it*, he told himself. "Let's do it again, John." Bogart turned the ruby ring just once.

The clapper man went through his routine.

"Do you know what you want, Rocco?" asked McCloud.

Robinson paused once more. "Sure. I want . . . I want . . ."

Bogart snarled. "You want more, don't you, Rocco?"

"Yeah," boasted Rocco/Robinson, with a catch of gleeful understanding. "That's it, I want more. More of everything."

The camera was moved behind and lower than Bogart's shoulder, looking slightly upward at Robinson. The entire process would commence again, with Bogart's back to the camera. Robinson's close-ups were also shot angled slightly upward.

Freund called for a few minor adjustments, particularly the fill light. Bogart noticed a studio executive talking to Huston and he could tell that the director was agitated. Huston made an angry gesture and then stomped over to the actors.

"Bogie, Jack L. just called. Wants you to meet him on the New York Street."

"Now?"

"*Now.* It's a good thing we're shooting Eddie's scene. We'll fake you in the shot."

"Think you can get away with it?"

Huston, both hands in his pockets, walked over to Freund. "Papa, Bogie's got an urgent call. Can you re-light for a double so that—"

"Certainly, John. I'll just lower the shadows a bit. Put the double slightly out of focus."

Bogart went to his dressing room, took his jacket and walked through the enormous double doors of the sound stage.

FOUR

Bogart stepped off Brownstone Street, turned right and found himself in the heart of New York City. Tenement houses lined one side, a theater and business district the other. The only signs of life were a stagehand pushing a klieg light into a bakery shop and an idling black Lincoln limousine parked beneath the overhang of the theater's marquee.

Bogart paused, flooded by memories that were not entirely pleasant. It was here, on this back-lot street, that he had acted in numerous Warner Brothers gangster films in the 1930s as part of "Murderer's Row." *Invisible Stripes* with George Raft, *Angels With Dirty Faces* and *The Roaring Twenties* with James Cagney. He had felt stagnation and was glad that phase of his career was behind him.

Bogart took his time reaching the limousine, deciding Jack L. could simmer in his own juices. He purposely paused near the rear door to light a cigarette. He flipped away the spent match and opened the door with an air of indifference, sliding into the backseat.

The man next to him was not Jack L. Warner.

"Hello, Bogart." Harry Cohn had changed considerably in four years. He was more bald than Bogart remembered—the hair was thinning at the top and had turned scraggly and gray. The china-blue eyes were still defiant. His nose was broad—too broad for his face—and Cohn's upper lip was almost totally absorbed by the lower.

Bogart immediately reached for the door handle.

"Hold it, Bogart," barked Cohn. "I went to a lot of trouble to talk that prick Warner into letting me on the lot. You think studio bosses just go driving around other studios without getting their heads blown off?"

"We've got nothing to say, Harry."

"About Johnny Hawks we do."

Bogart removed his hand from the handle.

Cohn sat against the luxuriously upholstered seat in a finely tailored blue serge suit, puffing on a fat brown cigar with a dictatorial air. "Johnny called me fifteen minutes before he got himself knocked off."

"You know who did it?"

"Maybe I know why."

"So why tell me? The cops'll be all ears."

"You're my only link."

The chauffeur shifted into first as Cohn closed a sliding glass that made the backseat soundproof. The Lincoln continued along New York Street, turned right onto French Avenue and then jogged into Midwestern Street. A location company was milling in front of the town square. Bogart recognized Dennis Morgan and Jack Carson rehearsing a scene for *Two Guys From Brooklyn.*

Cohn coughed on his own cigar smoke, eyeing Forrest Tucker and Dorothy Malone through the window.

"Johnny was okay," said Bogart. "The guy really loved this stinking business. What exactly happened?"

"Someone took a shot at Johnny at Vasquez Rocks. Grazed his hand. My special-effects boy, Edmundsen, confirmed it. Found a shell casing in some nearby rocks."

"Keep talking."

"Johnny was really shaken. He called me a few minutes later, pleading for protection. He was on his way back when someone filled his car full of slugs. They found his body just a few feet from the car."

"So why am I your only link?"

"You know Blake Richards."

"Sorry, pal. Never heard of the gentleman."

"Come on, Bogart, don't stiff me. You dropped the script on my desk."

"Much too fast, Harry, much too fast. Why don't you start with the day you were born and work up to it."

The limousine turned onto Western Street, which was completely deserted, and slowly moved past the Last Chance Saloon, the Dixieland Hotel, Spike's Livery Stable and the Wells Fargo Express Office.

"It was '44," began Cohn, snarling the words out of the corner of his mouth. "Right after *Sahara.* You clunked me with a script. *Hollywood Armageddon.* For your pal Blake Richards."

"That," said Bogart softly. "I'd almost forgotten."

"Start remembering," said Cohn. "I need to get in touch with this Richards. There's no record of him anywhere."

Bogart smiled gently, pulling on his earlobe. "There is no Blake Richards."

"What the fuck're you handing me, Bogart?"

"Richards is a pseudonym."

Some of the tension left Cohn. "A phony. Christ, no wonder my security boys couldn't trace him. So what's his real name?"

Bogart's silence was conspicuous. He arrogantly flicked ash onto the spotless seat covering.

"Goddamn it, Bogart." Cohn's face looked like a red balloon about to explode.

"I'm not betraying a confidence without good reason."

"I'll give you a fucking good reason, Bogart. Your pal Richards, or whatever the hell his name is, is getting ready to blow up the fucking Academy Awards show on Saturday night."

The limousine turned onto Valley Heart Drive and moved past a row of open-ended corrugated sheds—warehouses for thousands of breakaway walls and other remnants of movie sets long forgotten.

Cohn continued: "The way I understood it, Johnny read *Hollywood Armageddon* and started nosing around and found out something about Richards. More than was healthy."

Bogart's voice was filled with doubt. "And so Richards killed Johnny. Is that the way you figure it?"

"I don't know what to figure, Bogart. All I know is, Johnny was scared. And he was positive Richards was going to blow up Shrine Auditorium. And now Johnny's dead."

"I still don't see where the script fits in."

"You never read *Hollywood Armageddon?*" There was no sarcasm in Cohn's voice, only incredulity.

"You know I hate to read scripts unless I have to, Harry."

Cohn burst out in a fit of laughter. He shoved a fresh cigar into his mouth and lit it. Thick, obscuring smoke in the vicinity of Harry Cohn was perpetual.

"If you'd read that script," said Cohn accusingly, "you'd know what the hell this is all about. *Hollywood Armageddon* is the story of some asshole who blows up Shrine Auditorium on Oscar night."

"All right," said Bogart in a straight voice, the lisp very faint, "what facts did Johnny have? What was his proof?"

Cohn shrugged.

"Then all we've got are Johnny's assumptions. Nothing we can go to the cops with."

"The hell with the cops. I'll find this Blake Richards myself if I have to. Hell, Bogart, you knew Hawks better than anyone. Doesn't Johnny's word mean anything?"

Bogart sat in silence, surrounded by Cohn's smoke.

"I've got a corpse for a contract player. That's enough proof for me that Johnny was onto something solid. Now how about it, Bogart? Who's Blake Richards?"

"Neither love nor money, Harry."

"You'd put your loyalty for one man over the welfare of the entire film community? Damn it, Bogart, I helped make this town what it is and I sure as hell don't want to see nothing happen to it. And what if Johnny was right? Think what something like that'd do to this fucking town. The cream of Hollywood . . . wiped out in one fucking blast. There'd be pieces of John Huston as far as Wilshire Boulevard." Cohn leaned back into the seat, sighing in utter frustration.

"You sound off key today, Harry. Do I detect sentiment?"

"You don't think I got a heart?"

"A surgeon would have to prove that, Harry."

"You gotta stand in line to hate me, Bogart."

"And the line gets longer every day, Harry."

Cohn coughed again, this time with an air of defeat. "You're something special, Bogart. The most stubborn man I've ever known." He stared out the window at the mock-up interior of a spaceship, at a dilapidated bus leaning on a broken axle, at a collection of elegant and ornate staircases which all rose eight feet into the air and dead-ended.

"You know, Bogart," said Cohn softly, "we made a

lotta money off *Sahara*. Best damn picture about World War II any of them made. We coulda made a lot more pictures together. You oughta consider setting up your Santana production offices at Columbia. We could give you a helluva deal. Distribution, the works."

"Bribery never works with me," said Bogart. "Doesn't even appeal to my baser instincts." He rapped the glass, signaling the chauffeur to pull over. The Lincoln stopped at the foot of Valley Heart Drive in front of a green, two-story stucco building.

As Bogart climbed out, Cohn started snarling again. "I'm gonna find Richards," he forewarned, gripping Bogart's shoulder.

Bogart indignantly shook the clutching fingers away. "You do what you have to do, Harry."

Bogart watched the limousine until it disappeared behind the corrugated sheds. Around him the entertainment capital of the world dozed in mid-afternoon, smog-weakened sunlight. Its two dozen sound stages, laid out in stark military precision, reflected creamy yellow colors. There were unglamorous structures, resembling huge Quonset huts instead of working quarters for the most skilled craftsmen in Hollywood.

Dream factory . . . entertainment capital . . . to Bogart it was a place where he had worked steadily for more than ten years, and still there was nothing visually arresting about these 140 acres in Burbank, on the fringe of the San Fernando Valley.

Bogart still felt a deep-rooted respect for what Jack L. and his brothers, Sam and Harry, had brought to Hollywood with a new system called Vitaphone. To people that meant sound. And sound meant new dimensions in realism. "Wait a minute, you ain't heard nothin' yet," Al Jolson had prophetically roared in *The*

Jazz Singer—Bogart could vividly remember that first tingling wave of excitement in 1927 when he had sat in a New York theater balcony and heard those words. The Brothers Warner had reshaped the face of Hollywood.

Warner product, by the late 1930s, had become indelibly stamped with a special look, symbolized by the rousing Max Steiner fanfare that preceded each picture. Fast-paced crime sagas; splashy, bubbling Busby Berkeley musicals; and movies about the proleterian, though always within a framework of entertainment.

The nearest telephone was in the two-story cartoonists' building, and Bogart now headed there with a feeling of affection. He often came here, to this far corner of the studio, because he admired the animators for maintaining their autonomy from Jack L. Warner.

Bogart entered the ground floor, poking his head into a cluttered ten-by-ten cubicle in which a middle-aged man hunched over a drawing table, oblivious to everything except a full-color portrait of Yosemite Sam.

"Need to use your phone," Bogart told him, already taking the receiver off the hook.

"Sure, help yourself . . ." The artist wasn't about to be distracted; he continued to add refinements to the character's blustering face.

Bogart flipped through the pages of the small black notebook he always carried in his inside coat pocket, stopping at the name Dalt Brennan.

The number had been disconnected, with no referral.

His next call, to the main office of the Screen Actors' Guild, produced immediate results, for the sexy-voiced secretary seemed exceptionally eager to please Bogart.

He learned that Kitty Steele was working at Republic Studios in *Belle of the Wilderness*. Stunting and doubling for Vera Hruba Ralston.

Back at Sound Stage Five, Bogart casually informed Huston he was taking the remainder of the afternoon off. "You can shoot around me."

"You're resting on your laurels," Huston accused him with a faint suggestion of a smile; the director obviously enjoyed the way Bogart's eyebrows had arched. "You're going to spend the rest of your life living off the popularity of Fred C. Dobbs. Maybe you don't need pictures anymore."

"Maybe," replied Bogart not too convincingly as he started for the exit.

"There's only one problem with you, Bogie," Huston shouted after him. "You really believe you're Bogart."

FIVE

In the cool of the late afternoon, with gray rain clouds
hanging over the Santa Monica mountain range, Bogart drove due west along the southern edge of the
San Fernando Valley. Republic Studios was located in
Studio City, a small community that had been christened by Mack Sennett in the late 1920s. Herbert J.
Yates had taken over Sennett's studio in 1935 and in-
stigated a policy of fast production and faster profit.
It was this that had turned Republic into a profitable
factory of action films and serials.

Bogart had no difficulty at the main gate off Rad-
ford Drive. The middle-aged uniform guard gave him
directions to the *Belle of the Wilderness* sound stage.

No sooner had he cleared the gate than Bogart saw
John Wayne dressed as a sea captain: black pea coat,
dark bell-bottoms, double-breasted capn's coat, bosun's cap and canvas shoes. Wayne recognized him
and nodded, his expression unchanged. Bogart pulled
to the curb, rolling down his window. Wayne leaned
his towering frame down slightly. "Slumming?" he
asked Bogart, his calculating eyes sweeping the interior of the Cadillac.

"Here to visit a friend." Bogart nervously drummed
his fingers on the spotlight attached to the driver's
side.

Wayne, who had been in the process of rolling his
own cigarette, kept on eyeing Bogart with a hint of
suspicion.

Bogart felt there was a wall between him and

Wayne. "You fulfilling your yearly obligation to Yates?"

Wayne nodded, his eyes squinting to narrow, beady slits. He shifted his frame uncomfortably.

Wayne must see the same wall I do, thought Bogart.

"That's right," drawled Wayne, searching the pockets of his bosun's jacket for a match. "Picture called *Wake of the Red Witch.*"

"They tell me you're getting ten percent of the action."

Wayne's only reaction, for fifteen seconds or so, was to strike a match and light the grubby-looking stub in his mouth. Finally: "Piece of the action, that's the only way to travel in this town. Someday the rest of the community's gonna wake up to that fact. Time they stopped being pushed around and misused by the studio bosses."

"Come on over to Warners sometime. I'll introduce you to one of the sweetest."

"You tell Jack if he ever wants to see me around that studio of his, it'll be on my terms. Not his."

Bogart's fingers continued to drum idly on the spotlight. "Hear you've got a new picture just out. *Fort Apache.*"

"Been out about a week. Early to tell yet, but I think it's a good picture."

"John Ford's one of the best."

Wayne pushed his seacap farther back on his forehead. "Hear you've been busy in Mexico. They're talking about *Treasure of the Sierra Madre* for an Oscar."

"You know what they can do with the Oscar."

Wayne's coolness abated. "Just what I've been tellin' 'em for years. Well, this is costing Yates money. When it costs him, it costs me. Maybe I'll see you around Burbank someday." Wayne tipped his bosun's cap in a slightly exaggerated style and slipped like a silent panther into one of the sound stages.

Bogart parked at the side of the Mabel Normand Sound Stage, in a stall with the name *Wild Bill Elliott* stenciled across the pavement in large white letters. The red light flashing above the side door told Bogart a scene was in progress. While he waited he removed a fresh pack of cigarettes from the glove compartment and ripped open the seal. He took the time to light up even after the red had stopped rotating.

Inside, Bogart was greeted by familiar chaos. Stagehands scurried the length of the sound stage, stretching new electrical cables, shifting klieg lights and milling in general confusion. Bogart worked his way through breakaway walls onto a large saloon set littered with Faro and poker tables, chuckaluck games and one roulette wheel. Gaudy chandeliers hung from the ceiling; a curving staircase led to an upper landing. Several extras and supporting players, dressed as rugged lumberjacks, swapped stories or read *Variety* as they waited.

Bogart recognized Vera Hruba Ralston standing next to the bar counter, dressed in a low-cut, strapless, green taffeta dance-hall costume. She wore a feathered boa that streamed from a garish headpiece, black stockings and red high-heeled shoes with silver buckles.

Vera was a tall, buxom blond, a one-time Czechoslovakian skating champion who had fled Prague when Hitler marched into the Sudetenland. She had found refuge in films and, some rumor mongers insisted, in the arms of "happily married" Herbert J. Yates.

There was a woman dressed identically to Ralston. Bogart smiled as he recognized her. Kitty Steele took her place at the bar, giving Bogart a provocative smile and a swing of her hips.

Dalt Brennan was a lucky sonofabitch to have married a woman like her. Bogart was only sorry that Kitty's career as a character actress had failed to blossom. When it became apparent that she would never be a name in pictures, she had trained as a stuntwoman, learning to fall from horses and jump through raging infernos. In recent years she had doubled for such beauties as Marlene Dietrich, Ann Sheridan and Linda Darnell.

Kitty was joined on the saloon set by a tall, slender man with a screenplay tucked under his arm. He was Joe Kane, one of Republic's most prolific directors, with forty-three Roy Rogers programmers to his credit. Kane spoke briefly to Kitty, then ordered the cast to take a short break while the lighting was refined.

The next thing Bogart knew, Kitty Steele was at his side, sliding her arm through his and kissing him firmly on the lips. "How you doing, beautiful?" he asked.

"Dreamy . . . now that you're here."

"You're a married woman," quipped Bogart.

"Not anymore." The playfulness left her voice suddenly; Bogart realized she was utterly serious and he was startled enough not to speak for a moment while he studied Kitty.

Once beautiful, irresistible Kitty Steele had developed the hardness of a Joan Crawford or a Barbara Stanwyck. She was still hard-muscled, and there was a sultry tan on her skin. Her eyes stared at him in tired, wise fashion. Her breasts were still solid and self-uplifting, but her legs were starting to turn heavy from strenuous stunt work.

Bogart finally spoke. "You and Dalt—"

"—are all washed up."

"Dalt's why I'm here."

"Come on," said Kitty. "Let's talk."

They took refuge at Kitty's dressing table, one of several along a wall of the enormous sound stage.

"You've been out of touch," began Kitty, not accusingly, but with some hint of disappointment.

"You get caught up in this business. You know how it is."

"Too well," replied Kitty, accepting a cigarette. Bogart fumbled for a match, but Kitty shook her head. "Forget it. I know how you feel about a dame. She should be strong enough to light her own cigarette." She lit up and studied Bogart's face.

"What happened, Kitty?"

"We broke up last November."

"I can guess why."

"I just couldn't take it anymore, Bogie."

"Nobody's blaming you, Kitty."

"Dalt was getting worse. His violent outbursts. Those dark periods of depression. He was finally becoming paranoid, Bogie. I swear it. Absolutely paranoid."

"Still hating Hollywood?"

"And all the wrongs it had done to him. Do you remember Clive Donahue?"

"The producer who died about a year ago?"

"Dalt threatened Donahue. Threatened to kill him, Bogie."

"Donahue told you this?"

"I was there when Dalt picked up the phone and called him."

"Why would Dalt threaten Donahue?"

"It happened when Donahue was producing independent and releasing through Columbia. He'd bought one of Dalt's screenplays. It was the first thing Dalt had sold in almost three years. Since leaving Camp Pendleton."

"Which screenplay did Donahue buy?" asked Bogart keenly, leaning forward expectantly.

"*Embarkation Point.*"

Bogart relaxed. "I remember the picture. It was damn good. Just the thing for war-weary audiences. Departing soldiers and the wives and lovers they leave behind." He paused. "But I don't remember Dalt's name on the credits."

"There was no credit. That's why Dalt hated Donahue."

"Let me guess," said Bogart cynically. "The old Hollywood double-cross."

Kitty nodded. "Donahue brought in a writer and ordered him to alter the screenplay so drastically Dalt's name was dropped."

"Who was the writer?"

Kitty paused, as if she didn't want to continue, then: "Paul Fabrini." She nervously flicked ashes from her cigarette.

"Another Hollywood rat?"

Kitty frowned. "He's an okay guy, Bogie." She placed her hand on Bogart's. "He was just doing a job and got caught up in a very bad thing."

Bogart returned the frown. "Dalt's threatened people before, Kitty. He even got a little rough with me and Betty at the Garden of Allah that night we had to call you. But he's never killed anyone."

"I've never told you this, Bogie, but *Embarkation Point* is why Dalt came to you that night. He wanted to get it out of his system and you were the only friend he had to turn to. But then he lost his head . . ."

"There was something different about him that night, Kitty. It was the end of our relationship, but . . ."

"He scared me, Bogie, really scared me. I felt he *could* kill. I had to get away. I swear, if I had stayed . . ."

Bogart tightened his squeeze on Kitty's hand, and the emotional outburst he had sensed in her subdued. Kitty still looked tense when Bogart asked, "Ever hear of a script Dalt wrote called *Hollywood Armageddon*?"

Kitty shook her head. "There were a lot of things Dalt wrote he never showed me. You know how dark and moody he could get. Whole periods when he'd lock himself away at the typewriter. He'd write for hours, get it all out of his system. But he'd never show it to me. Not even *The Money Moguls*, the book he called his *tour de force*. And I never pried. There were some things totally private to Dalt. Even after seven years of marriage."

"Where can I find him, Kitty? It's important."

"I've lost all tabs, Bogie. I don't know where he is."

"That bad?"

"That bad," she echoed.

"Look, I need some kind of angle."

Kitty took a fresh pull on her cigarette. "He went to live with his brother Lloyd the week we split up. The next thing I knew, Lloyd was dead. Suicide . . . It seemed so unlike Lloyd."

"It's tough to figure, Kitty. When someone accuses you of being a Communist, and you know your career as a Hollywood writer is destroyed, there's no telling what makes you pick up a revolver and blow your brains out . . ."

Kitty shuddered. "I didn't go to the funeral. I didn't want to see Dalt."

"Any idea where Dalt might live now?"

"Lloyd's place? . . . I don't know. But if you find out, don't call. I don't want to know." Kitty paused, her brow furrowing. Before many more years, thought Bogart, there were going to be many more lines across Kitty's face.

Joe Kane, a broad smile on his thin lips, approached the makeup table. "Kitty, we're just about ready to roll for the fight."

"Still grinding out pictures, hey, Joe?" said Bogart, shaking the director's hand.

"They're pretty good old pictures," said Kane. "Yates is tight with a buck but we get a few good ones turned out. Yates saw Marlene Dietrich in *Destry Rides Again* and wanted something like it, so he had this cat fight written into the script."

"He-men and she-devils," quipped Kitty. "Come on, Bogie, get into the scene."

"What?"

"That's a helluva idea," agreed Kane.

"Just stand by the bar as one of the extras," suggested Kitty. "It'll be a great gag."

Phrased in another fashion, Kitty's idea might have been rejected, but Bogart enjoyed putting one over on anybody, and he accepted the offer. Very quickly he found himself slipping into a red-and-white checkered lumberman's jacket, a cowboy hat and black boots. No one recognized him as he took a position along the bar.

"Action," ordered Kane.

With his back to the turning Mitchell camera, Bogart poured himself a glass of tea (which would resemble rotgut whiskey on the Trucolor film stock) and pretended to be oblivious to the commotion.

Like rival tigresses, Kitty Steele and another stuntwoman, also dressed garishly as a saloon girl, rolled on the sawdust-covered hardwood in a bear hug, knocking over chairs with their flailing high heels and tearing at each other's dresses and petticoats. Kitty began throwing a flurry of punches at the woman's face, her fist grazing across Bogart's legs. He stumbled sideways along the bar, knocking over the only upright spittoon. Kitty held the top position in the struggle and pretended to rake her fingernails across her rival's face. She spat like an angry alley cat.

Kitty got so carried away that she ripped off the top half of the other woman's bodice, taking pieces of brassiere with it. The woman leaped up, aware that she was bare-breasted in a roomful of ogling technicians, and threw her arms protectively across her chest, cursing Kitty.

Kane wouldn't allow the cameraman to stop rolling until the woman had fled the set. "A helluva take," he roared, and the crew cheered her bravura performance.

"Print that," yelled Kane. "But make a note it'll have to be cut just before Kitty tears the dress. We'll cover the cut with a close-up of Vera down near the floor . . . Vera, darling, do you mind doing a close-up for us? . . . like she's struggling. Then we'll do a pickup from another master."

While the camera and lights were shifted, Kitty joined Bogart at the bar. "I don't know if this is any help, but when Dalt and I split up, he was thinking about going to see a producer at Columbia . . . Quinn Tayne . . . about some script ideas."

Bogart contemptuously blew smoke at the saloon

mirror. He said nothing to Kitty about his personal and professional dislike for Tayne.

"Know where I might find this Fabrini?" Bogart detected a jerk of Kitty's lower lip.

She shrugged and smiled hard. Maybe too hard, thought Bogart. "Haven't seen him. He must be around town . . ." Without saying another word she left him to readjust her hair.

Joe Kane joined Bogart at the bar counter. Bogart poured him a glass of tea. "I've made my share of B pictures," Bogart said, "always on a tight schedule, with a small amount of dough. So I know what you go through."

"It's always been my livelihood, the B picture," admitted Kane, "but now I'm getting worried. I just got back from New York. Saw my first TV show there. The screens're starting to get big. Saw one measuring eleven and a half inches. Imagine that. You put those boxes in homes and nobody's gonna go to a theater."

"If it happens," predicts Bogart, "it'll be Hollywood's own damn fault for not making better pictures, and for not buying into the medium before it catches hold. At least then it could have some control over the content. But I don't think Hollywood is that smart." Bogart set his glass on the bar. He shook hands with Kane. "Keep turning them out as long as you can, Joe."

"We're doing all right," said Kane. "Turning out good old pictures . . ."

Bogart wanted to say good-bye to Kitty but couldn't find her at the makeup table. Then he remembered how much she hated good-byes, so he stopped looking, turned in his wardrobe and found his own way out.

SIX

After leaving Republic Studios via the Hollywood Parkway, Bogart switched off the radio (Peggy Lee's "Golden Earrings" faded abruptly) and turned his thoughts to Harry Cohn.

Bogart hesitated to put complete stock in Cohn's theory. The studio boss was too often hysterical and unreasoning; yet it was difficult to dismiss Cohn entirely—not a man who had shrewdly engineered the growth of a major film studio.

Bogart dropped into Hollywood, turning from Highland onto Sunset and proceeding due east through Times Square. Not more than a mile ahead stood Columbia Pictures Corporation Studios, on the site of old Poverty Row.

In the 1920s Poverty Row had been the slums of the motion picture industry. Producers had thrown away their scruples to cash in on the profits of quickie motion pictures.

Ahead Bogart saw the high, prisonlike walls meeting at the corner of Sunset and Gower. They completely surrounded Cohn's fiefdom, stretching an entire block along Sunset between Gower and Beachwood and all the way to Fountain Avenue.

It was here that Harry Cohn, his brother Jack and Joe Brandt had launched CBC Corporation (derisively called Corned Beef 'n Cabbage). Like so many other tiny companies that ground out cheap one- and two-reelers, CBC had been housed in a faded yellow stucco house.

Slowly, by buying up property, they had converted

their humble beginnings into Columbia. Harry Cohn
had found his stride and sought out the best filmmakers, giving them independence instead of stifling their
creativity.

Bogart was aware of Cohn's other key trait: the uti-
lization of every conceivable dollar-saving device. He
dominated the studio and his belligerence had earned
Columbia the nickname "Bedlam Minor."

But Cohn produced money-making pictures, and
the free rein given Frank Capra to direct *It Happened
One Night*, with Clark Gable and Claudette Colbert,
brought Academy Awards to Cohn. At last Columbia
was a prestigious pin in the Hollywood map.

Bogart turned onto Gower and drove toward the
main entrance midway down the block. He was startled to see an orderly file of people in front of the
central gate, parading with posters on wooden sticks.
Most of the pickets looked like blue-collar workers; he
could read a few of the bobbing signs: PEACETIME
DRAFT A FRAUD . . . FASCIST FILMS UNDEMOCRATIC . . .
there were about a dozen protestors in all and they
parted amicably to allow Bogart through.

Frowning, Bogart pulled up at the gate, where he
was greeted by an elderly guard. "Welcome back to
Columbia, Mr. Bogart."

"Maybe, maybe not," said Bogart. "What's the
ruckus?"

The guard shrugged. "Protestors. Group called the
North America Committee for Democratic Action.
Commies if you ask me, hiding behind a name like
that."

"What's the beef?"

"Seems they object to one of our pictures."

"Wouldn't be Quinn Tayne's, would it?"

"Yup. *The Red Seduction*."

"Which stage is Tayne shooting on?" asked Bogart.

"Number Six."

"Yeah, it would be. Never mind an escort, I know my way."

The guard nodded, swung open the gate and waved Bogart through. He drove slowly along the narrow streets between sound stages, feeling mildly depressed. Columbia failed to generate the kind of excitement in him that he felt when he drove on the Warners lot. It was starkly barren and colorless. He passed technicians who walked like zombies as they trundled carts of cables and plugging boxes. They made no effort to acknowledge his presence.

Stage Six was the pride of Harry Cohn—where some of his classic films had been photographed, and where he always shot the film he considered to be his next blockbuster. It was just like him to turn it over to a film with the title *Red Seduction*.

He parked in an empty stall next to a gray Rolls-Royce limousine with wicker work on the body panels. On the driver's side stood a chauffeur, smoking a cigarette and contemplating nothing in particular. In stark contrast to his milk-white skin, he was dressed completely in black, from the driver's cap to his well-polished riding boots. His uniform, precision-fit to his lithe six-foot body, consisted of riding breeches tucked into boots at knee-height and a double-breasted jacket with a military collar. He wore dark glasses, but Bogart could see that he was strikingly handsome, probably in his late forties. The chauffeur's fetish for black extended to his thin leather driving gloves, which were spotlessly clean and stretched knuckle-tight over his slender hands.

Bogart sauntered up to the chauffeur. "You must drive for Quinn Tayne."

The man came to attention with his eyes if not his body, and snapped his cigarette away as if it were something diseased. "That's right, Mr. Bogart. I'm Valentine Corliss. How can I help you, sir?" ·

Bogart reached clumsily for a cigarette but Corliss moved with uncanny swiftness, producing a cigarette from a gold-plated case with the initials V.C. Bogart saw it wasn't his brand but accepted it with a quiet nod. "Nothing special . . . just wanted to talk to your boss for a minute."

"You'll find Mr. Tayne inside. He's in preproduction on a new film."

"*The Red Seduction.* I saw the poster jockeys at the gate."

Corliss grinned tightly. His teeth were small and very white. "Mr. Tayne does have a way of stirring up controversy."

"Controversy is good box office, especially if the film is lousy."

The red light was off as he reached for the door handle, but once again Corliss moved with lightning precision, snapping open the heavy-duty soundproof door. Bogart nodded as he entered. The door closed gratingly behind him, sending a shiver up his back.

He turned and experienced another shiver. For as his eyes adjusted to the dimness, he found himself on a massive prison set. In front of Bogart was an arched doorway with the hammer and sickle of the Soviet government emblazoned over it: Lubianka Prison, stronghold of the Russian secret police.

He knew it was papier mâché and plaster, yet he could easily imagine the smell of mold and decay.

Bogart walked through the archway into a dank corridor, the walls of which had built-in medieval-like sconces for unlighted torches. He wandered past interrogation rooms where lichen clung to water-damaged ceilings. Mesmerized, he wound his way into a chamber where iron fetters were chained to walls and a panoply of torturer's instruments littered the racks.

The illusion was disturbed only by the passing of set decorators and designers as they unrolled blueprints to check for accuracy. He became aware of the distant sound of hammers, saws and the cough of compressors feeding air power to spray guns.

Bogart reached the edge of the central set, which consisted of tier upon tier of cells rising up into the studio's catwalks. It was all gray, evil and enormous.

Now, thought Bogart, if Tayne has a script to match this set, he'll have one helluva picture, even if it is anti-Communist propaganda. But he had the hopeless feeling he was asking for too much when he saw Quinn Tayne standing in the heart of the cell block, talking in low tones to the craftsmen and laborers who surrounded him.

Tayne was very much as Bogart remembered him: a man who fulfilled the definition of "distinguished." He was still lean and slender, even at age fifty, although his once-blond, wavy hair had turned shocking white with sprinkled strands of gray. His nose was patrician, finely chiseled, separating fine china-blue eyes that managed to convey a sense of disdain even when he smiled.

A cobra's smile, Bogart decided. Tayne's face was well tanned, which emphasized the white hair and forced the solid jawline to stand out sharply. With Tayne, image was everything.

A costumer was showing armloads of Russian military uniforms to Tayne. As each costume was presented, Tayne inspected it against assorted photographs. Occasionally he fingered an epaulet or insignia; frequently he cocked an eye dubiously and shook his head. Everything that Tayne said, no matter how trivial, was taken down by a middle-aged stenographer. Bogart smiled sardonically. Tayne was going to need an even larger vault than David O. Selznick for storing memos.

Tayne began checking weapons provided by the property master. He held a 7.6-millimeter pistol with seeming disinterest, cocking it and dry-firing. He seemed satisfied. The prop man handed him several ugly-looking blackjacks, which were almost a foot long and had weighted ends.

Tayne smiled and commented on their realism, thumping the knobby ends against his palm.

A dapper, gray-haired man came out of the darkness of Lubianka and approached Tayne. As he came into the light, Bogart stiffened in recognition. Adolphe Menjou. Their voices carried to Bogart.

Tayne continually interrupted Menjou's cultured voice. Finally, "I don't wish to discuss script changes any further."

"But Mr. Tayne—"

"There's one rule I insist upon," said the producer, ignoring Menjou's interruption. "Lines are spoken as written. I've personally approved every word of this script."

"I don't wish to tone down the script; no indeed," insisted Menjou, stroking his mustache. "Rather the reverse. I'd like to see lines with more power, more force, more feeling. We need films like this to show the Communist menace."

Tayne listened politely, then rubbed his jaw. "I think I see what you mean . . . I think perhaps we could create stronger dialogue for the colonel."

Bogart watched from the shadows as Menjou's head bobbed eagerly. "It's only that I feel so strongly about the colonel. I want to be absolutely certain the message gets across . . ."

Yeah, Bogart thought. The message.

Bogart remembered John Lawson and the others—the Hollywood Ten. It had been only a short time ago when Menjou had stood, bright, shiny-eyed with patriotism, and pointed the finger at many of his coworkers, judging them to be left-wing fellow travelers of the Moscow party line.

Bogart doubted if Menjou had changed any.

And Tayne hadn't changed any, either; Bogart still felt a deep-rooted sense of contempt for him.

In 1941 Tayne had become part of the first Communist witch-hunting committee to thrust its tentacles into Hollywood. Bogart had been one of those accused of being a Communist, but Tayne and his committee cohorts could produce no solid evidence to back up the charge.

There had been no evidence to uncover.

Bogart had often wondered if Tayne hadn't joined that committee solely to get back at him for rejecting the lead in the Big Jim Blair series.

The year had been 1936, during the height of the Depression. From the initial reading, Bogart had hated the concept behind Tayne's proposed films. Blair was the president of a large manufacturing concern, who was always being thrust into political controversy and fighting corruption in the state capital. In each film Blair was framed or threatened by "people's" organizations attempting to usurp power.

To Bogart, Blair was a throwback to the robber barons, a man who looked upon the working man as an inept pawn to be manipulated by and for big busi-

ness. As far as Bogart was concerned, this rugged indi-
vidualist who pushed around the little guys smacked
of fascism.

If Bogart had accepted the Blair part, the series
might have had a fighting chance—Tayne had often
said as much—but with John Litel in the title role, the
films had flopped dismally.

His career at its lowest ebb, Tayne had languished,
making B Westerns until he resurfaced as a producer
at Columbia, releasing through Cohn's vast theater
chain.

Now he specialized in "timely" films decrying a
threat to national security.

Bogart stepped out of the shadows, a perverse smile
twisting his lips.

Menjou paled but regained his renowned aplomb.

Tayne smiled, the essence of sincerity. "Bogie,
Christ, I haven't seen you in years. In person, that is.
You're looking good."

"You don't look bad yourself, Quinn." Bogart's eyes
were unable to conceal his feelings. It was apparent
that his visit was not a social one.

Menjou cleared his throat, picked up his script, nodded indifferently to Tayne and disappeared into the
shadows of the set.

Bogart didn't bother to offer a handshake, but then
Tayne hadn't eagerly thrust his hand out, either.

Tayne gestured at the set, eagerly explaining, "What
do you think, Bogie? It's the most I've ever spent on a
single set."

Bogart noticed the steno woman was still taking
down every word. Prattle for posterity, he thought.

"We've even interviewed some Russian war refugees
and political exiles who survived Lubianka. But they

weren't much help on detail. Incredible, really, the difference in their ideology and ours."

There it was, thought Bogart. Just "theirs" and "ours." The simpleminded Tayne philosophy.

"But," continued Tayne, "I'm sure you didn't come here just to see the set."

"You're right. I'm looking for Dalt Brennan. I understand from his ex-wife you had some business with Dalt not long ago."

"That's right, I did."

"When did you see him?"

Tayne smoothed out the white hair spilling over his left ear. "First of the year. Right after he and Kitty Steele split up."

"How did he seem to you?"

"Not the greatest. He was angry with Kitty for not sticking by him. I'm afraid he became emotional during our session."

"Dalt was writing scripts for you?"

"We were trying out some concepts. Nothing that bowled me over."

"Maybe they were all too liberal," suggested Bogart. "Some of Lloyd's ideas might have rubbed off."

Tayne's face fell a notch, the sincerity draining away. "I would never subscribe to such a concept, Bogie. Just because one man is a Communist—"

"The charges against Lloyd were never proven," said Bogart.

"That depends on how much stock you put in HUAC."

"I don't put any stock in HUAC. But let's not get sidetracked. You say you didn't like Dalt's material . . ."

"I've always considered Dalt a minor talent."

"Let's just say he never hit it big," said Bogart.

"Let's say he just didn't meet my needs," said Tayne.

"Did Dalt ever mention a script called *Hollywood Armageddon?*"

"*Hollywood Armageddon.*" Tayne seemed to be weighing its sound. "Not exactly a box-office title, is it. No, he made no reference to it. Is it a hot property now?"

"In a special kind of way, yes."

"Tell me, Bogie, is Dalt in some kind of trouble?"

"Dalt's an old friend. We go back a long way."

"How like you, Bogie. To help another."

"I didn't say he needed help."

"Why are you looking for him, then?"

"That's personal."

Tayne gestured expansively. "I wish I could be of greater assistance. Consider me at your disposal, any hour." Tayne briefly flashed his unpleasant smile, turned and vanished into the darkness of Lubianka Prison.

SEVEN

At eight P.M. it started to rain in Beverly Hills. Bogart parked in front of the Brown Derby and stood briefly in the light downpour. He felt revitalized. Gone was the smog, gone was the hacking cough. He patted his coat pocket to make certain he had plenty of cigarettes, and turned. The Derby doorman began to make flourishing motions but Bogart ignored him. His destination was farther down the block, at 326 North Rodeo Drive.

Wedged between a number of exclusive clothing shops and jewelry stores which catered to the very rich was Romanoff's, which catered to the very Hollywood. The exterior was solid red brick framed by Roman pillars and enhanced by a massive door on which was centered the royal Romanoff coat of arms: an imperial gold-leafed double *R* set within a plaster shield.

Bogart passed through a small waiting room and entered the dining room and bar. Immediately his eyes fell upon the words *Imperial Greetings* scrawled above a charcoal portrait of the owner in a high top hat, tuxedo and bow tie. The caricature wore a monocle, smoked a pipe and stood before a giant champagne glass, as though contemplating a flying leap into eternal bubbles. In his hand was a Malacca walking stick.

To Bogart's left were seven upholstered booths known as Dress Circle. Bogart unfailingly demanded the second booth from the entrance and Romanoff unfailingly reserved it for him. The wallpaper above the booth was a flamboyant orange-yellow-green combination of abstract designs.

To Bogart's right was the air-conditioned bar, over which were hung paintings and caricatures. Along the bar sat several imbibers, including Clifton Webb and a young up-and-coming actress. Bogart spied Monty Woolley eating alone at his regular table behind the cash register, with a special reading light rigged overhead.

Jamieson, the distinguished maitre d'hotel, immediately recognized Bogart and rushed to greet him. "Monsieur Bogart, what a pleasure to see you back. *Où y a-t-il pour votre service?*"

"Hiya, Frenchie. Forget the seating for a minute. I want to see the big shot. It's customary in my country to acknowledge royalty before making a pig of yourself."

Jamieson led Bogart to the last booth of Dress Circle, where Romanoff was enjoying dinner, or, rather, enjoying the sight of two bibbed bulldogs lapping up huge platters of beefsteak and roast turkey.

Mr. Confucius, the bigger and older of the bulldogs, tossed his head, saw Bogart and barked once (very softly) as though to warn Romanoff. His companion, Socrates, remained interested only in a leg of turkey.

Prince Michael Alexandrovich Dimitri Obelensky Romanoff watched with dignified bemusement as Bogart slouched toward his booth. There was a polished European air about the restaurateur, and a distinct aura of snobbishness, which may have had something to do with the fact that he was more commonly known as Harry Gerguson.

Romanoff was five foot six, with closely clipped dark hair sprinkled with flakes of gray, a pencil-thin mustache and a leathery complexion. His nose, too bulbous for his face, was his one distracting feature—it almost shattered the Grand Illusion.

The prince was exquisitely dressed in an expensive blue-striped suit with wide lapels, the red ribbon of the *Legion d'Honneur* thrust through his buttonhole. He wore an old Etonian cravat, hugely knotted. His right hand was pushed into the pocket of his suit jacket.

Romanoff had once been a confidence man who posed as the cousin of Nicholas II; Prime Minister William Gladstone; William Rockefeller; and William K. Vanderbilt. It was also common knowledge he had once spent five months in The Tombs of New York City.

Such a colorful charlatan had won the heart of Hollywood, itself a 24-carat phony. Rumors indicated Romanoff still kept loose contacts with the Los Angeles underworld—a shadowy fact that only added to the prince's aura of mystery.

"Good evening, your royal phoniness," grunted Bogart with a derisive bow.

"You are not," breathed Romanoff accusingly, "wearing a tie."

"Ah," responded Bogart, "but I am. If you will kindly note . . ." Bogart produced a stark black bowtie, which he clipped to one side of his unbuttoned shirt. It was ridiculously askew, but he had conformed to Romanoff policy.

The prince gave a flip of his hand as if he were throwing a bone over his shoulder. "I believe you are becoming a fraud," said Romanoff in inaccurate Oxonian accent.

"It must rub off," countered Bogart, sliding into the booth. Mr. Confucius growled but showed more interest in his food than in protecting his master.

"What, old boy, is wrong with imposture in a community of make-believe?" asked Romanoff. "I was making no judgment, only an observation."

"You oughta teach these dogs manners," Bogart scolded Romanoff, wiping specks of gravy from his jacket. "Socrates is slobbering all over his bib again."

"I assure you, these magnificent creatures eat with greater refinement than most of my customers."

"You know, Prince, you oughta get out of this racket. You talk too much like a politician." Bogart ordered Scotch on the rocks when Jamieson stepped to the table. And he told him to make it snappy. *A corps perdu.*

Romanoff snuffed out his cigarette and reached for an embossed gold cigarette case emblazoned with the inevitable *R*.

"You oughta run for mayor of Beverly Hills," suggested Bogart.

"I am too restless and high-strung for civic office."

"Sell this dump and settle down, then."

"I would sell only to a proper party." Romanoff lit a new cigarette.

"Hey, the Duke of Windsor is a friend of mine. I'll tell him you want to dump this joint."

"I assure you, the duke's entirely lacking in background."

Jamieson returned with the Scotch for Bogart and a problem for Romanoff. The lobby was filling with clientele but there was a shortage of tables. Whom should be seated first? That, decided Romanoff, depended on the clientele.

"*A la bonne heure.* Alan Ladd has a party of five. Then there is Brian Donlevy and his wife . . . oh yes, the Gregory Pecks . . . and someone named Stuart. Hap Stuart."

"The character actor?" queried Romanoff. "I've heard he's been down on his luck since Iwo Jima."

"Hard to get roles," said Bogart, "with only one arm."

"Jamieson," ordered Romanoff, "see to it that Mr. Stuart and his party are seated ahead of the others."

"And make a show of it, Frenchie," added Bogart.

Jamieson chattered a reply in French, then scurried away. Socrates finished lapping the gravy off his platter and sat back on the upholstered seat, assuming a haughty pose. "Let the others wait," said Romanoff. "It will make them feel all that more important when they finally take their seats and I give them a curt nod or a few well-chosen words."

Bogart finished his Scotch quicker than usual. "Has Dalt been in lately, Prince?"

"Dalt? Really, Bogie. I haven't seen the man since . . . I recollect the war was still raging."

"Heard any word about him?"

"Only that nasty business about his brother Lloyd. But I have little time for idle gossip. I prefer to create my own. Well, if you'll excuse me I must do some performing. Live up to my rep—I daresay, old boy, I believe one of your acquaintances has crawled out of a hole somewhere."

Bogart squinted as a gnome of a man lurched through the entrance like the hunchback of Notre Dame and bee-lined toward Bogart's table. He walked like a leprechaun, and when he sat, he was poised like a toad on a lily pad.

Bogart walked to his private table. He towered above the diminutive figure seated on the outer right side of the booth, and looked down into eyes as big as eggs.

The rotund little man was unfashionably dressed in

wrinkled gabardine slacks and a brown wool sweater
pulled over an unstarched cotton shirt. His only colorful feature was a bright red bow tie neatly clipped
into place. One disheveled strand of his thinning, dark
hair hung down across the center of his forehead.
When he spoke, his voice was soft as butter but men-
acing, with just a trace of Viennese inflection. His
barrel-shaped torso seemed to quiver with anticipa-
tion.

"You are," commented Peter Lorre, "looking at a
man who has turned down several fortunes in his lifetime."

"But never a drink," retorted Bogart, snapping his
fingers to capture Jamieson's attention. The maitre d'
would not have to be told what to bring. Bogart slid
into the booth, touching a stack of envelopes resting
under Lorre's drumming fingertips. "Fan mail?"

Lorre gave Bogart a long, steady stare. Lorre had
often referred to this as his number-four look, and it
came during that awful interval between the striking
of a match and the lighting of a cigarette.

Jamieson brought the drinks, greeting Lorre with a
torrent of flowery French, then scampered off. Lorre
looked down into his bourbon and water like a man
who wanted to swim in it. He patted the bundle of
envelopes. "It is, as you so aptly put it, fan mail. But
there is only one letter of interest. It was penned by a
baroness and I quote: 'Dear Master: I would love to
be tortured by you.'"

"I assume you've replied," said Bogart, sipping his
Scotch.

"'My Dear Baroness: You've already been tortured
enough by seeing my pictures.'"

In that saddened face of Lorre's, Bogart recognized

a troubled air. "I get it," he said, stubbing out his cigarette. "Business has been slow."

"Business, dear Bogie, has been nonexistent. There comes a time when you must find the integrity to stand up and refuse certain types of roles."

"At least," said Bogart, "you can say you never played a frog that swallowed Cleveland."

"Precisely. I don't want to go down in history as a monster. I've played in *terror* films, not horror. I prefer the word *terror*. Let us say, dear Bogie, that in the future I want to do what is human, not what is profitable."

"You're doing all right," said Bogart. "You've got a new picture. I saw the ads. That Tony Martin thing."

"*Thing* is an appropriate appellation. Others call it *Casbah*. I play this jerk of a policeman—a kind of cheerful Inspector Javert—looking for another jerk, Pepe LeMoko. But I thought you were asking questions to cheer me up."

"It's that bad, huh, Peter? Look at the good side. You've got your independence from Warners."

"If only it were that simple. There are unignorable barriers, dear Bogie. Did I already mention integrity? It leads only to destitution and starvation . . . conditions I am familiar with. You forget I was born on the continent of Europe, without the silver spoon with which you were so fortuitously provided."

"Now who's insulting who?"

"Acting! To think that after studying for two years in Vienna with Sigmund Freud, I could have been someone important, someone special. If theater hadn't interfered with my life, I would undoubtedly be a world-famous psychoanalyst." Lorre cocked his head and for a moment resembled a small child with his baby face. It still amazed Bogart that this same man had so convincingly portrayed psychopaths, kidnappers and killers.

While Lorre paused to relight his cigarette and consume a hearty portion of bourbon, Bogart felt his usual affection, and concern, for Lorre.

They had first met at Warners shortly before World War II. Their immediate rapport, both on the set and on the screen in films like *The Maltese Falcon* and *Passage to Marseilles*, had led to a deep-rooted respect and a friendship shared in drinking and playing pranks on the stuffed shirts at Warners.

There had been times when Bogart, keenly aware of Lorre's psychiatric background, had wished the actor could peer into the recesses of his own brain. His fingers toyed with the glass, unconsciously pushing it away.

Lorre leaned forward curiously, a new hint of lucidity in his voice. "You're troubled, dear Bogie. You just pushed your glass away—a subtle gesture that did not go unnoticed by these soft-boiled eyes. I have so concerned myself with my own problems, I've neglected yours."

"Problem? You're very good, Peter."

"Empty out your troubles and I shall listen." Lorre leaned back inquisitively.

"Johnny Hawks was shot and killed today. By person or persons unknown."

Lorre said nothing for half a minute as his face turned ashen. His hand trembled as he drank the remainder of his bourbon. "That must have been a stake through the heart, to hear of Johnny's demise." Lorre's complexion began to return to its normal color. "Johnny was such a dedicated actor; and you sailed with him frequently. It would not be presumptuous of me to say that you knew Johnny as well as any man.

Surely you must have some idea who perpetrated such a heinous crime."

"There's the possibility it was Dalt Brennan."

Lorre gulped and turned ashen again. "You're coming at me with far more than I had bargained for tonight."

"It gets more complicated, Peter. Just before he was killed, Johnny called Harry Cohn and told him he suspected Dalt of—hang on, Peter, this is a dilly—of planning to blow up Shrine Auditorium on Saturday night."

Lorre could hardly remain seated. "Shrine Auditorium? Do you mean this coming Saturday night? Oscar night?"

Bogart nodded reluctantly. "Johnny believed that Dalt was going to follow the plot of a screenplay he'd written, *Hollywood Armageddon.*"

"You mean make his fiction a reality?" Lorre squirmed nervously, his saucer eyes homing in on Bogart. "This is incredible, dear Bogie. And that's why Johnny died? Because he's the man who knew too much?"

"According to Cohn, yes."

"And Harry is now seeking Dalt?"

"Cohn has no idea Dalt is involved. The screenplay was written under a pen name, Blake Richards."

"So." Lorre pressed forward eagerly, as though he were preparing to leap across the table. "Do you realize, dear Bogie, that you alone may possess the only clue to an incredible mystery? What other fabulous information do you possess? Quickly. What proof have you garnered to support—"

"Proof? Quit talking like a cop, Peter. I've got no proof. Just Johnny's word. Delivered secondhand by Harry Cohn."

"Johnny's word. That meant a great deal. His code of honor . . ."

"Exactly what I've been thinking."

"What do you intend doing about it, dear Bogie?"

"When a man's best friend has been shot and killed, he should do something about it."

"But," blurted Lorre, "what happens when the man who might have done it is also your best friend?"

"He should still do something about it. Maybe he doesn't like doing it, but . . ." Bogart's fist hammered the table and the remaining Scotch sloshed in his glass.

"What do you plan as your first move?" asked Lorre keenly.

"I've already taken it, Peter. I couldn't concentrate on the *Largo* set so I took a run over to Republic to see Kitty Steele."

"How is beautiful Kitty? Surely if anyone can speak for Dalt it's—"

"It's not that easy, Peter. First, Kitty is still beautiful. Second, she and Dalt are separated. For good. She's cut all strings. She told me Dalt went to live with Lloyd shortly before he committed suicide."

"The place in Topanga Beach? That would be worth checking."

"It's on my must list for tomorrow."

"You have my curiosity at a fever pitch," said Lorre. "Do you realize, dear Bogie, this is the first time I've felt uplifted—excited is the word—since I left Warners? But go on . . . surely Kitty must have told you more."

"She mentioned a writer named Paul Fabrini. Kitty heard Dalt threaten Fabrini. She didn't say it, but I got the feeling she was afraid for Fabrini."

"I well remember Dalt's temper, dear Bogie. Especially the night in Ciro's when Dalt went berserk. Some people thought he was doing an impression of me."

"Schizoid . . ."

"Hardly, dear Bogie. If he were a raving schizoid, he would have only irrational explanations of what the cruel world is doing to him. From what I recollect of Dalt, he could always logically put his finger on the people or circumstances doing him wrong. And he was so convincing, you had to pause and wonder if there really weren't a conspiracy. The word for it is *paranoia*. I would like to hear more about this writer . . . Fabrini."

"According to Kitty, he rewrote one of Dalt's screenplays."

"Another cross for Dalt to bear. Why don't you call this Fabrini?"

"Now?"

"Immediately. He is your only lead. Besides, it will give you peace of mind. Hell, it will give me peace of mind, now that you've stirred me up so."

"You know, Peter, you're getting better all the time."

Bogart flagged down Jamieson for use of a table phone. An operator told him Paul Fabrini lived in Santa Monica. He tried the number but connected only with an answering service. A bored voice promised to deliver the message, then perked up when the magical name *Bogart* was mentioned. Bogart hung up and looked despondently across the table at Lorre. "So much for peace of mind," he said.

Bogart ordered another Scotch. His thoughts settled firmly on Dalt for the first time since Johnny Hawks's death.

He felt only guilt.

He had turned his back on Dalt that hellish night at the Garden of Allah, cast him out of his life completely. It had been to protect Betty, but he still couldn't help feeling that his act of rejection might have led indirectly to the death of Johnny.

There was always the possibility that Johnny's suspicions about Dalt could be wrong, but Lorre had put it correctly: Bogart was the only one with the knowledge that Dalt might be linked to Johnny's death.

"I'm worried about one thing, Peter," said Bogart, after fortifying himself with more Scotch. "Harry Cohn. He's going to have his headhunters out beating the brush starting tomorrow. And if he finds Dalt before I do . . ."

Lorre sneered. "I wouldn't worry about that creeping blight. He's devious, but he's not clever. Have I never told you of my first experience with him? He had brought me from England to make *Mad Love*, in which I played a wonderfully awful madman. For my second picture Cohn kept offering me these terrible scripts and I, dear Bogie, kept turning them down. I suggested he put me in *Crime and Punishment*. You see, I wanted to play the part of Raskolnikov so badly. It was my ultimate dream as an actor. So I typed a two-page synopsis. Cohn was impressed—oh, was he impressed. He told me, 'A story like that, someone should write a book.' So you see, dear Bogie, I shouldn't worry about Cohn. We shall simply allow him to grope around in his ignorance."

It was now ten o'clock and Lorre was weaving slightly, even though there was no trace of drunkenness in his voice. Bogart suddenly realized that his own "thermostat" approach to drinking—consuming only so much every hour—had been forgotten in favor of a steadily increasing rate of consumption.

Bogart hated himself for losing discipline. He had discovered, some time after *Casablanca* but before *The Big Sleep*, that the insecurities that had fueled his drinking were no longer a threat.

"And who," boomed the bassoon voice of Romanoff, "is good enough for this?" He was standing at the head of the table, bill in hand.

"Nothing's free anymore," slurred Bogart contemptuously.

"If you've got it, I'll take it," said Romanoff. "If you don't have it, I'll give you credit."

"The man with the big heart," said Bogart, unfolding his wallet and placing several bills on the table. "I'm leaving one extra dime."

"Jamieson will be overwhelmed by your generosity."

"It's for the use of the phone."

"Consider it part of my public service."

Bogart stood up. "I'm gonna let the rest of the world catch up."

"Catch up?" pondered Romanoff.

"He means," interjected Lorre, sipping his fresh supply of bourbon, "that the rest of the world is always three drinks behind. It is a famous Humphrey Bogart expression."

EIGHT

From the moment he left Romanoff's, Bogart felt uneasy. The streets were wet, blinding in the glare of the neon storefronts, so he drove with extra caution. It was a few minutes after midnight when he edged up Rodeo Drive, carefully checking each intersection he passed in the rearview mirror.

He was acutely aware of the slight buzz from the alcohol in his system, but he knew that wasn't what was troubling him. The route was an easy one that he had driven countless times. Yet he couldn't shake his discomfort.

In the rearview mirror a pair of headlights swung out from a narrow side street just before he reached Sunset Boulevard. Bogart stiffened.

As he crossed Sunset, the car came up to speed and hung half a block behind him. As Bogart watched, he began to wonder if he was being followed.

A blaring horn startled him, and Bogart realized he was wandering into the opposite lane. He swung the wheel to the right. *Jesus, you idiot!*

Once he was on Benedict Canyon Road there was a distinct change in the neighborhood. The gloomy sidewalks were wider, the dark-green lawns more spacious, rolling like a midnight sea. The homes were more opulent, silhouetted against the night sky. The trees that lined the road—birch, spruce, weeping willows and a few eucalyptus—were ghostlike: black in shadow one moment, suddenly gray-white the next in the light of the high street lamps.

Bogart drove steadily, easing the Cadillac around long curves. Gradually the houses grew farther apart; the street lamps became fewer. His headlights flashed over wild empty lots and fields full of waving clumps of pampas grass. This far out the street was more like a country road, lined with tortured oak trees. Weeping willows dragged fingers across the top of the coupe.

Suddenly there was a dark, hurtling shape on Bogart's left. It was the sedan, a dark-blue Buick, trying to pass on a blind curve. Bogart cursed, knowing that he would have trouble giving the idiot the room he would need. He knew there was a ravine to his right.

There was a screeching, rending sound as the Buick sedan slammed into the side of the Cadillac. Bogart fought the wheel, felt the rear tires sliding on the wet road. Tree branches smacked into the windshield; his tires bounced on the loose shoulder.

The sedan forced the coupe farther to the right. Bogart was almost off the shoulder—a large utility pole loomed ahead suddenly. There was no room to avoid it! Unless . . .

Bogart stomped on the brakes, swung the Cadillac right for a split-second and then back to the left, threw the clutch out and jammed the gears down into second. The car went into a half-spin and almost turned turtle as it slid sideways and backward into the ditch. It came to rest at an angle to the road, the engine stalled. The utility pole was only inches from the front fender.

The dark-blue sedan roared up Benedict Canyon Road and out of sight.

Bogart let out a deep breath, slumped in his seat and wiped sweat from his forehead. After a half-minute he got out to survey the damage: It was minor, mostly scraped paint and dents. Bogart shook out a cigarette with a trembling hand. The match flame wavered before he could get it lit.

Bogart climbed back into his car and slowly pulled onto the asphalt. He kept a wary eye out for the return of the sedan. It didn't seem possible that the few questions he had asked would cause anyone to . . .

A few minutes later he turned left into a lane with thick grass and high weeds on either side. He drove up a steep incline, around a sharp curve, down a shallow dip and then up another incline onto a large, spacious knoll.

Atop the knoll was Hedgerow Farm, a rambling, three-level house with peaked roofs at either end. The house was dark, lit only by a few exterior lamps. He parked in the rear driveway, where the main entrance was located.

Bogart got out, tossed the cigarette into the wet grass, took the 16-millimeter film cans from the rear seat and turned at the sound of running feet.

"Hiya, Harvey," Bogart said, tousling the head and clipped ears of an eager, playful boxer. "Everything safe and sound?"

The dog wagged a stub of a tail and followed Bogart past the white picket fence that framed the lawn and swimming pool. Using his latchkey, Bogart entered an oval-shaped entrance hall. Harvey followed. Bogart shrugged off his coat, stepped left and flicked on the lights in the walnut-paneled living room. He flung his coat over one of a pair of wingback chairs that faced a huge fireplace. He placed his hands on the large, hand-carved English mantel and stared into the ashes of a dead fire.

Harvey climbed onto a divan under bay windows in the opposite wall and placed his head between his paws, watching his master. Bogart's hand still trembled. Suddenly home—so beautifully decorated by Betty in a mixture of Dutch, early American and French Provincial—didn't seem as comforting. He sighed and walked through double doors to the right of the fireplace and crossed to the built-in bar in the den. He mixed Scotch and soda and sat on a leather bar stool, staring at his mirrored reflection behind the counter.

He sipped his Scotch and tried to shake the feelings of depression and uncertainty that stole over him. He felt the urge to thread up *Birth of a Nation*—it might be one way of getting his mind away from the day's events—when his eyes fell on a gallery of framed photographs on the wall. Bogart slid off the stool, a smile creeping over his face. Betty Bacall, in one of her rare cheesecake photographs, smiled back at him. He wished she were back from New York.

He stepped closer to study Betty's high-cheeked, sultry gaze when his attention was caught by the photograph below.

It was an age-browned photograph of Dalt Brennan.

Thirty years ago. Dalt in a seaman's uniform. Lithe body; small, close-set eyes shining eagerly over a bulby nose. All the youth, enthusiasm and innocence in that round, corn-fed, Ohio face had not yet been lost in the classrooms of reality.

Another photograph. Bogart standing next to Dalt, both of them in uniform. Silly smiles. Young Bogart also full of the same naiveté. The photograph had been taken on the deck of the *Leviathan* before they had reached the coast of France. Abaft the ammunition lockers, Bogart remembered. *Nineteen eighteen.* A long time ago.

Below was another picture of them together. Dalt hadn't changed much—a few more pounds maybe. No hay bales to lift in New York. Bogart remembered the occasion: New York, 1927, an illicit nightclub. When they were both getting started, Bogart in theater, Brennan writing plays. Dalt still had the same country-boy look: round face; small, intelligent eyes. His tuxedo was just a shade too tight. A homburg, rakishly tilted over one eye, hid the unbrushed, puppy-dog hair that always seemed to fly in all directions. They were surrounded by other aspiring actors and actresses. Bootleg bottles of booze littered the table. Bogart's hair was slicked down, the same glossy look as his tuxedo, and his teeth jutted out in a smirk.

God, how the years go. The ticking of a nearby wall clock split time into minuscule fragments. Bogart lit another cigarette, sipped more of the Scotch and let memories sweep up and over . . .

NINE

It is a time of mass slaughter, madness and patriotism. Yet back in the U.S. there are still those who regard the war as some sort of sporting event. They sing "When It's Apple Blossom Time in Normandy" and George M. Cohan's "Over There," and speak petulantly of chasing the Kaiser clear to Berlin.

At eighteen Bogart is as brash and optimistic as they come. His experience has been limited to the luxuries of the Upper West Side of New York and the privileges that go with being the son of a physician some people call eminent and a mother who is a famed magazine illustrator.

Even after failing Andover Academy, the family alma mater, Bogart is no less brash when he stands before his glaring father one afternoon early in 1918. Dr. Belmont DeForest Bogart pulls the pince-nez from the bridge of his broad nose. "I had deep hopes, Humphrey, that you might amount to something one day."

"I am going to amount to something," promises Bogart, "but first I'm joining the navy." Indifferent to his parents' objections, he pulls on his chesterfield overcoat and throws down the butt of a Sweet Caporal cigarette. He walks determinedly from the three-story limestone house on 103rd Street without looking back.

Seaman First Class Humphrey Bogart dons his uniform like a quarterback preparing to charge onto a gridiron. In boot camp he finds the company of his New York peers dull and is attracted instead to Dalt Brennan, the gangling son of an Ohio corn farmer.

Dalt is far from a hayseed or a dullard. He has struggled hard to educate himself. The hardships of Dalt's upbringing can be seen in his face, but Bogart also sees eagerness and exuberance and, before training is completed, he and Dalt are inseparable. Dalt jokes of sinking a pig boat single-handedly; Bogart brags about storming Berlin. Both have trouble learning how to tie knots.

Their first tour of duty is aboard the troopship *Leviathan*, and their assignment is to ferry Yanks to the front lines of France and return the wounded to Liverpool.

When they reach the shores of France and hear the distant whine of bullets and see the lingering, foul smoke of mortar shells, they suddenly realize that death is looking over their shoulders. They both look pale, and the battle-hardened medics who carry the blood-soaked stretchers laugh derisively and call them greenhorns.

Klaxon horns clang urgently. On that first day the bodies number in the hundreds. The wounded fill the sick bays and litter the decks above. Many of the casualties are suffering from phosphorous burns or from flame-thrower bursts. It is a baptism in blood. Bogart swallows the bile building in his throat, but Dalt, his face a sickly green, vomits over the starboard side.

Bogart and Dalt hurry from victim to victim, helping corpsmen apply unguent to the ruptured, blistering flesh.

Nothing can expunge the sickeningly sweet odor of charred flesh. It clings to their uniforms like a whore's perfume, long after they have unloaded the wounded on British docks.

Dalt keeps his mind occupied by identifying the guns always growling in the distance. "Thirty-

millimeter mortar, Humph. Hear those heavy sounds?
Machine guns. There, a Hotchkiss. And that. Water-
cooled Browning. That jerky popping? Vickers gun.
That springy rattle? Lewis guns." What begins as a
form of escape for Dalt turns into an obsession with
weaponry.

Afternoon. Hundreds of walking wounded limp and
hobble up the gangplank from the docks of Brest. "Jesus, sweet Jesus, Humph. I don't think I can take
much more of this."

"Me either, Dalt. It's enough to—"

A scream splinters the air. Standish, the bosun's
mate, is flailing his arms and cursing unintelligibily.
Bogart and Dalt watch in fascinated horror. Six burly
seamen drag Standish down the stairwell and throw
him into the brig.

"Did you see that?" asks Dalt.

"I saw it," says Bogart. But he wishes he hadn't. It is
a restless night aboard the *Leviathan*; it is difficult
for men to sleep when one of their shipmates is raving. In the morning the captain decides Standish
should be removed to a military stockade and the
transfer is assigned to Bogart and Dalt, who strap on
their puttees and Colt .45 automatics with a naive air
of adventure, eager to be free of the ship's ungodly
routine.

"Help me prop him up, Dalt." Bogart, his British-
style gas mask flapping against his chest, pushes Standish down into the cockpit of the motorcycle's sidecar.
Dalt straps in the catatonic prisoner, securing the
handcuffs. "Can you drive this thing, Humph?"

Pushing goggles over his eyes, Bogart hitches up his
leather driving jacket and straddles the seat. "There's

no time like the present to learn. Hang onto your steel pot, pal."

Dalt jumps onto a makeshift seat behind the sidecar and the motorcycle jerks erratically to life and lurches drunkenly across the dock area. Dalt is holding on dearly but Standish, his large body limp, continues to stare with vacant eyes. He begins a dirge for his long-dead mother.

The motorcycle gambols wildly as Bogart familiarizes himself with the controls. His grin soon shifts to a frown as they pass retreating British troops. Many are injured—red-stained bandages on legs, chests, heads. Standish groans.

They approach a field hospital. Standish tenses up at the sight of the Tommies littering the entrance. Men without arms and legs lie groaning or unconscious, awaiting their turn to go under the surgeon's tools.

Beyond the hospital, an orchard has been blasted and shredded by cannon fire. Birds chirp among broken hemlock trunks. Two horses lie in the crater-pocked road, a horde of bloated blowflies rising from their ruptured stomachs.

Standish explodes.

Bogart hears a bullish roar and turns to see the steel handcuffs swinging toward his head. Standish strikes him solidly in the mouth and Bogart tastes blood and salt. Tears leap from his eyes and the landscape whirls. A sensation of falling, of spinning, is acute and he is terrified by the kaleidoscope of light and dark. His fingers touch a piece of lip dangling from the right corner of his mouth. Pain. Excruciating pain.

Pressure against his side. Someone is taking the .45

from his holster. Bogart can't find the strength to prevent it.

There's a lurching sensation as the motorcycle rams against an embankment. He feels himself being flung to the ground and finally he can see Standish, .45 in hand, staggering away from the overturned cycle, a deep cut on his forehead. A warm breeze washes across Bogart. A stream of blood flows from the cut as Standish swings the .45 toward Bogart in slow motion.

An explosion. The bullet punctures only gray sky. Dalt is twisting Standish's arm. Bogart hears heavy breathing, loud grunts, and the splashing sound of his .45 dropping into a puddle. The grunts turn to groans as Dalt draws his own Colt and beats Standish across the skull. The crazed sailor staggers and sinks lower under each impact.

Supporting himself on a shell-splintered tree trunk, Bogart gets groggily to his feet. Standish's eyes are glazed and he falls into the mud in a fetal position, softly crooning to his mother.

Dalt thumbs back the hammer of his Colt and aims at Standish. Bogart staggers to him and throws his hand over the muzzle, looking Dalt in the eye. Bogart sees only senseless fury at first, but finally a glimmer of humanity returns. Dalt eases off the hammer and reholsters his automatic. Although dazed and disoriented, Bogart helps Dalt right the dented motorcycle and restrap the semiconscious Standish into the sidecar.

At the nearby field hospital Bogart's lip is examined indifferently by a British medic whose apron is spotted with bloodstains. "It's hardly worth my time, compared to some of the chaps I've sewn up today, Yank. I'll have to do my stitching without anesthetic. Afraid we're all out."

"Just clam up, Doc, and go to work." Bogart can barely slip the words through his throbbing mouth.

"You might have some trouble later on, Yank. That's a big chunk of lip the Huns have hammered on. Could affect your speech."

As the doctor plies his needle, Bogart tries to keep his mind off the pain by staring at Dalt, who stands grimly before him, hump-shouldered. There is something dark and foreboding about him that unnerves Bogart.

"Sweet Jesus, Humph," says Dalt later, "that sawbones never missed a stitch. He closed you up like my grandma used to weave rugs."

Soon after the incident, Dalt seems his old self. Bogart feels indebted to him for saving his life—an act he may never be able to repay. The lip heals properly but is noticeably scarred, and Bogart learns to control the resulting lisp.

Dalt is assigned to a supply ship and for the duration transports artillery and mortar shells, learning the fundamentals of explosives and ordnance. He makes voluntary forays into the trenches to learn from seasoned sappers the handling of land mines, grenades and TNT.

"It should scare the hell out of me," he writes to Bogart, "but it's fascinating. There's an awesome sense of power when you handle this stuff. It's strange, but I seem to be able to control my own worst fears when I work with explosives."

Bogart shudders, but any fears he may have about Dalt are forgotten with the coming of peace. As the *Leviathan* steams into New York harbor, Bogart and Dalt vow to help each other. If there are obstacles, they will overcome them together. They have seen enough death; now they will contribute something positive.

On January 16, 1920, the Prohibition Act ushers in a new decade that will give birth to speakeasies, bathtub gin and a dance craze called the Charleston. Bumming around on Houston Street, jobless, Bogart buys his Scotch in bottles with hand-printed labels. He increases his smoking to disguise the foul breath the hooch gives him.

With smooth-pomaded hair, Bogart purposely walks the streets to ogle the new knee-length dresses and silk stockings. He reads about the Al Capone gang wars in Chicago, and he loves the movies of Gloria Swanson and Clara Bow with their new bobbed-cloched hairdos. The postwar generation is said to be "lost," and the times are described as "roaring," but Bogart is utterly bored.

. . . Until an old family friend, Broadway producer Bill Brady, gives him a job moving scenery in the Playhouse Theatre on Forty-eighth Street. Bogart is immediately stagestruck. Brady sees latent charisma in Bogart and, despite his lack of formal training, throws him into a play called *Experience*. It is not an auspicious debut. Theater critic Alexander Woolcott singles out Bogart as the kind of performer who is "usually and mercifully known as inadequate."

A peculiar streak of luck clings to the fledgling actor and he is cast in several roles, usually as a dandy or juvenile lead. He develops a sleek, dapper style, can read lines effectively and projects a strong, self-assured masculinity that women find attractive.

On the opening night of *Cradle Snatchers* in 1925, Bogart is finally singled out favorably by critics. ". . . Bogart created a furor as one of the hired lovers

. . . young and handsome as Valentino . . . as graceful as our best romantic actors."

It is during the run of *Cradle Snatchers* that Dalt
appears backstage. He's a few pounds heavier but the
inquisitive face and the eager attitude are still
strongly in evidence.

In Bogart's favorite speakeasy, they get drunk on
the worst Scotch imaginable as revelers sing "Bye Bye
Blackbird" and "Cecilia." Bogart learns that Dalt has
spent his postwar years in Paris, bumming the boule-
vards with the likes of F. Scott Fitzgerald, whoring,
drinking and occasionally putting words to paper. To
get the war out of his system, Dalt has written a lavish
antiwar novel, *Farewell to Flanders*. And he has several "rousing" ideas for Broadway plays.

Bogart introduces Dalt to one of his co-stars in *Cradle Snatchers*, a redheaded, sexy ingenue named
Sherry Scott. The booze flows. Dalt's arm slides
around Sherry's waist and Bogart knows the evening
will end warmly for his old war buddy. They relive
the good times and the bad times. Bogart hasn't forgotten their vow. "Take your eyes off that beautiful
dame and listen, Dalt . . . You knock out the plays
and I'll peddle 'em. I know a lot of people in this business."

They shake on it. There is no reason to anticipate
anything but the very best of times.

By the time Bogart finishes reading *Farewell to
Flanders*, Dalt and Sherry are engaged. Bogart finds
the book a powerful antiwar novel, full of literary
promise but raggedly written. Dalt has no luck with
publishers but isn't disappointed. Bogart finds Dalt's
playwriting has strong social overtones. But this is a

gay season of sophisticated comedies and the only interest in Dalt comes from insignificant neighborhood playhouses, where audiences are minuscule and critics never seen. Bogart is a little startled when Dalt sets a marriage date with Sherry—she has a reputation for playing around. But Bogart is best man at their wedding and he drowns his misgivings in a plethora of champagne.

For a year Dalt sustains himself by selling pulp adventure yarns to *Sea Stories, War Birds* and *Daredevil Aces.* Sherry, whose career is limited to chorus lines, is easily disenchanted. Her desire for better material things leads to constant arguments.

Then Dalt writes *Day of the Leviathan,* a comedy-drama about boredom and war aboard a U.S. troopship. Bogart feels it is a brilliant play and submits it to Linus Larrabee, a visionary producer noted for taking risks. *Leviathan* is turned into an extravagant production, its large male cast headed by Paul Kelly, Sidney Toler and Porter Hall.

The critics roast the production as "overdone" and "disoriented" and *Leviathan* sinks after only seven performances.

On closing night Bogart is backstage to witness Dalt accuse Larrabee of having an affair with Sherry. She refuses to deny it and says she's through with Dalt. In a rage, Dalt goes for Larrabee; Bogart and the stage manager must pull him away.

This is the first time Bogart has seen Dalt slip into heavy drinking and manic depression. With Bogart's help, Dalt finally snaps out of his despondency.

He refuses to divorce Sherry, feeling bound by his deep-rooted Midwest-puritan ethics. By now Sherry is running around with several men and drinking heavily. Too drunk for auditions, her career ends dismally about the time she divorces Dalt.

Bogart's own marital status is no better. His marriage to actress Helen Menken ends in divorce after only a year, and Menken is quickly replaced by another Broadway ingenue, Mary Philips. But she and Bogart are devoted professionals, and they spend too much time on the stage to make anything solid of their marriage.

Mary Philips Bogart compresses her lips and shakes her head emphatically. "I refuse to go, Humphrey, and that's the last word."

"Listen, angel," pleads Bogart, "the talkies are taking over. Didn't I tell you when that Jolson picture was released? Now look, baby, I've got the Fox contract right here in my pocket. Seven hundred and fifty a week. That's real dough, and I've got the train tickets. I want you in Hollywood with me. Hell, I *need* you."

Mary's voice is firm, uncaring. "I have my career here on the stage to consider. And I refuse to give it up. But don't be so upset, honey." Mary slides an arm around Bogart and kisses him tenderly. Bogart's expression of disappointment doesn't change. "After all, Humphrey, we are a modern couple. A few months apart might do us some good."

Bogart's eyes turn as cold as Mary's voice. "Yeah, sure, sweetheart. Whatever you say."

"Sorry about this, Mr. Bogart, you losing the part in *The Man Who Came Back*. The stock market collapse hasn't helped the picture business either. It isn't as if we're terminating your contract. We have extensive plans to use you in our low-budget films. Right now the name Humphrey Bogart just doesn't have any drawing power. You understand."

Bogart's eyes are cold. "Sure, I understand."

Bogart commences a string of small, inconsequential films—usually with tenth billing. He finds filmmaking technically fascinating but is easily bored on the set. For the first time he begins to drink heavily.

"Howzit, Bogart?" Spencer Tracy rubs a thumb and forefinger across the bridge of his big nose and glances at a parade of half-dressed dance starlets walking between sound stages at Warners. "Hear you're doing some nice stuff with Bette Davis in *Three on a Match*."

"Nice stuff? I think I'm going backward, Spence," snorts Bogart. "Now they got me playing a gangster. How low can you get? They don't even have a name for the character. Just 'The Mug.'"

Before scurrying away Tracy thumps Bogart on the arm and counsels him to keep working—exposure is everything in the motion picture business. Bogart is about to return to the set when he sees a familiar figure striding toward him.

Dalt is a few pounds heavier but his good spirits indicate he has recovered from his marital problems. He introduces Bogart to his twenty-year-old "kid" brother Lloyd.

Bogart senses that Lloyd is an aloof, high-strung young man, likable but distant, with a strong desire to be a writer.

While Dalt was in Europe, Lloyd left the farm at sixteen to work in Chicago as a copyboy and cub reporter on the *Tribune*. Now they're together in Hollywood. So far they've lived off Dalt's pulp stories, which he now writes under pen names so Sherry can't claim half through alimony payments.

"So," says Bogart, "you're going to try your luck in the Land of Fantasy."

"I can't do any worse than you," says Dalt. "I was hoping you could introduce me to the story editors. The way I figure it, this is a visual medium that calls for visual stories. Action stuff. I've learned my lesson about trying to save the world—I'll keep that for the books. For Hollywood, make it move and you're in."

"These are hard times," Bogart warns him. "And it doesn't look like it's going to change until we kick Hoover out of office. But I'll see what I can do. Maybe we can kill them yet."

"You know," says Dalt, "we aren't getting any younger."

Producers at Fox gauge Dalt's outdoor adventures too difficult to handle. Hollywood is still experimenting and fumbling with the techniques of sound recording. Most films are nothing more than photographed stage plays. Dalt must accept this as one of the maddening anomalies of Hollywood. He subsists on his pulp writing, which has now been elevated to *Black Mask* and *Argosy,* and starts a new novel based on his Broadway experiences entitled *The Hopeless White Way*.

Lloyd returns to Fox to pick Bogart's brain about scriptwriting; Bogart does his best to dissuade him. Bogart still thinks Lloyd is too gentle and sensitive to survive in such a tough profession.

Bogart is no less stunned than Dalt when Lloyd's first screenplay is purchased for a record-breaking price at MGM. They celebrate the sale, but Bogart detects in Dalt a deep-seated jealousy. Lloyd tries to be casual and urbane, but Bogart can sense the strain.

Dalt's pain is slightly anesthetized when Bogart convinces a Fox producer to buy one of Dalt's Western scripts. *The Wayward Trigger* is made into a low-budget second feature with George O'Brien.

It is the *open sesame* Dalt so desperately needs. He continues to write mystery, adventure and Western scripts. *The Hopeless White Way* is purchased by a publisher, who goes bankrupt before press time. Rights are caught up in litigation and the novel never sees print.

Meanwhile, almost effortlessly, Lloyd ascends to the MGM apex, where he is groomed by Irving Thalberg and embraced by Louis B. Mayer as a distinguished writer of sophisticated comedies. Soon Lloyd is being compared to Charles MacArthur and Noel Coward. To become part of the movie world intelligentsia, Lloyd moves to Topanga Beach. It is then that Bogart's suspicions are confirmed about Lloyd's homosexuality: He lives openly with his lover, untouched by Dalt's embarrassment.

If Bogart fails to make an impression on the film-going public, he wallops his fellow workers. He is a fast study and he always arrives prepared—something almost unheard of among his peers. He develops a reputation as a loner who refuses to attend snobbish Hollywood parties and who voices iconoclastic opinions.

Fox continues to cast Bogart in uninteresting, often inept films. Bogart is hardly shocked when his option is not renewed. He decides he's washed up and tells

Dalt he is returning to Broadway. Dalt is working slavishly at Mascot and Victory, grinding out wretched Western serials. At night he toils into the early hours on his own original screenplays. Bogart, who detects improvement in Dalt's style, urges him to try his luck on Broadway again. But Dalt sees his future in Hollywood. The same week that Bogart leaves for the East, Lloyd publishes his first book, *Sit Down Laughing*, a collection of whimsical sketches about Hollywood.

The Depression forces hundreds of thousands of Americans to seek escapism in movie theaters. It is ironic that just when those swelling audiences need new movie heroes, Bogart is leaving Hollywood to return to Broadway.

It is not the Broadway he once knew. Prohibition has been repealed and now nightclubs like the Stork Club, El Morocco and Twenty-One are respectable "joints" for the Astors and Vanderbilts and slinky women in strapless evening gowns.

Producers have also changed. Plays close faster than they open and, because Bogart is almost an unknown commodity again, he is jobless for several months. His dying father summons him to his deathbed and gives Bogart his ruby ring—and numerous debts. In an effort to pay them, Bogart works in a penny arcade, challenging chess players at fifty cents a game. His perseverance pays off and soon he regains his reputation as a stage actor. He stars in *I Love You Wednesday* and *Chrysalis* and is glad Hollywood is behind him. He considers *Invitation to Murder*, when it opens in May 1934, his worst play despite solid support from Walter Abel and Gale Sondergaard.

*   *   *

". . . the hip hooray and ballyhoo . . . the Lullaby of Broadway . . . when the Broadway baby says goodnight, it's early in the morning . . ."

Bogart snaps off his Stromberg-Carlson console and resumes writing: "You won't believe this, Dalt, but 150 plays flopped on Broadway last year. For a while I thought I was going to have to stand in the soup-kitchen lines with everyone else. Then this play, *Invitation to Murder*. What a clunker. Yet something crazy and wonderful is happening. A producer named Arthur Hopkins saw me in the damned thing and told Robert Sherwood I'd be perfect for the role of a gangster in something they're planning called *The Petrified Forest*. That terrific British actor, Leslie Howard, is playing the lead. The plot's probably petrified too but in three days I'm auditioning. Incidentally, I saw that Klondike picture you wrote about the kids and the wolf dog and I thought there were some nice touches in the dialogue, but the plot . . . sure wish you could sell one of your gems and get out of the sweat factory . . ."

Robert Sherwood scowls and slumps in his center-section loge in the Broadhurst Theater. "What's his name again?"

Arthur Hopkins, Sherwood's producer, squirms nervously. "Bogart. Humphrey Bogart."

"Never heard of him. You heard of him, Leslie?"

The slender actor leaning languidly against the orchestra pit, Leslie Howard, smooths back his blond hair, staring off at some distant point as though distracted. Vaguely, "Can't say that I have."

Hopkins speaks with enthusiasm. "He's done scads of plays. Even was in pictures for a time."

"None of the pictures I've seen," said Sherwood.

"Well," says Howard vacuously, "as long as he's backstage."

"If you're insistent, Arthur, flag him on."

Bogart ambles onto a stage that is totally bare. He has spent the past three nights prowling the Bowery, absorbing the milieu of derelicts. He shuffles to avoid the spotlight, which floats to find him, and always deliberately stays inside its shadow. He hasn't shaved for three days and his once-sleek hair is cut short and brushed straight up. He is sallow-face, world-weary and grim-jawed. His eyes stare brutally into the darkness of the wings. "You better just stay where you are, pal. My friend's got the itch between his fingers and he might blast you. I guess we're all a lot of saps."

It is the voice, and it is not the voice, of Humphrey Bogart. There is a harshness to every word, a cynicism that twists the vowels and wrings the consonants. What emerges is not so much a voice as a character, a hated outcast of society, venomous and callous.

". . . I'll spend the rest of my life dead . . ."

Leslie Howard no longer looks faraway or distracted. He has been totally absorbed by Bogart's performance.

Sherwood leans forward to whisper in Hopkins's ear. "What'd you say his name was?"

"Bogart. Humphrey Bogart."

"That isn't Bogart," breathes Sherwood. "That's Duke Mantee."

When Bogart first steps onto the Broadhurst stage, unshaven and uncouth, an "ah" ripples through the startled audience. He plays Duke Mantee one hundred and eighty consecutive times opposite Howard and is applauded for the singular villainy and the sympathy he evokes for an escaped criminal warped

by the injustices of society. Bogart's performance becomes the high point of the season. The actor is
viewed with new reverence. No longer is he the sleek
leading man in tuxedo and top hat.

He is raw and real.

"Telegram, Mr. Bogart."

"Just leave it on the makeup table, junior."

"They told me it was really important. I'm to hand
it to you personally."

"Sure you just aren't looking for a bigger tip? Okay,
junior, hand it over."

> HUMPHREY BOGART BROADHURST THEATER NEW
> YORK CITY NEW YORK OVERHEARD IN STEAM ROOM:
> WARNERS BUYING SCREEN RIGHTS PETRIFIED STOP
> ROBINSON OR RAFT FIRST CHOICE FOR MANTEE STOP
> BETTER HUSTLE ASS STOP DALT BRENNAN HOLLY-
> WOOD USA

"Any reply, Mr. Bogart?"

"No, but hand me that phone, junior, and you'll
really get a tip. . . . Hello, Mabel, give me Leslie
Howard and quick . . ."

Leslie Howard places his hands together tepee-
fashion and, in his soothing, cultured English voice
says flatly: "I'm sorry, Mr. Warner, but I must be insistent. I've given Mr. Bogart my assurance that he
will play Duke Mantee in the film version."

Jack L. Warner looks like a troubled man with a
quickly forming ulcer. He squirms in his high-backed
swivel chair and glares across the spacious office at
Bogart. "This is a big picture, Leslie. And when we

make a big picture, we use big stars, such as yourself. *Not unknowns.*"

"Put Mr. Bogart in this picture," promises Howard, "and he *will* be a star."

Warner is ominously silent, contemplating his ceiling.

Howard straightens up in his chair, his gentle features hardening. "Mr. Bogart and his wife Mary have driven all the way from the East in an old Chevrolet. As much as I despise old clunkers, I shall be accompanying them on their return . . . should your answer be no."

"Now wait just a minute," says Warner, losing interest in the ceiling. "Now wait just a minute . . ." He stares at Howard like a man personally offended. Then a smile brightens his face and he sighs obsequiously. "I wanted Eddie Robinson, but if that's the way *you* want it. . . ."

There is a long silence as Bogart tries to comprehend what has just happened. It isn't until later that night, while he and Howard are celebrating over glasses of Scotch, that he lets loose with a shout of triumph and smothers Mary with kisses.

The film version of *The Petrified Forest* has all the plus factors of the Broadway play and Bogart's career as a heavy is underway. Forthwith he becomes a principal inmate of Warners' "Murderers' Row" (Paul Muni, James Cagney, Edward G. Robinson, George Raft, John Garfield) and he describes himself to the press as The Little Lord Fauntleroy of the studio. He jokingly informs reporters that he experiments with novel ways to croak the line "Get over against the wall and don't move or I'll plug you"; new ways to gasp; new ways to clutch his bullet-riddled stomach. The story goes over the wire services as though Bogart were serious. Thereafter it is difficult to separate Bogart fact from Bogart fiction. The legend of Bogie (as he is now affectionately called) begins its unprecedented ascent.

"Would you call yourself a character actor, Mr. Bogart?"

"I better have character. Character is the only thing a man *ever* has."

"How would you describe yourself, Mr. Bogart?"

"Romantic, idealistic, gallant. Only none of it's on the surface. I like it that way."

"How do you feel about women?"

"A dame should be small enough to fit into your hip pocket, pal. Then when you want to see her she'll fit into the palm of your hand. Then if she gets out of hand, back into the pocket she goes."

"A lot of people say you have class."

"I was born with it. But I sure as hell can live without it."

Dalt is in a rotten mood and sits dejected in Bogart's dressing room. Bogart is eating his usual lunch: baloney and cheese sandwich on plain white Langendorf and one bottle of beer. Bogart is aware that Dalt has been unable to make a transition to A pictures. Sherry has continued to suck up half his earnings, and his career setbacks have led to many flare-ups with producers. It is becoming harder and harder for Dalt to control his temper, and he has begun to see a psychiatrist—a new phase of the Hollywood syndrome. Bogart decides to josh Dalt into a happier frame of mind.

"You talk about *Wayward Trigger* and *Six to the*

Yukon. Hell, all you did was write them, Dalt. Me, I've had to appear in some of the worst pictures in Hollywood history. *Isle of Fury. Two Against the World. The Great O'Malley. The Return of Dr. X.* I've been shot, knifed, garroted I don't know how many times. But the secret in this business is to keep coming back and hoping for something better."

Dalt jerks his head up, a look of hope forcing away his depression. "Who said anything about giving up? I've started another book, *September Wheat.* I'm going to get my childhood out of my system and maybe even give the critics something to write about. And, to keep Sherry in booze, I've got some new synopses I'd like you to show around. Class-A stuff."

"I'll deliver to Jack L. personally," promises Bogart.

"Do whatever you can," urges Dalt, "but do something, Humph. I told Lloyd I wasn't taking any more of those assignments he was arranging for me through the minor independents. I just couldn't keep taking the kid's handouts forever."

Warners increases Bogart's yearly salary but not the quality of his roles. The only film he considers worthwhile during this period is *Dead End,* in which he essays Baby Face Martin, a Brooklyn tenement hoodlum. Ironically, it's not even a Warners film. He makes it on loan-out to Samuel Goldwyn.

On Bogart's return, Warners looks bleaker than ever. His drinking increases and he spends many nights getting drunk with Dalt. One day he is missing from the set and studio police find him stewed to the gills, riding a bicycle around the back lot, clad in dirty pajamas. He looks the fool and, embarrassed, faces Jack L., promising never again to conduct himself so unprofessionally. He keeps the promise, confining his drinking to home and nightclubs.

Bogart's marriage to Mary Philips finally ends in divorce. At a Hollywood party he meets a buxom actress in a flaming red dress named Mayo Methot and it is instant love. Unlike his other wives, Mayo enjoys drinking as much as Bogart and any illusion of an idyllic marriage is quickly shattered by marathon drinking bouts followed by bruising slugfests. The columnists dub them "The Battlin' Bogarts." Yet the more savage their physical abuse, the stronger their lovemaking afterward. Mayo sacrifices her minimal screen career to devote herself solely to Bogart, but so much idle time leads inevitably to heavier drinking.

Their love-war continues and so does Bogart's career as a movie bad guy. He chalks up hits in *Angels With Dirty Faces, The Roaring Twenties,* and *They Drive By Night.* But the unique qualities he displayed in *The Petrified Forest* are submerged and lost in stereotypes.

Dalt remains adrift in his private despair, grinding out an endless string of action pictures. *September Wheat* is accepted by a major New York publisher but it sells only fifteen hundred copies. Rave reviews in the *Atlantic Monthly* and *American Mercury* hardly make up for the indifference of the reading public.

Bogart notices that Dalt is drinking more heavily and is still easily inflamed. Things look good when Fox purchases one of his best scripts, *The Ohio Adventurer,* but disagreement among executive producers over story development leads to such extensive rewriting that Dalt receives only story credit. Half of everything he earns goes to Sherry. He returns to his psychiatrist for one more meeting, then storms out of the office. Every time Bogart sees Dalt he is lost in an alcoholic haze, and his writing has come to a stand-still.

Critics are excited about Lloyd Brennan's new book, *At Home with the Wanderers,* a departure from his usual lighthearted, witty character sketches and farces. This is a serious novel about Ohio farm boys maturing during the Depression and it reads, to Bogart, like a thinly disguised autobiography.

Dalt is livid when he reads the book and he accuses Lloyd, in Bogart's presence, of stealing the idea. This very story was to have been Dalt's next project. Lloyd is flabbergasted and denies it, but Dalt curses him and storms away. Bogart attempts to reconcile the brothers, but fails. Dalt will no longer speak to Lloyd.

These are years of drudgery for Bogart, too infrequently rewarded by a decent screenplay. Then . . . a break. George Raft refuses the role of Roy "Mad Dog" Earle in Raoul Walsh's *High Sierra* because he must die in the final scene. Bogart accepts it as merely another assignment, unaware that his portrayal of a psychopathic killer with a soft streak for a crippled girl will win him new accolades from critics and spark Warners to reevaluate his worth as an actor.

Dalt suffers a complete breakdown. He spends six months undergoing psychiatric treatment. Bogart and Lloyd join in assuming the expenses. When Dalt emerges from the clinic, he is a shattered hulk of his former self. Bogart's efforts to find him writing assignments are met with opposition; however, Bogart's positive stance sways opinions and Dalt is hired to write a series of anti-Nazi melodramas. He frowns on these assignments (*I Stalked the Fuhrer, London Blitz, Dictator from Within, Fascist Confession*) but brings to them a level of literacy and depth that makes them minor classics overnight.

Six months later Sherry dies penniless in a New York City alcoholic ward. For the first time in almost fifteen years, Dalt dates some of Hollywood's most beautiful starlets and his name appears as an item in the gossip columns.

But the casual affairs end the day he meets a struggling young actress, Kitty Steele. Bogart is amazed to see how she bolsters his spirits and inspires him to begin writing another book. Impetuous in matters of matrimony, Dalt and Kitty are quickly married.

Kitty is instrumental in reconciling the differences between Dalt and Lloyd. They spend many weekends, often with Bogart and Mayo in tow, at the Topanga Beach cottage. Lloyd has mellowed considerably and no longer lives openly with a lover, but it is a well-kept secret in the inner circle of Hollywood that he and Geoffrey Carroll are lovers.

America goes to war. Japanese-Americans are herded into concentration camps. Mechanics' overalls become the garb of thousands of women working in shipyards, and skirts are shortened because of fabric shortages.

Teenagers in saddle shoes and bobby socks sip strawberry sodas while listening to Frank Sinatra records. Gas is rationed, junk is turned into tanks and the Hollywood Canteen entertains thousands of men in uniform.

Bogart goes to war, too. He machine-guns Japanese fifth columnists in Huston's *Across the Pacific,* he upholds French traditions in *Passage to Marseilles,* he captures a German battalion in Zoltan Korda's *Sahara*. And he stars in what become instant classics. By the time he has played Sam Spade in Huston's *The Maltese Falcon* and Rick, the cynical café owner, in Curtiz's *Casablanca*, Bogart is a recognized, international star.

Bogart's success is dimmed only by the loss of Leslie Howard on a trans-Atlantic flight that is shot down by Nazis in 1943, and by the behavior of Dalt Brennan.

Dalt has recovered, yet he has not recovered. He seems to be sinking ever deeper into a black morass of pessimism and depression. He no longer pounds his typewriter with frenzied determination. The pulp-magazine editors no longer request his stories, and the screen assignments he does garner tax his diminishing strength.

One of the big hits in late 1942 is *Cantina Blues*, produced by Linus Larrabee, Dalt's old Broadway nemesis, who has made the transition to motion pictures. At Warners, Larrabee turns out a series of profitable musicals and service comedies to relieve war-weary audiences. *You're Out of Step, Private Jones* is a well-received comedy about the USO in the Pacific. One afternoon on the set of *Action in the North Atlantic*, Dalt storms in to inform Bogart that Larrabee has stolen ideas for *Private Jones* out of a story outline he once submitted to Warners. But there is no record of the outline in the story-department files, and Larrabee denies the charge, accusing Dalt of trying to get back at him for his long-ago affair with Sherry. Bogart wonders . . . this is the second time Dalt has charged plagiarism—first against his own brother, now against a rival.

The Screenwriters' Guild arbitrates in Larrabee's favor, and Bogart sees marked deterioration in Dalt. Bogart realizes that over the years Dalt has built up a seething rancor for the movie-making system.

Bogart tells Dalt that he must accept the good with the bad, and above all else he must continue to write. Bogart has no apparent effect on Dalt's unshakable alienation.

Dalt resumes his heavy drinking. His fierce temper is beyond self-control; and he is charged in two minor assault-and-battery cases. Kitty is his one stabilizing factor, but even she tells Bogart she wonders how much longer she can hold their marriage together.

For a short period in 1943, Dalt is employed at Columbia. Every project he develops is eventually shelved. Dalt's growing contempt is reflected in his sloppy work habits, and he shows up to work late once too often. Cohn whirlwinds into the Writers' Building and angrily fires Dalt. From that day on Cohn becomes a personal symbol for Dalt's growing hatred.

The war enters its darkest moments. Hollywood is stripped of its leading men, its technicians, its artists. Too old to fight overseas, Dalt volunteers his services to the Marine Corps. He is assigned to nearby Camp Pendleton as a demolitions instructor.

Bogart is pleased when Dalt finds some minor satisfaction in writing Marine training films. Dalt instructs in the use of Bangalore torpedoes, satchel charges, primacord, flame throwers and hand grenades.

But his satisfaction is short-lived. Upon his return to Hollywood Dalt is again depressed because Kitty's career has stagnated and she has turned to stunting at Republic for the Queen of the Cliffhangers, Linda Sterling.

* * *

Bogart celebrates Dalt's forty-fourth birthday at Ciro's, but it is not a happy occasion. After several drinks Dalt sees Linus Larrabee in another booth and attempts to strangle the producer. As Bogart pulls Dalt away, he is reminded of how Dalt almost pistol-whipped Standish to death in 1918. It is finally the pleading, broken voice of Kitty Steele that calms Dalt. Larrabee, always the gentleman, refuses to press charges. Bogart still wonders who really wrote *You're Out of Step, Private Jones.*

Later that night, sobering up on coffee, Dalt apologizes. "I don't know what came over me, Humph."

"You've had a lot of things coming over you lately, Dalt. You better get a better grip on things. If you want to survive in this business, you can't let it grind you down."

For a moment Dalt can't bring himself to look at Bogart, and Bogart can sense his shame and confusion. For the first time Bogart feels a gap widening between them.

"What can I do, Dalt? I'm scheduled to go overseas soon to entertain the troops."

"I've just finished *Hollywood Armageddon* . . . it's a helluva screenplay. I tried to expose the film industry for what it is."

Bogart frowns. "More catharsis, Dalt? Don't you think you need something more commercial right now?"

"If you don't want to handle it . . ."

"Hold it, kid. I want to do it. If you think it'll make a helluva picture, that's enough for me."

"I'd like you to start with Harry Cohn."

"As bastards go," says Bogart, "you couldn't have picked a better one."

❋   ❋   ❋

Bogart throws Dalt's screenplay on the kitchen table. Mayo begins to recite the lyrics of "Embraceable You"—which means she's in a drunken mood and ready for battle. Between articulate curses ("you two-bit ham actor, go to hell"), she hurls her finest china at Bogart. He throws a bowlful of Caesar salad back at her and war is officially declared. Shards of broken dishes litter the kitchen by the time Bogart storms from the villa, shouldering depression as he has never felt it before. Because he's between pictures he can go on a monumental bender. He stays drunk for three days. Mayo remains drunk for a week.

Hollywood Armageddon is still lying on the kitchen table, its surface spattered with stains from Mayo's bourbon glass, when Dalt casually drops by one evening to see Bogart. Bogart is trying to sober up on coffee and offers a cup to Dalt.

He sees the screenplay and instantly sizes up the situation. "You said you were going to deliver." It flows out of Dalt before even he realizes what he's said. The floodgates burst.

Bogart blushes with embarrassment. "Jesus, I'm sorry, Dalt. Things around here have been—"

"You're no different from the rest of the crap heads in this goddamn town."

"Now don't start that business again, Dalt. I thought—"

"You don't think. You don't give a damn about a guy who sweats his guts out to write something decent. You accept the crap and you're happy."

"Jesus, Dalt, I'll get the script to Cohn first thing in the morning."

"Don't do me any favors." Dalt rushes from the villa.

Bogart stares at the bourbon stains on the screenplay. He pours the coffee into the sink and finishes out the week in a state of drunkenness.

After he sobers up Bogart leaves the screenplay, *Hollywood Armageddon*, with Cohn's receptionist. Harry is in New York on business and she assures him he'll get right on it. Bogart tries to reach Cohn the following week, but Harry is still tied up on the East Coast.

Bogart has a few belts one night and decides Dalt has been unfair and unnecessarily abrasive. To hell with Dalt Brennan, he decides.

He stays drunk for a week. When he wakes up, the taste in his mouth is awful and he has forgotten about Dalt's screenplay.

In 1944 producer-director Howard Hawks introduces Bogart to his new leading lady in *To Have and Have Not*. She is a young, smoldering, sexy New York actress, only eighteen years old. This is her first picture, yet Bogart is immediately attracted to her sophisticated acting style, her bedroom eyes and her seductive, throaty voice. Just as quickly, he falls in love with Lauren "Betty" Bacall. Their dialogue in the Hemingway story is filled with racy double entendres and their presence together is instant box-office magic.

Bogart and Bacall refuse to hide their love from the rest of the world, and Mayo, now an overweight alcholic, falls into one of her jealous, destructive tantrums. Bogart attempts one last reconciliation but it ends disastrously in flying dishes and hurtling insults. Bogart walks the lonely beaches of Malibu and spends too many nights at Lorre's home on Mandeville Canyon Road.

In May 1945, Betty Bacall becomes the fourth Mrs.

Bogart. Broken-hearted and still drunk, Mayo packs her bags and leaves for Seattle.

"This town is full of women," says Bogart, "but me—I married a lady."

Bogart and Bacall are hastily cast in Hawks's next picture, *The Big Sleep*, in which Bogart plays Raymond Chandler's hard-nosed gumshoe Philip Marlowe. It is another masterful portrayal, lending new dimensions to the genre of the code-bound private investigator he first played in *The Maltese Falcon*.

It has been a year and a half since Dalt stormed out of Bogart's life. Bogart makes infrequent attempts to contact Dalt, but they go unanswered. Bogart even invites Dalt and Kitty to the premiere of *The Big Sleep*, but they never show. The next morning Kitty calls to say Dalt is sorry and wants to apologize, but is too ashamed and can't bring himself to face Bogart.

September 1946. A frantic pounding on the door of their bungalow at the Garden of Allah awakens Bogart and Betty. Bogart recognizes the incoherent voice of Dalt and opens the door.

He wishes he hadn't. Dalt is waving his army .45 as he hurries across the threshold. "Sweet Jesus, Humph, this time they went too far." There is no trace of whiskey on Dalt's breath. Dalt is breathless, on the verge of panic. In his frantic carelessness he points the automatic in Betty's direction.

"Now wait a minute, Dalt," Bogart says as calmly as possible. "Put the gun down and let's talk."

"The both of them, they schemed it from the start. *Embarkation Point*, my script! Donahue ripped it apart and Fabrini put it back together and there was

nothing left of me. Do you know what something like
that does to a writer?"

Bogart can guess: another Hollywood double-cross
with Dalt caught in the middle.

Recklessly, Dalt marches through the rooms of the
villa, arms flying as he curses the parasites of the film
industry. He knocks over a table; one of Betty's
flower pots is shattered. Betty makes a sincere attempt to reason with Dalt and he turns on her, inad-
vertently striking her across the shoulder with the .45.
That's more than Bogart can stand. He shoves Dalt
into a corner and tries to wrest the automatic from his
deathlike grasp. A bullet thuds into the ceiling. Betty
turns pale and scrambles to call the police.

"Put down that phone," Bogart manages over his
shoulder.

Once again Bogart finds himself staring into Dalt's
straining face. But this time he sees neither a glimmer
of intelligence nor humanity. There is only blind, un-
controllable fury.

And madness.

Finally the automatic falls from Dalt's hand and he
drops limply into a sofa, covering his face with his
hands.

Bogart nods affirmatively at Betty, who phones
Kitty. Dressed in a fur overcoat over her nightgown,
her face a flushed mixture of embarrassment and concern, Kitty leads Dalt to her car. Bogart suggests that
Dalt should start seeing a psychiatrist again—he'll even
foot the bills. Kitty refuses the offer.

"Seeing a doctor," she replies, "is something Dalt
has to decide for himself. I can't tell him anything.
Not anymore."

Bogart studies Dalt, who has fallen silent. Thoughts
about the years of friendship and camaraderie well up

within Bogart and some of their best experiences together flash before him.

As much as he hates himself, it is crystal clear what Bogart must do. "We go back a long way, Dalt," he says, "but that still doesn't condone what you've done tonight. You've terrorized the hell out of Betty, you've turned my bungalow into a shooting gallery and frankly I don't mind saying you've scared the pants off me. I think we better just part company and let the rest of it be a memory. It can be a pleasant memory or an unpleasant memory. That's up to you."

Dalt says nothing. His face is empty of emotion.

He never speaks another word to Bogart.

DAY TWO

Wednesday, March 17, 1948

ARAB GUERRILLAS RAID A KIBBUTZ ON THE ISRAELI BORDER, KILLING TEN AND TAKING SIX CHILDREN AS HOSTAGES. PRESIDENT TRUMAN CONFERS WITH TOP ADVISORS ON THE LATEST CLASHES IN THE MIDDLE EAST . . .

NEW YORK DETECTIVES APPREHEND PRIMARY SUSPECT IN THE RECENT BOMB THREAT TO DESTROY THE CITY'S RAILROAD STATIONS, FERRIES AND NEWSPAPER PLANTS. SEVERAL STICKS OF DYNAMITE ARE FOUND IN THE HOME OF THE SUSPECT, A MILD-MANNERED CLOCKMAKER NOW UNDERGOING PSYCHIATRIC TREATMENT . . .

NEW FUNDING APPROVED FOR MASSIVE FREEWAY SYSTEM THROUGHOUT LOS ANGELES AREA . . .

LOS ANGELES POLICE INVESTIGATE DEATH OF COLUMBIA CONTRACT PLAYER JOHNNY HAWKS, SHOT TO DEATH NEAR WELL-KNOWN MOVIE LOCATION, VASQUEZ ROCKS.

TEN

"You're in trouble, pal," Bogart said in a flat, nasal voice. He smiled slightly and slowly rubbed his earlobe.

Max Steiner stared at the chess pieces before him on the checkered dark- and light-brown board. Bogart had boxed him in with a variation of the Sicilian defense and it was taking longer than usual for Steiner to make a countermove.

The chess games with Steiner always went well, absorbing the time that it took for a large movie crew to prepare a set. Bogart lit a cigarette and blew smoke in Steiner's direction. The composer waved it away unconsciously, adding to it with desperate puffs on his own Havana cigar.

"What's on your mind, Max? It sure as hell isn't on this," Bogart said, indicating the chess board.

Steiner withdrew the cigar and shrugged. "Ach, Bogie, *ich habe viele sachen im kopf.* The scoring that still has to be done on *Don Juan.* Errol Flynn is ill—"

"Sure he is," Bogart said sardonically.

"Whatever he has done in the past, I think Flynn is doing his best to finish *Don Juan,* but the inescapable fact is I cannot complete the scoring until I can see more of a rough cut. Soon I am to begin *Johnny Belinda* for RKO and if *Don Juan* overlaps . . ." He shrugged again and dragged roughly on his cigar. A wave of sadness crept over his intense features. "And there is the sorrow about Forbstein. You've heard about Leo?"

"Only that he'd had that heart attack last Sunday. How's he doing?"

Steiner slowly shook his head. "*Has du gehort. Didn't you hear? Ehr ist todt.* Dead. Another attack of his heart. Everyone in the music department is quite saddened. Twenty-two years he had been with Warners as musical director."

"That's rough."

"Saturday night Leo was going to conduct the orchestra at the Academy Awards."

"Who's going to take his place?"

"Ray Heindorf . . . he will conduct the academy orchestra. No doubt he will he named department head also."

Bogart glanced out the dressing-room door. The next setup was almost ready. He had been called on to repeat yesterday's shot, since the dailies had shown Huston that Bogart's double hadn't worked out. "Papa" Freund had thrown up his hands; only the real Humphrey Bogart would do.

"The Academy Awards—" began Steiner.

"—is the bunk, Max," finished Bogart. He dragged on his cigarette. "The only true test is to have all the silly actors in this town put on black tights and recite *Hamlet.* That'd separate the phonies from the real thing."

Steiner chuckled and finally moved a knight two places and one over.

Bogart gleamed evilly.

The phone rang. Bogart picked it up, motioning to Steiner to close the door, keeping out the set voices and clatter.

"*Mr. Bogart, this is the studio switchboard again . . .*"

"Yeah, I recognize your velvet voice, sweetheart."

There was an appreciative giggle. *"We have a party on the line. Says she's your wife."*

"Betty? Put her on."

"No, Mr. Bogart. I know Lauren Bacall's voice and this isn't it."

"Well, come on, sweetheart. I only have four wives. Which one is it?"

There was a mumbled conversation on the line and in a few seconds the operator was back. *"She says her name is 'Sluggy.' Do you want—"*

"Mayo, for Christ's sake! Sure, put her on."

There was a familiar voice on the line. *"Bogie . . ."* And a long pause.

Bogart also paused. *"Sluggy . . ."*

"Hey, it's your old sparring partner."

"I thought you and Seattle were inseparable . . . ?"

"Ambition rides high, Bogie. It's tough to shake off the movies—I was pretty good once. Remember?"

"Yeah, you were, angel. Where you staying?"

"You'll never believe it, but I'm at the Garden, and sentimental dame that I am, I'm in our old villa."

"The Garden of Allah? Christ, talk about scraping up the past—you're damn good at it, angel, damn good."

"I'd like to see you, today if possible. It's important to me, Bogie."

"Well, I don't know, Mayo. You know what this town is like. All Louella or Hedda needs is a nice juicy item."

"Come on, for old time's sake. What do you care what people think? Doesn't sound like the Bogie I know . . ."

. . . the Mayo he knew had been a hell-cat, fighting and scratching. Vividly etched in his mind was the time she had picked up a wicked-looking kitchen knife and tried to slice him alive with it. Jesus, what a little wildcat.

"Look, Mayo, I've got some important things to do this afternoon. How about after that? Say around two-thirty."

"I'll be waiting."

There was a knock on the dressing-room door and Steiner turned in irritation.

Bogart opened the door to a stocky, friendly-looking man.

"Hey, Bogie, can I talk to you for a minute?"

Bogart recognized Chuck Jones, a chief animator from the cartoon building. "Sure, Chuck."

Max Steiner rose, his cigar between two fingers. "This dressing room is getting to be Union Station. We're never going to get a respectable game going."

"You're saying that," said Bogart, "because you don't often get a chance to win."

Steiner pointed the cigar at the chess board. *"Mach dir nichts draus*—Don't concern yourself. You had me in only three moves anyway."

"Two," Bogart said emphatically.

Steiner laughed, his depression momentarily forgotten. "Tomorrow, the same time?"

"Probably."

Jones stepped aside as Bogart left the dressing room.

As the two men walked to the *Key Largo* set, Bogart scanned the activity. It was apparent that Huston was going to need him in a few minutes.

"We got this great idea for another cartoon," said Jones enthusiastically. "With you, Bugs, and Elmer Fudd. See, you come into this restaurant, Fudd's the waiter, he falls all over himself to take your order.

Problem is, you want rabbit stew . . . get it? Bob Clampett's already working on Elmer, but I want some new material from you: appropriate gestures, facial expressions."

Bogart lowered himself into his canvas chair. "Just draw your brains out, kid."

Jones unleashed his drawing pad, sat in a canvas chair, took out a Wolfe carbon drawing pencil, laid the pad across his knees and began rapidly sketching the upside-down V of Bogart's brow. He stroked in a suggestion of five-o'clock shadow.

Huston strolled over. "Bogie, we're all set for the scene where Robinson slaps the shit out of you."

"Damn it, John, we did that weeks ago."

"It's the breaks. The lab screwed up the negative. Besides, it gives me a chance to do it again from a different angle. Some of the actors had their eye lines wrong. Fehr didn't like the way they intercut."

Huston gestured him onto the set and positioned Bogart on the tape marks.

Robinson stood opposite Bogart as the dolly grips moved the Mitchell in closer. Freund, watching the placement with Teutonic precision, accepted a martini from his assistant.

Robinson looked pleased. "Don't fret, Bogie. I don't mind the overtime. My contract calls for penalties this week. It's Warners' money, and if they want to waste it, who am I to gainsay it?"

Bogart grinned. "Yeah, Eddie, I bet you'll pick up another Grant Wood with that dough."

"Now, boys," said Huston, "I want this to be completely realistic. No fake slaps."

"I dislike violence, John," said Robinson. "It's only a movie; let us do it the usual way."

Huston shook his head emphatically. "Audiences will respond to the real thing, Eddie. I want 'em to feel it."

Bogart hooked his thumbs into his belt. "Go ahead, Eddie . . . anything for art."

Robinson hesitated.

"Go ahead, Eddie. If you can dish it out, I can take it."

Bogart had twisted a line from *Little Caesar* and Robinson acknowledged it with a soft smile. "It's gonna hurt you more than it's gonna hurt me."

Huston rubbed his hands together. He called for the clapper routine. The camera rolled, the sound was up to speed, and Huston called for action.

Whack—whack—whack. Rocco/Robinson slapped McCloud/Bogart in one direction, then back again. Left, right, left, right, first to the side of one cheek, then back, fast, to the other cheek. Right, left, right, left. Whack—whack—whack—

McCloud/Bogart just stood there and took it. Each time the scene was retaken, Freund had the camera moved just slightly.

"Didn't I tell you I could dish it out," said Robinson in the mock-snarling voice of *Little Caesar*.

Bogart's face burned. For someone who protested against violence, Robinson was taking an unusual delight in the scene. Finally there was a break, and Bogart dropped into his chair. Jones began to sketch once again. Bogart closed his eyes; Dalt Brennan thrust into his thoughts—he was never far from the surface of Bogart's mind. Would it be stretching the imagination to believe that Dalt would try to blow up the Oscars? If so, where was he now? . . . Still at his brother's home? Lloyd and Dalt had always been close, despite their mutual rivalry . . .

"Humvrey, I vould like vords vit you."

Bogart looked up into the familiar face of a balding, six-foot man with piercing china-blue eyes and a firm mouth. The fifty-five-year-old man wore boots, riding jodhpurs and a flowing, open-necked shirt and carried a riding crop tucked under one arm.

"Sure, Mike. What's up?"

Michael Curtiz was ranked as one of Warners' finest directors. He was a taut, unyielding craftsman. At first Bogart had found him to be an arrogant, driven man. But brilliant. They could do no wrong together: *Virginia City, Angels with Dirty Faces, Passage to Marseilles.* And their milestone film had been *Casablanca.*

Curtiz handed Bogart a thick script.

"This looks fatter than DeMille's version of the Bible. What is it, Mike?"

Curtiz looked down his large nose. His voice boomed out in a Hungarian accent that had declared war on the English language. "A terrivic for you a part. Anodder Oscar nomination. A study ov a gangster. The vorst sort—"

"Not again," moaned Bogart. He winked at Chuck Jones, who continued to draw.

". . . a dangerous psychopathic. Loves his modder, who travels vith him . . . robbink, stealink. Has selv-induced splatting headaches. Terrorizes nut only girl friend, poliz of chievs, but also the men in his gang. Vun juizzy part! Raoul Walsh vants it. Howard Hawks has his eye upon it. I vant it. I vant you."

"I don't know, Mike. I've gotten away from doing bad guys. My public might not go for it. I suppose the guy dies at the end?"

Curtiz waved his arms extravagantly. "Stupendously! He kills himselv to hell by blasting avay at valves on top oil storage tank. Blows whole thing to sky. Marvelous! A man on top ov the vorld."

Bogart idly leafed through the pages. "I don't think it's for me, but why don't you let me read it."

Curtiz nodded energetically. "Sure, Bogie, read it carevully when you don't haff time." He turned with military precision and marched away.

Bogart stared at the bulky script. Because screenplays came in from the front office by the dozens, he had learned to skim-read and could do a thorough job per script in less than an hour.

Yeah, thought Bogart . . . there was a lot to do. He lit a cigarette and thoughtfully let smoke escape from his lips.

Where the hell is Dalt? Topanga Beach seemed the most likely place to continue his search.

He turned and looked absently at Chuck Jones, who was drawing as quickly as possible.

Bogart rose from his chair. There was indeed a lot to do.

Art Luecker, Huston's assistant director, youngish and eager, sauntered over to Jones. "How ya, Chuck. Huston wants Bogie on the set. Seen 'im?"

Jones slid his sketching materials under his arm. "He was here . . . I was drawing away, just about done—looked up . . . bang, he was gone."

John Huston's face became gloomy when Luecker reported back. "Gone? Gone where, in God's name? I can't believe my ears," he said loudly, his rolling *rs* muted by disbelief. "Where does he think he is . . . at Monogram?"

ELEVEN

The smog burned Bogart's sinuses until he reached the junction of Ventura Boulevard and Topanga Canyon Road and began climbing into the pure air of the northern Santa Monica Mountains. At the head of Topanga Canyon Bogart was greeted by an unsurpassed view of the Santa Susana Mountains to the north.

He shifted down and guided the Cadillac into Topanga Canyon. It was a gradual nine-mile descent, made picturesque by the towering peaks on both sides of the tortuous road. Occasionally he caught a glimpse of the Pacific Ocean below. He passed the heavily wooded picnic areas of Topanga Mineral Springs and reached sea level at Topanga Beach.

The town had been heavily populated by the movie community in the twenties. But later Malibu Beach had become popular, and now Topanga was a minor settlement for surf lovers, film writers and those not yet rich enough for Malibu. Bogart had no trouble finding the old Lloyd Brennan house—it was a simple, one-story stucco cottage with a red tile roof, facing onto the beach.

Dalt had brought Bogart and Mayo here frequently during the war years, when the house had been immaculate. Now Bogart could see signs of advanced deterioration: The house needed a thorough paint job, the once-yellow shutters were peeling and the picket fence had finally lost its battle against the strong winds from the Pacific.

Bogart enjoyed the roar of the surf and the taste of salt spray as he walked up the cobblestone walkway.

The front door was slightly ajar, but Bogart rapped
anyway. When there was no answer, he pushed it
open and stepped inside. The living room was in darkness, the venetian blinds lowered.

Thanks to narrow beams of light leaking through
the blinds, he could make out, amid the clutter of
pre-Depression furniture, the remnants of an all-night
party. A trail of panties and bras led to Lloyd's old
master bedroom. There were several seminude orgy-
spent bodies sprawled about. He accidentally kicked
an empty bourbon bottle across the floor and it was
only after it stopped rolling that he heard the sound of
typewriter keys.

Bogart followed the sound. He passed through a
swinging door and found himself in a grease-stained
kitchen. There were stacks of dirty dishes and high-
ball glasses on a table; more plates were piled in the
porcelain sink. Bogart wrinkled his nose, recognizing
the smell of rotting cheese.

There was just enough space on the table for a
typewriter, and behind it sat a paunchy, sleepy man,
nearly forty, who stared with doleful gray eyes at the
dog-eared paper in the machine. Next to his elbow
was a stack of well-read pulp magazines, and Bogart
could see several thick screenplays scattered atop the
dishes. One of them bore the title *Ka-Shana, Jungle
Goddess*.

Bogart heard a giggle and turned. Standing in front
of a half-open refrigerator was a young woman—
buxom, blond and leggy—a bottle of Royal Crown
Cola halfway to her pouty lips. She had the kind of
figure, Bogart decided, that casting directors wanted
to put on their couches, not in their pictures. She was
wearing one of those new two-piece French bathing
suits, what they were calling the bikini.

"I've got it, Trixie," the man at the table was saying, his voice rising with inspiration. "We get Mokolo to short-circuit Rocket Man's power-pack and then they're fighting like crazy on the edge of the cliff and bam, over the edge goes Rocket Man. Continued next week. Only next week Rocket Man doesn't go over. There's a bush below the rim, see, and he's hanging there for dear life—"

But Trixie was pointing mutely toward Bogart. Finally she managed, "We got company, Whit."

"What the hell—" Whit glared at Bogart.

"You look like . . . like . . . " said Trixie. The Royal Crown bottle was still tilted in midair, her thirst forgotten.

"Maybe, maybe not," said Bogart. "A lotta people look alike these days, what with plastic surgery." He turned to the typist. "You own the place?"

"Sure do. Name's Whitney McCord. I write for the movies. Hey, maybe you saw a thing I did, *G-Man Versus the Leopard Woman.* Some of the best tough-guy dialogue around." McCord stood up nervously, knocking several copies of *Bluebook, Thrilling Wonder Stories* and *Fantastic Adventures* to the dirty linoleum. He obviously wanted to come around the table and shake Bogart's hand, but he hesitated, perhaps intimidated by Bogart's officious attitude.

"Sorry, I've been out of town and missed it." Bogart shrugged.

"Maybe you could use a writer. I've got a lot of tough-guy scripts in the closet."

"Let's keep them there, pal. I'm here about the house. You must have bought it recently."

"Matter of fact, I did. First of the year."

"Whit bought it from the guy who owned it before," Trixie said.

Bogart frowned. "You must have all joined hands to reach the spirit world. The owner's dead."

"What Trixie means is, we bought it from Mr. Brennan's executor. His name was Carroll. You should know him," said McCord suggestively. "He's one of Hollywood's leading hairstylists."

"Geoffrey Carroll?"

McCord scratched his bulbous nose and nodded. "Lloyd Brennan and Carroll were close. I mean, *close*. If you know what I mean."

Bogart arched his eyebrows again. "You should save the subtleties for Rocket Man."

"Say, I've got some great tough-cop ideas—"

But Bogart was already through the swinging kitchen door. It was a full thirty seconds before Trixie, whose mouth was hanging open, realized that her Royal Crown had dripped onto her bikini, down her leg and onto her sandals.

TWELVE

All roads lead back to Beverly Hills, Bogart thought. He maintained a steady twenty-five miles an hour as he drew close to Beverly Drive. On his right were block-long hedges of fuchsia and geraniums. He slowed for the turn, then accelerated.

Dark clouds were coming in from the northwest, throwing a gray, shifting pattern over the pink bungalows of the Beverly Hills Hotel.

Vast, tree-lined Beverly Drive eventually branched off to the left. Bogart swung to the right, up Coldwater Canyon Road, passing the vast estates and sprawling mansions with their long, sweeping drives and electronically operated gates.

At the Lago Vista marker he turned and sped down a narrow asphalt road which paralleled the shimmering waters of a reservoir. He drove through a pair of miniature gates. He continued along a curving gravel road, parking in front of a sparkling-white pocket edition of the Palace of Versailles with powder-blue trim around the arched windows.

The hairdressing business must pay very well, he thought with a brief chuckle. He punched the doorbell.

Bogart was surprised when Geoffrey Carroll himself opened the door.

"Well, well, this is a pleasant surprise," said Carroll, his bemused voice a high tenor's. He was inches taller than Bogart, much slimmer, and in his early forties, with bright gray eyes. His silver hair was coiffed in a romantic style that swept over his ears and curled over his collar. He looked very much like what he was: the most successful hairdresser in Hollywood.

"Come in, Bogie, come in." Carroll wore pleated gray slacks, a yellow silk shirt with the sleeves rolled up just above the elbow and a short artist's smock.

Bogart stepped into a cool interior: marble floors, checked with alternate white and gray square slabs, white walls, white rattan peacock chairs and potted palm fronds. All the rooms, white and glistening, were furnished in authentic eighteenth-century French pieces. The walls were spotted with Old-Master style paintings and enlarged photos of leading movie actresses.

"We had a party last night and poor George, he's not up to replying to shrill-ringing bells. I'm very democratic, you see, and insist that my staff join me and my guests in my little amusements."

He guided Bogart through a series of large, white, airy rooms. The dining room had tall mirrors that ran to the ceiling, reflecting the two men as they walked. Bogart could see that Carroll was in good physical shape, despite the very slight tippy-toe walk.

"What can I do for you?" asked Carroll. "I'm sure you didn't come to see me about doing your hair?"

"I wanted to talk about Dalt Brennan."

"Not a happy subject," said Carroll.

They came into the middle of what was obviously Carroll's workroom. It too was white, with a large platform raised six inches off the floor, on which was a luxurious barber's chair.

In the chair a red-haired woman sat admiring herself in a full-length mirror. She was about thirty, with wide green eyes. She wore a white lace dress, cut low over milky-white breasts.

Bogart appreciated a full figure like Susan Hayward's.

Hayward caught Bogart's reflection. "Bogie!" she cried, jumping out of the barber's chair.

She hugged Bogart, stepped back and did a short twirl, allowing the many layers of flossy white lace to spread like a cloud, pearls and shimmering crystal beads catching the light. "Like it? I'm wearing it to the Academy Awards. Don Loper designed it and I just think it's the most elegant dress I've had in months."

"Yeah, Susan, it's a knockout." He admired the way Hayward enjoyed life. Some actresses could barely handle fame, but Hayward was one that both managed it and savored it. Actress, star, woman, wife and mother were wrapped into one personality.

Susan smiled charmingly and ran a hand up to her flame-red hair. "Geoffrey's helping me select a hairdo for Saturday night."

"Bogie and I will be having a private conversation, my dear," Carroll said. "Won't be long."

"Don't stand on ceremony on my account." Hayward plunked herself down into the barber chair and picked up a copy of *Life* magazine.

Carroll and Bogart walked out onto a garden patio festooned with hanging ivy. There was a pond with golden carp darting in and out among the lily pads. Off to one side was a mirrored portable bar that reflected the high wall surrounding the garden.

Bogart settled into a white-painted metal garden chair. Carroll poured Scotch over ice and a pony of brandy for himself, and sat in a twin chair next to Bogart.

Bogart sipped the Scotch appreciatively. "About

Dalt. He's dropped out of sight and frankly I'm about three months in the dark."

Carroll tasted his brandy. "Dalt showed up at Lloyd's last year. He'd split up with his wife—"

"Kitty Steele . . . I've seen her."

". . . he had nowhere else to go. He stayed there for a while . . . Lloyd's suicide was a shock."

"Who found the body?"

"Dalt."

"Who did he call first?"

"The police, naturally."

"And then he called you?"

Carroll nodded. "I was grateful to Dalt for that."

"What did you do after he called?"

"Naturally I went right to Lloyd's."

Bogart nodded in understanding. "And that was the last you saw of Dalt?"

"Heavens no, Bogie. You have been out of touch, or you'd have known I took care of him."

"He stayed here?"

Carroll sighed. "For a while. After that Dalt went all to pieces pretty fast. He couldn't find work writing . . . He seemed, well, off balance." Carroll swirled his brandy and sniffed the aroma meditatively. "It all led to a breakdown."

"Breakdown? When did that happen?"

"Not long after the funeral."

"Lloyd's suicide must have really hit him hard."

"If you ask me, it really started with *Embarkation Point*."

"Kitty mentioned that. Where do you fit in?"

"I was the hairstylist on the picture."

Bogart leaned forward. "Tell me about it."

"What I saw . . . Let me tell you, it was hell just

watching Dalt come unglued because of Donahue and Fabrini."

"I'm very curious about those two."

Carroll was silent, as though dredging up the past painfully. "Two years ago I received a script of *Embarkation Point* with Dalt's name on the cover. It seemed a good script . . . but Donahue needed more money for a top-notch actor in the lead. At first it was going to be a limited-budget production, but suddenly Donahue got what he wanted—enough money to hire two stars—Tyrone Power and Joan Crawford. From then on, Bogie, there was a—a different atmosphere on the set. Donahue's point of view about the script seemed to shift drastically. Crawford's part had to be expanded, and Paul Fabrini was brought in to rewrite her scenes . . ."

"That happens a lot."

"Well, Donahue apparently liked what Fabrini was doing, so he kept on shifting the emphasis. The woman's story became almost as strong as Power's. I'll never forget the day Dalt came on the set. He blew up when he saw what Donahue and Fabrini had done—raging uncontrollably—Dalt almost killed Fabrini. Grabbed a steel helmet from one of the extras and laid into Fabrini, beating him over the head . . . Fabrini was a bloody mess before they could pull him off. Donahue had him subdued and forcibly ejected from the set. Dalt never came back."

"And Dalt never got a screen credit," said Bogart.

"It was downhill from that day on. Dalt went under treatment with a psychiatrist. Lloyd was footing most of the bills—"

Bogart sat up straight. "Dalt was under treatment again? Kitty didn't tell me that."

"Dalt apparently didn't want Kitty to know."

Bogart digested that. "Who paid for all the psychiatric help after Lloyd's suicide?"

"I did. After selling Lloyd's house, there was plenty of money."

"But it was still rough?"

Carroll nodded. "Dalt kept on drinking heavily . . . One night he was raving about Fabrini ruining his screenplay—"

"That must have been the night Kitty overheard him threatening Fabrini."

"After that Dalt tried to keep his anger in check, but he knew it was a losing battle." Carroll tossed down half of the remaining brandy. ". . . So Dalt had himself committed."

Bogart stared at Carroll and whistled under his breath. "So . . . Dalt's in a hospital. Where?"

"I honestly don't know, Bogie."

"Come on, Geoffrey, you were paying the bills . . ."

"Dalt didn't want anyone to know . . . wanted to handle his own problems. His doctor was the only person who knew where Dalt was sent, and he refused to tell me."

"Who was this doctor?"

"Doctor Marshall Quesne. A Beverly Hills type."

"What type is that?"

Carroll looked uncomfortable. "You know the sort . . . a distraught actress comes in and gets happy pills to perk her up. Other pills to put her out. Almost any problem that could be solved with . . ." Carroll paused. "You know, anything for a buck."

Bogart tugged slowly at his earlobe. "Drugs?"

"There *have* been rumors."

Bogart stood up and angrily threw his cigarette into the lily pond. "Why the hell did you let Dalt get mixed up with a creep like that?"

"Bogie, please, I didn't pick him. Quesne was Dalt's choice. I tried my best to dissuade him, but you know how stubborn he can be."

There was a moment of silence as Bogart finished the Scotch and Carroll stared at the goldfish, sipping his brandy.

"Tell me," Bogart said finally, "about Lloyd's suicide."

Bogart thought he saw tears in Carroll's eyes. His voice choked. "I could never understand it. Shooting himself simply wasn't in Lloyd's character. I know for a fact that he laughed at the HUAC investigation. He was going to form a committee and fight back with his own kind of weapon: humor. Lloyd wanted to have the whole country laughing *at* them."

Bogart put out his hand and felt raindrops. Carroll took the glasses and put them away. As they started to walk inside, Bogart paused at the white workroom entrance. "Did you ever hear Dalt mention a script he wrote called *Hollywood Armageddon?*"

Carroll was thoughtful. "As a matter of fact, yes. I overheard Lloyd and Dalt discussing it. Lloyd didn't think much of it, as I recall. It was a long time ago. Must have been . . . oh, three or four years ago. Is it important?"

Bogart shrugged.

"I guess you're going to see Doctor Quesne?" asked Carroll.

Bogart looked at his watch. "Yeah, I'll see him today."

"Would you tell me when you find Dalt? I'd like to see him."

"What's up, fellas?" asked Susan Hayward.

"It's getting ready to come down again," said Carroll, wriggling his hand down through the air, miming the rain.

Hayward got down from the barber's chair, brushing water droplets from Bogart's coat sleeve. "I hope it clears up by Saturday night."

"I'll lay ten to one odds," said Carroll, "that it doesn't rain Saturday night. My creation for Susan will be outstanding and Jupiter Pluvius wouldn't dare to wet a masterpiece."

"That's telling the gods where to get off, Geoffrey," said Hayward.

"Yeah," said Bogart thoughtfully. Rain had better be the *only* thing that could ruin things Saturday night.

It was a short drive from Carroll's Beverly Hills home to Bogart's new destination: 8150 Sunset Boulevard.

At Havenhurst, Bogart slowed for a right turn. There he saw the curving wall, set back from the sidewalk, which declared *GARDEN OF ALLAH* in Persian script.

It was a two-and-a-half acre home-office-bedroom-romping ground for those who toiled in the sweet-sour vineyards of Hollywood. Shaded by tall evergreens, Hawaiian pines and bamboo trees, it covered most of a city block, bordered by Sunset, Havenhurst, Crescent and Fountain.

Bogart parked as the rain stopped, locked the coupe and hurried through a Spanish-style wrought iron gate. He walked along the flagstone path that wound among the twenty-five bungalows. Soft, diffused light cast dappled shadows on his face.

Bogart had lived here with Mayo Methot, slugging it out in some of their classic bouts. Later he and

Betty had moved in, proving to be more sedate dwellers, before buying Hedgerow Farm.

Since the war the Garden of Allah had begun to go seedy. Gone were most of the flamboyant personalities. Now it was just another place to live, with ghosts and memories rapidly diminishing into the past. Bogart recalled the time when character actor Charles Butterworth had pushed Benchley across the lawn in a wheelbarrow. It had been funny then—it seemed to make little sense now.

The swimming pool was empty of people, forlornly empty, except for floating unlit lily pad candles.

There was nothing left but memories.

He stopped at the familiar door, the pool to his back, and knocked lightly. He slid a forefinger across the brim of his hat, getting the angle just right.

The door opened and Bogart forced a smile. Then it became a natural smile.

Mayo had changed.

He had expected to see her as he last remembered: a gin-bloated, foul-mouthed woman, ready to tear Bogart's heart out.

What he saw instead was radiant, coiffured blonde hair and a wide infectious smile. The once-stained teeth were pearly clean. The baby-blue eyes hadn't changed, but now they looked unpolluted and unstrained. Her skin was fresh and lightly powdered. She was wearing a dark-green taffeta dress and a tailored, ruffled pale-yellow blouse.

"Hello, Bogie."

"It's good to see you, Sluggy."

Mayo stepped aside and motioned Bogart into the villa, her smile indicating a bemused attitude.

The bungalow conveyed a Spanish motif with blue peacock tiles and arched doorways. Mayo had tossed her open suitcase onto a divan and he noticed the edges of rumpled petticoats and other disheveled clothing. Bogart removed his hat and turned it nervously in his hands.

Mayo locked the door and leaned against the jamb in a provocative pose. The stance didn't bother Bogart—he found it just exaggerated enough to be amusing.

"You act like I'm going to bite, sweetheart," said Mayo.

"Just tell me how deep and if you draw blood."

Mayo laughed, exaggeratedly. Bogart was reminded of an actress trying desperately to play a role beyond her limits. "I've changed," she said bluntly.

She moved catlike across the cool living room, each move calculated to accentuate her flowing body. Her large breasts were extra-taut against her blouse.

Mayo pushed her hair back and stood next to a small fireplace, where they had often lounged in silk pajamas—before the fighting had started. "Got a light?" she asked, producing her own cigarette.

The lighting routine had been a part of their sexual foreplay—a moment when they were close but not touching. Bogart lit the match and moved the flame close to her face. Mayo inhaled and removed a speck of tobacco from her lower lip. "I was damn good in my day, wasn't I, sweetheart?"

"Yeah," he nodded. "You were very good."

"I was *damn* good in *Marked Woman*. I think I even gave Bette Davis a run for her dough. I'm sure I can do it again. I'd be better than that broad."

She saw Bogart's doubt and his silence fell on her accusingly. She tossed back her hair. "It isn't easy to pick up where you left off without a little help."

"So you want me to make some calls for you."

She turned, smiling, looking ready to leap into his arms. It was a good performance, thought Bogart, but it was missing a touch of finesse.

"One chance. Is that asking too much, sweetheart? For old time's sake. Look at me. I haven't had a drop of sauce in a month of Sundays."

"I believe you, angel, but that's not the big trouble. It's a different kind of town than when you worked in it. It's tough to make a start with the business in the doldrums."

"Is that the only reason?"

"No," said Bogart emphatically. "I've got my personal life to consider."

"How is Betty?"

"She's good for me."

"And I wasn't . . . ?"

"I didn't say that, angel. You said that."

She became flirtatious again. "Gee, Bogie, we had some swell times together. All around the world. Hey, remember Algeria, baby? That poor waitress in that cheap rundown hotel who thought I was trying to hustle you. She almost threw me out on my ass." Mayo laughed and sat down on a heavy settee. She looked deeply into Bogart's impassive face.

Her forlorn look reached across the room and touched Bogart and pulled him toward the settee.

"Look," said Mayo, "I know I've made a lot of mistakes. But a woman has to wise up sooner or later."

Bogart settled onto the settee next to her, remembering the old days, not the drag-out fights, not the bickering, not the drinking . . . all that was forgotten in a flood of pleasant images: days with Mayo aboard their cabin cruiser *Sluggy*; evenings together with good friends; nights at the theatre or in high-class restaurants. Those had been good times.

Bogart was almost unaware that Mayo had placed her hand over his. The warmth of her flesh felt soothing.

"Look, angel," he said, "I'll do what I can, but I won't lie for you . . . or to you. Fair enough?"

"Fair enough." Her fingers gently massaged the surface of his hand, working around onto the palm. The tingling sensation Bogart felt brought back memories of their passionate foreplay.

Too many memories, he finally told himself, and casually removed Mayo's hand. He turned deliberately to the phone and dialed, asking for Jerry Wald's office at Paramount. It took only a minute to get through to the producer.

It was a good conversation until Bogart got around to the actual object of the call—Mayo's return.

"You gotta be kidding, Bogie. Talk about a bad penny."

"She wants a test, Jerry," said Bogart loudly and enthusiastically. "Another crack at the business. I said I'd see what I could do."

The silence from Wald was ominous. Bogart turned his back to Mayo, just in case his disappointment was showing.

Finally Wald's voice sprang to life again. *"Listen, Bogie, for you I'll do it, but I want to see her first, make up my own mind. Understand?"*

"Yeah," said Bogart spiritedly, "that's right, Jerry."

"Tomorrow. Have her in my office at one o'clock. Sharp."

"She'll be there." Bogart turned to Mayo after hanging up. "You've got a date, angel. Tomorrow, one o'clock."

Mayo's smile wasn't contrived. "With Jerry Wald? I

can't believe it." She fondled his hand and he didn't try to pull away. "Oh, Bogie, I won't forget this."

She came to him and Bogart assumed it would be an innocuous kiss. Her lips breathed warmly against his sideburns, and her tongue playfully flicked at his ear. And then her lips were pressed to his ear, soft and moist. "Oh, Bogie, I've missed you. Day and night for the last three years. I *had* to come back—had to see you. Tell you how much I still love you. I knew it would be like this . . . so good between us."

Mayo's lips left a sugary moisture as they worked from his ear down across his cheek. Then they were pressing against his lips. Bogart felt her physical need surge into him. Her arms were on his shoulders, caressing his neck, working their way sinuously through his hair and she was mashing her face against his.

Her tongue darted out, probing the inside of his mouth, seeking a response from his own tongue. Bogart's tongue slid against hers and they were locked together, his body a contradiction of impulses and urges. He knew he should pull away, but he was enjoying her nectareous kisses.

Something deep within made the decision—he couldn't even remember thinking it. He jerked his head back. Mayo's passionate eyes went suddenly from ecstasy to surprised disappointment.

Bogart didn't push her away; that would have been cruel. Instead he removed her fingers from his neck, and stepped backward.

His expression was hard and uncompromising.

"Some things can't change, angel. I tried to tell you that."

"I only thought . . ."

"I know what you thought. And I appreciate the offer. But you're going to have to forget it."

"I'm pretty stupid, I guess," confessed Mayo, fighting the tears, the emotion building in her throat. She managed a new, nervous, baby-girl, flirtatious smile and said, "I forgot that you only sleep with women you're married to. I guess that makes me a first-class chump."

She paused, ran a hand nervously through her hair. "Got a light, Bogie?"

She held a cigarette between her lips, waiting. He struck the match and held it to the tip; her eyes didn't leave his as she inhaled.

Mayo was trying to assume an objective, unaffected smile, one that hid the heartbreak he knew she was feeling.

"You're still the greatest, Bogie. I want you to remember that. Whatever happens."

"Thanks, kid. Just remember we have a date tomorrow with Wald. I'll pick you up at twelve-thirty sharp. Have your best duds on."

"For you I'll always be ready," she replied.

Bogart closed the door and turned to walk down the pathway. He looked down at his hands. They were trembling, and he let out a mild chuckle.

The rain had come again, and it spattered at the puddles already formed. As he hurried past the two-story villa where F. Scott Fitzgerald had written *A Diamond as Big as the Ritz*, other Garden of Allah memories began to wash over him. But he wanted to forget memories now. He'd had enough for one afternoon.

Bogart slid behind the wheel of the car. He put the coupe into first and pulled away from the curb. Geoffrey Carroll had given him Quesne's address. Westwood Village.

Bogart didn't look back at the Garden of Allah.

He should have. He would have noticed a dark-blue Buick with a scraped right fender pulling into the traffic and following closely.

THIRTEEN

The sky threatened rain as Bogart drove west on Santa Monica Boulevard. He passed beauty parlors, antique shops and several examples of a new business phenomonen: the self-service Laundramat.

He turned right at Wilshire, winding through the lush landscape of the Los Angeles Country Club. On the other side of the club greens, the area changed character again.

Even under the brooding gray sky, the shops and apartments were dazzling white with red-tiled roofs. The service stations featured high towers and smartly uniformed attendants. The Chamber of Commerce bragged about Westwood's plethora of parks and the fact that it had more "friendly people" than anyplace else in Los Angeles. No doubt Dr. Quesne spearheaded all those smiling faces.

Bogart sensed he was up against a formidable problem. He was about to ask a doctor to breach his oath and reveal a confidential matter. But what would be the most effective approach? He could play the hardboiled dick as he had done so successfully on the screen, but that would be obvious. Geoffrey Carroll had pointed to the more-than-likely possibility that Quesne provided illegal drugs for his patients. If he could simply strike at that chink in the armor . . .

The streets turned to green parkways, with swaying palms overhead. The meticulous cleanliness was disrupted only by an unsightly Giant Orange refreshment stand rising twenty feet into the air.

Then he was into the village, a shopping haven for

the wealthy, the influential and the famous of Bel-Air to the north.

Bogart turned on Malcolm Street and parked opposite Westwood Memorial Park. For a moment he was soothed by the glades of cool shrubbery. A cold wind scattered leaves and debris along the streets. From the backseat Bogart picked up his favorite trench coat. He slid into it effortlessly, adjusting the belt so it was rakishly knotted and its buckle dangling. He smoothed the crown of his hat: The man and the actor were skillfully blended.

Pulling up his deep collar, he ambled along Wellworth Street. Knots of students, their heads down against the cold wind, hurried from the University of California at Los Angeles campus. Bogart could see the mock-Mediterranean-styled Royce Hall six blocks in the distance.

At Glendon he found the address: a four-story building set back from the sidewalk, braced by taller buildings on either side. This created a cold, permanently shaded walkway to the entrance.

Dr. Quesne was on the fourth floor.

The office was a cold, white imitation of Bauhaus modern, unenhanced by zig-zag motifs edging the reception desk and floor lamps. On a black leather sofa sat a sloppily dressed young woman, wringing her hands.

Bogart recognized her as a B-picture actress. She looked up at Bogart and did a classic double-take, her red-rimmed eyes widening. Her shoulder trembled and she licked her lips nervously. Her flowered print dress was wrinkled as if she had slept in it. From her handbag the woman picked a copy of *Colliers* and hid behind it.

The mousy-haired receptionist was so busy reading

Photoplay she never heard Bogart enter. "What can I do for you?" she asked, absorbed in a photo portrait of Clark Gable dancing at the Mocambo.

"It's more what can I do for you."

She gasped at the familiar voice, looked up and shot him an embarrassed look. Her voice faltered. "Ah, you don't have an appointment . . . do you . . . ?"

"It's the doctor," said Bogart, "who has an appointment with *me*." He allowed a slight grin to dance across his face.

The receptionist glanced apprehensively at the door behind her. Bogart followed her gaze. There it was: the inner sanctum.

She coughed. "Uh, Doctor Quesne's in consultation right now and wouldn't want to be—"

"I wouldn't dream of disturbing the good doctor," said Bogart, walking deliberately past her and thrusting open the frosted glass door.

Like the reception area, the office was cold white, with a black-glass-topped desk, a modern gunmetal filing cabinet in the corner and, near the desk, an overlong black leather reclining couch.

Dr. Quesne, two hundred and seventy pounds of obesity, squatted behind the desk. Thick, blubbery jowls gave his face a puffy, froglike appearance. Above his piggish lips a nose protruded like a toadstool. Oily beads of perspiration shimmered on his wrinkled forehead. His hair was gray, with a striking erratic white streak through it.

Quesne's fingers were poised in midair, coiling protectively around a pile of large bills on the desk. Quesne had been discovered *in flagrante delicto* with money.

Bogart decided that Carroll couldn't have been too

far wrong in his evaulation of the doctor. Even in a well-lit room, Quesne would look shady.

Quesne licked his lips, then with a dredging motion scooped the money into the central drawer of the desk.

"Keeping up with the Joneses, I see," said Bogart.

"What the hell do you mean, barging in here like this?" Quesne demanded.

Bogart's voice feigned innocence. "Didn't you hear my knock?" He stepped closer to the desk. "You must have been concentrating very hard on your . . . 'patient.'"

"Please make an appointment with my receptionist . . . *Mr. Bogart.*"

"But I did make an appointment," said Bogart. "And the appointment was for now. Right this minute."

"What is it, Mr. Bogart? I'm a very busy . . ."

"See, Doctor, you have a patient who's a friend of mine. You put him in a hospital. My friend forgot to tell me the name of the hospital."

"You want me to tell you where he is."

Bogart snapped his fingers. "I *knew* you could tell me. You come highly recommended, Doctor."

"*Who* recommended me?"

"People. Good friends. In the business."

"What business?" Quesne's eyebrows arched.

"Why, the healing of the mentally sick. What other kind of business would I be talking about, Doctor?"

"Who is this friend you're looking for?"

"Dalt Brennan."

"Yes, yes, Brennan was a patient. But his present whereabouts is confidential information."

"And," said Bogart, "in good conscience you can't divulge it at this time."

Quesne nodded. "I *am* a professional man, Bogart."

Bogart ambled to the reclining couch. "Exactly why I'm here, Dr. Quesne. You see, I have this problem I want you to help me with." Bogart eased himself back on the black leather surface of the couch. "It's a problem of guilt. A professional man like yourself, you must surely understand guilt. You see, I *need* to find Dalt Brennan."

"I've taken as much of this mockery as I care to," snarled Quesne. "I'm calling the police."

Bogart stood. Quesne reached for the phone but Bogart's hand closed gently over his—very gently. The tone of innocence in Bogart's voice never shifted.

"You got me all wrong, Doc. I love your profession. Didn't I already call you a professional? I have a great admiration for the way you provide special treatment for certain patients."

"Patients? Which patients? What are you talking about?" Quesne removed his hand from the receiver.

"Oh, they wouldn't want me to mention their names, Doctor. They're a little shy. But . . . you know the ones I mean. The ones who have these strange daily urges. It comes on them suddenly. A . . . craving, you might call it."

"What . . . what about . . . them?"

"Oh, nothing very important. Just the relief you bring them with your special treatment."

"Treatment . . . ?"

"You know what I mean," Bogart said affably. "Take the blond girl, the one with the depressive fits. Nice kid, actually. Now her—you've done wonders with her. She doesn't even get the shakes anymore. You know about the shakes, Doctor. Maybe you can help me . . . get rid of all this guilt I'm carrying around."

Quesne paused and tried to wring out a friendly face. "Yes, well, I think I can do something for you. I believe you said you wanted some information about Mr. Brennan."

"I don't know . . . I've thought it over, and well, maybe that *would* be asking for too much. A lot to ask of a man with an oath hanging over his head."

"No, no, I insist. After all, you are a close friend of Mr. Brennan's."

"We're like brothers, Doctor. Inseparable."

"Uh, well, Mr. Bogart, there are times when . . . Mr. Brennan might need the companionship of an old friend right now. You know, it might be just the thing for a fast cure."

Quesne hurried to the gunmetal-gray filing cabinet and extracted a card. Bogart took it from the doctor's clammy grasp.

SAINTS AND SINNERS
SANITARIUM

| Bel-Air | Martha Pearce |
| California | Administrator |

The card went into Bogart's pocket and he walked toward the door. He paused. "You oughta go easy on how you spend all that dough, Doctor. I have a feeling you just might need it for a rainy day."

The receptionist was again absorbed in *Photoplay* as Bogart stepped into the anteroom.

The black leather sofa with the chrome armrests was empty. The copy of *Colliers* was on the floor. There was no sign of the actress.

Bogart would have to compliment Geoffrey Carroll on his accurate judgment of character.

* * *

A crisp wind whipped the lapels of Bogart's trench coat as he slid into the phone booth near the corner of Ashton and Malcolm. He dropped in his nickel and soon had Fabrini's answering service.

The same affectionate, warming voice. *"Oh, yes, Mr. Bogart, I personally gave Mr. Fabrini your message this morning."*

"Do you know where I can reach him right now?"

"I am sorry, but he left no number and we have no means of reaching him."

"Damn. It's important—"

"He left you a message . . . 'I'm giving you the option on Hollywood Armageddon.'"

If the voice said anything further, Bogart didn't hear it.

A chill seemed to invade the interior of the booth. Bogart was watching a familiar shape slowly turning at Malcolm and Ashton.

A dark sedan. A Buick Roadmaster. With a scraped right fender.

He left the receiver dangling and jerked the hinged double doors open, running for the intersection. It had to be the same car . . . following him! Watching his every move.

At the corner Bogart skidded to a stop. The dark sedan had accelerated and was disappearing into heavy traffic.

Ten seconds later it was gone.

FOURTEEN

Bogart ate, but showed no signs of enjoying, an early dinner at Romanoff's. The prince, wearing a bright red British blazer and flannel trousers, insisted he indulge in Russian beluga caviar and royal squab, but Bogart wrinkled his nose and ordered a medium-rare New York cut and baked potato.

Afterward, he savored his usual glass of Drambuie while Romanoff joined him at the booth. The prince smoked a decorative pipe stuffed with Royal Yacht, which was priced at ten dollars a pound. "I picked up the habit from the Prince of Wales," claimed Romanoff.

Before long he and Bogart were discussing the terrible trench warfare of World War I. Bogart listened patiently to Romanoff's involvement in the battles, then commented, "You're the only man alive who was a British lieutenant on the Western front, a Cossack colonel on the Eastern front and a member of Allenby's forces in Palestine—simultaneously."

Romanoff chatted on insufferably about the brutality of war but Bogart only half-listened, his mind preoccupied with his encounter with Dr. Quesne. He knew what he had to do next, yet somehow he was afraid to face it. Bogart edged the check Jamieson had brought closer to Romanoff's elbow. Romanoff indelicately edged it right back. "You know how I feel about those things, old man. If you've got it, flash it." Bogart reached for his wallet.

On his way out of Romanoff's, Bogart bumped into a familiar, rotund figure wearing an unpressed suit and a garish blue bow tie sprinkled with orange polka dots and carelessly clipped into place. Before Peter Lorre could object he was grabbed by the shoulder and led to Bogart's car. Shoving him into the front seat, Bogart said, "You're tagging along with me, pal. I need someone to talk to."

"Why didn't you tell me we were going somewhere? Why do you do this to me? Always grabbing, always pushing. Why?" Lorre clutched at the safety strap over his head.

"I want you around because you're a genius."

"If I am such a genius, why am I out of work?"

"You're working now. For me."

Bogart pulled onto North Rodeo Drive and hung a hard right onto Wilshire Boulevard. Across the street was the Beverly Wilshire Hotel, its arched openings reminiscent of an Italian facade. He drove due west, passing the exclusive shops and showcases of Beverly Hills.

"Peter, someone tried to run me off the road last night. It was no accident."

"Dear Bogie, you attract the most charming people."

"You shoulda been with me today and met some of them. A writer who must dream up some of those cheap pictures you make. A hairstylist who could do wonders for that curly top of yours. And finally a greasy little doctor your friend Freud wouldn't give an id for."

"And now you know where Dalt is."

"Saints and Sinners Sanitarium."

"The Martha Pearce place in Bel-Air?"

"You know Saints and Sinners?"

"I know many of the latter, but alas, none of the former."

Bogart swung off Wilshire, taking Beverly Glen north through the fringes of Westwood Village. Soon they could see the Los Angeles Country Club to their right. Beverly Glen snaked through one of the most beautifully landscaped areas of Los Angeles. Bel-Air was definitely for the elite; numerous exclusive estates were surrounded by iron fences or lost behind thick groves of trees. The road was lined with eucalyptuses, pines, acacias, jacarandas and feathery peppers.

"Who's this Martha Pearce you mentioned?" asked Bogart.

"She was a wonderful comedienne during the silent days," began Lorre. "You've probably seen some of her old pictures. She had a flair for comedy and she was even good in a dramatic role. You know how they loved innocence in those days, but it was just as fashionable for a pretty young actress to get hooked. Remember Olive Thomas?"

"The Ziegfeld Follies queen?"

"The ideal American girl . . . dead in her prime. And others. All junkies. Barbara LaMarr, Alma Reubens, Juanita Hansen."

"And then there was Martha Pearce."

"You're anticipating me again, dear Bogie. I wish you'd allow me to tell the story. Yes, and then there was Martha Pearce. As tightly hooked as Mae West's brassiere. And then a nervous breakdown. There was noplace for her to turn. She was alone and destroyed."

"You can always find someone . . ." said Bogart.

"Martha did, finally. It must have been someone in the industry who knew where many of the skeletons were closeted. Anyway, Martha made a comeback in 1928 in some of the last of the silent comedies."

"Sounds like the story had a happy ending."

"Not quite. Martha had a terrible voice. Worse than

mine. Worse than yours. Are you beginning to get an idea of just how terrible it was? And then, just when she was hitting her stride—"

"—sound came in," intruded Bogart. "Which meant Martha was out again."

"Indeed. Martha remembered how alone and empty her life had been when she needed help, and she assumed there were other movie people in the same fix. Hooked on drugs, booze. Nowhere to go, nobody to turn to. She had a bold theme: a sanitarium for movie people."

"That makes Saints and Sinners very exclusive."

"Stars, supporting players, character actors, bit players, extras. If you've got a SAG or SEG card, you're in."

"We've talked about Martha Pearce. Let's talk about Dalt."

"Psychotic, dear Bogie. If he's retreated from reality, we can assume schizophrenia."

"What if he still sounds logical?"

"If his personality is relatively intact, but he persists in saying that there is a plot against him in a convincing fashion, he's paranoid."

"You haven't mentioned delusions, Doc."

"Doc? That appellation, it sounds condescending."

"Yet it touches your ego, right, Doc? The part that always wanted to be a psychiatrist."

"Are you attempting to flatter me now?"

"Keep talking about delusions, Doc."

"It isn't easy with your constant interruptions. Yes . . . delusions of persecution. That would fit."

"What can we expect?"

"Depressive or manic behavior."

"Now you're getting too clinical, Doc. Can you clarify?"

"Always I must clarify. Depressive, depressive. It means what it means. Why do you constantly torment me, force me to explain the least significant detail?"

"You say it so beautifully."

"Gloom, morbidity, feelings of worthlessness. His speech will be slow, impeded, lazy. He'll talk about committing suicide or about his great internal suffering."

"And that other . . . manic?"

"He'll reach a high level of excitement very quickly. He will be as restless as you often are. He'll make speeches."

"Like you're doing right now?"

"Speeches and dramatic gestures. He might even get violent."

"Well, we're about to find out." Bogart suddenly turned off Beverly Glen. Lorre was thrown across the seat. As he clutched for the safety strap:

"Must you drive like a madman? You know I hate careless driving. You must stop this incessant irritating behavior."

The Cadillac eased along a one-lane road through an expanse of rolling green lawns and tranquil, deep-blue lakes surrounded by blooming snowdrops and budding daffodils. Spotlights positioned in trees and on hillsides illuminated the landscape and gave it a parklike quality. A paper-thin mist hung over the grounds like a gossamer wedding veil. The air had turned chilly, and Lorre buttoned his coat.

Bogart followed a sharp bend in the lane. Once the car cleared a grove of American firs, they had their first impressive view of Saints and Sinners.

The air turned colder.

Surrealistic and dreamlike, the Victorian two-story

mansion sat isolated on a manicured hillock, shrouded by the fog.

A spiked steel fence surrounded the front of Saints and Sinners, and Bogart swung into one of the parking stalls marked for visitors. He and Lorre passed through the Directoire gates and ambled along a crushed-stone *allée* edged with clipped laurel. Bogart studied the Corinthian columns, the Greek pediment and the Italian-style ornamentation; over the main entrance was a Tiffany stained-glass dome roof.

Bogart could still not shake his uneasiness. There was no external sign indicating that this was a sanitarium.

They passed through massive oak doors into an alcove. The small room was painted a warm blue and parquet hardwood gleamed beneath their feet. A sculptured lioness on a pedestal, its mouth open in a perpetual roar, was their only welcome. Next to the door was an antique motion picture camera on a wooden tripod. The walls were lined with large photographic blowups of film crews at work, the styles of clothing, hairdos and equipment all from the twenties. The feature that Bogart and Lorre noticed most was the uncanny silence.

The woman who finally came to meet them was dressed in a French crepe blouse and black velveteen skirt that fell nearly to her ankles. The pearl-and-gold belt gracing her slender waist managed to suggest a uniform—the first subtle clue of what Saints and Sinners really was. The woman was nearing fifty, and her dark-brown hair was swept atop her head in a severe bun. She introduced herself as Josephine Rossi, program director for Martha Pearce. Then, "Are you here to see one of our patients?" she asked in a warm tone.

"A friend. Dalt Brennan."

Josephine blanched just slightly. "I'm . . . I'm afraid no one can see Mr. Brennan without special approval from Mrs. Pearce."

"Can we see Mrs. Pearce then?"

"Certainly. Right this way, please."

She led them from the entrance hall into a corridor. Again the walls were a mixture of pre-Raphaelite paintings and large, glass-encased photographs of Mack Sennett, William Ince, Erich Von Stroheim and other filmmakers of previous eras. There were giant blowups of several film stars of the twenties; some Bogart recognized, some he didn't.

Josephine opened a door leading off the hallway and ushered them inside. "Mrs. Pearce will be with you shortly."

Bogart and Lorre stood in a cavernous study. "The sanitarium business is good," said Bogart in awe.

"I haven't seen this much opulence since I left Vienna."

The walls were lined with built-in mahogany bookcases stuffed with old medical and psychiatric volumes, as well as a collection of histories on Hollywood and film: *From Caligari to Hitler, Magic and Myth of the Movies, The Rise and Decline of Silent Comedy,* and others. The parquet floors were largely covered by Turkish rugs. Dutch paintings by Kuyper hung above a black ivory fireplace. But the core of the room remained the enormous maple desk and the gigantic photographic portrait on the beige wall above it. It was a portrait of a young woman in a white, filmy nightgown, her head thrown back in ecstasy. It was an erotic and sensual image and for the moment Bogart was mesmerized by its wistful, wanton quality.

In contrast to the formality of the rest of the room, the mahogany desk was littered with ledgers, medical volumes, stacks of reports and an overturned water glass spilling out pencils and pens.

Presently the door burst open and a matronly woman swooped in. She was obviously accustomed to show-business flair, for she was dressed in a multicolored, floor-length, loose-fitting evening gown that concealed her bulky figure. She was in her late sixties, Bogart guessed, and although her skin was saggy and she had developed a double chin, Bogart immediately recognized her as the woman in the photograph.

"Mr. Bogart . . . Mr. Lorre, this is a privilege. I loved the pictures you did together; *Passage to Marseilles* is one of my favorites." Lorre had been right about her voice—it was hoarse, gravelly and awful.

"I'm impressed with *your* layout," complimented Bogart, shaking her beefy hand. "But I have the feeling I'm in a museum, not a sanitarium."

"Exactly. There's nothing I hate worse than hospitals. Antiseptic smells, sterile white walls—you'll find none of those distasteful things here at Saints and Sinners."

"Where did you acquire such movie-world memorabilia, Mrs. Pearce? I've seen nothing like it."

"I love the movies, Mr. Lorre. I loved making them for many years. I've loved watching them for as long as I can remember. As you may know, we allow only industry people into Saints and Sinners, and by having Hollywood's historic past on display, we hope to make the atmosphere comfortable for our guests."

"You've studied your human psychology," said Lorre admiringly.

"A soothed mind is the first step in a new direction," she replied. "Now then, I'm told you wish to see Mr. Brennan."

"He's a very old friend," said Bogart.

"Normally there'd be no problem . . . but there was an accident."

"Dalt's not hurt?"

"I'm afraid he's been badly burned, Mr. Bogart. We had a fire recently. It swept through the south wing, through Dalt's ward."

"How badly burned?"

"Second degree, I'm afraid. On his face, neck, hands . . . he's heavily bandaged and we've had him under sedation."

"It's imperative I talk to Dalt."

"I'd rather you came later, when he's—"

"This is important. It can't wait until later."

"Very well, but only for a few minutes. Maybe it would lift his spirits to see some friends."

Martha Pearce led Bogart and Lorre along the corridor and finally up a carpeted spiral stairway. At the top were tall Ionic columns and a coffered ceiling. They were proceeding along the second-floor corridor when a door eased open and the face of a man in his sixties peered at them.

Bogart and Lorre stopped. The aging man who stepped into the hallway was dressed in baggy black pants in desperate need of pressing, shoes three sizes too big, a black derby and a badly worn walking cane. The oldster twirled his bushy mustache and began to perform what appeared to be a vigorous vaudeville jig. He pantomimed the words.

"That'll be enough, Charlie," ordered Martha crisply, her expression unchanging.

The old man stomped one foot and applauded himself. "That's a bit from *Dough and Dynamite*," he said in the exaggerated style of a ringmaster or carnival barker. "Maybe you'd like to see something from *Easy Street*."

"Charlie!" admonished Martha.

The old man jauntily slipped back into his room, still affecting a debonair, shuffling walk. Pearce shook her head helplessly. "We call him Charlie, but his real name is Jimmy Leonard."

"The silent-screen comedian?" asked Bogart incredulously. "When I was in knee pants, I used to fall down laughing. That man was funny."

"He still is," agreed Martha, "in his own special way, though some people might call it pathetic."

"It would appear," commented Lorre, "that, like most actors, he is suffering from delusions of grandeur."

They all laughed mildly. "With Jimmy it started as adulation. Charlie Chaplin was his idol. He studied every film featuring The Tramp. And at one time he was as funny as Charlie. But then his career soured. When he couldn't face the fact that he was all washed up, he had his breakdown. We haven't been able to do much with him. He has the run of the grounds, and he never gives us any trouble."

Martha paused before a door at the end of the hallway. She knocked lightly. Bogart and Lorre became immobile at the sight of the young woman who opened it.

Honey-blond hair fell gently to caress soft shoulders, and two inquisitive green eyes gazed wonderingly at Bogart. A yellow cotton sweater was pulled tantalizingly across her swelling breasts, and she wore a slinky pleated wool skirt, also yellow, that clung to her fleshy, nyloned legs. She was thrust provocatively upward on bright-red Balenciaga suede high heels.

But it was the face that held Bogart, and Lorre in his own enigmatic way, enthralled. The moist lips suggested sexual games yet the eyes shone at Bogart with beguiling innocence. He detected a redness around her eyelids that told him she had been crying.

"This is Nurse Baker," explained Martha.

"Nurse?"

"I also detest white uniforms, Mr. Bogart. And those awful white hose and shoes. It's still possible to be sanitary *and* glamorous."

"I won't argue the glamorous aspect," said Bogart, stepping into the room.

"How's our patient?" Martha asked the nurse.

Nurse Baker shrugged. "He's been fine . . . I guess."

Bogart frowned. Nurse Baker didn't seem to fit the image—but what did at Saints and Sinners?

The room was small yet comfortable, the aqua walls and the carpeted floor giving it a distinctly unclinical feeling. Bogart and Lorre followed Martha to the bed on which Dalt Brennan's six-foot-long figure was stretched and covered with blankets.

Nurse Baker dabbed at her eyes with a tear-stained handkerchief as Bogart studied Dalt's shape on the bed. The head was completely swathed in bandages except for small openings for eyes and mouth. To Bogart they seemed obscene black holes. He felt a touch of nausea and experienced a strange sense of detachment. He could not bring himself to believe that this was the man he had once known.

He tried to shake off the feeling by smiling and saying to Dalt, "Hey, old buddy. You awake? It's me, Bogie. I thought I'd drop around and see how—"

The hands that had been buried under the blankets—hands with thick, powerful fingers—suddenly came alive, rose up and gripped Bogart by the throat.

But the hands were bandaged and unable to secure a solid grip. Bogart pulled away in surprise, stumbling against Lorre. Bogart's own hands flew to his throat, which throbbed where the thumbs had tried to gouge into his neck.

Dalt was grunting, throwing himself violently up and down on the sheets. The sounds coming from him were barely human, more like the cries of a trapped animal. Bogart felt his stomach sinking. Martha herded them out of the room, but Bogart moved reluctantly, fascinated by the unholy sight of Dalt Brennan.

Dalt tried to rise from the bed but kept falling back. Finally he was too exhausted to continue. Nurse Baker stood helplessly by the door.

In the corridor Bogart heard Dalt's grunts and then the consoling voice of Nurse Baker. Martha Pearce was pale. "I should have warned you," she said. "Dalt gets violent at times. Clinically speaking, it's part of his behavioral pattern. But I know how you must feel, seeing him like this . . ."

Bogart didn't speak. He was tense yet he also felt some relief; seeing Dalt had been traumatic, but at least it laid to rest Cohn's crazy theories. On the other hand, that deepened the mystery behind Johnny Hawks's death. What the hell did it mean? If Dalt was not at the bottom of the mystery, then why the dark sedan?

Bogart lit a cigarette, realizing his hand was trembling slightly. Lorre bummed a light from Bogart. His hand was trembling, too.

Respecting Bogart's silence, Martha led them back along the corridor. The last thing Bogart saw before descending the spiral stairway was the face of ex-comedian Jimmy Leonard staring out at him. An eye was winked, a derby tipped and a cane twirled before the door closed soundlessly.

"I tell you, Doc, something's really bugging me."

"It's the owner of this despicable establishment," volunteered Lorre, nodding his head toward Romanoff. "He forces his customers to *pay* for their drinks. Uncivilized."

Bogart pounded the surface of his booth in Dress Circle. "Damn it, something back there . . ."

It was nearly eleven P.M. and Bogart had been drinking steadily since their return from Saints and Sinners. He had insisted that Jamieson keep the empty glasses on the table so he could keep count and know when to quit. But he hadn't bothered to count.

"Nobody likes to see someone go berserk, dear Bogie. Especially when it's a friend and he tries to choke the life out of you."

"For once in your life, Lorre, old man, you're right," said Romanoff. "It's not unlike having good customers who don't pay for their drinks." Most of his clientele had cleared out for the evening, and he had decided to kibbitz at Bogart's table until closing time. He was bored and he looked it.

"Dalt trying to strangle me isn't what I'm worried about," explained Bogart, finishing another glass of Scotch and consigning the empty to the ever-growing graveyard before him. "Something about that room . . ."

"The room?" Lorre closed his saucer eyes, in deep thought. "I recall it being quite ordinary. A bed of no special detail. A stand for the food tray, a night table with a box of Kleenex. Some paper cups . . . bandages . . . blankets . . . and of course that lovely little thing who called herself a nurse. If it's the nurse bothering you, I understand . . ."

"Bandages," repeated Bogart, more to himself than the others.

"Ordinary white," responded Lorre, unimpressed.

"We used to treat burn victims on the *Leviathan*," said Bogart.

"Can't say I've ever cruised on her," said Romanoff. "Liner or yacht?"

"Troop ship," replied Bogart. "They'd be wrapped in bandages . . . only there was something . . . a smell."

"Of burnt flesh?" Romanoff looked revolted. "I say, old man, that's positively morbid."

"Something stronger than burnt flesh, Prince. Something that canceled out the smell of flesh. Unguent. Salve. It was all over those bodies and the smell of it was all over the ship. We lived with it for days, for weeks. For a year."

"I smelled nothing in the room," said Lorre. "Not even antiseptic."

"That's just it, Doc. If Dalt was suffering from second-degree burns like Pearce said, we should have smelled it. It should have been overpowering."

Lorre placed his elbows on the table. "Are you suggesting Martha Pearce was lying about the fire?"

"Maybe that wasn't Dalt on the bed."

"I say, who was on the bed?" asked Romanoff.

"A substitute—so no one would know the real Dalt was gone."

Bogart gripped Romanoff's arm. "It's a long story, Prince. We'll tell you about it in the car."

"A ride? At this late hour? Really, it's almost my bedtime . . ."

"We're going back to Saints and Sinners to talk to Dalt—or whoever's in that bed."

"I must say you're arousing my curiosity. I wouldn't miss this excitement for anything, but I must insist on taking Socrates and Mr. Confucius. They haven't had their midnight walk yet."

"Have it your way, Prince. Just make sure they don't pee on my backseat."

"I assure you," intoned Romanoff indignantly, "that if the urge came upon them, they would pee only on the front seat. After all, it is a Cadillac."

Bogart was drunk and he sped recklessly around corners, tires squealing in open defiance of the community's private security force.

Lorre clutched the safety strap; Romanoff, having heard the full details surrounding Hawks's murder, confined himself to the backseat—but not his bulldogs. Socrates bounded across Lorre's lap and thrust his head through the open window—taking the air, as Romanoff phrased it. Meanwhile, Mr. Confucius had sprawled his body across Bogart's and had his moist nose pressed against the rolled-up window.

Lorre was furious. "Why do you permit these ugly beasts the freedom of the car? You know how I feel about such brutes."

Lorre's indignation only seemed to have the wrong effect on Bogart, who drove faster by the minute. Bogart felt nothing but intense anger for allowing himself to be played for a sucker at Saints and Sinners. He hardly noticed Lorre and the dogs and continued to follow winding Beverly Glen into the heart of Bel-Air.

"Dogs, bah." Lorre flipped a half-smoked cigarette

out the window, then wiped the slobber from his hand that had dripped from Socrates' extended tongue. "I have reason to hate dogs. Since 1929."

"Is that designed to pique our curiosity?" asked Romanoff, who was filling the car with the smell of Royal Yacht as he puffed his pipe.

"I was walking along the Schleuterstrasse in Berlin, minding my own business. The Schabanerjamm Theatre was showing *M* at the time, and I loved to stroll past the marquee and see my picture on the posters.

"Suddenly a cobble whizzed past my head. I was then struck on the shoulder and felt considerable pain. I looked back to see a crowd of people yelling vile, evil things."

"No doubt," said Romanoff, "they were excited fans who thoroughly loved your portrayal of a child murderer."

"And then one of them unleashed an Alsatian."

"You fled for your life."

"Posthaste. But not nearly quickly enough, dear Prince. The filthy beast bit me squarely on the ass. It was only the strong stick of a passing *Polizei* that saved me. And then the policeman had the audacity to say to me, 'Ah, you should not have given such a realistic performance, Herr Lorre.' "

"I suspect that story to be apocryphal," said Romanoff.

"Believe what you will, our royal phoniness, but anytime you wish to inspect the scar, I will be most happy to pull down my pants—preferably in the middle of your beautiful dining room."

"We shall have to arrange precisely that," agreed Romanoff. "Business has been frightfully dull of late."

"You're driving too fast again, dear Bogie. Why must you always drive so recklessly? And you've had too much to drink. Why do you incessantly behave in this childish manner?"

Bogart's reply was to accelerate the car, the tires squealing as he negotiated a difficult curve.

"Now you've done it," said Lorre accusingly.

Bogart glanced into his rearview mirror to see a flashing red light. It was followed by the sound of a siren.

Lorre sighed. "I tried to tell you. I tried to warn you, *didn't I?* Admit I did everything in my power to make you slow down."

Cursing under his breath, Bogart pulled the Cadillac under a grove of pepper trees. Socrates began to bark when the siren grew louder.

The police car sped past, followed by an ambulance.

Mr. Confucius licked Lorre's face and bayed at the diminishing siren. Lorre picked up the dog and threw him into the backseat. "Control your charges," he barked at Romanoff.

Considerably sobered, Bogart resumed driving. What he saw next sobered him more and he slammed on the brakes, bringing the car to an abrupt halt in the center of the road.

"Now what the hell's wrong?" asked Lorre.

Then Lorre realized.

The squad car and ambulance had turned left off the highway. Left onto the one-lane asphalt road that led to Saints and Sinners.

FIFTEEN

The twirling red light of the patrol car flung bursts of light through the fog that still clung eerily to Saints and Sinners As Bogart drew up. He saw that another black-and-white patrol car and an unmarked maroon sedan had already parked in front. Bogart realized it was not an ambulance that had passed them but a coroner's wagon.

Bogart's anger had vanished and was slowly being replaced by fear.

Lorre turned on Romanoff accusingly as they neared the Directoire gate. "There're already enough crazy people inside. I suggest you take your filthy animals for a walk."

Romanoff gave no reply but whirled Socrates and Mr. Confucius on their short leashes and walked them toward one of the lakes.

A uniformed policeman ushered them into the waiting room. Slumped in one of the leather chairs was Josephine Rossi, whose mascara was now terribly tear-streaked. A plainclothesman was taking down her statement.

Slightly bent over, his bulbous nose pushed inquisitively against the lens of the antique movie camera, was another plainclothesman with a pipe thrust in his mouth. The rotund man maneuvered deliberately, almost ponderously. Bogart surmised he was only five foot three, about fifty-five years old. The diminutive man finally took notice of the new arrivals and turned slowly, removing the pipe from his mouth with a sigh and staring curiously at Bogart through thin-rimmed spectacles.

"I'm Inspector Fitzgerald," he said, his Irish brogue as disarmingly soft as his face. "Arthur Fitzgerald, to be precise."

I bet that voice has fooled a lot of crooks, thought Bogart as Fitzgerald shook his hand warmly.

"Sure now, Mr. Lorre, I can't say I've seen many of your terror pictures." The two squat figures stared at each other. Fitzgerald's eyes seemed full of weariness and wisdom.

"And I," responded Lorre, "cannot say I have heard of many cases you've solved." He spoke with a peculiar uplifting cheerfulness that kept it from sounding like an insult. If Fitzgerald could be deceptively charming, so could Lorre.

"And you, Mr. Bogart—I admire your pictures—they're quite enjoyable—but I find your characterizations of policemen a bit hard to swallow."

"I play *private* detectives," corrected Bogart. "Playing cops would be bad for my image."

"Romantic, your private detectives."

"And real cops are hard-nosed realists . . ."

"I deal in facts, Mr. Bogart. And right now a fact I would like to know is, where have you been during the past two hours?"

"Why? . . . if you don't mind *me* asking."

"Sure now, you two were the last to see Martha Pearce alive."

There was a moment's silence. Fitzgerald puffed his pipe with patience.

Finally Bogart said, "She's been murdered?"

"I didn't say that." The brogue remained soothing, gentle. Not even movie cops were this cool, decided Bogart.

"But she is dead." Lorre's moon-shaped eyes saddened.

Fitzgerald nodded. "Miss Rossi says she heard a shot shortly before nine-fifty." Fitzgerald studied his watch. "About two hours ago. She entered the study and found the unfortunate woman slumped over her desk. Apparent suicide."

"You say apparent."

"There was a note. Suicide is always apparent until all the facts are in."

"I forgot . . . you're a man who doesn't deal in theory."

The inspector beckoned for them to follow him.

The study-library was as Bogart remembered it. The only difference now was the form of Martha Pearce—still dressed in her gown—sprawled disconcertingly across the surface of the desk.

"I don't know if this means anything," said Bogart, nervously twisting his ruby ring, "but that glass of pencils . . . it was overturned when we were here last."

"You've a remarkable eye for detail, Mr. Bogart," said Fitzgerald with wry admiration.

"An actor has to be aware of detail. Otherwise he gets upstaged. Even by cops."

"How did she . . . er . . . die?" asked Lorre, who had turned several shades paler.

"You probably can't see it from your angle, Mr. Lorre, but Mrs. Pearce placed a .32 revolver—registered in her name, I might add—against her left temple and pulled the trigger. Or so it appears. If you come around here, you can see the pool of—"

"If you don't mind," said Lorre, running his fingers around his shirt collar, "I'd rather not bother."

"You said left temple?" queried Bogart, forcing himself to take a closer glance at the pool of blood under her face. Martha Pearce's eyes were open and stared down into an accounts-receivable ledger with seeming indifference. Bogart straightened up, relieved that he could now shift his attention to the portrait on the wall. He studied it, feeling his melancholia returning, then said, "That would mean she was left-handed. Maybe this is insignificant, Inspector, but wouldn't a left-handed person keep her pencil glass on the *left* side of her desk? Instead of always having to reach across?"

"A very excellent point, Mr. Bogart. I've underestimated you. It's a common flaw of us Dubliners."

"Do you mind if we step into the hallway?" asked Lorre, who was still quite pale. "It is growing extremely warm in here."

"Of course," said Fitzgerald cordially, opening the door. "I'm curious about one thing. Just why did you gentlemen visit Mrs. Pearce tonight?"

"Actually," explained Bogart, "we came to see one of her patients. Dalt Brennan."

"And you saw him?"

"Yes and no."

"Yes and no," repeated Fitzgerald, drawing deeply on his pipe.

"What I mean is, Pearce told us Dalt'd been burned in a fire here. He was covered with bandages. Head to toe. When Dalt saw us, he got violent. We left."

"What I'm really curious about, Mr. Bogart, is why you've returned, with Mr. Lorre, at such a late hour."

They stood in the hallway, occasionally stepping aside for the crime lab investigators who came and went from the study-library. Bogart could hear the *pop-pop-pop-pop* of flash bulbs as a photographer snapped Martha Pearce's death position.

"I had my suspicions that it wasn't Dalt in the bed."

"A curious attitude," said Fitzgerald. There was no change in his expression.

"Just a feeling, nothing you'd call fact, Inspector. But it does make me wonder if there's any connection between that and Mrs. Pearce's death."

There was a glimmer of agreement in Fitzgerald's blue-green eyes. "Why don't we check Mr. Brennan's room to see if he can shed any light on this theory of yours."

The moment Bogart saw the door to Dalt's room ajar, he knew something was wrong. The bed was empty and there was no sign of Nurse Baker.

Back in the waiting room, Josephine Rossi, between sobs, could provide no explanation. Nurse Baker had been hired on the previous Friday. By Mrs. Pearce personally—which was unusual, because normally Josephine did all the hiring. There was no personnel record in the files and Rossi had thought it strange: The young woman had demonstrated no knowledge of nursing whatsoever. As for a fire, there had been none at Saints and Sinners. Ever. Dalt Brennan? Mrs. Pearce had insisted on no visitors.

Fitzgerald said he would put out an APB on Brennan, now wanted for questioning in connection with the death of Martha Pearce. And with that he dismissed Bogart and Lorre.

"I'm disappointed," said Lorre, walking down the steps. "He didn't even ask us not to leave town." Lorre paused, peering into the misty darkness. "I believe that one of *their* nuts has found one of *our* nuts."

He was referring to the familiar shape of Romanoff, who stood in a sunken garden located against the right wing of the main building and lined with walkways wide enough for two passing wheelchairs. The labyrinth of flower beds and paths was illuminated by floodlights fastened to tall oaks, the tops of which were lost in swirling fog. Bogart could see someone standing near Romanoff and the tugging bulldogs.

Comedian Jimmy Leonard. No, not Leonard. Charlie Chaplin.

The old man was gesturing wildly with his hands and performing a routine from *The Gold Rush* in front of a fountain surrounded by Japanese cherry trees.

As they approached Romanoff through the mist, Socrates plunged into a bed of azaleas in order to lap at the water spurting from a marble birdbath, pulling his hapless owner with him. Ignoring the fact that he was trampling flowers, Romanoff gestured for Bogart to hurry. "I say, what kept you so long? I've walked into something big over here."

"I warned you to watch where you're stepping when those two beasts are running rampant," admonished Lorre.

"I've met a chap who fancies himself Chaplin."

"I'm reminded of a chap I know who thinks he's a prince," said Lorre.

"This is no laughing matter," insisted Romanoff. "He's been telling me how he intends to help in the destruction of the Academy Awards on Saturday night. *He's going to blow them up.*"

Bogart was frozen like a statue in the center of the walkway, speechless. Lorre stumbled against the base of a crabapple tree, clutching its trunk for support. His egg-sized eyes had grown one size larger. Finally Bogart managed, "Now maybe we can get more than theories."

It took little persuasion on Bogart's part to get Leonard/Chaplin to tell him everything he knew. Bo-

gart simply promised Leonard a part in a forthcoming
picture that would reunite all the stars of silent-screen
comedy. Bogart knew he would hate himself in the
morning, but it was also heartwarming, he thought
sardonically, the way he'd lit up that man's eyes.

"It's the nice man down the hall," began the Chap-
linesque old man.

"What nice man?"

"Down what hall?"

"The hall isn't important, Prince; please be still."

"My friend Dalt. Only he wasn't my friend after the
game."

"The game?"

"The one I played with Martha. We pretended there
was a fire."

"Before the fire . . . what happened, Charlie?"

"Dalt was going to let me help him. I was to have
second billing. Only he didn't tell me about the black
car."

"Tell *us* about the black car, Charlie."

"It always came in the back way. It always parked
behind the studio."

"He means the sanitarium," explained Lorre softly.

"They met," continued Charlie. "They met inside
the black car."

"Who met?"

"My friend Dalt."

"And . . . ?"

"Another man."

"What other man?"

"The director." Leonard thought for a moment. "Or
maybe he was the producer."

"He doesn't know," whispered Lorre. "He thinks it's
all part of a movie project."

"It was my secret." Leonard danced a jig to express

his delight. "I didn't tell anyone. Not even Dalt knew I was watching the black car. Dalt, he had it all written down." Leonard continued to dance, spinning in the shadows of the tall oaks.

"The screenplay," breathed Bogart.

Socrates began to bark. Romanoff quieted him and the old man resumed. "And then Dalt put on the bandages and he didn't talk to me the same way any more."

"That's when the switch was made," assumed Bogart.

"And then the other man came, the birdman who took the scenario away."

"Birdman? I say, this is enigmatic." Socrates barked in agreement, still lapping at the water in the bird-bath.

"Try to be quiet, Prince." Lorre's voice was genuinely annoyed. Bogart could sense Lorre was deep in thought. Then Lorre snapped his fingers; his eyes flickered with revelation. "Of course . . . birdman. He's talking about Johnny *Hawks*. Don't you see?"

"I certainly do not, my good man."

"How does Johnny Hawks fit with the sanitarium?" wondered Bogart.

Leonard continued his happy dance, breaking his pantomime to sing. "Oh, the birdman came to see the nurse/And to sing to her his pretty verse/But he really wanted to make her/This beautiful girl named Baker." Leonard danced off into the fog, skipping across the flower beds and disappearing behind a stone wall.

"No wonder vaudeville died," snapped Romanoff, gripping the leashes of his dogs.

Bogart turned to Lorre. "The nurse. She must have been Johnny's girl friend."

"Having seen the girl, I would say it figures," agreed Lorre.

Bogart thought: Why hadn't Johnny told him about the girl? Usually he enjoyed bragging about his latest conquests during their weekend cruises on the *Santana.* "Let's see what we have, Doc. First Johnny visits the sanitarium to see this Baker dame. Charlie, thinking the man in the bed is Dalt, returns the copy of *Hollywood Armageddon.* Johnny reads the script. What happens then?"

"Something tips him off to the bomb plot," said Lorre. "Maybe he also talks to Charlie and puts two and two together."

"So he cops the script."

"Now he knows too much," said Lorre.

"And then," contributed Romanoff, "Johnny gets himself killed."

"A brilliant observation, Prince, brilliant. Perhaps you will enlighten us as to the killer's identity."

"Pearce? Dalt?" But Romanoff's voice wavered with uncertainty.

"We don't have enough yet," said Bogart.

"I know one thing," said Lorre. "Finding a copy of *Hollywood Armageddon* is now very vital."

"What good is a piece of fiction?" asked Romanoff.

"It might prove to be more than fiction. It could be the key to Dalt's psychology. Maybe it will give us some idea of how he intends to carry out his threat."

"*If* he carries out the threat," corrected Bogart.

"You still have doubts?" asked Lorre.

Bogart paused. No answer.

"Or is it that you don't want to believe . . ."

Bogart looked Lorre fully in the eye. "I think something is going to happen Saturday night. I'm not convinced yet that Dalt is behind it."

"But he's part of it," said Lorre. "He has to be. Otherwise they wouldn't have gone to the trouble to make the substitution."

"Maybe it's time we told some of this to Fitzgerald."

"You're wasting your time," said Lorre. "He'll demand proof. We don't have it. Not yet."

"Hate to admit it, old man, but for once in his life Lorre is correct. In all my dealings with officers of the law, none of which was all that pleasant, I have yet to find one who knows how to listen objectively."

Bogart rubbed his chin thoughtfully. "You know, that's the first time you two have agreed on something. But what you say makes sense. I'm going to have to work alone to get that proof."

"What do you mean, *you'll* get the proof?" snapped Lorre. "You wanted me along for the ride, to build your ego, to be your walking textbook on psychoses. Now, dear Bogie, you're stuck with me."

Socrates' barking sealed the pact.

SIXTEEN

The man at the wheel of the Dodge pickup drove with intense purpose. His tiny gray-bluish eyes looked dejectedly at the passing slums. His face was jowly, unshaven, with a gray-streaked mustache and long-ignored tousled dark-brown hair.

He listened to the droning radio with disinterest. His hands closed around a whiskey bottle in the dash compartment and twisted off the cap. He drank deeply.

A radio voice, familiar and evocative: *"This is Jimmy Fiddler from Hollywood with the latest about the greatest in filmland. Flash! The House Un-American Activities Committee hasn't even begun to get under the skin of Hollywood and prove its subversion, according to my Washington contacts. The 'Hollywood Ten' could easily become 'The Hollywood Score.' And knowing the score in Hollywood just might not be such a good idea in these days of alleged Communist infiltration . . . A tribute to Susan Peters, that beautiful young actress who suffered a terrible shooting accident in 1945 that left her paralyzed. But it hasn't kept her from pursuing her greatest love, acting. I've just seen her in* Sign of the Ram *and she's terrific. Best wishes to a girl who had the spunk to come back against overwhelming odds—Wait, I've just been handed a late bulletin. Ex-movie great Martha Pearce, a queen of the silent comedy days, was found dead tonight in her Bel-Air sanitarium, Saints and Sinners."*

The man's foot came off the gas pedal and stayed glued to the floor, unmotivated, uncaring. His hands were leaden weights that handled the wheel with equal indifference. The wheel spun wildly on its own volition.

"Police report she died of a self-inflicted gunshot wound. Her suicide coincides with the strange disappearance of screenwriter Dalton Brennan from Saints and Sinners. So far, the police report no connection between the two incidents."

The pickup veered sharply to the right, leaped viciously over a red-painted curb and careened against a telephone pole. The man's body rocked in unison with the jarring impact, his head striking the windshield. The Garand M-1 military rifle banged in its scabbard over the rear window and slid partway out.

The man snapped off the radio with a savage twist of the knob.

The engine stalled and died. The tousle-haired man pressed his forehead down on the chipped plastic of the broken horn button. Teardrops moved slowly down his face, forming a parenthesis around his reddening nose.

He finally raised his head and pushed the rifle back into the leather scabbard. He turned on the ignition and the motor purred back at him uninjured. New-found strength flowed into his feet and hands.

The Dodge backed away from the telephone pole and proceeded along the avenue. One headlight was dead—a broken heap of glass and filaments lying on the sidewalk behind him—the other was askew, raking to the left.

He rolled down the window and allowed the cool night air to wash over his face.

The pickup made a left turn onto Jefferson and nosed to the empty curb, jerking to a stop. To the right was a bulky, shadowy building, eerily projecting Moorish domes and Arabesque decor. Flickering shadows traced across dark tiles on the wall near the ticket windows.

Dalt Brennan had found his way to Shrine Auditorium.

DAY THREE

Thursday, March 18, 1948

SECRETARY OF DEFENSE FORRESTAL SAYS EVENTS IN PALESTINE MAY FORCE CURTAILMENT OF STEEL PIPELINES FOR SAUDI ARABIA OIL FIELDS . . .

SWASTIKAS FOUND PAINTED ON EXTERIOR WALLS OF SANTA MONICA THEATER CURRENTLY SHOWING OSCAR CONTENDER *Gentleman's Agreement*. TWENTIETH-CENTURY FOX SPOKESMAN SAYS SECRET FASCIST ORGANIZATION IS RESPONSIBLE . . .

FILM WRITER LESTER COLE IS GIVEN HOPE BY U.S. JUDGE YANKWICH THAT HIS $1500-PER-WEEK JOB AT MGM WILL BE REINSTATED. JUDGE YANKWICH SAYS HOUSE UN-AMERICAN ACTIVITIES COMMITTEE HAS NO RIGHT TO DEMAND YES-OR-NO ANSWER TO THE QUESTION: "ARE YOU A COMMUNIST?" . . .

HOLLYWOOD FILM COMMUNITY MOURNS DEATH OF CHARACTER ACTOR JOHNNY HAWKS.

SEVENTEEN

Gray dawn broke over Benedict Canyon. Bogart was aroused from a troubled sleep by the petulant jingling of the phone. He was badly in need of a shave and rubbed away granules of sleep from his eyes. Yawning and stretching, he threw back the deep-beige chintz bedspread. He slid out of the large double bed, brushing aside the draperies which hung from a false valance, and answered the phone on Betty's vanity.

Bogart winced when he recognized the prattling voice of Louella O. Parsons, movie columnist for the Los Angeles *Examiner*. She was alleged to be at the top of her profession—or the bottom, depending on one's point of view.

Thanks to the power of her publisher, William Randolph Hearst, Parsons had elevated herself to such a height in the Hollywood hierarchy that she had a stranglehold over the film community, threatening the stars with bad publicity—or worse. There was a rumor that Parsons suffered from a weak bladder and Bogart had often referred to her as "the peeing one." At this hour of the morning he felt ready to call her just that, but he bit his tongue.

"*I was calling*," Parsons said cattily, "*about Hedda's interview in this morning's* Times." Jealousy was oozing out of the receiver.

"What do you expect, Louella?" Bogart asked grumpily, still rubbing his eyes. "She came to Warners. I happened to be making a picture there. So . . ."

She edged her venom ahead of Bogart's. "*The least*

you could do to make up is give me some information about why you were at the Martha Pearce Sanitarium last night."

Bogart was suddenly wide awake. The goddamn broad must never sleep, he thought.

"How did I know?" her pseudosweet voice purred. *"Louella has spies everywhere, dear."*

"Uh, look, Louella, I'm going to have a really hot item for you soon."

"I hope it isn't just about silly old business."

"Oh no, Louella dear, this is very personal. It's a real scoop. I'll get back to you at the end of the week."

"Oh, Bogie, that's wonderful. I knew we could still be good friends. In the meantime we'll just drop that other little matter regarding Hedda. Bygones will be bygones."

Bogart slapped down the receiver. Of all the Hollywood gossip columnists, he hated Louella the most. Not even simpering Sheila Graham was that bad . . .

Lorre was already stirring when Bogart gave his rotund, sheet-covered form a solid whack on the backside and told him to get out of bed.

Lorre rolled over and glared at Bogart. "Don't you realize I need my beauty sleep? Why do you treat me with utter disregard at such an ungodly hour?"

"On you all that beauty looks bad," retorted Bogart. "Get your fat ass out of the sack. The predators are already on the prod this morning. You'll be nothing but a bleached carcass by noon if you don't get out of bed and protect yourself."

"For once in my life I wish you'd leave me alone."

"Out of bed, Doc. I'm gonna fix you a helluva breakfast."

Lorre groaned loudly. "Now I know I'm going to stay in bed."

Bogart threw his wrinkled pajamas against the bleached wood paneling and reached for his white terry-cloth jumpsuit and Indian moccasins. He jammed a weatherbeaten black peaked yachting cap onto his tousled hair and shambled from the room.

Harvey greeted Bogart at the back door with a wet nose and a hungry yipping. Bogart picked up a pail from the porch and walked behind the house, where eight coops were aligned on the rear slope. In all, the Bogarts had fifteen chickens, two roosters and six ducks. He found the usual six eggs and returned to the house with Harvey at his heels.

Still bleary-eyed, Bogart found his way into the kitchen. The sink was tiled a gleaming yellow and the cupboards were of assorted hues, bearing numerous patterns and tyrolean figures.

First he fed Harvey, then he buttered a skillet. Lorre, wearing the same clothes from the night before except for a red-and-white bow tie he had pulled from a pocket, stumbled into the kitchen and spread the Los Angeles *Times* on the table.

Bogart was just cracking the last of the six eggs into the skillet when the phone rang. Lorre answered it indifferently, then covered the mouthpiece. "It's White Fang himself," he revealed, handing the receiver to Bogart.

"Doc, flip those eggs. I'm making you my special, Eggs Benedict Canyon," he said. Lorre looked disapprovingly at the kitchen stove, shrugged his shoulders impassively and shuffled to the stove.

Bogart recognized Cohn's gravelly voice. *"All hell's cutting loose and you're still in bed. Say, was that Lorre who answered the phone?"*

"Get to the point, Harry."

"The point is, I want your ass over here quick.".

"Say please, Harry."

"All right, so please get your ass over here quick."

"Why should I?"

"Damn it." Lorre had broken one of the yolks and was looking at Bogart like a man in need of the Seventh Cavalry.

"This Johnny Hawks business is about to drive me nuts, Bogart. And right now you're the only joker who can help me straighten it out."

"You and me, we have nothing in common, Harry."

"After all that farting around you did last night at Pearce's headshrinking joint, we sure as hell do! Just come over before I go stark raving fucking nuts."

So old Harry was wise to last night. But how much had he figured out on his own?

"White Fang sounded like his fun-loving self," commented Lorre, bursting another yolk. "I wish you would cook the breakfast yourself, dear Bogie. You know how clumsy I am around the kitchen. For once would you finish something you start?"

"Did you read the paper?" asked Bogart, his attention suddenly riveted to the front pages of the *Times.* Beneath the major headline TRUMAN DEMANDS U.S. ARM AGAINST SOVIET WAR THREAT was a smaller item: BEL-AIR SANITARIUM SUICIDE PROBE. "There's a story about Martha Pearce's death."

"Really," pleaded Lorre, "we must do something about these eggs."

"Here's something else. VASQUEZ MURDER VICTIM MOURNED BY FILMLAND. It's an update on Johnny Hawks . . . 'Hawks's bullet-riddled car was impounded by police . . .' Hey, you know, Doc . . ." Bogart brought up his fingers and tugged at his earlobe. "I think . . . maybe you should check out that impounded car today."

"First you ask me to be your private chef. Now you want me to be your errand boy, your stooge."

"Drop by the L.A. Police Department. I'll meet you later at Johnny's funeral."

"Would you mind telling me where?"

"Forest Lawn, that great sound stage in the sky. Where else?"

"Don't joke about such a thing," snapped Lorre. Then morosely: "I have a feeling we may both end up there. And in the not-too-distant future." Lorre looked balefully into the frying pan. "You're going to have to settle for something a little different this morning."

"Oh?" queried Bogart.

"Yes," said Lorre, his saucer eyes wide. "Scrambled eggs."

EIGHTEEN

The North American Committee for Democratic Action was increasing its pressure. While before there had been only a handful of protestors, pickets now lined the walls of Columbia not only on North Gower but on Fountain as well.

Counterprotests were being generated by Columbia, which had recruited its own line of demonstrators: At least fifty employees paraded with placards which proclaimed the right of free expression. One man at the gate had the sole task of passing out brochures. Bogart accepted one and saw that it was propaganda from Tayne's production office, beautifully printed on glossy paper with the Tayne emblem embossed in gold.

"The American way of life is imperiled by insidious forces from within and without," it began pompously. "The Communist cause is endangering our democratic ideals . . ."

Bogart could read no further and tossed the brochure into the backseat.

Bogart parked the coupe and hurried toward the main administration building. He passed Gene Autry coming out the door dressed in Levi's and a gaudy cowboy shirt. Pat Buttram was at his side, carrying a script labeled *The Strawberry Roan*. Though Bogart thought Autry's musical Westerns somewhat ridiculous, Middle America loved them, and so did Columbia, which enjoyed a healthy box-office gross.

Bogart climbed to the second floor and entered Cohn's outer office, which was sparsely furnished and staffed by a single receptionist. The primly dressed young brunette immediately stopped filing her fingernails and cleared him through to the inner office. This was also sparsely furnished and staffed by a head secretary and one assistant, both as prim and well coiffed as the outer receptionist. Some producers had been known to wait here several hours—others several days.

As he waited indifferently, aware that the assistant was watching him over the top of her Underwood, Bogart studied the door leading to Cohn's office. The soundproof barrier had neither keyhole nor knob, being controlled by a buzzer at the secretary's fingertips. Bogart noticed smudge marks on the edge of the door at mid-height left by the sweating palms of those passing into the "inner sanctum."

Bogart was kept waiting exactly one minute.

Cohn's office was as he remembered it—intimidating to the visitor and fittingly awesome. Cohn had patterned these private chambers after Benito Mussolini's in Rome, and for years had kept an autographed photograph of Il Duce on the wall—until it had become unfashionable and unthinkable.

Bogart stood in an elongated room which was paneled in dark woods, richly furnished and thickly carpeted. At the far end was Cohn's overwhelming semicircular desk, raised slightly above floor level. On the wall behind Cohn were the Academy Awards his studio had garnered. A telephone and an intercom box were the only objects on the desk—the latter enabled Cohn to contact any department of the studio with the flip of a switch.

At first Bogart had difficulty making out Cohn behind the desk. It was customary for Cohn's end of the office to be shadowy and dim, while the entrance was brightly lit. Finally Bogart's eyes adjusted and he saw two figures standing next to the desk. One was a beautiful blond in a light worsted plaid skirt with a matching cape and a red blouse. The face and figure were unforgettable.

Nurse Baker.

She had been crying again, Bogart noted. Her mascara was running hopelessly. Otherwise she was her same beautiful self.

The man was six feet in height and had a rounded face with bright, smiling eyes and a bushy mustache that enhanced his bourbon cheeks. The sculptured, streamlined nose was as red as those cheeks. When he saw Bogart, the smile left his eyes and an attitude of embarrassment settled into the wrinkled lines of his face.

Bogart recognized him: Ray Teal, a decent-enough character actor who was usually relegated to playing small roles—sheriffs, mayors, bankers. His most memorable bit had been as the loud-mouthed bigot who had been knocked through a plate-glass window by Harold Russell in *The Best Years of Our Lives*.

"You took your goddamn time getting here," accused Cohn, rising imperiously from his swivel chair.

"I'm sorry about this whole thing, Mr. Bogart," said Teal with deep sincerity.

"Quiet, Ray," ordered Cohn, like a growling bulldog. He turned the growl on Bogart: "I was hoping maybe you could give me some answers, because frankly, I don't know what this is all about . . . yet." Cohn leaned forward in his chair to light a fresh cigar.

"Start with the girl," said Bogart. "She interests me the most."

"I thought she might. Meet Norma Jean Baker. Max Arnow just signed her to a six-month contract."

"With standard options," added Norma Jean, dabbing at her eyes with a red handkerchief that matched her blouse.

"I wish you'd stop that crying," simpered Cohn. "Crying women make me nervous."

"Forget the introductions, Harry," said Bogart. "*Nurse* Baker and I have already met." The young woman smiled, but Bogart could sense she was holding in her grief.

"And this," continued Cohn, "is Ray Teal. He's doing a hunk of . . . a film we're making called *The Black Arrow*. With Louis Hayward clankin' around in armor, for Chrissake. Ray's one of our contract players." Cohn leaned back and looked somewhat puzzled as he said: "The way these two told it to me, they were hired free-lance, without the knowledge of the studio, by Martha Pearce."

"Let me guess," said Bogart. "Norma Jean was hired to play a nurse and Teal, a guy wrapped up in bandages, Dalt Brennan."

"As a practical joke," said Teal.

"I don't think it turned out very funny," said Norma Jean.

Cohn resumed: "Then you came along last night, Bogart. That's the part where I get lost. I also wanna know how all this fits in with Johnny getting himself knocked . . . I mean, murdered. Norma Jean just told me they were going steady."

Norma Jean looked as if she might break into tears again. "Johnny and me, we were gonna get hitched."

"I'm sorry about Johnny," said Bogart.

"He talked a lot about you, Mr. Bogart. All the time, he talked about you and how you and he were gonna make pictures together."

"Well," said Cohn, "I'm waiting for someone to get

off their . . . uh, to tell me what the hell's happening."

Bogart paused to light a Chesterfield. Let the sonof-abitch wait. Finally, after blowing smoke in Cohn's direction, Bogart explained that Blake Richards, author of *Hollywood Armageddon*, and Dalt Brennan were one and the same.

Bogart expected a fresh outburst from Cohn, but the studio president eased back into the gripping comfort of his gargantuan swivel chair and brooded.

It was Norma Jean who broke the pause. "You really threw us last night, Mr. Bogart. Nobody said anything about you coming around to Saints and Sinners."

"I was the one fly in the ointment. How long were you two masquerading?"

"Since the weekend," said Teal.

"You knew you were impersonating Dalt Brennan?"

"But that's all I knew, Mr. Bogart. I didn't ask too many questions. Sometimes it's not enough, working bit parts in pictures."

"What Martha was paying was no joke," said Norma Jean.

Bogart studied Teal closely for a moment. "Yeah, I can see why Pearce hired you. You look enough like Dalt. Enough to pass under the circumstances, anyway."

"Would someone please get to the point," chimed in Cohn.

Teal animated his words with broad sweeps of his thickset arms. "Everything went well at first because there were no visitors to the room. Then an old man kept coming in, wanting to talk."

"An old man who thought he was Charlie Chaplin?"

Teal nodded. "Norma Jean kept shooing him out.

Once he left a script behind—I guess he was convinced I was Dalt."

"What happened to the script?"

"I gave it to Johnny," said Norma Jean. "I knew he'd been looking for new properties."

"Johnny knew about this charade all along?"

"Oh no. Not until he sneaked in to see me. But he thought the whole thing was kinda funny."

"He read the script?"

"Yeah, then he came right back to the sanitarium to talk to Martha Pearce."

"What about?" queried Bogart.

Norma Jean shrugged. "I never had a chance to talk to Johnny about it. But he sure was acting funny after that."

"Blackmail, that's what Johnny saw Pearce about," interjected Cohn, suddenly rising from his desk. "Johnny must've been threatening to expose their plot."

"*Their* plot?" challenged Bogart.

"Yeah, Pearce and Brennan's. They must've been in on it together. And they knocked off . . . er, shot Johnny to keep him quiet and to get back the screenplay. And then you came snooping around last night, Bogart. By God, you did listen to me, after all."

"Just following the end of my nose, Harry."

Cohn had a smirk on his face; he was apparently quite proud of his rationalizing. "So the real Brennan decided things were getting too warm and silenced the one person who was already in on the plot: Martha Pearce."

"All very logical, Harry, but there's no proof whatsoever that Brennan killed either Hawks or Pearce. For all we know, Brennan might have been abducted. Perhaps even killed." It was possible, but it seemed unlikely to Bogart. He turned to Teal, whose bourbon cheeks had begun to glow again. "What happened at the sanitarium before Lorre and I got there?"

"What the hell does Lorre have to do with this?" barked Cohn. "That sneaky little bas—eh, little guy can't be trusted."

"Just shut up and listen, Harry."

Teal swallowed a lump in his throat. "Martha Pearce hurried down and told us you'd be coming in. I almost jumped out of my bandages. I figured I'd never fool a close friend of Brennan's."

"So you decided feigning violence was the only way to keep me away. It was a damn good performance. You had me believing it."

"After you and Lorre left, Pearce came back in and paid us off."

"That was no joke either," said Norma Jean.

"Told us to get the hell out and not to come back. To keep our mouths shut. Then this morning when I read about Pearce's suicide, I realized we were caught up in something bad. I called Norma Jean and told her to get right over here. I figured if anyone could protect us, it'd be the studio."

"Yeah," agreed Cohn, "I pay plenty to keep my players' names out of the papers." He pressed a button on his intercom system.

A mousy-looking young man in a gray flannel suit, wearing steel-rimmed glasses and carrying an alligator-skin briefcase, darted into the office and stood before Cohn's desk.

"This is Peterson," said Cohn. "He's one of the best when it comes to keeping names out of the rags."

"That's right," said Peterson proudly. "You can count—"

"Be quiet, Peterson. You just do your job and leave the rest to me."

Bogart didn't bother to return Peterson's smile. "I'd better warn you, Peterson. There's a damn smart cop by the name of Fitzgerald who's gonna strip the hide right off that beautiful little carrying case of yours. No matter how good you think you are at hushing up scandals."

Cohn jerked his head toward the door, the signal that Peterson was to take the contract players out. Teal apologized to Bogart one final time, and Norma Jean took more swipes at her mascara and walked toward the door.

After they were gone, Cohn coughed on his own cigar smoke. "You ever see anything like that Norma Jean, Bogart? By God, I think we really got something there."

"Just make sure it's all for the screen, Harry."

A door in the side of the office opened and a middle-aged, bewhiskered man in a white apron stepped out holding a strop and razor. "Good morning, Mr. Cohn. It's that time again."

The door led to a small room that served as Cohn's private bath. There was a toilet, wash basin, small shower stall and barber's chair. It was here that every morning Cohn had his shave and, once every two weeks, a haircut.

The barber threw a striped towel around Cohn's head and shoulders and immediately began to apply a thick lather. "I remember the bastard now," said Cohn.

"Which bastard? In this town you have to be specific, Harry."

"That sonofabitching Brennan. I don't care if he was your navy buddy, his work for me was the shits.

He was always late. I hate people who're late, Bogart. I run a studio and if it's gonna profit, it's gotta have people who're dependable."

"So you fired the bastard," said Bogart unemotionally.

"No wonder he had to use that pen name and *your* friendship to get that goddamn script to me. You two guys musta had the same case of crabs in the navy." Cohn stirred restlessly and the barber froze in position, the razor poised against Cohn's jugular vein.

"I wish I were holding that razor right now," fantasized Bogart.

"You and about fifty thousand others in this town. Like I said before, Bogart, you gotta stand in line . . ."

"Dalt stood in line, too, only he wrote *Hollywood Armageddon*. As a sick joke . . . as a way of getting back at you."

Cohn popped his head forward and the barber popped the razor back. Too late. A tiny trickle of blood appeared on his neck. But Cohn had felt nothing.

"You must believe me by now, Bogart. About Brennan blowing up the Oscars."

"Let's say I'm curious. Can you remember any details about the screenplay?"

"I put all that crap outta my mind."

"It's important, Harry. Lorre thinks—"

"Lorre? So that little sonofabitch *is* involved. I thought that was his voice this morning. That bastard tricked me once into letting him make a picture about some Russian jerk who went around killing peasants and shopkeepers. That Lorre is a clever little foreigner, with those goddamn eyes of his rolling around in his head. Devious as hell, I warn you. Is he on our side?"

"He's on *my* side, Harry. And he thinks the screenplay is very important."

"All I can remember is that some idiot writer blows up the Oscars. More I can't tell you."

"Come on, Harry. Give me something to work with. Don't you keep files of old screenplays? Personnel records?"

"Maybe they got something in the Writers' Building."

"You mean you haven't checked it yet?"

"We'll check it, we'll check it."

"Hurry up, I'm a busy man, Harry."

"At least let me finish my shave in peace, Bogart. That's the least you could do. You know, sometimes I think you ain't human, Bogart. You just ain't human at all."

The files were so old they were covered by a layer of dust an eighth of an inch thick. Bogart rifled through the cardboard boxes, and delighted to see Cohn down on his hands and knees in this isolated part of the Writers' Building, flipping through retired files as if he were a secretary. Occasionally a puff of dust would rise and hit Cohn in the face.

It was Cohn, choking from just such an attack, who found the Dalt Brennan employment file.

The only script was one Brennan had begun but never finished, *The Love Factor.* "We shelved that dog after a month," explained Cohn. "Like a million other projects that never see the inside of a theater."

Cohn waved Dalt's personal correspondence in Bogart's face, giving Bogart a look which said "I told you so."

The file was full of Communist pamphlets, inflammatory literature, fund-raising appeals, rally an-

nouncements, documents and letters bearing the logos
of known Communist-front organizations. All were
dated pre-1940.

"This proves it," raved Cohn. "It proves your pal
Brennan is a stinko Commie. And that screenplay you
call a joke—hell, that's no joke, that's part of his
warped ideology."

Before Bogart could reply, Cohn launched into one
of his diatribes. He called upon the HUAC committee
to expose the Communist menace in Hollywood,
waxed hysterical about the "patriotic, daring" producers now engaged in making such quintessential Communist exposés as Tayne's *The Red Seduction* (naturally he mentioned that film first), George Sidney's
The Red Danube and Sol Seigel's *The Iron Curtain*.

Bogart calmly smoked and waited for Cohn to un-
wind. When he finally paused to relight his extin-
guished cigar, Bogart said, "If Brennan's a Commie,
Harry, he's pretty dumb to have left behind all this
incriminating evidence."

Cohn maintained his smugness. "Someday," he said,
"the world's gonna praise us for cleaning up our own
house."

"HUAC is going after the wrong cockroaches,"
countered Bogart. "All that wind and fury in Washington hasn't proven anything to me. And," said Bogart,
standing up to leave and crushing his cigarette underfoot, "congratulations to you, Harry."

"What the hell did I do?"

"Nothing, Harry; you did nothing. You just let them
sail John Lawson down the river."

Cohn coldly ignored Bogart's remark. "Hey, don't
forget Johnny's funeral this afternoon. People say I
got no heart, but I want you to know I've issued a
memo to all my top producers and directors and or-

dered them to turn up for this thing. Or else. You can't say I don't have feelings, Bogart."

As Bogart left, Cohn was still down on his hands and knees, sending clouds of dust up around himself. Bogart decided it was exactly where Cohn belonged.

NINETEEN

"*Mr. Bogart?*"

"Yeah, but make it quick. Your call caught me at a busy moment."

"*My name is Paul Fabrini . . . still in a hurry?*"

"Who's in a hurry? I'm listening."

"*You received my message . . .*"

"*Hollywood Armageddon* has a special ring to it."

"*The way you've been asking questions, I thought it might.*"

"I'm concerned about Dalt Brennan. I'm also concerned about anyone whose life he's threatened."

"*You're an inquisitive man, Mr. Bogart. Just how much do you know?*"

"Two minutes, Bogie."

"What? . . . Okay, Art, tell Huston I'll be there in a minute. It's my sick grandma from Peoria. . . . Fabrini? Just how much do *you* know?"

"*About Martha Pearce, for instance?*"

"How does Saints and Sinners fit into your life?"

"*Not as a place of residence, I assure you.*"

"You knew Martha?"

"*Now there's a fascinating woman. Imagine. Dying like that.*"

"The cops say suicide."

"*And little turds roll out of Hedda Hopper's typewriter every morning.*"

"You sound like a man with a theory about murder."

"*Not a theory, Mr. Bogart. Facts. Enough to set this town on its can. Speculation I leave for screenplays.*"

"I thought you screenwriters were supposed to be rich and carefree. You sound like you might be involved—right up to your neck."

"*If knowing facts is 'being involved,' then you're right, Mr. Bogart.*"

"I have some facts, too, Fabrini. Fact one: Dalt threatened your life. Fact two: A good friend of mine named Johnny Hawks is dead. Fact three: Martha Pearce is dead. Fact four: Facts one, two and three all seem to be touched, directly or indirectly, by Brennan's screenplay."

"*No matter how you add them up, Mr. Bogart, you still have only conjecture.*"

"Here's some more conjecture. If Dalt is running loose, your life could be in danger."

"*And you could be right—only not in the fashion you imagine. The same might be said for your life, Mr. Bogart. And perhaps even those close to you. If you keep nosing around openly like you have.*"

"Is that a threat?"

"*It's a threat—but not from me.*"

"I think it's time we met face to face, Mr. Fabrini. Romanoff's is a place of considerable charm and atmosphere."

"*Charm and atmosphere bore me. You'll be contacted.*"

"Now wait a minute, Fabrini. Give me some idea—"

"*I said you'd be contacted, Mr. Bogart.*"

The line went dead.

Bogart replaced the receiver. He was now convinced that whatever had happened on the set of *Embarkation Point* was only a small part of something bigger that was just now coming into focus. Danger . . .

* * *

"Did you hear the big crash?" asked John Huston. "The temples of all the Rialtos of the world are falling down right now. Humphrey Bogart has decided to come to work again . . . It's obvious something's eating you, and the camera's catching every nuance of it."

"Children," muttered Edward G. Robinson, rising from his canvas chair. "That's all we are. So are the saps who pay to see our movies. We're all just a bunch of kids—Bogie, me, Cagney, Raft—just a bunch of guys that never grew up, playing cops and robbers. Yeahhh."

"But well-paid children, Eddie," added Huston.

Chuck Jones was on the fringes of the set, drawing again while Bogart waited for the camera routine to begin. Huston called for action, the camera dollied in and tracked alongside Bogart and Robinson. Huston called "cut" and "print it," and the flurry of activity for another scene began.

Art Luecker strolled up urgently and informed Bogart that he had made three calls to the Garden of Allah in the last thirty minutes and there had been no answer.

The scene had been Bogart's final one. Now there remained only a few pickup shots of Robinson with Thomas Gomez. An electrician angled one of the four-sided barn doors on a Senior light high in the rafters. He jumped with a yell when, ten feet away, one of the 225-amp Brute Arcs exploded, throwing a shower of glass from a Fresnel lens and a puff of smoke out of its heat chimney.

In disbelief Huston stared upward at the ruined piece of equipment. Karl Freund placed his light meter close to his eye as though it were a monocle.

"We need it. Get another carbon and lens on that

thing, Lee," Freund called. "And check the cables for a melt-down."

Huston stood in exasperation. "Papa," he said to Freund, "someone doesn't want us to finish this picture before noon."

Freund remained unruffled and sipped a martini.

Everyone waited as Lee Wilson and his men scurried to fix the lamp. The telephone on the set-stand jangled; it was a call from Bogart's business agent, urging him and Betty to accept a weekly radio series, to be syndicated by Santana Productions, in which they would portray two characters running a saloon and a fishing boat out of Key West: a thinly disguised *To Have and Have Not*. Bogart said it sounded good and he would consider it. Next Bogart was offered an opportunity to portray Sam Spade in a one-hour *Suspense* show, "The Kandy Tooth," a sequel to *The Maltese Falcon*. Bogart turned it down flat on the premise that Howard Duff was already established as radio's Sam Spade.

He had just turned away from the telephone when it rang again. Another business call—an offer to star in a *Lux Radio Theater* version of *The Treasure of the Sierra Madre*. He said that he would seriously consider the offer if Walter Huston and Tim Holt were also in the cast.

He left the telephone, his mind juggling business with his personal involvement with Dalt Brennan. Everything and everyone he had been in contact with in the last few days were more and more embroiled in the twisted affair. Again, Fabrini's voice came to him.

Danger . . .

Luecker caught Bogart's eye, pointed to a wall phone and shook his head—still no Mayo. Bogart glanced at his watch. He had to be at the Garden of

Allah in less than forty minutes to pick up Mayo. Why hadn't she answered?

"Hello, Bogie. You haff a vew minutes?"

"Hiya, Mike. What's on your mind?"

"Haff you read the script?" asked Curtiz.

"Checked it out this morning, Mike."

"You zeem empty of enthusiasm for it. You are diztractioned? Maybe there is nodding I can do for you?"

Bogart smiled. "Sorry, Mike. There are a lot of things piling up. I like the script, but I just don't know if I'll have the time to fit it in. That's the best I can promise you."

"Vonderful. Vhat more can I azk, I azk you. I must be going, but I vould like much to ztay for the wrapped pardy."

"Yeah, Huston shouldn't mind."

Huston walked over to them, nodding to Curtiz. "Bogie, don't leave just yet. I've got an idea for a picture I want to discuss. *Key Largo* is my last film for Warners and Sam Spiegel and I are forming an independent company."

"Is this that African thing you're always bending my ear about?"

"I tell you, Bogie, it's one helluva story. C. S. Forester can really write them."

"I tell *you*, John, me playing an old drunken river rat trying to sail a beat-up old tub down a river full of crocodiles would never go over. I'd look dumb."

"We can talk about it, can't we?"

"Maybe, but I can give you my answer already."

"Just keep an open mind, that's all I ask."

Danger.

Could Lorre be in danger? Maybe he had been wrong to send him looking for Johnny's car. And Romanoff? Was he in danger too? Bogart rolled the ruby ring around on his finger. And Mayo . . . the black sedan might have followed him to the Garden of Allah . . . Was Mayo . . . ?

"Now, everybody," said Huston, "this is important. We can wrap this whole thing up in just a few more scenes, get it done quickly and efficiently." He paused, his long face solemn. "And of course with artistry."

The crew and actors laughed.

Thomas Gomez and Marc Lawrence were on their marks. Bogart watched as the camera came in for their insert close-ups. Art Luecker tapped Huston on the arm, who shrugged him away. Art tapped again. Huston turned, exasperation on his face.

Art held up his wrist watch. "I'm sorry, John. Orders. Two minutes of silence."

Luecker blew the whistle hanging around his neck and all activity on the sound stage ceased. Huston stood like a man battling unseen forces. Finally he threw up his hands in despair and stalked to the sidelines, where he stared at the blank walls.

Bogart thought it odd that the entire studio complex would dedicate two minutes of silence to honor Leo Forbstein, a man whose entire life had been devoted passionately to music, to sound. *Two minutes of silence?*

At the end of the tribute, Art Luecker blew the silver whistle again and normal activities resumed.

The noon whistle blew.

The clamoring of carpenters, grips and electricians ceased once again. Huston stood in a disbelieving posture, hands clenched at his sides.

Bogart picked up the telephone. "Angel, try that number for me again."

"*The Garden of Allah, Mr. Bogart? Right away.*"

The phone buzzed and buzzed repeatedly, then there was the sound of the receiver being lifted. Clumsily, thought Bogart.

"Mayo . . . ?"

There was no reply, only the sound of a crash, of muffled thuds.

"Mayo?"

He left the phone dangling, whipped up his coat and threw it on. Huston looked at him, opened his mouth to speak but Bogart was already running.

In minutes he was at the studio parking lot, gunning the engine and speeding the car through the gate.

The cluster of stop signals at every corner conspired against him all the way to Sunset Boulevard. Each intersection seemed to drag at the wheels like chewing gum as Bogart was forced to wait precious minutes. He maneuvered through traffic, weaving in and out, edging out caution lights and sliding perilously through arterial stop signs.

Near Havenhurst he transgressed the traffic lanes in front of a stampede of oncoming autos. Honks and beeps cursed him as he made the left turn. He parked and ran to the gate. He pounded along the paths, sloshing through rain puddles.

The skies had cleared, but sparkly drops still fell from the corners of the red-tiled roofs. A brisk wind wobbled the glass-sided lanterns in the loquat trees.

The villa was ominously dark as Bogart came to a skidding halt at the door. He pounded on it, waited hesitantly, then stepped back. No answer. Damnit. He kicked out at the lock. The door groaned but resisted. Bogart kicked again. In the villas surrounding the pool curtains were pulled back. He kicked again. The door lock splintered. With one final kick, slamming the door hard against the wall, Bogart rushed inside in a crouch.

The interior was dark and cool.

"Mayo!" he called.

There was a blur, a flash of light. Bogart ducked. Shards of glass exploded beside his head and he fell heavily across a footstool.

There was a musical, desperate laugh.

Bogart stared incredulously. Mayo Methot was crouched on the floor, her hair in disarray, stains spotting the front of her pink blouse. He could see a rip in the seam of Mayo's slacks. The stench of alcohol filled the corners of the room. She laughed giddily.

"I see you, Bogie, I see you. Comin' through the door like the vice-squad after Robert Mitchum." She tried to get up but fell on her side.

Bogart got to his feet, his coat ripped along the underarm. "Goddamn it, Mayo!" He tried to help her to her feet, but she jabbed viciously at his midsection and swung at him with her high-heeled shoe.

The impact on Bogart's shin sent stabbing pains up his leg. He grabbed at her waist; she tried to duck under his arms. Her hand struck at the side of his face.

Bogart cursed again.

She had twisted a heavy leather chair out of position and pushed it desperately at him across the waxed floor. Bogart leaped to one side, using the fireplace mantel for support.

"Screw you, Bogart," Mayo screamed shrilly. "I don't want your goddamn handouts!"

"You called me, remember?"

"Who cares," she yelled, throwing another ashtray at him. She ran into the kitchen, twisting away from his reaching arms.

Bogart ducked. A rain of hurtling china, pewter and glass splattered on the wall behind him. He dropped to all fours, taking cover behind chairs and tables.

A six-foot, bead-shaded floor lamp crashed down beside his legs. He twisted quickly and rose to his feet in a half-crouch. An end table lamp whipped through the air. He knocked it aside with a quick flash of his left hand.

"Mayo, you crazy bitch!"

Mayo stood in the kitchen doorway clutching a ten-inch butcher knife, wild-eyed and slack-mouthed.

Bogart stepped forward, his hand outstretched. "Give me that knife, Mayo. Come on, it's me, Bogie."

It had been the wrong thing to say.

She snarled and lunged crookedly with the knife. Bogart leaped back quickly, threw a hand across her face to confuse her and wrapped a hand over her wrist. He twisted hard and Mayo uttered a short, sharp cry. The knife clattered to the floor. She twisted away from him, her legs flailing.

Mayo hurled a half-empty whiskey bottle. It shattered only inches from Bogart's face. Small slivers of glass rained over his head and the cheap booze splashed onto his coat.

She tottered lopsidedly and began laughing.

Bogart drew his lips back. His instinct was almost automatic. In three steps he was in front of Mayo. His hand came up in a short arc, curled into a fist and connected solidly to Mayo's jaw.

She tumbled backward, sprawling into a chair. Bogart stood over her, his feet apart. He picked up the phone, jiggled the cradle and dialed Jerry Wald's office.

"Sister, this is Humphrey Bogart. I've got a message for Jerry Wald. Tell him his one o'clock appointment is cancelled."

Mayo groaned. Bogart stood over her, thumbs hooked into his belt. He watched, his anger in check, as she tried to focus. Tears welled up in her eyes and streamed down her cheeks. She tried to wipe them away with trembling hands.

Bogart took a handkerchief from his pocket, wiped his hands and ran it over his face. His hands trembled.

"Mayo, you lied to me. Worst of all, you lied to yourself. You said you came back to get into pictures again. You came back because you thought you could wind me around that pretty little pinkie of yours. And yesterday, when that didn't work you reverted to type, baby."

He stepped outside without a backward glance. He looked up at the trees and sky. Clouds gathered. It was going to rain again. He walked jaggedly through puddles, his head consumed with dull fury, like raked-over coals.

In a minute he was behind the wheel of the coupe and moving left on Fountain Avenue, left again on Crescent, then right onto Sunset. As he passed Schwab's drugstore he glanced into the rearview mirror.

A black pre-war Packard sedan was following him onto Sunset. Bogart watched it carefully as it maintained a discreet distance. A clammy feeling tickled the back of his neck. It *wasn't* the car that had run him off the road and that he had chased outside Dr. Quesne's office.

A second car.

At Highland, Bogart got into the left lane and turned, steadily increasing his speed.

The black Packard maintained the same steady distance.

TWENTY

Bogart drove to Glendale, a wooded community in the narrow southeastern corner of the San Fernando Valley, bordered on the east by Griffith Park. He sped through the residential area of bungalows and white stucco homes. Everywhere he looked he saw well-manicured lawns and palm trees lining the streets.

But there was no sign of the black Packard.

At the major intersection of San Fernando Road and Glendale Avenue, Bogart swung the Cadillac through an impressive pair of wrought-iron gates. He eased into Forest Lawn Memorial Park, a 306-acre cemetery designed by Dr. Hubert Eaton, whose "Happy Eternal Life" creed had spawned this parklike format. Its landscaping consisted of groves of trees, sweeping lawns, bubbling fountains, statuary which never depicted pain or suffering and several churches. In keeping with Dr. Eaton's wishes, there were no "misshapen" monuments or "jutting" tombstones.

After passing through the gates Bogart saw to his immediate left a lake aswarm with white ducks and swans and ringed with statuary. To the right: a quaint Tudor-style cottage with the sign Forest Lawn Life Insurance Company.

Bogart followed Cathedral Drive, lined with pine and oak trees, past a sculpture depicting the Pharaoh's daughter finding Moses in the bullrushes. Then he branched to his left onto another macadam road, passing the *Temple of Santa Sabina*, a sarcophagus of marble inlaid with gold mosaic. Everywhere he looked Bogart saw rolling knolls and dells of evergreen lawn. It was one garden and court after another as he maintained a steady climb.

Bogart bore right onto Valley Way Road and immediately saw a cluster of automobiles—assorted limousines, several Continentals and a Rolls-Royce he recognized as Tayne's—parked near *A Mother's Compassion*, a sculpture of maternity set beneath a grove of spruce trees.

The burial of Johnny Hawks was taking place on Sunrise Slope, two rows back from a marble statue of Apollo and Daphne. Junipers flanked the statue; pines swayed softly overhead. Bogart saw that the service was already in progress and cursed Mayo for fouling up his afternoon schedule.

Bogart parked on Memory Lane next to Tayne's Rolls. The chauffeur, Valentine Corliss, was leaning against the front fender, smoking a cigarette and seemingly absorbing the serenity of Forest Lawn. He gave the chauffeur a brisk wave, then hurried to join the crowd on the slope.

He was too late. The minister had already thrown in the first handful of dirt and the entourage was breaking up. Standing out from the others was the tall, lanky figure of Basil Rathbone; beside him, speaking in subdued tones, was writer-director William Castle. Bogart also recognized Glenn Ford, who had made several Columbia Westerns with Johnny. Other fellow performers who had come to pay their final respects were Ann Savage, Gerald Mohr, Noah Beery, Jr., and Evelyn Keyes. There were at least three beautiful starlets Johnny had once carried the torch for.

Cohn was out ahead of the others. He saw Bogart, snorted lightly under his breath and angled to join him. Together they walked briskly toward Cohn's limousine.

"I been thinking over that screenplay of Brennan's," rasped Cohn. "We shoulda found it somewhere by now. Someone musta tossed it into the garbage years ago, or it's been copped."

"Copped?" echoed Bogart. "Swell. Then maybe whoever *copped* the script also planted that crap in Brennan's personal files."

Cohn whirled and threw a piercing look at Bogart, thoughtlessly blowing cigar smoke into the actor's face. In retaliation, Bogart fumbled for a Chesterfield but came up only with an empty, crumpled pack. For a moment he refused to believe he had allowed that to happen, then recalled how disconcerting his afternoon had been—first finding Mayo drunk out of her mind, then discovering that he was being followed by a black Packard.

Had the Packard followed him into Forest Lawn? He whirled to scan the top of Sunrise Slope and saw a black sedan perched behind a statue, half-hidden from view. But then it moved off, out of sight, and he couldn't be sure if it was the same car or not.

"You ain't the only one researching this monkey business, Bogart," said Cohn.

"I heard your headhunters are out beating the brush, Harry."

"Yeah, that's cute, Bogart. Only they found out that your pal Brennan was a Marine Corps specialist in firearms and explosives at Pendleton. That sure gives him the know-how."

"I could have told you that, Harry. All you had to do was ask."

"Kiss my ass," growled Cohn, climbing into his limousine. Settled into the seat, he rolled down the window and told Bogart, "Stay in touch, goddamn it. You tell me what you find, I'll do the same."

Sam Katzman was the next man off Sunrise Slope and he leaned against Cohn's limousine, his eyes pleading for mercy. "Damn it, Harry, I'm gonna have to reshoot all of Johnny's footage for *Raiders.*"

Cohn shook his finger at Katzman. "Listen, Sam, you're gonna have to make do. I've already slashed studio personnel by one-third. In only six months, Sam, one-third. I gotta compensate for lousy box office."

"But all my pictures make money. I never miss," Katzman pleaded.

"Sure, sure. But what about all those other deadbeats who ruined it for me last year? *Down to Earth. Guilt of Janet Ames. Lady From Shanghai.* Your crap, those Blondie pictures and Autry are all that's saving me from total bankruptcy."

"The whole industry is hurting, Harry. For the first time in history, it's really hurting."

"You think I don't know that, Sam? I'll tell you how much Columbia is hurting. We don't have a single picture in the Oscar race." He paused, glancing at Bogart. "Not that it matters, maybe." Cohn's limousine lurched forward, swinging in a wide U and returning up Valley Way Road.

Bogart turned to find Geoffrey Carroll standing before him, a towering monument to black except for a red carnation thrust through the breast of his turtleneck sweater. Carroll still affected the slightly tippytoe walk as he stepped up to Bogart.

"I wasn't aware you knew Johnny."

"We met on the set of *Buccaneer's Gold.* Johnny had an insatiable desire to know everything about film. . . . Still looking for Dalt?"

"I tracked his doctor. You had Quesne pegged."

"In Hollywood, everyone is typecast."

"I tracked Dalt to Saints and Sinners in Bel-Air."

"Before Martha Pearce shot herself?"

"That same night."

"Dalt was already gone?"

"Martha had substituted an actor in his place. I almost fell for it."

Carroll shrugged in dismay. "Don't ask me to understand it. I'm afraid even *The Thin Man* was more than I could follow."

Carroll walked to the driver's side of his white 1941 Lincoln Continental. Bogart admired the long hood and the low-slung interior, then said, "It keeps coming back to *Embarkation Point*. Geoffrey, tell me one thing. You said Clive Donahue originally was going to shoot the picture on a limited budget?"

"That's right. It was going to be a modest picture when he first hired me. Then suddenly the production escalated."

"And that's when he hired Power and Crawford . . . Any idea who his new backer was?"

"Rumors had it to be Harry Cohn, since the picture was finally released through Columbia. But how much stock can you put in Hollywood rumors?"

"Do you suppose Harry might have been trying to cut himself in on the action for the sole purpose of changing Dalt's script?"

"You mean control the purse strings first, then control the script rewrites?"

"Exactly. And effect a rewrite that would completely deprive Dalt of screenplay credit."

"If Harry did that, he's a bigger bastard than I ever in my wildest dreams imagined. You might have something though, Bogie. Donahue acted strangely after he hired Power and Crawford—as though he didn't have the same control anymore."

"Like a puppet on a string," mused Bogart.

"Cohn would have had to really hate Dalt to do that."

"Or want Dalt in a special frame of mind."

"What are you getting at?"

"It could be Dalt is being manipulated. But there I go again, Geoffrey, speculating. Refresh my memory. Did you clean Lloyd's place out?"

"Yes. It was painful. But I managed it."

"Did you find many manuscripts, screenplays?"

"Did I! There were several boxes."

"Is it possible some of Dalt's writing was mixed in with Lloyd's?"

"It's a good possibility. Lloyd willed all his literary materials to Raymond Chandler. He always did consider Chandler one of his mentors. Even though he never wrote a private-eye novel in his life. But he loved to read them, Bogie. It was one way he had of clearing his mind. Lloyd felt Chandler had elevated the private-detective novel to new literary levels."

"Where is Chandler these days? Still in La Jolla?"

"As I recall. I had the boxes shipped. Yes, I'm sure it was La Jolla."

"Thanks, Geoffrey. You may know more about *The Thin Man* than you realize."

Bogart hurried toward Tayne's limousine, his need for a cigarette becoming an obsession. Tayne was still lingering on the hillside with his stenographer, who was obediently taking down every word. Corliss waited patiently, staring at the silhouetted steeple of the *Wee Kirk o' the Heather,* a re-creation of an ancient church near Glencairn.

"I need a coffin nail, real fast," he told Corliss. The

chauffeur eyed him curiously while reaching for his gold-plated case with the initials *V.C.* Bogart accepted one of the Lucky Strikes but was sorry after the first puff. Indiscreetly, he crushed the butt under his foot. And coughed.

"Perhaps you should see a doctor," suggested Corliss.

"Every time I do, he says I should switch to Kools."

Bogart turned at the sound of Tayne's voice. The producer was finally coming off the slope, followed by his madly scribbling steno girl.

". . . I think it imperative that the House Un-American Activities Committee be given full congressional powers to further its investigative procedures. Furthermore, it is my intention as a producer, specifically of the forthcoming motion picture *The Red Seduction* . . ." Tayne stopped at the sight of Bogart, then angled directly toward his Rolls, his face betraying no emotion. Neither man offered his hand.

"Still flushing out Hollywood Commies?" asked Bogart cheerfully.

Tayne smiled, although Bogart assumed he was boiling inside. Tayne's voice was soft raindrops falling on lily pads. "Flushing out Communists?" he repeated slowly, deliberately. Tayne straightened the lapels of his austere navy-blue suit. "I doubt that, Bogie. That would seem to be a waste of time, since most actors have only the barest and most rudimentary political sense." Bogart knew he had been included among "most actors."

Tayne went on, the steno girl jotting down every word. "Hollywood stars spend too much energy on their careers to worry about politics. As for writers, it's ludicrous even to speculate. They all write for studio bosses, who keep them under rigid control. Don't forget, the studio bosses wield the power in this town. They censor what goes into a picture."

A solemn shade of gray fell over Tayne's features as he offered Bogart a cigarette. Still not replying, Bogart accepted it and leaned forward for a light.

Tayne nervously cleared his throat. "I've never had the opportunity to say this before, but I'm truly sorry about 1940—I'm afraid I was caught up in the fervor of the times . . ."

Fervor of the times . . . even then the crusaders and headhunters had been out in force, beating the movie brush for scapegoats. Anyone who imagined witch-hunts were new to Hollywood in 1947 had neglected history.

It had actually started in May 1938, when Texas Democrat Representative Martin Dies had established the House Un-American Activities Committee. Their first target had been Hollywood. If the film community was guilty of sex and drug scandals, surely it could be found guilty of political scandal, too.

The committee's initial attack had been leveled at Lionel Stander, Gale Sondergaard, playwright Clifford Odets and director Herbert Biberman. The list continued to grow: Fredric March, Francis Lederer, James Cagney, Franchot Tone . . .

. . . and Humphrey Bogart.

Tayne had served on the committee as its sole Hollywood representative, and during the hearings he had remained clearly unsympathetic toward the accused.

Especially Bogart.

Bogart drew on his cigarette, angling toward the steno girl and catching her eye. "I made a statement back then; I'll repeat it now, just for the record." The girl continued to take down every word dutifully.

"'The charges were without foundation. They're absurd and ridiculous.'"

Tayne shifted his weight casually, but Bogart detected a faint nervousness in his eyes. "I remember your statement most vividly. At the time the committee was forced to admit it had failed to uncover enough significant evidence of subversive activities among those accused."

"Enough, my ass. Not a single shred."

The steno girl blushed but was faithful to her shorthand.

"I want you to know one thing," said Tayne. "I joined that committee because I sincerely felt I was protecting the motion picture business."

"Yeah? Are you sure about that?" Bogart glared at Tayne through narrow eyes as tendrils of smoke drifted in front of his face. "Are you sure it had nothing to do with me turning down the Big Jim Blair series?"

"I'd have been a fool to allow my personal feelings to interfere with a committee investigation. Why can't we let bygones be bygones?"

For a brief second Bogart felt as though Tayne genuinely meant it.

"Surely we can overlook the mistakes of our youth," Tayne said. "You know, Bogie, I'd still like to discuss a film project with you. It has nothing to do with communism. Strictly an adventure—"

"Tayne, in my book there are some things a man can never forgive. There's no margin for lack of judgment when someone's career is at stake. You lacked the basic decency to understand that in 1940; I'm convinced you still lack it. You'd be the last man in this town I'd want to work for." For emphasis, Bogart crushed the cigarette underfoot.

Corliss, holding the door open for Tayne and the steno girl, shot a glance at Bogart that was as blank as his employer's. Mirror to the master, reflected Bogart, as the Rolls spit gravel at him and shot away.

Johnny Hawks's grave site was deserted except for a lone figure standing in the shadow of the Apollo-Daphne statue. As Bogart approached, he saw that it was Norma Jean Baker. She was dressed in an all-black moire suit with a cutaway jacket adorned with scalloped lacing and silver buttons. Most of her blond hair was beneath a black bandana tightly knotted at her throat. She dabbed at her eyes with an embroidered handkerchief.

Bogart paused at the side of the grave, staring down at the coffin. He decided it was one of the medium-priced Forest Lawn selections—a suitable match for the medium-priced burial ground.

Bogart felt there was a part of him that would never be fulfilled now that Johnny was gone. Whatever might have happened between them—films, weekend cruises, races—were things irretrievably lost. The anger surged up in him and he felt new determination to find Dalt.

Bogart heart a light footfall behind him. For just a moment he had forgotten he wasn't alone on Sunrise Slope.

Norma Jean paused at his side to look down into the open grave. "When I was a kid . . . I never liked going to funerals. Now . . ."

"It's tough when you lose someone close. Parents . . . lovers . . ."

"After someone's gone, you realize maybe you didn't know them at all. But it still hurts."

"Yeah, it hurts."

Grief had done nothing to spoil Norma Jean's

beauty. Once again Bogart found himself enraptured by it. Surely she was the ultimate answer to any man's dreams. Yet there was something about Norma Jean that transcended mere physical beauty.

Behind that sparkling, uncomplicated personality was the glimmering promise that she could deliver if called upon—and Bogart wasn't just thinking of sex. She looked as though she had the intelligence to buck the system, to walk around casting couches. It was the key which might one day unlock the door to where she wanted to go. Maybe all the way to the top.

At this moment she was emotionally at the bottom. Her tears started again and he felt her body faltering against his. He steadied her by gently grasping her arm and shoulder.

"How long had you known Johnny?"

"Only six months . . . yet it seems like a lifetime."

"At Columbia?"

"Fox. I was under contract; Johnny was on loan from Columbia."

"Was that the comedy picture about the mules?"

Norma Jean nodded. "*Scudda Hoo! Scudda Hay!* I had one line. I said 'Hello, Peggy' to June Haver, but they cut the scene."

"Welcome to Hollywood. They did the same thing to me on my first picture."

"No kidding? . . . Johnny was a little upset when he heard about it. But he *was* wonderful; he used to take me to all the best places. Then he'd hang around the Actor's Lab. I tried to take it seriously, Stanislavsky and all, and Johnny'd kid the daylights out of me. He was a great kidder."

"You need a sense of humor, Norma Jean."

"Johnny used to say you were a legend, Mr. Bogart."

"I'm no legend, Norma Jean."

"Johnny used to say if you were a star you couldn't be normal. You had to be something special. Godlike. I'd like to be a star someday," said Norma Jean. "That probably sounds silly to you."

"Not at all. It's the very thing you have to keep telling yourself if you do want to make it. And maybe you will make it."

"Johnny used to say that too but I always thought he was kidding."

"Depends on how bad you really want it." Bogart tightened his grip when he felt her swaying slightly. "Hey, you okay?"

"Yeah, I'll . . . be okay. Thanks, Mr. Bogart."

"Can I give you a lift somewhere?"

"No, I'd rather stay for a while. It's quiet here."

Bogart stared down into the open grave again. "I want you to know one thing. There are a lot of unanswered questions about what happened to Johnny. And I intend to get those answers."

"Are you . . . there isn't any danger, is there . . . Bogie?"

"Danger? I live with danger in every one of my pictures."

For the first time that afternoon, Bogart saw Norma Jean smile. Bogart kissed her lightly on the cheek and hurried to his Cadillac. He could feel her eyes following him.

As he drove up Valley Way Road, he saw a black Packard poised atop Sunrise Hill. There was no mistaking that it was the same automobile.

Before starting down Cathedral Drive to the main gate, the last thing he saw was the solitary figure of Norma Jean Baker on the slope of Sunrise Hill, the handkerchief pressed against her face.

TWENTY-ONE

The bomb-gutted French village lay in ruin somewhere between Freshman Drive and Stocker Street,
on Back Lot number 2 of Metro-Goldwyn-Mayer in
Culver City. The village church was only an empty
shell, its surviving steeple rising above the debris.
Fifty feet beyond the last crumbling chateau wall
stood the now-decaying facade of Tara Plantation as
it was used in *Gone With the Wind*. Behind the pillars
where Vivien Leigh and Olivia de Havilland had once
stood while the South died around them, a figure
stirred slightly, watching the activity in the village.

A whistle blew. A hundred extras dressed in olive
drab charged through the village streets. Mounds of
earth erupted around the attackers, showering them
with harmless Fuller's earth, sand and peat moss;
black smoke billowed skyward. Several soldiers flung
away their rifles and collapsed.

Bayonets gleamed in the afternoon sun but they
were not real bayonets. Rifles and submachine guns
and pistols and carbines issued only the hollow bang
of blank cartridges and puffs of dark, photogenic
smoke.

Helmets rolled across the central plaza as the men
charged. Out of the gutted ruins of storefronts, the two
forces came together, lashing out with phony bayonets.

Some soldiers simulated death so realistically that
William O. Wellman, the white-haired, gangling director, forgot to yell CUT. But finally the cameras stopped
and the men in the square were no longer death-

dealing soldiers but extras eager to return to their pinochle.

"Goddamn, that was good," enthused Wellman,
slapping John Hodiak on the back. Hodiak was in the
uniform of a colonel and had the weary look of an
officer who must send his men on a suicide mission.

Wellman turned his attention to the powder men
stringing Cordtex detonating wires to mortar pots buried in the ground. The pots were then packed with
Fuller's earth and two ounces of gunpowder and
smoothed over with sand and peat moss. Some of the
holes were loaded with fougasse charges made with
fifty-gallon petrol drums which were vertically positioned so the blast would rise straight up to create a
fireball effect. On cue, these would be detonated
from a central controlboard.

Dalt Brennan waited until Wellman and Hodiak
had wandered back to the plaza, then he came out
from behind the Tara pillars and casually worked his
way toward the special-effects trucks. The powder
men carried their detonating fuses and their flash
powder and their blasting caps as they hurried back
to the location to connect all the wires.

Brennan stood on the sidelines, blending in with the
rest of the crew. He heard Wellman shout an order
and watched as everyone scrambled into position.
This would be a continuation of the action, explained
the director, but with tighter camera angles.

The cameras were soon whirring, the extras engaged each other in hand-to-hand combat and new explosions erupted in the square.

Brennan, pulling his duckbill cap tighter onto his
head, sauntered to the nearest dirty-gray Ford truck
and climbed into the cab. The sound of the grinding

engine was lost amid mortar bursts and the cries of "dying" men.

The truck turned onto Rue de Marmont, speeding past production assistants, the catering van and an MGM security patrol car. Brennan heard startled voices above the din of battle but he only slammed harder on the accelerator. Rue de Marmont suddenly came to a dead end and Brennan swerved the Ford onto an unpaved road lined with old German tanks and jeeps mounted on blocks.

The dirt road led straight toward an Olympic-sized swimming pool where Esther Williams and her aqua-cade queens were somersaulting through water lay-ered with red, green, blue and purple smoke. The Ford was heading straight for the pool; already pro-duction assistants were waving him away and the sound mixer was cursing.

Brennan saw an opening in a wire-mesh fence and he veered off. The dirty-gray Ford bounced over un-paved terrain, past sheds stuffed with breakaway walls. Brennan glanced back and saw that the security patrol car—a red-white-and-blue Nash sedan with the MGM logo on its doors—was also swinging past the pool and through the break in the fence, leaving a tell-tale trail of dust.

Brennan drove straight into the front yard of a farmhouse, searching desperately for an escape. He saw it to his left—an opening between two barns. Dangerously narrow, but an opening. Chickens scur-ried to either side as he roared past a camera team and aimed for the opening.

The truck squeezed through with only inches to spare—but he was free again. He looked back to see the security car brush against one of the buildings.

Sparks flew; the impact was too great for the false-fronted barn and it collapsed on its side. Dust was everywhere. Yet the security car kept coming.

The rush of air was cold against Brennan's face and his hands felt soldered to the wheel. The dirt road was pocked with potholes and repeatedly he flew upward off the seat, banging his head against the roof of the cab. In the rear of the truck, the crates of special-effects explosives shifted from side to side and banged against the tailgate. Perspiration broke out on his forehead; huge circles of sweat clung to the khaki under his armpits. He heard the siren of the security car wail mournfully.

Brennan stepped on the gas harder, angling the truck always left in his attempt to reach the northern edge of Back Lot number 2 and escape via Sopho-more Drive. He was racing along a midwestern com-munity street which he recognized as the main set of the Andy Hardy series. Again he turned left at the first intersection, tires squealing, onto a seventeenth-century Parisian street.

Ahead of him, in the middle of the boulevard, stood part of a camera crew and several men in bright Mus-keteer costumes, dueling with ill-dressed ruffians. The grip, realizing the truck had no intention of stopping, began pushing the dolly into an alleyway. Other men were waving and shouting angrily, their faces falling from anger to dismay as the truck kept coming.

Brennan recognized Gene Kelly and Van Heflin and began beeping his horn as a warning. The two actors, their swords still raised, watched the truck bear down. Only at the last moment did they dive aside.

Brennan took a hard right and sped onto a Western

street, sighing with relief when he saw there was nothing in production there.

The siren was wailing louder now, and he assumed that the security car was gaining. He glanced again into the rearview mirror but could see nothing.

Brennan realized the patrol car was taking a different route—was coming at him from another angle—might overtake him if he didn't reach the street first.

The pickup thundered across a flat expanse of ground littered with cannons and other medieval props. Ahead, to his right, Brennan saw the mock-up of a castle exterior, which was paralleled by a deep moat. To his left Brennan could now see the security police speeding toward him on an access road that led directly to the castle's raised drawbridge. If they were to pull up in front of him, his escape onto Sophomore would be cut off.

Brennan accelerated, hearing the crates shifting and banging in the back. His head throbbed from the roar of the engine.

The red-white-and-blue security car sped directly toward the drawbridge, coming up rapidly from the left. Brennan pushed the Ford to its limit and sped past the castle entrance. A full second later the security car arrived. The guard hit his brakes . . . too late. The Nash leaped from the dirt road, flew across the moat and smashed against the castle wall. It was wood and plaster and dissolved before the bumper of the airborne Nash. The vehicle passed through to the other side, where it came down with a jolt and a rushing of air as the tires went flat.

Now there was nothing to stop Brennan. He crashed through the wire-mesh fence that completely surrounded Back Lot number 2 and barreled away from Culver City, pointing the truck northward toward central Los Angeles.

He remained hunched over the wheel, driving like a man possessed.

TWENTY-TWO

It was noisy at Romanoff's, but the sounds were a
minimal annoyance to Bogart, who by six-thirty had
put away five stiff shots of Scotch. Finding Mayo in
her drunken condition that afternoon still troubled
him.

Bogart unloaded some of his troubles on Romanoff,
who was distracted slightly by the volume of early
customers but still lent an attentive ear and a sympathetic shoulder. Myrna Loy, Walter Wanger and Jennifer Jones with David O. Selznick were diners, along
with Alfred Hitchcock and George Burns and Gracie
Allen. Bogart heard a familiar voice in the booth next
to his and glanced over to see Gregory Peck. Peck politely returned the look and complimented Romanoff
on the banana shortcake.

Romanoff smiled. "It is not a chef who makes a
good restaurant, but the personality of its owner."

Jamieson, somewhat indifferently, brought a check
for the prince's close scrutiny. Romanoff held the thin
paper up against the light of the chandelier. "Mori-
bund," he proclaimed, and ordered "the charlatan" to
be thrown from the restaurant into the center of
North Rodeo Drive.

"How can you spot a phony like that?" asked Bogart.

"It takes one to know one," answered Romanoff
slyly.

A hulking brute of a man, at least six foot six, suddenly towered above the Bogart booth in Dress Cir-

cle. His biceps bulged threateningly and he directed a defiant stare at Bogart. Bogart gritted his teeth.

The 250-pound hulk wasted no time. "You don't look so tough to me, Bogart. I bet you're a pansy. A sissified mama's boy."

"Sir," protested Romanoff, starting to rise, "I must insist that—"

"Mama's boy can handle this." Bogart quieted him with a gentle wave of his hand. Nonchalantly he finished his sixth glass of Scotch and rose to his maximum height of five feet seven inches. It wasn't high enough.

"I'll take you on any day of the week," Bogart informed the hulk, his voice lisping its menace. "But not in here. I have too much respect for Prince Romanoff's furniture and decor. We'll settle this matter in the parking lot."

The hulk accepted and started for the main entrance, assuming that Bogart was following.

Bogart didn't follow. Instead, he signaled for Jamieson, who scuttled across the room. Bogart said, "A Texan just went out the front door and the chances are very good that he'll attempt to reenter. If he does, have him thrown out."

Romanoff gestured at the maitre d'. "It'll be my personal pleasure if you throw him out yourself, Jamieson."

"I shall consider it *my* personal pleasure, m'sieur."

Lorre arrived two Scotches later, out of breath, wearing the same wrinkled suit and a bow tie patterned with silver stars on black velvet. Bogart wanted to know why he had failed to show up for Johnny's funeral.

"You should not so freely insult someone who has gone to the troubles I have gone to, dear Bogie . . .

your impertinence is exceeded only by your rudeness. I need bourbon, quickly, good prince. As strong and as qualitative as you stock."

When Lorre had finally quieted down, he told Bogart about the police red tape in which he had become hopelessly ensnared. "In order to examine Johnny's impounded car, dear Bogie, I was forced to wander like a street waif from department to department. And still some of our most esteemed law enforcers had the unbridled audacity to request my autograph. To ask for that and then to keep me waiting like some proletariat off the street . . . I tell you, it was almost more than I could bear."

"You're gonna make me cry, Doc."

"Keep your bawling muffled so you can hear what else I have to tell you. Prince, keep your hankie handy. Finally, after I mentioned Inspector Fitzgerald's name enough times, they cleared me through."

"Get to the part about the car," insisted Bogart.

"You must learn patience, dear Bogie. I'm trying to tell you about the car. Instead you interrupt and ask me to tell you about the car."

"I won't interrupt again, I promise."

"At first I thought I had it."

"It? What's it?"

"The screenplay—what else would I be talking about?"

"And did you?"

"Did I what?"

"Have the screenplay, damn it."

"Yes I did and no I did not."

Bogart went limp with frustration.

"Oh," smiled Lorre, "I located a screenplay all right. On the backseat of Johnny's car. Adorned with the cover of *Hollywood Armageddon*."

"Then you *do* have it."

"Not exactly. You see, between the covers I found *Raiders of the Badlands*."

"A peculiar development," interjected Romanoff, looking more puzzled than Bogart.

"Peculiar only if you didn't know Johnny Hawks," replied Bogart, rubbing his chin. "I think I have a pretty good idea where we're going to find *Hollywood Armageddon*."

Bogart was interrupted by a hearty laugh and a solid slap on the back. He turned to see the familiar face of Van Heflin with a newly grown goatee.

"Wentzel," cried Bogart. Wentzel was a private nickname which Heflin often used whenever he wanted to avoid notoriety.

"Welcome aboard, Admiral," said Helfin. They both loved the sea and had spent many weekends together aboard the *Santana*. Bogart noticed several bruises and a deep scratch across Heflin's left cheek.

"What the hell happened to you? Did you fall overboard?"

"Hell no, I almost got run down by a madman today on the back lot at Metro."

"It must've been Louie Mayer driving."

"If it had been Louie, he would have finished the job. No, this was a guy who was twice as crazy. Almost ran down Gene Kelly and me right in the middle of a dueling scene."

"Does the cinema really need another version of *The Three Musketeers*?" asked Romanoff. "My great-great-grand-uncle, Alexandre Dumas, would be spinning in his mausoleum."

"Turns out," resumed Heflin, "that it was some guy stealing a truck full of special-effects explosives. They chased the bastard across the lot but he busted through a fence and got away. Anyway, I'm celebrating the fact that I'm still alive." He nodded at Bogart's row of empty glasses. "Looks like you're already celebrating."

"Please," grimaced Lorre, "do not give him the opportunity to comment that the rest of the world is still three drinks behind. I cannot bear to hear it again."

As Heflin hurried away to his own table, Jamieson glided to Bogart's side and whispered confidentially, "*Pardonnez-moi*, Monsieur Bogart, but there is a beautiful woman here to see you."

"Isn't there always, Frenchie? Give her a number and have her wait in line with the others."

"This woman is special, *bon ami*. She says she is an old friend. She wishes to speak to you *en particulier*. A private conversation. I said that I would speak to you. She awaits . . ." Jamieson's hand gestured toward the entrance as if it were a magic wand.

But the appearance of Kitty Steele was no illusion.

As Bogart moved toward the doorway, he saw no hint of a smile. There was only worry tearing at Kitty's face; the wonderful contours of her supple body remained hidden beneath a long black overcoat.

Without a word he took her hand. It was clammy—something he had never felt in Kitty before. He kissed her gently on the lips; they too were cold and unresponsive. He pulled back to look into her eyes; what he saw was what he had felt. Worry and fear. Not the same Kitty he had seen two days earlier on the set of *Belle of the Wilderness*.

"Have you found Dalt?" she asked expectantly.

"You didn't want me to tell you about that, remember, beautiful?" He tried to sound lighthearted but it had no visible effect. "No, Kitty, I haven't found Dalt."

Disappointment remained locked on Kitty's face. He continued to grip her hand, sensing she needed some token physical support. "But not because I haven't tried. I wish you had told me Dalt suffered another breakdown."

"I didn't know myself until yesterday. There were a lot of things I didn't know until yesterday."

"Why're you here, Kitty?"

"*Hollywood Armageddon*. Paul said you'd be contacted."

"Paul? . . . Fabrini?"

She nodded. "Buy me a drink, Bogie?"

"I need a drink. Let's go to the bar. It's the only place in the joint I won't allow Romanoff to bug."

He still sensed her reluctance when they reached the bar. He ordered two Drambuies. She showed no interest in the liqueur, only continued to look carefully into Bogart's eyes.

"Now I know," he said, "why you came to Paul's defense when I called him a Hollywood rat. Being in love with someone isn't an easy thing to hide, Kitty."

"I want you to know, Bogie, that I never cheated on Dalt."

"You don't have to explain anything, Kitty."

"Sure, Paul and I became good friends during the filming of *Embarkation Point*, but that was as far as it went. Then."

"What you've done is your own business."

"It wasn't until I had separated from Dalt that . . . well, I had to turn to someone, Bogie."

"They call it the fast rebound, Kitty. Part of human nature." He sipped his Drambuie, but tasted nothing.

"We were good for each other, Paul and I. It worked. Paul was what I needed after seven years of internal hell. For the first time I was happy . . . until yesterday."

"How have things changed, Kitty?"

"From the moment Paul read about Martha Pearce's death, he was a different man. He wouldn't talk to me. Then when I told him you'd been asking questions about Dalt, he left the house in a hurry. When he came back last night, he was evasive, frightened."

"And he told you nothing?"

"He kept saying it was better I didn't know."

"Is he worried something might happen to you? Does he think Dalt—"

She shook her head. "Martha Pearce's death—it seems to be the key to something. Whatever started between Dalt and Paul on the *Embarkation Point* set is still happening."

"He said that?"

Her face clouded over with vagueness. "I could only get bits and pieces, Bogie. Somehow it's all connected to the death of Johnny Hawks."

"That much I already know."

"It's also tied in with Lloyd Brennan's death."

"Lloyd? Sweet Jesus, Kitty. You're moving too fast for me."

"I swear, Bogie, I don't know any more than that."

Bogart was unaware that his clenched fist had slammed on the bar top; his Drambuie sloshed but didn't spill. For just a moment the other drinkers paused to watch him curiously.

"Damn it, Kitty. I need some straight answers. Just tell me where he is. I'll drag it out of Paul, goddamn it."

"You won't have to. Paul wants to tell you everything."

"Why me?"

"He trusts you, Bogie."

"Why should Paul trust me?"

"Because I trust you."

"All right . . . When?"

"Tonight. One o'clock sharp at this address. Try not to be late."

Bogart glanced at the slip of paper Kitty handed him. He shoved it into his pocket and took her hand in his again.

Their eyes met and Kitty forced a smile onto her face. "I think that deep down I still love Dalt. I think I was the first woman who ever did. I had Dalt writing again and we were in love . . . So crazy in love you wouldn't believe it."

"Hey, you're reminiscing with a man who's been married four times. You think I don't know what you're talking about? I wrote the book on love, beautiful."

"Bogie . . ." She squeezed his hand in response, then pulled free, whirled and rushed from the dining room. Kitty hadn't even touched her Drambuie. He returned to his booth, where Lorre and Romanoff waited curiously.

"Kitty's still a marvelous-looking woman," said Lorre.

"I say, old man, were you enlightened?" asked Romanoff.

"Kitty's given me a lead to Fabrini."

"But still no answers . . . ?" asked Lorre.

"It always comes back to that, doesn't it, Doc. No direct answers. No packages with pretty little bows."

"Not quite the way it happens in films, old man," said Romanoff.

"*Never* believe what you see in the movies, Prince.

Right now me and the Doc have some checking to do."

"Another one of your wild goose chases, dear Bogie?"

"Relax, Doc. You can claim the carcass when I'm finished."

"Such generosity."

"Do be careful," warned Romanoff.

"Of what?" asked Bogart.

"Of the Texan sprawled in front of my door. I wouldn't want you to step on him. It might give my place a bad reputation."

The Cadillac coupe turned right at the coast highway. Bogart kept his mind in neutral, unaffected by the rows of white combers sweeping in from the darkening horizon of the Pacific. Off to the left, the Municipal Pier was a long-fingered silhouette jutting into the water. The sinking sun swept orange over the water.

On the inland side towered the cliffs of the Palisades, somber, eroded, brown, relieved only by an overhanging crown of purple dwarf lupine.

Bogart kept his eyes on the road and gave only an occasional glance to acknowledge Lorre's chattering. Dark clouds gusted by high winds lent a purple-red cast to the sky.

The miles unwound.

At Las Tunas Beach, a small community of artists, writers and musicians, Bogart watched two figures standing upright on long boards riding the waves. It seemed to him an odd, precarious sport, not attractive enough to gain much in popularity. He and Lorre watched the golden surfers balanced on the silvered waves, backlit by the setting sun.

A few miles beyond Los Flores they sped past Malibu Beach Colony, a sand spit serving as a residential area guarded by the Malibu Seashore Patrol. A heavy chain and a guard house barred the access road.

In Malibu proper they passed four-plexes in disrepair, a few stores, bait shops and one coffee shop. The last shreds of dark sunlight raked across the cream-colored buildings.

Lorre nudged Bogart's arm. "That's it. On the right."

Bogart parked in front of a four-plex apartment house. The address revealed that Johnny Hawks's main interest had not been deluxe living. The stucco exterior was flaking and needed a fresh coat of paint. Bogart noticed several broken windows. The building answered a developer's prayer: cheap to build and appealing to actors and actresses, would-be starlets, and seekers of sun, sand and surf.

They walked to the entranceway. Bogart thumbed the bell opposite the manager's number.

The glass-paned door snapped open.

"Yeah? Whaddya wan'?"

The manager was about forty; beefy. Matted chest hairs curled out of the top of a tank-style shirt. He wore cream-colored slacks and his unwashed feet were jammed into a pair of frayed Mexican huaraches. The man's mouth slowly came open in recognition as he shifted his eyes hurriedly from Bogart to Lorre, Lorre to Bogart, Bogart to Lorre . . .

"Geez," the manager said.

"Johnny Hawks was going to leave something for me in his room," said Bogart.

"Geez, sure, Mr. Bogart, sure. Too bad about Johnny. He told me all 'bout youse guys sailin' together. Sure, come on in. Geez."

He led the way to the second floor and unlocked the door. "This is Johnny's. Not much, but he liked it, geez he liked it."

Bogart stood in the middle of the room as Lorre raised the window shades. The room went from gloomy purple to dark gray.

The manager lingered in the doorway, the door keys jingling in his hand. Bogart clicked on the overhead lights and took a fast inventory: living room, kitchenette, bedroom.

The walls were pale green and covered with movie posters of Johnny's first Hollywood films: *Raid on Manila, Rommel Must Die, Mojave Justice*. There were photos personally autographed by Western stars Randolph Scott, Joel McCrea and Glenn Ford. Yakima Canutt and Tom Tyler had scrawled their names on production stills that had begun to curl at the edges. The rooms were littered with director's chairs with Johnny's name stenciled on the canvas backs. Beyond sliding glass doors was a narrow deck overlooking the ocean.

Lorre looked behind the dresser and checked the kitchenette and the cabinets. Bogart looked behind a cheap reproduction of a Leeteg painting and under the mattress. On the wall next to the bed were snapshots of Johnny: in swimming trunks, at the beach, aboard small powerboats and winding rope on the deck of the *Santana*. In one of them, Bogart recognized himself at the wheel in the background.

In the bathroom hamper he found a discarded bra, a woman's one-piece bathing suit and hosiery. In the medicine cabinet the only things out of place were vials of inexpensive but nice perfume.

Then they searched the closet.

It contained few clothes: two pairs of slacks, four dress shirts, one sport jacket. Several ties.

They found the box of manuscripts on the floor.

"Now we're getting somewhere," said Bogart.

They spent several minutes rummaging through all the screenplays. In each, Johnny's dialogue had been underlined in red. They also found a copy of *The Purloined Letter*, a screenplay developed by Johnny and scripted by William Castle.

But nowhere did they find a copy of *Hollywood Armageddon*.

"Nothing, dear Bogie," said Lorre.

Something nagged at the back of Bogart's brain.

"The cops didn't find nuttin' either," said the burly manager.

"We've come up with another goose egg, Doc." Bogart stabbed out his cigarette in a cheap blue ceramic ashtray. His glance traveled over a small bookshelf. There were books on sailing and navigation, and anthologies by Edgar Allan Poe, Ambrose Bierce, Algernon Blackwood and Arthur Machen. On top of the bookcase was a framed photograph of Basil Rathbone, autographed: "To Johnny Hawks: Nevermore. Sherlock Holmes."

They headed back along the coast highway. The headlights cut ovals out of the dark, shadowy landscape. Bogart drove in silence, the oncoming traffic alternately slicing bright, then dark. Finally he said, "You know what struck me back there?"

"The apartment hardly seemed lived in, dear Bogie. Only the bare essentials."

"You saw what was in the closet? Practically nothing. Johnny liked to dress well. Where are his clothes?

I know he had at least a dozen suits, including two tuxedos."

"Your powers of observation are improving, dear Bogie. What do you make of that?"

Bogart drove in silence for a long time. Then: "How about if I just drop you off? I'm going on down the coast to La Jolla."

Lorre yawned. "La Jolla? Why? It's a long drive, almost to San Diego."

"I've got to see Raymond Chandler before I see Fabrini."

Lorre nodded. "It's going to take you almost four hours. You don't think Chandler will know anything about Dalt?"

Bogart shrugged. "He might have some ideas. He's good with ideas."

"On paper, Bogie. But he has no professional background in detective work."

"But he has a hell of a mind."

"It can't be any more hellish than yours."

"Thanks for the compliment, Doc."

TWENTY-THREE

Dalt Brennan sat alone, slowly freezing to death.

He had bundled himself in a rain-stained overcoat, wrapped a muffler tightly around his neck and pulled a woolen cap with earflaps firmly onto his head.

Still the cold seeped in.

His fingers remained exposed to the numbing cold and he breathed warm air on them to comfort them, keep them flexible. The steamy moisture escaping his mouth eddied like bursts of smoke toward the workbench, dissipating among the glass tubes scattered there. The tubes trailed like corkscrews out of larger glass retorts.

Chugga . . . chugga . . . chugga . . .

The compressor air conditioner that was tucked into a storage closet worked overtime to send the temperature plummeting. Though frost had accumulated on the smeared windows of the insulated shed, Brennan could see beyond into the night—could see the hulking, deformed shapes that perpetually bobbed up and down. Hour after hour, day after day, the humping machines sucked oil out of the earth. Yet their monotonous sound never reached inside the thick-walled shed to shatter the solitude that Brennan needed.

Noxious fumes rose from a yellow, oily liquid in the bottom of a porcelain bowl. Brennan waved away the fumes, trying to concentrate.

He dipped a measuring cup into a coffee can: ten percent proportion of sawdust . . . one percent of calcium carbonate . . . twenty-nine percent sodium nitrate. Just right . . .

Into the granular compound he cautiously measured an amount of ethyl glycerol. He waited until the material was thoroughly coagulated. By the time he had added a colloidal compound that quickly formed a gelatinous mass, his fingers were completely numb.

Brennan glanced at an old alarm clock on the bench, waiting out the minutes. He stomped his feet again and beat his hands against his sides. Despite the numbness, he flipped the dog-eared pages of an old note pad, its cover embossed with the faded insignia of the U.S. Marine Corps.

Patiently, one eye still on the clock, he picked up a can of blasting powder and mixed it into the compound. The granules stuck under his fingernails as he slowly, carefully, kneaded it like bread dough.

He scooped some of the new compound into the oily liquid, and continued to add new materials from the stolen cans marked with the MGM emblems.

Dalt Brennan sat in a room, slowly freezing to death. Yet it all seemed worth it.

TWENTY-FOUR

La Jolla was a small retirement community north of San Diego which could boast of gingerbread window boxes but not of industry. The wide streets were kept spotless and the trees and shrubbery lining them well trimmed. La Jolla dozed in the daytime and hibernated at night.

The single-story, gray-painted house on the corner lot at 6005 Camino de la Costa stood on a slight slope and was bathed in moonlight as Bogart parked directly in front. The tedious drive from Los Angeles had tired him and he was not in an exuberant mood when he climbed out of his car. He paused on the walkway to admire the front courtyard, which contained a fish pond and rock garden. But the building itself seemed foreboding; a funereal air made him feel ill at ease. All the windows were covered with heavy, dark draperies and there was a feeling of murkiness about the house.

Bogart waited a two full minutes before his ring was answered. The man who stood at the threshold staring into Bogart's face with a certain defiance, as if he resented being disturbed, was almost sixty years of age. Strands of dark-brown hair, snowflaked with specks of milk white, hung down his furrowed forehead as if to caress the tortoiseshell reading glasses that enlarged his penetrating hazel eyes. He wore dark-gray slacks, a jet-black turtleneck pullover and decaying leather slippers. The man refused to speak. He just kept staring at Bogart.

Bogart pulled at an earlobe, a habitual gesture.

"Are you the star of the first magnitude in the constellation of modern mystery writers?" Bogart's hardened features were suddenly altered by a satiric grin.

Raymond Chandler stepped back and smiled, but there remained a chilliness about his manner. As Bogart crossed the threshold to find himself in a massive, darkened living room, Chandler said: "Still being the tough guy without a gun, I see."

"A gun's for a fall guy," said Bogart. "It only gets you *in* trouble—not out of it."

"You're starting to sound like Philip Marlowe again."

"Not *enough* like him. They make nothing but bad imitations these days."

"Now you know why I left Hollywood."

"So haul yourself back. Someone's gotta put decent dialogue back into our mouths."

"The town stinks."

"So do most movies. So what?"

"They won't get any better."

"Sometimes I think I should stock the *Santana* with a year's provisions and set sail for the edge of nowhere. But then they'd offer me another picture and a few hundred thou, and I'd go back."

"You're nuts."

"I'm an actor."

"Didn't I say you were nuts?"

"You're a writer—are you any different?"

"No; I'd come back from the edge of nowhere too."

They broke into laughter simultaneously, realizing they were still facing each other as strangers instead of friends. Bogart extended his hand and warmly accepted Chandler's. It was an enthusiastic grasp and Bogart, for the first time, saw a glimmer of friendliness and a dissipation of Chandler's glacial reserve. "How are you, Ray?"

Chandler shrugged.

The living room was darkly furnished with mahogany furniture, a grand piano in the corner (its ivory keys seemed to Bogart the only bright objects in sight) and a large RCA Victor console radio. A bay window offered what might have normally been a panoramic view of Point Loma but tonight, in moonlight, it reminded Bogart of the rolling, tombstoneless dales of Forest Lawn.

Chandler shoved his hands into his pockets. "I see your name all over the marquees. You're busy."

"I'm still conning them, if that's what you mean."

"You always had something the others didn't."

"Yeah, a three-hundred-and-fifty-thousand-dollar contract."

"Alan Ladd, he's hard on the outside, but underneath he's all jelly, a little boy playing a tough gangster. You, you're tough on the outside—*and* the inside." It was said not as a compliment but as a fact.

Chandler navigated an unlit corridor that was glassed on one side and looked out onto the landscaped grounds; the moonlight cast shadows that struck Bogart as misshapen; it was like a shrouded haven for unseen gargoyles and lurking demons.

At the end of the hallway, branching to the left, was Chandler's study. It was an intimate but masculine room lined with cabinets and bookcases. One window overlooked a garden. "I prefer it to a view of the sea," volunteered Chandler when he noticed Bogart studying the flower beds illuminated by night lights. Again there were gloomy, deformed shadows. "The sea," said Chandler, "reminds me of a lot of men who never came back."

Bogart recalled that during World War I Chandler had been the sole survivor of his Canadian infantry

unit. Lucky to be alive . . . but Chandler hadn't always looked at it that way. There had been numerous
times he had cursed his "good fortune."

On an oak desk near the window was a typewriter
loaded with paper, and next to it were the strewn
pages of a manuscript, many passages savagely
crossed out by black pen. Chandler had often said he
was not a writer but a rewriter. He labored many
months on each of his Marlowe novels.

Atop the scattered pages, purring contentedly, was
a black Persian cat. Chandler petted the cat and massaged her ears. "I like to have Taki around. She
doesn't give a damn about anyone." Certainly Taki
didn't give a damn about Bogart, for her head hit the
first page of Chapter Six as she resumed her slumber-
ing.

Because Chandler's body had fleshed out and his
eyes and cheeks were no longer puffy, Bogart decided
that the writer had stopped drinking. How long had it
been since they'd last met? Bogart's memories wandered to 1946; to the time of Howard Hawks's *The
Big Sleep*. Chandler, depressingly disenchanted with
the Hollywood system, had moved to La Jolla, where
he had ensconced himself in a self-imposed reclusive
existence. From that time on he seldom saw old
friends, only infrequently journeying to Los Angeles
on business, and had sunk deeper each year into melancholia brought on by his lack of faith in others.

"How's Cissy?" asked Bogart, his voice expressing
concern.

Chandler shrugged and looked a little lost. "Getting
older. She's seventy-eight now. Sick most of the time.
Usually in bed by seven. I doubt if you'll be seeing
her tonight."

"That makes for long evenings," said Bogart.

"I have my typewriter. And Taki. You might call me a reluctant recluse."

"You should think about returning to civilization. They'd hire you in a minute."

"Would they? . . . Everyone in Hollywood thinks he's a writer. It's an impossible climate to work in. Everyone has all the answers. They have nothing. Working with Billy Wilder on *Double Indemnity* was bad enough. After *The Blue Dahlia* I couldn't stand it. At least here I can write what I want."

"What's in the chopper?" Bogart fingered the sheet of bond paper rolled into the typewriter slightly askew. "A new Marlowe caper?"

Chandler nodded almost sorrowfully. "Can't escape his popularity. He's all a publisher ever asks for."

"What's it called?"

"*Little Sister.* But God knows they'll change the title."

"They always do."

"It's a Hollywood story."

"Getting the movie business out of your system?"

Chandler shook his head. "Not about the movies, but about the different strata of Hollywood life. Con man, up-and-coming actress, blackmailer, prostitute."

Bogart smiled. "Everything the reader likes to find Marlowe wallowing in. They love the dirt, don't they?"

"Right now I'm drafting a scene where Marlowe goes to a film studio and listens to a lot of actors trying to steal scenes from each other."

"Sounds like a picture I just worked on."

"I've got one producer who struts around with a walking stick. I'll let you figure out who that is."

Bogart didn't have to figure. Chandler had never got along well with Billy Wilder and especially resented Wilder's habit of shaking his walking cane as though it were a loaded shotgun.

As Chandler continued to describe his novel, Bogart detected a self-effacing cynicism and was overwhelmed by a sense of tragedy. Here was a man considered to be the finest detective-fiction author in the world, yet who remained untouched by, and aloof from, his successes. It was as though Chandler were turned off by his books.

Bogart knew that Chandler's personal life with his wife Cissy, an older woman who was chronically ill, had led to his restricted living pattern. Nor was Chandler's own health all that encouraging. He suffered from insomnia, bronchitis, swollen throat and allergies.

Chandler had frequently voiced his disapproval of the indifferent manner in which New York publishers seemed to handle his Philip Marlowe novels despite the mystery writers' awards and critical approval from all over the world.

Bogart didn't feel like talking about old times, or asking about old friends. He was beginning to feel as dark and somber as the house. So he told Chandler about Dalt Brennan. All of it. Chandler listened contemplatively, puffing on a narrow-stemmed pipe.

When Bogart finished, Chandler stroked Taki's back. The cat's tail swished languidly and a soft purring filled the small study. Then: "The fact that Dalt's a close friend of yours notwithstanding, I've never considered Dalt anything more than a second-rate writer. Lloyd was something else again. He was everything Dalt wanted to be but couldn't. Sometimes you've got the talent and sometimes you don't, and no amount of hacking will change that. As for Dalt wanting to blow up the Oscars, more power to him. Oscars exist for and by Hollywood, their purpose is to maintain the supremacy of Hollywood, their standards and problems are the standards and problems of Hollywood and their phoniness is the phoniness of Hollywood."

"That sounds very literary," said Bogart.

"It better," retorted Chandler. "It's part of an article I'm preparing for the *Atlantic Monthly*."

They laughed simultaneously again and it was an uplifting laugh. The study didn't seem so dark to Bogart now.

"Those boxes of material Lloyd left you . . ."

"Haven't even had the time to look at them. They're in the closet behind you. Help yourself."

Bogart spent almost half an hour rummaging through the material. There were screenplays by both Dalt and Lloyd. All of Lloyd's had been produced by MGM: *They Wandered From Eden, Key to Paradise, The Countess and the Lion, Four's Not Company.* Most of Dalt's scenarios had not been produced and represented the free-lance material he had never been able to sell: *Cavern of Fear, The Trench Fighters, The Way of Life*— and a screen version of *Day of the Leviathan,* updated to World War II.

Bogart came across a collection of poetry by Lloyd. As he flipped through the sheets, he realized why it had never been submitted for publication. It was entirely of a homosexual nature. One of the poems was titled: "An Ode to Geoffrey."

As had been the case in Johnny Hawks's apartment, he found no copy of *Hollywood Armageddon.*

Then Bogart came across several pieces of Communist-inspired propaganda, similar to what Cohn had discovered in the Columbia files. Bogart wondered if someone hadn't salted both the Columbia boxes and the material in Lloyd's home before Geoffrey Carroll had bundled it up. Would anyone go to such elaborate lengths? Yes, he decided. Especially if that someone was planning to blow up the Oscars and needed a clay pigeon to take the fall. Maybe Dalt had been kidnapped after all, and was being framed. That would make any bomb threat look Communist-inspired.

Bogart's speculative reverie was jarred by the incisive voice of Chandler, who crouched down next to Bogart, staring at the manuscripts and the Communist literature in particular. Chandler leafed through the literature, then contemptuously shoved the boxes back into the closet.

"I don't buy the Commie angle," said Bogart.

"Neither do I," agreed Chandler. "About Lloyd *or* Dalt. Something else: Lloyd killing himself like that? It doesn't wash."

There it was again. The unanimous opinion that Lloyd would never have taken his own life. First Kitty, then Geoffrey, now Chandler. If Lloyd wasn't a suicide, that left only murder. Why murder? Perhaps for the same reason *Embarkation Point* was rewritten. Dalt's mental instability was common knowledge to the entire film community. Someone could be using that knowledge . . . The maddening series of questions pounded away at Bogart.

Finally they stood up and Chandler relit his pipe, pausing again to scratch Taki's back. "From the beginning I personally never bought any of that HUAC claptrap. You know, Lloyd called and asked if I would serve on a special anti-HUAC committee. That was shortly before he died."

"Lloyd had me included, but never got around to calling."

"Lloyd was ready to fight those bastards. Suicide? Bah."

Bogart closed the closet door. He'd come back for the boxes later, if it turned out they were condemning proof. Otherwise they were best left forgotten.

"What a loss to Hollywood, the death of Lloyd Brennan," lamented Chandler. "Even more tragic is the fact that Lloyd'll never write all those books he had stored up in him. I don't know how many times he told me he wanted to escape the monetary lure of Hollywood. He often said he wished he had my backbone. That's a laugh; a good, hearty laugh."

Before Bogart could reply, a haggard old woman appeared at the door dressed in a rumpled black nightgown tattered along the sleeves. She seemed to cast darkness with her eyes, which touched all things in the study, including Bogart.

It was Cissy Chandler, and although she knew Bogart well, she looked right past him and beckoned to her husband with a wizened hand. "I think I need another of my pills. I just can't sleep . . ."

"Yes, darling," said Chandler soothingly. "I'll have it for you in a moment." He placed his pipe in an ashtray and turned toward Bogart, the smile no longer on his face. Bogart felt a chilliness and shivered.

Cissy turned, zombielike, and shuffled back into the corridor. Chandler said nothing further, only shrugged his shoulders helplessly and followed her. It was the last Bogart saw of them: two lonely, separated figures moving along the darkened corridor. They vanished into a bedroom and closed the door—and everything out of their lives.

Bogart waited for ten minutes before he realized Chandler wasn't going to return.

He found his own way out and began the wearisome drive back to Los Angeles.

TWENTY-FIVE

Gusts of harsh winds spattered wet gravel against the tires of the Cadillac as it passed through two immense iron gates. Bogart followed the oval driveway and parked between a Rolls-Royce Silver Wraith and another Cadillac. There were nine other very expensive cars parked nearby.

The three-story white mansion was nestled in seclusion on the low slope of the Hollywood hills, just above Sunset. The rolling lawn that bordered the driveway featured several splashing fountains. Subtly concealed floodlights illuminated the six tall, fluted pillars that graced the front. Ivy wound maternally around the base of the pillars and climbed to the shuttered second-story windows. The fanlight over the front double doors spilled rosy hue onto the driveway.

The architect had taken vast pains with the details and decor to achieve a mood of ante-bellum Louisiana. On the veranda, lanterns cast romantically soft shadows that added to the Southern-plantation atmosphere.

Bogart was dead tired from the long drive from La Jolla, but the spirit of the mansion invigorated him; it seemed wonderfully alive. He could see silhouettes of people drifting behind the lighted, lace-curtained windows. Some rooms were lit by flickering candlelight, other rooms by soft, pink-shaded lamps.

Bogart walked between the central pillars of the veranda and pushed the bell button. Within seconds the double doors opened. Bogart's eyes widened a fraction. The Negro butler wore white satin knee

breeches and a red jacket with shiny brass buttons.
His brown face was topped with a powdered white
wig, its queue tied with a black velvet bow. The perfect eighteenth-century butler.

"Yes, sire, what do you wish?"

Bogart couldn't tell if the butler recognized him or
not. He seemed quite blasé. Bogart stepped in.

The foyer was varnished hardwood and white-
painted walls, the floor dark-gray polished stone. Ferns
were planted in pots next to wall niches that contained small ivory and marble statues of wood
nymphs and archer-Dianas. To the left was a grand
staircase of white banisters and crimson carpet that
wound gracefully, majestically, to the upper floor.

Overhead, a heavy gilt chain supported a massive
chandelier, a magic beacon of layered, teardrop-
shaped crystals and lights. It winked and blinked,
sending specular highlights into all the corners of the
foyer; a steady draft created tinkling and plinking
musical notes.

All the grand doors leading from the foyer were
closed, but Bogart could hear the subdued sound of
merriment and conversation. There was a pleasant
smell in the air, suggesting fine Havana cigars, fine
old sherry, fine old brandy and bourbon.

Bogart gazed casually around the foyer, as it finally
hit him. What a place for Fabrini to choose for a meeting!

A whorehouse!

One of the best Bogart had ever seen—and smack in
the middle of Hollywood. Hemingway would have approved. Bogart turned to the butler. "I'm looking for a
gentleman—Paul Fabrini. Supposed to meet him
here."

Before the butler could reply, double doors leading

to a drawing room burst open and a busty, plump woman glided cheerfully into the foyer. Behind her, Bogart glimpsed a cloud of cigar smoke, pools of pink light, easy chairs, a fireplace and billowing curtains. He could hear faint giggles amid clinking glassware.

"Good evening, Mr. Bogart," the woman said exuberantly. "We are honored. I am Madame Czinara. Welcome to the Plantation."

Bogart guessed the woman to be nearly fifty. She was more than slightly plump, her muscular tummy jutting against a marvelous, frilly, layered gown. She didn't walk; she swirled in a sea of garish taffeta, a compliment to the Confederacy.

Her fiery-red hair was stacked high, with long curls dangling down to her broad, naked shoulders. She reminded Bogart of an aging Scarlett O'Hara who had long ago kissed her lover—and her prime—good-bye.

"You act as though you expected me," said Bogart softly, with a trace of suspicion.

She smiled bemusedly. "Well, now that you mention it . . . Paul did say you might be dropping in. As a matter of fact . . . you're ten minutes late."

Kitty had warned him not to be late.

Bogart cleared his throat nervously. "I'm impressed, Madame . . ."

"Czinara. Madame Czinara."

"Czinara," he repeated, trying to familiarize himself with the sound. "This is quite a layout."

"We do try to accommodate any and all of our clients' tastes. As long as they behave themselves, of course. This is your first visit, I believe."

"I believe."

Where was Fabrini?

"Step into the drawing room, Mr. Bogart. Have a cocktail. Drambuie is a favorite of yours."

"Now I'm *very* impressed. You know your clientele."

"Intimately."

Down the curving grand staircase paraded a group of men dressed in period costumes ranging from American Revolutionary through the Civil War. The women clutching their arms wore Southern-belle hoop skirts and looked childlike with their heavily rouged cheeks and curly blond wigs.

Madame Czinara took Bogart's elbow and smilingly guided him into the large drawing room.

He thought he would find Fabrini there. He was wrong.

Bogart stopped involuntarily. Oh, it was a whorehouse all right, but one with a difference. Bogart was very, very impressed. Madame had created the ultimate fantasy.

"Ann Sheridan" looked up with interest at the new arrival.

"Linda Darnell" stopped stroking the forehead of a portly gentleman and smiled provocatively at Bogart.

He took in a sharp breath. Another familiar-looking woman gestured seductively, peeking through a fall of dark hair over a smooth forehead. She stood near the fireplace, drink in hand, three handsome middle-aged men sitting around her. A pale blue gown clung to the woman's lithe, catlike body. She stepped toward Bogart, her body speaking a language all its own, and she sang a few throaty lines of a song.

> . . . and her tears flowed like wine—
> she's a real sad tomata—she's a
> busted valentine . . .

Bogart recognized the song from *The Big Sleep*, and the singer raised her glass to toast him and smiled, appreciating the joke.

Madame Czinara laughed with adolescent innocence, her red curls dancing. "See, Mr. Bogart, we offer only the best."

Where else but in Hollywood would you find a whorehouse that offered the women the rest of the world could only dream about.

"The secret," confided Madame Czinara, "is a good eye for young women who resemble their counterparts and an excellent touch of makeup . . . a private projection room where they can watch their alter egos, copying mannerisms, voices, movements."

"The makeup is damn good," lisped Bogart, tugging at his earlobe, "but some of the girls could stand more acting lessons."

Madame Czinara laughed musically again. "I assure you, our clients are more interested in other talents."

"I'm letting my professional instincts get the better of me."

"Surely there are other instincts," she said, winking.
Ten minutes late.

"I'm going to have to sample the merchandise some other time. Right now I'd better see Paul."

"Imagine that. Humphrey Bogart coming to the Plantation to meet a man. Well, it takes all kinds . . ."

She laughed mockingly as she led him back outside the smoky drawing room. The girl waved at him.

Madame Czinara pointed up the curving staircase. "Fabrini's in the Crystal Room. I'd be honored to escort you—"

"'Don't bother. I'll find it."

Madame Czinara shrugged disappointedly and watched Bogart climb the stairs.

The upper floor was romantically lit by rose-shaded lamps. The walls were painted a lustrous white and the red plush carpet was soft underfoot. Despite the white walls, the corridors were dim and dreamlike.

Bogart opened a door in the hope that it was the Crystal Room.

He was wrong.

A blond with well-rounded legs, wearing a white one-piece bathing suit that was partially unzipped, turned and glowered at the intruder. "Betty Grable" said, "Close the door, buster."

Bogart recognized the man pulling the zipper—one of Grable's co-stars of a few years back. He looked sheepishly at Bogart from his compromising position on the satin-covered bed. His fingers were frozen on the zipper.

"I'm looking for the Crystal Room," Bogart said to "Grable."

She put one hand on her hip and pointed with the other. "Down the hall, buster. Can't miss it. The door's got a crystal knocker. You know what a knocker is . . ."

As Bogart passed doors, he heard soft moanings, mutterings and occasional muted bursts of giggles and laughter. He stopped when he saw the crystal knocker. It was a room at the end of a hall; Fabrini had picked a good spot for a quiet conversation. Bogart knocked and waited. He knocked again, then turned the knob. The door wasn't locked.

He went inside.

The room was dark. Bogart felt along the wall and found the light switch. A chandelier glittered, illuminating the mirrored walls.

In the center of the room was a mahogany four-poster bed. Rich cloth brocaded in hues of pink and gold cascaded from above, tied back in sections to each of the hand-carved mahogany corner posts. The bed was covered with a densely patterned brocade spread, shamelessly scarlet in color. Everywhere he looked Bogart saw mirrors that had been cleverly angled to allow the occupants of the bed to see themselves.

But it was the scarlet bedspread that kept Bogart riveted at the doorway. Diagonally across the bed lay a middle-aged, dark-haired man in a blue serge business suit. His right hand rested on a fluffy pink pillow as though caressing it affectionately. He lay face upward, staring at a mirror, but Bogart knew he could see nothing.

He also knew the man was Paul Fabrini.

There was a dark, curving arc that ran from the man's right cheekbone, under his neck and back up again to the left cheekbone, and it glittered in the lights of the chandelier. Streams of blood were flowing down behind Fabrini's head.

They matched the color of the bedspread perfectly.

TWENTY-SIX

The blast of blinding light from a Speed Graphic bleached the already drained face of Paul Fabrini. Bogart felt his stomach twisting nauseously and he turned toward the wall of the bedroom. A hundred Humphrey Bogarts glared back at him in the network of mirrors; a hundred pale faces protested their revulsion.

Fitzgerald placed a reassuring but authoritative arm on his shoulder. "Sure enough now, you should be getting used to these kinds of things, Mr. Bogart. Bodies seem to turn up around you as faithfully as your fans."

They edged away from the four-poster to allow room for Fitzgerald's homicide team—two photographers, two men dusting for prints and two coroner's attendants wheeling in a gurney.

"Sorry, Inspector, but I've just decided I don't have the stomach for your line of work."

"Understandable," responded Fitzgerald, pausing to pull deeply on his rosewood pipe, "since you deal in only make-believe and I . . . well, I must face the mundane day-to-day realities. . . ."

Bogart's legs turned wobbly. Near the wall he saw a scarlet footstool and he settled onto it, wiping moisture from his forehead with a handkerchief. He could hear the muted voices of a detective and Madame Czinara drifting in from the corridor.

"Well now, you did the right thing, Mr. Bogart, calling us so promptly. I hope you didn't go nosing about the scene of the crime as you've been nosing around town these past few days."

"You'll find my prints on the door, but I didn't touch anything else. . . . So *I've* been nosing around . . . sounds like you've had your bloodhounds out for a stroll."

"You did cross our line of vision now and again."

Bogart arched an eyebrow. "Do any of your boys drive a Packard? Black?"

"A Packard, you say. Well now, you'd have to ask the man who owns one, Mr. Bogart. I'm afraid the department couldn't afford the luxury. It would appear you've crossed someone else's line of vision as well."

"Someone forced me off the road the other night."

"Packard?"

"A different car."

"Accident?"

"More like a warning."

"It would seem you've attracted an element of danger to yourself, Mr. Bogart. Suppose you fill me in on just how you came to be here tonight with the late Mr. Fabrini."

"Fabrini called. Said he wanted to see me."

"Why you?"

"A mutual friend informed him I was looking for Dalt."

"And Fabrini said what?"

"Over the phone, not much. Said he had information. Something that would link the murders of Johnny Hawks and Martha Pearce to Dalt Brennan's disappearance."

"The *murder* of Martha Pearce?" This time it was Fitzgerald's eyebrow that arched. "How did he know that?"

"He sounded pretty sure of himself. Maybe he was only guessing."

"He wasn't guessing, Mr. Bogart. The lab has confirmed it. Martha Pearce did not take her own life."

"Then that overturned pencil glass . . ."

"Just one of several clues, Mr. Bogart. Still, the department thanks you. What else did Fabrini tell you?"

"That the death of Lloyd Brennan fitted into this somehow."

"Lloyd Brennan, you say." A special twinkle lit up Fitzgerald's face. "And just what was this fascinating link among all these people?"

"I never found out. Fabrini was like that when I got here."

"You didn't pass anyone in the hallway?"

"No, but when I came in there were quite a few people coming down the stairs in costumes. The killer might have slipped in and out without being noticed."

"A likely possibility. And nothing was moved?"

"Only my emotions, Inspector."

"Surely you must know of some link between Fabrini and all these fine people we've been talking about."

Bogart nodded. "It all stems back to the making of a film during the war called *Embarkation Point*. Fabrini did a rewrite on Dalt's screenplay. Dalt got pretty upset."

"And Dalt harbored a grudge?"

"Enough to threaten Fabrini."

"You heard these threats?"

"The contact did." Bogart paused while one of the fingerprint men dusted the legs of the footstool. The attendants were still waiting patiently for the photographers to finish their portraits. The voice of Madame Czinara continued to float in from the hallway.

"Well now," said Fitzgerald, "that might account for why Dalt busted out of Saints and Sinners. To do in Mr. Fabrini as we now see him."

"I don't buy Dalt murdering anyone."

"Now on that point I might have to agree with you. I've done some looking at Dalt's police file—"

"Dalt has a record?"

"All minor offenses. Assault and battery, drunken driving, insulting an officer of the law with profane language, disorderly conduct in assorted saloons. Nothing more serious than that. But please, carry on with your thoughts about Mr. Brennan."

"I think he's being manipulated, whether he knows it or not. *Embarkation Point* might have been part of someone's plan to get Dalt into a particular frame of mind. Maybe Lloyd's death was another contribution."

"Manipulated to do what?"

"To go after bigger game than Paul Fabrini."

"Perhaps," said Fitzgerald drily, almost in a bored voice, "to blow up Shrine Auditorium on Saturday night?"

Bogart felt a new surge of hope; his giddiness left him. "So you've been talking to Harry."

"Rather, Harry's been talking to us. Seems he has an uncommon respect for authority, when pressed in a forceful fashion."

"And you bought Harry's story?"

"Well now, let's examine the facts. *Something* is happening, or Dalt wouldn't be missing, now would he. And according to Norma Jean, there's a definite link between Johnny Hawks and the sanitarium. And we must assume there's some connection between Martha Pearce's death and Dalt's absence from the sanitarium. All of these elements connect together,

Mr. Bogart, but nowhere is there any proof that Dalt might be planning a bomb plot."

"Ah," said Bogart, "but there might be proof. A screenplay."

"Ah, yes, the screenplay. Cohn mentioned it at length, and Norma Jean made reference to Johnny reading a screenplay at the sanitarium."

"They're one and the same. *Hollywood Armageddon.* Dalt's way of getting all his hatred and frustration out of his system. And Johnny's dead, isn't he? He was on his way to Cohn with what he knew about the bomb plot when he was killed. What more do you need?"

"I can think of other reasons a script might be worth murdering for."

"Such as?"

"Such as screenplays sell for large sums of money. As much as a few hundred thousand. Am I bandying about the proper figures?"

Bogart said nothing.

Fitzgerald continued: "Rival producers fighting over ownership of a script . . . greed . . . avarice . . . Now those are motives I can understand, Mr. Bogart. I live with those things every day."

"I agree, it does sound farfetched, someone using a screenplay as a blueprint. But we're living in a changing world, Inspector. There's a lot of hate and bitterness these days. Hell, only last week someone made a threat to blow up every railroad station, ferry and newspaper plant in New York City."

"I remember the incident well, Mr. Bogart, but in no case was a bomb discovered. All the work of cranks."

"You're forgetting the Fox Theatre in San Francisco last week. That lobby blast was real enough."

"Aye, now you've touched a nerve," Fitzgerald sighed. "If you could just give me something concrete, Mr. Bogart. The connection between this missing screenplay and our dead participants is too tenuous."

Bogart slapped his knee, suppressing his disappointment. Fitzgerald was sympathetic, but it didn't look as though he was going to be much help. "By the way, Inspector, even if I can't get through that thick Irish skull of yours, thanks for helping Lorre cut the red tape this afternoon."

"It was that sinister glance he gave the station sergeant, I believe."

"I was hoping he'd find something in Johnny's car, but—"

"Johnny's car? Sometimes you're hopelessly misinformed, Mr. Bogart. Who told you it was Johnny's car?"

"I assumed . . ."

"If we're discussing the yellow Oldsmobile in which Johnny Hawks met his untimely end, we're discussing the property of Norma Jean Baker—no other."

"Norma Jean's car?"

Fitzgerald emitted a thin chuckle at Bogart's surprise. "What's so strange about that, now, I ask you? When two people live together—"

"Wait a minute; I'm way behind you, Inspector."

"Well, we didn't exactly announce it to the press. We saw no reason to bring Norma Jean into the matter . . ."

"They lived together?"

"At the Malibu address."

"In Johnny's apartment?"

"No, no, Johnny only kept that as a front. They lived in Norma Jean's place. On the same floor, in the back."

"No wonder Lorre and I found so little clothing in Johnny's apartment . . ." He blurted it out before he realized it.

Fitzgerald cocked his head and clucked his tongue. "So you've searched Johnny's apartment. With or without a search warrant, might I ask?"

Bogart ignored the question and glanced at his watch. "Inspector, whether I'm right or not about Dalt, I've got just forty-two hours before the Oscar show Saturday night."

The photographers were turning to leave when Bogart wiped his forehead, again seeing himself duplicated a hundredfold in the mirrors.

A hundred Kitty Steeles stared back.

Bogart leaped up, knocking over the footstool.

A uniformed policeman slipped past her and approached Fitzgerald. "Lady says she's Kitty Steele. Says she dropped off the deceased. Says she came back to pick him up. Figured you wouldn't mind me bringing her up."

"It's all right, George, I'll take care of it," said Fitzgerald.

"*I'll* take care of it, Inspector," corrected Bogart.

"You know her?"

"Fabrini's contact."

"We'll be wanting to ask her some questions."

"Later," said Bogart forcefully.

"Of course. Tomorrow will be soon enough."

Kitty refused to enter the room; she stood at the threshold, staring disbelievingly at the four-poster while the two attendants lifted the corpse from the stained brocade bedspread. One of them pulled a white sheet up and over Fabrini's outstretched form.

"Kitty . . ." Bogart hurried to the doorway, his eyes

locked onto hers. A tiny tear glistened at the corner of her right eye; her body became rigid and he knew she was fighting off the grief threatening to burst within her.

She turned slowly, watching the sheeted form being trundled past Madame Czinara and the detective.

How the hell did this woman do it? Bogart asked himself. The strength she displayed as a stuntwoman had also manifested itself in an inner strength, a resiliency against life's toughest slaps.

There were a hundred things Bogart wanted to say, but he said nothing. He gently took Kitty's arm and guided her slowly down the corridor, the rose-shaded wall lamps casting a soft glow over her somnambulistic figure. Without stopping, they descended the curving staircase, the overhead crystals creating a musical accompaniment to each step. The foyer and vestibule were filled with the "actresses" and "clientele" of the Plantation, each impatiently waiting to be interrogated. The smells of old sherry and Havana cigars were no longer in the air. Lilac time was finished.

The butler in eighteenth-century livery remained dutifully stationed at the massive mahogany doors. He ushered them out, bowing graciously.

They passed between the pillars and stepped down onto the oval driveway now littered with police cars, unmarked maroon sedans and the coroner's wagon. A thin mist of rain and a raw wind whipped at the weeping willows and bougainvillea. The dampness had a reviving effect on Bogart; he no longer felt wobbly or lightheaded.

Ignoring the mist on his face, Bogart turned to Kitty, taking her hand in his. It was a piece of ice. "I'll take you home, Kitty."

Suddenly the tears were flowing without restraint

and she was sobbing and throwing herself against Bogart. He held her tightly against his chest. His trembling fingers delicately patted Kitty's shoulder, then climbed to stroke her hair. Her head remained pressed deeply against his breast.

Finally the spasms subsided and Kitty released a deep sigh and looked into his face. "I'd . . . I'd rather you didn't drive me, Bogie."

"I'd feel better if you'd let me—"

"I need to drive for a while by myself. Think things out."

"If that's the way you really want it."

She nodded, adjusting the strap of her purse over her shoulder. Stoically she walked to her prewar La-Salle parked at the foot of the oval driveway and climbed in. Bogart closed the door for her.

"Kitty, there's one thing you've got to know. I'm convinced Dalt had nothing to do with Paul's death."

"I never believed for a moment . . ."

"I'm convinced Dalt is being manipulated. Used."

"By whom?"

"That I don't know yet. Paul . . . well, he died before he could tell me."

"It doesn't matter, Bogie. It's finished. They're both out of my life now."

"I'll call you, Kitty, I'll . . ." But Bogart didn't know what else to say. She gave him a wave, started the engine and pulled away. Bogart watched the bright-blue LaSalle swing onto the street and pick up speed, the thin layer of rain pattering softly against the hood.

"That you, Doc?"

"What? . . . My God, must you persecute me even

at this unsaintly hour? Do you have any concept of the time?"

"Time is something that's running out, Doc."

"Do you realize how nerve-shattering a phone sounds at two in the morning?"

"I've got a new lead on our missing screenplay. You ever read Poe's 'The Purloined Letter'?"

"You dare to present me with a literary examination at this hour? You know I've read every word Poe has written. What does it matter?"

"Meet me at Johnny Hawks's apartment in Malibu."

"Now?"

"Immediately."

"Now that you've dangled the carrot before my nose, I seem to have no choice. But it will take me time to dress."

"All right, but make it quick."

"My wife has urged me never to hurry in your case. She has already threatened to divorce me should I continue my nocturnal association with you."

"Tell her you're performing a public service. Tell her anything . . . just get to Johnny's."

"In an hour . . . if I make it at all."

"You'll make it, Doc. That analytical brain of yours won't let you stay away."

TWENTY-SEVEN

Oncoming headlights illuminated Bogart as he sat behind the wheel of his parked coupe, smoking a cigarette. The twin beams swept across the stucco apartment building and then went out. A car door slammed. Bogart turned to see the grimacing countenance of Lorre. Apparently he had dressed hastily after all: His beige camel-hair coat was misbuttoned over a rumpled gabardine suit, which in turn had been hastily pulled over black-and-white pajamas, the tips of which were visible at Lorre's waist and at his cuffs. A bow tie covered with miniature arrowhead designs stuck out of a coat pocket.

Bogart climbed out and threw his cigarette into the gutter. "More bad news, Doc. Paul Fabrini was killed tonight before he could tell me what he knew. I found the body."

"Killed?"

"Murdered."

Lorre's grimace gave way to surprise. "And that's what brings us out here to Johnny's?"

"We're both a couple of chumps for not figuring this angle sooner, Doc. I learned from Fitzgerald that Johnny's car wasn't Johnny's car. It belonged to Norma Jean. She was living with Johnny. Right here in this building. He kept his own room as a front."

"Which explains the lack of clothing."

"That much I figured, Doc."

"But *I* have yet to figure how Poe fits in. Or would you care to enlighten me?"

"I'm going to let you find out firsthand, Doc."

While Lorre fumed, Bogart walked to the entranceway of the building, found the buzzer for the rear apartment and pressed it.

"The Ogre awakens the Sleeping Beauty," muttered Lorre, huddling against the cold air. "Things are moving fast, dear Bogie."

Bogart grinned; the buzzer sounded shrilly and he pushed open the front door. They hurried up the stairs, turned into a central corridor and proceeded to the rear, where light fell onto the carpet through an open doorway.

Bogart came to a standstill in mid-corridor. So did Lorre.

Norma Jean Baker stood framed in the doorway, soft yellow light from the apartment silhouetting her body. She wore a virgin-white negligee of crushed crepe which swept to the floor and clung to every intriguing nuance of her body. The nightgown was precariously tied around her neck by a band of thin pink satin, which looked inadequate. Although she had obviously been rudely awakened and her hair was rumpled, she still radiated warm sexual energy.

Bogart and Lorre overcame their inertia and approached the apartment.

"My God," breathed Norma Jean accusingly, "do you know what time it is?"

Lorre sighed. "He is quite indifferent to the beauty rest of others, sweet creature. He is wallowing in the excitement of the hunt."

Norma Jean held back a yawn, her fingers caressing the smooth skin of her neck. Suddenly she snapped awake. "Bogie," she said, "oh, Bogie. Oh, it must be about Johnny . . ."

Bogart nodded and she immediately stepped back. Bogart brushed lightly against Norma Jean; the combined softness of the crepe material and her body took some of the urgency out of his mission.

It was an apartment similar to Johnny's, although furnished to a woman's taste. The chairs were covered in hues of ocher and tan; the divan was a soothing lemon yellow. The table lamps were pink, with ruffled shades. The effect was a relaxing softness.

"Excuse my rudeness, Norma Jean. This is someone I bumped into. His name is Peter Lorre."

"Oh, Mr. Lorre." Norma Jean extended a warm hand, which Lorre fondled gently in his own and bent to kiss.

"The pleasure, despite the impossible hour and the crudity of my companion, is all mine."

Bogart gave Lorre the eye to finish his nonsense. Then to Norma Jean: "Did Johnny leave anything with you? Books . . . notes . . . a script, perhaps?"

Norma Jean looked oddly at Bogart. "Johnny was always giving me something to read. He liked to read . . . tried to get me interested in literature. Some of the plays he gave me were wonderful. Right now I'm reading *Death of a Salesman*. Have you read it? By someone named Arthur Miller."

"This might have been something special. Something he asked you to take care of."

She thought for a moment, then: "On Monday night, I remember he left a box on the kitchen table. I haven't touched it."

"Would you get it, Norma Jean?"

She returned from the kitchen with a cardboard box that had once contained a ream of typing paper. Inside was a manila envelope. Bogart opened the folded flaps, turning to Lorre. "Do you remember, Doc, I asked you on the phone—"

"—if I had read 'The Purloined Letter.' Of course. A

man leaves an envelope in plain sight on a mantel, and no one notices, even though a thorough search is conducted for it."

Bogart pulled a bound screenplay from the envelope. The gummed label on its cover read *Raiders of the Badlands*.

Lorre studied it, emitting a low sigh and a glance of admiration. "I'm beginning to understand. Johnny just left the script lying around."

"But he pulled a switch," said Bogart. "He changed the covers. *Raiders of the Badlands* to *Hollywood Armageddon*, and vice versa. What you found in the back of the car was the decoy, Doc."

"Ingeniously simple," marveled Lorre.

Bogart leafed through the papers. "Yeah, this is it." He sank heavily into the sofa and leaned back against the cushions.

Lorre cleared a space on the low table as Norma Jean placed a tray of coffee before them. She took a position on the far end of the couch, the nightgown clinging to her.

Bogart lit a cigarette and looked accusingly at Lorre. "Now we're going to find out if any of your theories about Dalt Brennan hold water, Doc."

Bogart sipped coffee, Lorre tried to conceal his pajamas by tucking them into his waistband, and Norma Jean remained curled on the couch, a ball of fluffy innocence waiting, wide-eyed. Bogart turned to the first page.

They read . . .

Something hitting the carpet brought Norma Jean awake. The *Hollywood Armageddon* screenplay lay at Bogart's feet and he was staring at it as if it were a time bomb. A pall hung over him and Lorre; neither of them spoke.

Norma Jean stirred, yawned and excused herself for falling asleep. "I dropped off just when Albert Danan was about to be cheated out of an Oscar by that writer, Redfield. What happened then?"

"Danan continues to get cheated," capsulized Bogart. "By unscrupulous studio bosses, by unfeeling directors, by clawing actresses."

"He is," expounded Lorre, "subjected to abuse, betrayal and outright malevolence."

Norma Jean cocked her head and closed her gaping mouth.

"Finally," resumed Bogart, "it boils down to Redfield, who cops the Oscar that should rightfully have been Danan's, a beautiful actress bitch, Wanda Lovecraft, and a fat-cat producer named Sidney Winestock—a carbon copy of Harry Cohn. Danan decides to have his revenge—by blowing up the Academy Awards. Everyone—Danan included—gets blown to hell. The last ten pages describe what happens to those in the auditorium. Engulfed by the blast, killed by falling debris, trampled in the stampede that follows. The shattered aisles of Shrine Auditorium are littered with famous corpses."

"Why must you be so melodramatic?" accused Lorre.

"Then the camera lingers on a golden statuette, which suddenly bursts into flames . . . and we fade to black."

There was a sharp intake of breath as the impact of the idea got through to Norma Jean. "Does that have something to do with why Johnny died?"

"Johnny died," said Bogart, "because he knew someone was intending to use this script as a blueprint."

"To really blow up the Academy Awards?" whispered Norma Jean.

There was silence for a long while. Lorre picked up the script, riffling its pages. "This is certain to give me nightmares, dear Bogie. This screenplay is a perfect Rorschach test of Brennan's personality—an escape valve for his festering hatred. The idea of blowing up the Oscars must have become a subconscious fixation; something Dalt was finally compelled to carry out after Lloyd's suicide. Albert Danan . . . even the name is a twisted anagram of Dalt Brennan. Do you see, dear Bogie, they are one and the same."

"So now we're both convinced Brennan could do it."

"Not *could* do it, dear Bogie. *Will* do it. *Must* do it. Unless he's stopped."

"One thing, Doc. How's he going to follow the screenplay? Isn't that going to be tough?"

"He can't possibly follow it step by step; he'll have to fit his own plan to the realities of here and now. But Dalt may stick to certain key elements."

"In other words, he'll adapt what he can from the original and improvise the rest?"

"Precisely."

"You know, Doc," said Bogart, "there's one theme running all through this thing."

"Yes—the Oscar. In Dalt's eyes it is a vile object, something loathsome and repugnant."

"If his hatred is that keen," reasoned Bogart, "he just might stick to the script and rig the statuettes with explosives. It might not be a bad idea for me to drop into Shrine Auditorium and see Jean Hersholt, the academy president. He might see reason enough to close down the ceremony until Dalt is found."

"Good luck," wished Lorre dubiously.

"And good luck to you, Doc. You, you're going to

drop into the main branch of the academy on Melrose as soon as the sun is up and check out where they keep those Oscars."

Lorre had already left for Mandeville Canyon by the time Norma Jean returned from the kitchen with newly brewed coffee. She poured out two cups and curled up on the sofa. Bogart caught a glimpse of thigh as she rearranged billowy clouds of crepe material around her. He felt greatly distracted by Norma Jean's presence. Ever since Lorre had left, he had felt strangely vulnerable.

"Do you think any of this will give you a lead to who killed Johnny?" she asked.

"Lorre thinks so."

"And you?"

"I'm not sure what I believe anymore." He sipped the strong coffee, feeling the stimulant push away his growing fatigue. It was still less stimulating than Norma Jean's presence.

"What makes a man write a story like that? How could anyone come to hate Hollywood so much?"

"There are two sides to this film industry. The good side is what you young people see: glamour, fortune, world recognition . . ."

"And the other side?"

"The side you never know about until it's too late. Until you've been sucked into the business. Jealous rivalry . . . plagiarism . . . back-stabbing . . . broken promises . . . unmade pictures . . . a lot of bad breaks that can turn a person bitter, hateful, destructive . . ."

"Not a pretty picture."

"It's not a pretty town."

"How did you get started in pictures, Bogie?"

"By not knowing any better. Naiveté can be the

best thing going for you. For a while. Then you have to wise up to protect yourself. You have to work hard. And relax."

"How do you mean, relax?"

"Don't drive yourself so you burn out before you're thirty. If you have talent, somebody'll recognize it. Concentrate on acting, learn your trade. You've got to develop confidence, and confidence comes from knowing the ropes. You're in a helluva fix, wanting to be an actress, but keep trying, keep working . . ."

Norma Jean sipped her coffee. Even her ordinary motions and actions were unconsciously sensual. "What happens when other people start using you? Pushing you around?"

"Like the guy who wants to audition you, but all he has in his office is a couch? Giving in to jerks like that won't get you anywhere, Norma Jean. The minute you give in they lose respect for you and won't give you the part anyway. You've got to be honest to yourself first. You've got to believe in your career and fight for it."

"Sometimes I think I'm nuts, trying to crack such a tough business."

"There're a lot of good reasons for sticking it out, and I'm not talking about dough. You become a star to do something special in life; to be someone special. You set yourself apart from the mob. They all know your name, what you look like, how your voice sounds, how you walk across a room, how you light a cigarette. Baby, that's magic."

"I'd like a piece of that magic someday." Norma Jean slid across the couch to within a foot of Bogart and leaned back into the cushions. The hem of the nightgown had crept above her knees; her breasts jutted tautly against her thin, frilly bodice. She gazed endearingly at Bogart. God, she was lovely.

Desire for Norma Jean swelled within him. The opportunity was here and now and it was overwhelming—alone in her apartment, Betty out of town, nowhere to go until morning . . . no one to answer to . . . except himself.

Her eyes innocently invited him.

He felt himself starting to close the gap on the sofa. Felt the undeniable urge to reach out and take her tightly in his arms, press her flushed face against his and kiss her. Hold her and caress her smooth body and stroke her breasts . . .

What the hell was he doing?

That single thought gave him the strength to break eye contact and turn away. He took a mouthful of coffee to break her spell for good. He set the saucer and cup down and looked at his watch, purposely keeping his eyes averted from Norma Jean's. If he looked at her again . . . he didn't want to imagine what might happen.

Norma Jean jerked alert, spilling coffee onto the yellow sofa. She became a flurry of fussy activity, cleaning up the spilt liquid.

"I've . . . I've got to be going, Norma Jean. I'm dead on my feet. And I've got a busy day tomorrow with the academy."

"I . . . I wish you'd stay a little longer, Bogie. Maybe I could put on some music. I've got some terrific Peggy Lee ballads."

He waved away the suggestion indifferently, even though he felt newly threatened on the inside. Music and Norma Jean together might be more than any mortal man could resist . . .

He excused himself and hurried for the door, taking the copy of *Hollywood Armageddon* with him. He never even turned to give her a farewell kiss. He could feel her eyes following his every movement down the stairs.

Betty, he screamed to himself, if you don't hurry and get home fast, I'm going to become the horniest actor in Hollywood.

TWENTY-EIGHT

Rain and wind blew across the compound of the Semaphore Oil Company's utility shed, its windows rattling against the gusts.

Brennan pulled his muffler tighter against his throat and stared at the small blobs of explosive material spread across the long workbench. A wooden base about twelve inches square supported a wooden cone three inches high and two inches wide at the bottom.

Cautiously he pressed the first lump onto the cone, plucked it off and then forced a small brass cone into the newly formed cavity. Just as cautiously he scooped a handful of tiny iron pellets out of a bucket and poured them into the brass-lined cavity. He methodically sealed it with a layer of the explosive.

He reached for another blob.

In two hours Brennan had cleared the bench of all the explosives. The irregular cubes of gray modeling clay stood in rows like children's toy blocks.

He stepped to a cabinet and poured a small amount of whiskey into a jelly glass and drank slowly, savoring it, letting it bite the back of his tongue before he swallowed it. The warmth spread through his body.

Tick . . . tick . . . tick . . . tick . . . He carried two ordinary alarm clocks back to the bench. He tied insulating wires leading to a fulminate of mercury cap, twisted them down and inserted the detonating cap into one of the gray-colored charges. He put the first one aside and repeated the action. After the two charges were completed, he twisted two wires to the soldered terminals behind each of the two alarm clocks.

Brennan brought to the bench two six-sided 35-millimeter film canisters. He unlatched one, blew out the dust with a few blasts of chilly breath and began to place the cubes of hardened explosive inside. The last cube had the detonating cap with two-foot trailing wires.

He repeated the operation with the second film can, then closed and locked both of them. The two dry-cell batteries and the two cheap alarm clocks went into the pockets of the stained raincoat.

He opened the closet door and pulled the compressor's operating switch to Off and the chugging spluttered and died.

He picked up the M-1 rifle, slung it over his shoulder, then picked up the film cans and carried them from the shed to the pickup outside. The wind whipped at his clothing, the flapping sound merging with the thumping rhythm of the nearby oil-pumping rigs. Even against the night sky, Brennan could see their shapes rising and falling.

In the bed of the pickup was an old mattress. Brennan heaved the 35-millimeter film canisters onto it and, using a length of stout cord, rolled the mattress over and tied it into a roll.

Head down against the wind, Brennan unlocked the gate of the cyclone fence. In less than a minute he had driven through and relocked the gate. He squinted at the sign:

SEMAPHORE OIL COMPANY
UTILITY SHED—KEEP OUT
PRIVATE PROPERTY

The wind and the dark-gray morning sent a chill through Brennan as he slipped the rifle into its scabbard over the rear window. He started the engine, went one block and turned onto Henry Ford Avenue.

He sighed. The forest of derricks began to thin out; he slowed for a turn onto Highway 101. Soon he would be in view of a new forest—the tall masts and spars of the sailboats docked at Newport Beach.

Brennan began to hum to himself, keeping his red-rimmed eyes open for an all-night coffee shop.

TWENTY-NINE

At 4 A.M., with his brain groggy from lack of sleep, Hedgerow Farm was a welcome sight in the glare of Bogart's headlights. He had pushed himself to the brink of exhaustion and he now needed nothing but the warmth of his bed.

But the instant he snapped off his motor and lights, an instinct within him came alive. The house looked orderly, yet he was overwhelmed by an uneasy feeling. And Harvey . . . his bark was too shrill and his behavior too agitated.

Inside the house he found a shambles. Drawers had been emptied out, chairs and tables overturned, photographs pulled down from the walls. Even the print of Griffith's film had been dumped from its tin and lay in a spaghetti mess.

His private sanctum, the place christened Bogart's Mad Room, had been invaded. He clicked on the lamp made from a giant Bavarian beer mug. The glassy plaque which Betty had designed was on the floor. Even upside down he could read:

DANGER—BOGART AT WORK*!*
DO NOT DISCUSS: POLITICS—RELIGION
WOMEN—MEN—PICTURES—THEATER
OR ANYTHING ELSE*!*

Bogart picked it up, then surveyed the intruder's work. The model of the *Santana* was tossed into a corner. The divan, which could be made into a spare bed, was pulled aside, the covers tossed onto the floor, and little mugs with naked women forming the handles were scattered over the floor.

Anger crowded into his tired mind. He stared blankly at the red plaid wallpaper, then kicked savagely at one of the mugs.

The master bedroom was in no better shape. Someone had crumpled the blankets and sheets into a giant ball. In the clothes closet he found his racks of suits undisturbed, but someone had scattered the shoe boxes on the top shelf.

Betty's vanity had been frightfully rifled. After straightening up some of the mess, Bogart decided they—or he—hadn't bothered to take any of Betty's more expensive jewelry. Obviously his visitor had been looking for something special.

Hollywood Armageddon?

His life was in danger. He knew that to be a cold, undeniable fact. With the cleverness of a club-footed elephant walking through a crowded square, he had fumbled from lead to lead. Some investigator . . .

He found the .45 automatic where he had discarded it—in a kitchen drawer, buried among butcher knives, eggbeaters and potato peelers. It was the same .45 he had carried throughout the war years.

There were unloaded clips in the bottom of the drawer. He rummaged through cookie cutters and pie tins until he uncovered a box of ammunition. He tried to shove the bullets down against the clip spring. Repeatedly he fumbled; bullets rolled around on the kitchen floor, making clattering noises that jarred his thinking. He was too tired even to curse his own clumsiness.

Finally he managed to fill one clip and he shoved it into the handle, sliding the top cartridge into the chamber.

In the bedroom he rearranged a few of the blankets on the bed, ignored the sheets and found a discarded pillow in the closet. It was covered with a ruffled yellow silk casing. He slid the automatic under the sea of yellow and, without even undressing, dropped onto the mattress and instantly fell asleep.

DAY FOUR

Friday, March 19, 1948

ARAB GUERRILLAS BLOW UP THREE ISRAELI BRIDGES, KILLING AT LEAST THIRTY . . .

CLOCKMAKER HELD BY NEW YORK POLICE IN CONNECTION WITH RECENT BOMB THREAT TO SUBWAY SYSTEMS REVEALED TO BE ONE-TIME CITY EMPLOYEE WHO WAS FIRED AND THEN THREATENED REVENGE AGAINST GOTHAM ADMINISTRATION . . .

MGM SPOKESMAN ANNOUNCES THAT LESTER COLE, SCREENWRITER INDICTED BY HUAC, WILL NOT BE AUTOMATICALLY REHIRED UNTIL STUDIO HAS REEVALUATED COLE'S POLITICAL RECORD . . .

AGNES MOOREHEAD AND DICK POWELL TO SERVE AS EMCEES DURING OSCAR SHOW AT SHRINE AUDITORIUM ON SATURDAY NIGHT . . .

THIRTY

The phone rang twice before Bogart finished his breakfast.

The first call was from Louella O. Parsons. The lilting, petulant voice almost made Bogart choke on his fried eggs. He stalled her off on the promised exclusive story, wondering, after he had put down the phone, just what the hell it would be.

The second call was the one that made him put down his coffee cup and watch the remainder of his eggs turn cold. It consisted of only one word, but it might have been ten thousand.

It was the familiar voice of Mayo. All she said was "Bogie," in a tone that was hopelessly lost.

Within five minutes he was dressed and out of the house.

The dark branches of the Hawaiian pines clashed like swords, crossing, recrossing, en garde, thrusting, parrying. An intense shower of rain rippled across the turbulent surface of the swimming pool. The air carried a chill that penetrated Bogart's skin as he jammed his hands into the slash pockets of his trench coat.

His face was somber—a reflection of the dull gray skies. The door to Mayo's villa was cracked open and Bogart once again found himself standing in gloominess.

He sniffed the air; there was the smell of alcohol. Lingering from yesterday? Bogart doubted it. There was the sound of movement in the bedroom. A faint prickling rose up over his neck.

"Mayo?" he called, his hand on the doorknob. He realized that he had unconsciously set his body in a reflexive stance, ready for anything.

"In here, Bogie," Mayo called.

He let out a soft sigh.

He opened the bedroom door and found her packing her suitcase. He saw that the closets were empty and the dresser drawers were pulled out askew. Mayo thrust downward, and there was a sharp click.

"There, done," she said and turned to face Bogart.

He had expected Mayo to look her worst—he was glad to see he had been wrong.

She wore a slim navy-blue traveling suit with a pleated skirt and a pale yellow blouse, all nicely pressed and form-fitting. She was thrust upward on blue velvet step-shoes and her nylon seams were slightly off-center. Mayo's eyes were reddened, her cheeks puffy; a trace of mascara trickled from her left eye.

"I'm going back."

"Seattle?"

"There's sure as hell nothing to keep me here." She walked to the ornate dresser, picked up a silver flask and tipped the contents into a thick-sided glass. She turned and stared at Bogart, drinking the whiskey defiantly. "I'd had it in Hollywood, but I came back . . . to make one last stab at being someone."

Bogart straightened his shoulders.

"Nothing to say, Bogie? Well, I guess . . . it doesn't matter."

"Yeah, angel, I have something to say. Hollywood's a great big game. You can't take it seriously, can't let it get you down."

Mayo choked back a bitter smile. "Sure. Don't let it get you down. Come on. I've got a train to catch. You can carry my bag . . ."

"I'll drive you to the station," said Bogart as he picked up the leather suitcase from the bed.

She swallowed the last of the whiskey and shoved the silver flask into her purse.

In the living room, Bogart stopped at the door as Mayo gazed about her, her eyes lingering on the fireplace.

Clutching her handbag, she took out a pack of cigarettes, shook two out and moved next to Bogart. She slid one between his lips.

"Got a light?" she asked.

Bogart lit her cigarette, then his. She blew a cloud of smoke at the ceiling, inhaled and removed a speck of tobacco from her lower lip. Her large eyes fluttered nervously.

Outside, the wind rattled the windows, the trees made sharp scraping sounds, and far away, beyond the Santa Monica mountains, there was a muted rumble of thunder.

"I was damn good in my day, wasn't I, Bogie?"

"You were very good, angel. Very good."

Reporters jostled, photographers clicked their heavy Speed Graphics and flashbulbs lit up the ribbed contours of the train like sheets of lightning.

Bogart steered Mayo around the crowd gathered on the station platform of cavernous, cream-yellow Union Station. He kept his hat pulled low.

"What's going on, Bogie?" asked Mayo.

Bogart shook his head.

They paused at the edge of the crowd. There was a cheer as a pretty young woman, wearing a Scottish checkered shawl cape over her shoulder, stepped from the train. Bogart recognized her as Jean Simmons—

here to represent the British Empire at the Academy Awards.

More flashbulbs exploded. "Smile, Miss Simmons," cried the photographers. They tossed burnt-out bulbs onto the concrete platform, inserting new ones with professional speed.

Bogart watched with wry amusement. Hollywood-Welcomes-You-With-Open-Arms. The routine had been done to death for decades. Bogart saw other familiar faces in the crowd: the full flower of "The British Colony." Sir C. Aubrey Smith towered over most of them, stroking his full, gray moustache and patting his plaid waistcoat; Reginald Owens jostled Reginald Gardner's arms, which were filled with long-stemmed red roses.

George Sanders tipped his homburg rakishly as he extended a hand to Jean Simmons. More flashbulbs went off. Claude Rains, in a fine pinstriped suit, looked up at the girl standing on the steps and was joined by Ronald Colman and his wife, Benita. Nigel Bruce shouldered his way through the crowd, harumphing and apologizing as he collided against others. Eric Blore snarled like a whipped dog when Bruce landed on a tender bunion.

Bogart pulled Mayo away from the crowd and they hurried along the platform. Her train waited, puffing steam and emitting sounds as the Pullman doors slammed and opened. They passed a gaggle of young servicemen and porters pushing carts piled high with luggage. Steam rose in whooshing puffs, creating a dense wooly fog over the heaps of suitcases and bags.

A sailor and his girl friend strolled by, arm in arm, their eyes aware that precious time was running out. Three air force men stood by their duffel bags, smoking cigarettes, absorbed in their own thoughts.

Steam drifted and eddied around the feet of the travelers. Bogart held Mayo by the elbow as she mounted the steps leading to her compartment. Bogart put the suitcase beside Mayo just as she reached down and touched his arm with unexpected tenderness. Moisture gathered in her eyes.

"Yeah, angel, I know. It's a tough break."

"We . . . we're never going to see each other again . . . are we, Bogie?"

Bogart took off his hat and held it in one hand. He touched her outstretched arm firmly. "It's a big crazy world, angel, but we don't have to say good-bye with a lot of regrets."

"No," she choked, looking at him. "I'll *remember*. I'm sorry I made things so wrong."

Bogart waited for a second, then Mayo leaned down. He kissed her lips, which quivered under his own. He knew she was on the verge of crying. His arm tightened on hers.

After a long moment he pulled back. Mayo's eyes went down and a shuddering ripple went through her body. Bogart slowly took his arm away. Mayo turned partway, climbed the last of the steps and pulled a handkerchief from her handbag.

The loudspeaker announced the departure of the northbound train: last call, last call.

Bogart stepped back. Mayo clung to the chromed handles of the doors, refusing to move. Conductors swung on board, bells clanged, the sailor broke from his girl friend and leaped aboard several coaches ahead. Windows were thrust open as travelers leaned out to see a last glimpse of those staying behind.

There was a tinny, ear-piercing whistle . . . the train lurched, metal wheels squealed against steel tracks, springs and air-hose connections jerked and protested. Slowly the train moved forward. Mayo remained frozen, looking down at Bogart. He walked steadily beside the train. For over fifty feet he kept apace with Mayo, but gradually the train pulled away. The steam swirled and drifted in ever-increasing trails.

Bogart waved and Mayo lifted a tentative hand in return. He put on his hat, sliding a finger along the brim. He stopped walking when a billowing cloud of steam obscured Mayo.

Bogart was unaware of the red caps and porters hurrying by. With his head down, he walked toward the gates. He slowed his steps and glanced back again as the train picked up speed.

He pulled the collar of his trench coat around his neck as a chill wind blew down the platform, breaking up the last remnants of swirling steam. There was the shriek of a whistle.

It was over.

THIRTY-ONE

With no great ease, Bogart fought to shut off any lingering memories of Mayo Methot. His drive through central Los Angeles was an uneasy one. He saw no sign of the black Packard, but a feeling of apprehension clung to him as he swung past the University of Southern California and pulled up at 665 West Jefferson Boulevard.

Shrine Civic Auditorium.

He paused at the sidewalk to admire the ocher-color concrete building, four times larger than any theater in the City of Angels, known officially as the Al Malaikah Temple. The exterior impressed him with its Moorish domes, high and narrow arches and elaborate Arabesque filigree.

Bogart passed into the spacious main lobby, which maintained the Moorish motif. He noticed a hat-check booth and a first-aid station; seldom did an event pass during which emergency oxygen or wheelchairs were not needed.

The vomitories into the main auditorium were labeled *A* through *D*, in right-to-left sequence, and there was one central corridor which ascended to the balcony. Stairs led to the rest rooms on a lower level, and eventually to the depths of the Catacombs. He chose *B* and found himself immersed in darkness—his eyes would need about half a minute to adjust to the inky gloom.

He felt tiny in the vast, empty auditorium. Shrine filled many needs: grand operas, musical productions, concerts, ballets and even motion-picture filming. In

1943 Darryl Zanuck had re-created here the 1912 Baltimore Democratic Convention for his biographical drama *Wilson*. The auditorium seated nearly six thousand five hundred persons and had served six times previously as a showcase for the academy presentations.

The full implications of the bomb plot struck a new chord of horror within him.

Bogart massaged the back of his neck, studying the auditorium.

Hundreds of feet above, hanging from the domed ceiling, was a spectacular chandelier filled with blue, amber and white bulbs which threw flickering, multicolored light onto a scene of the Nativity handpainted across the ceiling.

He estimated the stage to be two hundred feet wide and seventy feet deep. The orchestra pit could easily accommodate a full symphony orchestra. To the right of the stage he saw the giant Moehler pipe organ.

Already the stage had been partially dressed for Saturday night's presentations. In its center, bathed in a spotlight that poured from the projection booth behind him, stood a giant replica of a two-layer birthday cake. Facsimiles of Oscars were arranged candlefashion around the two levels. Rising up from the center of the "cake" was a giant version of Oscar.

Workmen were still in the process of shuffling props. Hammering came from behind a gold contour curtain hanging at the rear of the stage.

It was behind that curtain that Bogart found Jean Hersholt, who was overseeing carpenters in the construction of two giant Oscar replicas. He was engaged in an involved explanation of how these would stand on each side of the stage during the show, and Bogart had to wait impatiently.

Hersholt, a character actor from Denmark, had originally found success in Hollywood portraying Dr.
Christian in a series of low-budget, highly popular
films for Fox. Now he immersed himself in running
the Academy and the Motion Picture Relief Fund,
and eschewed acting except for his weekly radio appearance as Dr. Christian.

Hersholt was almost six feet tall, with a kindly face.
His blue eyes bespoke their friendliness and his curly
black hair gave him a special boyish look. He had a
habit of smoking outrageous pipes, and today he
puffed sedately on a pinewood concoction with a tortuous stem. He wore a conservative tweed suit.

Finally Hersholt turned and they shook hands
warmly. Bogart came directly to the point.

"Jean, I realize this may sound a little off-center, so
please bear with me. But I've got good reason to believe someone wants to set off a bomb in here tomorrow night."

Hersholt's pipe almost fell from his lips. Finally
Hersholt composed himself well enough to comment:
"The academy's received no such threats."

"I'm aware of that. This is private information."

"What do you propose?"

"Cancel the Oscar show until I can find the man
who's posing the threat."

Hersholt's Scandinavian accent harshened. "It would
be unthinkable to delay the Academy Awards—not
when the entire film community is eagerly awaiting the event and its outcome. The whole world, for
that matter. Careers, and in turn box-office fortunes,
are dependent on who wins on Saturday night. Do
you realize how many theaters across America are
ready—eager, I might add—to book tomorrow night's
winners? Why, cancellation, any kind of postponement

for a single minute, would be a disastrous setback for all concerned."

"Have you stopped to think," responded Bogart harshly, "that if I'm right it could also be very tragic for some sixty-five hundred of Hollywood's finest?"

"Let's assume for a moment you're really onto something," acquiesced Hersholt. "What evidence do you have?"

"That's the problem, Jean. I don't have any evidence. At least nothing I could take into court. Just a lot of conjecture, a helluva lot of suspicion. But surely you can see the advantages of playing it safe."

Hersholt could see no advantages. "If the police were to order me to close down, that would be another matter entirely."

"It could take me days to gather evidence, Jean. Assuming I could do it at all. By then it would be an academic point . . ."

Bogart could sense that it was useless arguing. Hersholt, in his benevolent way, was loyally keeping to his cliche show business belief that the show had to go on. Bogart argued for the next ten minutes and got nowhere. But he did detect an undercurrent of uneasiness in Hersholt's manner, as though the thought of six thousand lives in jeopardy had finally penetrated. Hersholt stopped smoking his pipe and slid it into his pocket with a worried frown.

I've shaken the boat, thought Bogart, even if the waves are minor.

"You bring me something tangible," said Hersholt, "and I'll listen, Bogie. In the meantime, I have work to do . . ."

As Bogart walked from the stage he thought of the similarities between Hersholt and Fitzgerald—both were men who believed only in what they could see.

Bogart had reached the end of the center aisle when he bumped head-on into a delivery man in khaki coveralls. The light was very dim—so dim that Bogart almost didn't see the man's face.

But he felt foolish for being so careless and he wanted to apologize.

That was why he bothered to turn and look the man in the eye.

And found himself staring into the face of Dalt Brennan.

THIRTY-TWO

For a moment Bogart stood in the center of the aisle, no longer hearing the noises from the stage, suspended in time. He absorbed the recognizable but changed features of Dalt Brennan.

Unshaven jaw. Sunken cheeks. Hollow, glaring, accusing eyes. A haunted face. A tangled mass of curly black hair. Slumped, tired body. He reminded Bogart of a concentration camp survivor.

Bogart's instinct was to reach out and touch Dalt and help him. But he was frozen.

"Humph! It's great to see you. Sweet Jesus, you look good."

"Dalt. I've been looking for you. I want to help you."

"Help?"

"You're sick."

"How do you know I'm sick?"

"Just look at yourself, Dalt. Look at what you're doing."

"You better stay back, Humph. No use lying. It's all there."

"What's all there?"

"In your face. The plan . . . you know it all. Don't try to kid me, Humph. Damn it, you don't understand. About all those years."

"I'm trying to understand, Dalt. Sweet Jesus, I'm trying to understand."

"You don't understand anything."

"Maybe I understand *Hollywood Armageddon*.".

"Then you understand what I have to do."

Bogart recognized the fear that flashed with clarity across Dalt's haggard face. He saw the thin body tensing to spring and run. There was no time to think—just to act. Bogart dived at Dalt, but his body moved slowly and he lumbered across empty space.

Dalt Brennan fled.

Bogart fell across the carpet like a dead weight, his elbows taking the brunt of the fall. Some of the air was knocked from his stomach. Brennan was already out of sight by the time Bogart awkwardly picked himself up and ran after him.

As Bogart emerged from the mouth of the rampway, Brennan was racing across the spacious foyer, knocking aside a janitor and his push broom. A bucket of soapy, dirty water skidded across the marble floor. Bogart was unaccustomed to physical exertion and his lungs suddenly felt congested.

Brennan took the stairway to the lower level and Bogart, taking care not to slide in the sudsy water, was directly on his heels. He could hear the echo of footfalls coming from below and it was inspiration to his struggling body, even if the cadence was faster than his own.

Bogart reached the lower level where the corridor ran east and west.

He could discern the dimly lit figure of Brennan rushing west along the corridor, which soon began to curve downward at a gradual angle. Brennan was leading him into the depths of the building. Blindly? Or diabolically?

He tried not to think about the immensity of Shrine Auditorium, but the farther he ran, the more he realized that a man unfamiliar with its design could easily become lost in its Catacombs.

As Bogart ran, he passed chambers, storage rooms,

huge electrical switchboards, boiler cubicles and numerous interlocking corridors. It was a giant, complex labyrinth.

The ceilings were speckled with heating ducts that led to the seats above; there were numerous crawl spaces and narrow, one-man passageways honeycombing the lower level. He even saw trap doors set into the walls. Hundreds of hiding places.

To his own amazement, he was moving swiftly, aided by the gradual descent of the corridor. Brennan loomed ahead and Bogart realized that for the first time he wasn't just keeping apace—he was gaining.

As he ran deeper into the Catacombs, Bogart became more conscious of the atmosphere. Years' worth of dust had built up along the floor and walls; the cobwebbed corners and the dimness filled him with gloom.

Twenty years of accumulated darkness and dust carried with it twenty years of a theater's history; he felt inundated by ghosts, of Shriners dead or forgotten.

Abruptly Brennan branched off the corridor and rocketed through a door marked Dressing Room.

Bogart was right behind him. It was a massive, high-ceilinged chamber, the walls lined with yards of mirrors and dozens of makeup tables. He stumbled awkardly against a row of washbasins, fearful for a moment that he had lost Brennan.

His luck was holding. He spied an ajar door and charged through it, not bothering to consider what danger lay on the other side. He still refused to believe that Brennan would harm him.

Now he was in a boiler room, the concrete walls starkly lit by a single overhead bulb. His head almost banged against a maze of overhead plumbing pipes. He searched behind a row of water heaters, thinking

Brennan might be hiding, but he was wrong. The Birchfield Boiler was a baffling mystery of valves, hoses . . . He swung about in confusion, seeing a huge blower-heater with an enormous wheel and maze of fan belts. He saw another open door. His heart beating madly, he barged ahead.

Supply room. Cleaning gear, large buckets stuffed with push brooms. Scores of light holders, seat cushions with their insides bursting; folding chairs; card tables; carpet cleaners; bottles of solvent. There was only one door and he took it on the fly.

Another central corridor. Brennan was in sight again, tired now from the pounding ordeal, his run-down body taking a beating similar to Bogart's. It was a question of who had an extra ounce of reserve stamina. Bogart accepted the challenge, and continued to gain.

His lungs felt as if they were going to burst; he was wheezing like a dying horse, and yet he pushed himself on through the eldritch gloom.

His socks were drenched in sweat. He became aware of the blisters forming under his toes, so he redirected his mental focus to the back of Brennan's receding figure. The sweat was rolling off his forehead into his eyes but he just kept reminding himself that Brennan was also human and subject to the same torturous limitations.

Each thrusting step was taking more effort now; each leg was becoming a lead weight that didn't want to be picked up again. He could feel his heart tripping too fast but the sound propelled him onward.

Bogart now had the distance down to ten yards . . . just one final burst and he'd nab Brennan.

That's when Brennan, without warning, threw his shoulder against a door. Bogart felt a rush of colder air as he followed Brennan through the opening; the musty smell was revolting but the coolness was refreshing to his sweaty face. They were in an elongated storage room. The ceiling was low and crawling with water pipes; in the murkiness they resembled entwined snakes. Along the wall, dark with seepage stains, were racks of Shriners' uniforms—what looked to Bogart like marching or band costumes.

Bogart called on his tired body to provide him with more power. He could see Brennan stumble and fall, and clumsily get up again and run on. By God, he thought, now I'll nab him. His heart stammered . . . his legs were not responding . . .

Bogart promised to all the gods who might be listening that he would never touch another cigarette, that he would exercise faithfully every remaining morning of his life.

But the gods must have known that Bogart was a grand liar.

Suddenly he was strangling on his own saliva and the lead weights he knew to be his legs refused to move again. Bogart felt a vicelike grip tighten around his windpipe. There was neither breath nor strength left in him.

He fell forward on his face. As he lay there, his lungs returning to normal, he cursed his smoking and his blatant disregard for his body.

He twisted his head to stare into a portrait photograph hanging from the ceiling on a frayed cord: the Imperial Potentate of Shrine. The middle-aged, bespectacled man looked back with an accusing face.

Bogart grimaced and listened to the diminishing cadence of Brennan's footfalls as they receded into the greater depths of Shrine Auditorium.

THIRTY-THREE

Bogart felt alone on the stage of Shrine Auditorium despite the fuss of activity behind him. Workmen were putting away their tools and the janitor Brennan had knocked down in the lobby was sweeping up sawdust and wood shavings. His sense of isolation was not relieved by the presence of Inspector Fitzgerald, who paced back and forth with cadenced regularity, and Jean Hersholt, who worked a tiny pocket-knife blade over a small piece of oak he was fashioning into the shape of a cross.

Bogart couldn't understand why he felt so alone. Fitzgerald had hardly been lax in responding to Bogart's news that Dalt Brennan was loose in the Catacombs: He had immediately ordered a full-scale search.

With Bogart acting as his personal escort, Fitzgerald had explored the roof, examined the chandelier's interior through a trap door, checked out the projection booth and investigated the Moehler Organ housing unit.

After two hours his special squads were still attempting to reach the farthest regions of the building. So far no one had reported any sign of Brennan.

And that, Bogart decided, was the cause of his desolate feeling.

So he was alone again—still working partially in the dark, still unable to prove conclusively to Fitzgerald just what Dalt Brennan had intended to do.

Bogart studied Fitzgerald's face and saw only the

same misleading cherub smile and rosy, leprechaun cheeks. Fitzgerald leaned over in his unassuming way and borrowed a light from Hersholt. Fitzgerald stopped pacing and came to stand near Bogart's side. "To put your mind at rest, Mr. Bogart, I've done everything you've suggested, plus a few things I thought of myself. I hope you don't mind me taking such liberties."

"I'm just slumming, Inspector. Don't mind me."

Bogart, in defiance of the gods who had refused to help him in the storage room, lit up a Chesterfield. He drew in the smoke deeply and for the first time noticed circles under Fitzgerald's eyes.

"Furthermore, Mr. Bogart," continued Fitzgerald, "I've had a bomb squad sweep over this stage thoroughly."

"That I saw with my own eyes, Inspector."

"Just wanted to make certain you were satisfied. They examined every object and found nothing. Once the main auditorium and Catacombs have been completely searched, I'll feel confident there's no bomb."

"Dalt's hands were empty," said Bogart. "How do we know he didn't plant something *before* I saw him?"

"Everything points to some nefarious activity, of that we can be sure," said Fitzgerald, staring gloomily off across the immense auditorium.

Together they walked slowly out into the main foyer, which was deserted except for one uniformed officer stationed at the doors. "We've already checked the first-aid station," commented Fitzgerald in his attempt to remain one step ahead of Bogart. "Mr. Bogart has some strong points, so, as a precaution, I'm ordering a heavy guard placed around the theater tonight and all day tomorrow, right up to the time of the show. That way, should Mr. Brennan attempt to reenter—"

"It all seems so unnecessary, Inspector," protested Hersholt.

"You might also keep a bomb squad handy tomorrow night," suggested Bogart forcefully.

"My department's thorough, Mr. Bogart. I've already taken the liberty to order such a bomb squad for tomorrow night."

"Really, Inspector," said an incensed Hersholt.

"I'm sure having a few of the boys on the premises won't affect the outcome of your little show tomorrow night, Mr. Hersholt."

"It's hardly a little show, Inspector."

"Jean," said Bogart accusingly, "I think you've taken this whole matter too lightly."

Bogart looked pleadingly at Fitzgerald, who shrugged his shoulders and said to Hersholt: "I can't force you to close the building. It's entirely up to you."

Hersholt spent the next few minutes putting away his pocket knife and studying the curving stem of his pinewood pipe.

The look he gave Bogart was benevolent. "You should have seen the negative mail I received when I played a villain in the last Mr. Moto film with Peter Lorre a few years ago, Bogie. I realized then I had to stop playing villains. Audiences would only accept me as Doctor Christian. Now you're asking me to be a villain again—to stop the most important annual event in Hollywood. To make a decision that would generate adverse publicity all over the world."

That's it, thought Bogart, taking a deep breath. It's

going to be up to me to find Dalt. Fitzgerald was good and his men were good, but he had the sinking sensation that Brennan would remain one step ahead of them.

THIRTY-FOUR

"It's quite impossible, dear Bogie. No one at the academy would discuss the whereabouts of the Oscar statuettes. They're treating it not unlike the Manhattan Project."

Bogart unconsciously twisted his ruby ring while Jamieson elegantly cleared away his uneaten dinner and placed a glass of Drambuie over ice on the table in Dress Circle. He glanced at Lorre, who was wearing a checkered sport coat, unpressed corduroy pants and an azure-blue bow tie adorned with tiny champagne glasses.

"The academy certainly likes to play its little game of secrecy." Lorre reached for one of Bogart's cigarettes and deftly slid it into his ivory holder. "However, I put out some feelers."

"Who got pinched?"

"Oh, some associates of mine. In the Academy of Motion Picture Arts and Sciences. Very high up."

"And were these . . . associates sympathetic?"

"Enough to provide me with information. In this case, *inside* information . . . such as where the Oscars are kept just prior to the presentations."

"Damn, Doc, you got the information!"

"Information! I have an address."

"Toss it over, Doc."

Lorre complied.

"What about security?" asked Bogart.

"According to my associates, very light. And what about you? What did you run into?"

"Dalt Brennan. Literally."

Lorre froze, the cigarette halfway to his lips. "You found Dalt? Actually found him?"

"Found him and lost him—all in the space of five minutes." Bogart told Lorre everything that had happened. Lorre listened, smoking his cigarette thoughtfully.

"Fitzgerald sounds like he's softening," said Lorre.

"Like margarine on an iceberg. Doc, we've only got about twenty-four hours to wrap this up."

They sat in silence. Lorre kept glancing toward the bar, where Romanoff stood alone, ignoring the customers around him. Clutching the holder between his teeth, Lorre said, "Have you noticed the good prince lately?"

"Unless he's buying the drinks, I'd rather ignore him."

Lorre tapped away another quarter-inch of ash. "He seems quite—how shall I describe it—nervous, apprehensive."

"Maybe the loan company is foreclosing on the joint."

"The prince has been standing there, almost in the same pose as his graphic caricature, for the last few minutes. I would say that he has a task to carry out that leaves him feeling uncomfortable."

"Maybe business is so bad he has to start busing tables with the rest of the cheap help."

Bogart stole an investigative glance at Romanoff. The restaurateur was stroking his mustache as he leaned against the black leather bar. After a moment he shot his cuffs.

Bogart leaned back. "Get that, with the cuffs. He'll be here in about five seconds."

Lorre lifted an appreciative eyebrow.

Bogart stared down into his Drambuie. Five seconds later he heard a throat being cleared and looked up to see Romanoff two feet from the table, straightening his tie nervously.

"Come on, Mike, spill it. Something's been eating you for the last few minutes."

"It concerns a matter of trust, old friend," said Romanoff.

"Here it comes, Doc." Bogart winked at Lorre. "The old 'Mister, can you spare a dry shoulder, a sympathetic ear or a hundred bucks.' "

Romanoff rose up on the heels of his patent leathers and peered down his nose at Bogart. "Come, come, Bogie, surely I'd wait for a more propitious moment than this for such mundanities."

"So I'm sorry if I offended you, Prince. Had I known it was this serious I'd have consulted my banker."

Romanoff leaned forward and darted his eyes surreptitiously back and forth. "This is a . . . delicate matter. I must have your implicit trust."

"Didn't I give that to you once? As I recall, you forgot to return it. Prince, if I can't trust you, who can I trust?"

Romanoff looked mildly relieved. "I'm sure you won't regret your decision."

"No doubt I'll hate myself in the morning."

"There are two . . . gentlemen outside who . . . well, they wish to see you. They'd like to take you with them."

"Take me? You mean for a ride, Prince?"

Romanoff stepped back imperiously, gesturing toward the entrance. "Two-way, I guarantee you . . . Please." His tone was deliberate, not pleading.

Bogart climbed out of the booth. "Take care of things, Doc. I'll call you tomorrow . . . if I'm still around. If I don't come back, you inherit this booth."

Bogart paused at the entrance as Jamieson personally retrieved his trench coat and hat. Bogart stepped outside. A gust of wind whipped his coat as he pulled the hat down tightly, snapping the brim with his fingers.

He took six steps and stopped. He clenched his hands into fists and felt the blood race to his face.

A black prewar Packard limousine was at the curb, waiting.

There were two men stationed on each side of the entrance to Romanoff's. The man on the right was taller by a few inches, very lean, with a beak nose and sharp gray eyes. He wore a black homburg, a tuxedo with a glossy bow tie, a ruffled blue shirt and a heavy, dark overcoat. The man on Bogart's left was stocky and muscular, with slick black hair and hooded snakelike eyes. He wore light tan slacks, a checked racetrack-tout's sport coat, a white shirt and a purple tie, decorated with a hand-painted hula-hula girl.

"Hello, Mr. Bogart," said the man on the right, a cheerfulness in his gruff voice. "You're looking good these days."

"It's the makeup I use."

"He's a great kidder, isn't he, Fenner?" To Bogart: "We'd like to request that you come along with us on a little errand, Mr. Bogart."

The man named Fenner scowled, his eyes raking Bogart. "Sometimes Morgan's a little too polite for his own good. We're not asking you to get in the car— we're tellin' you."

"Yeah," said Morgan, holding open the back door of the Packard. "It's kinda like a request, sorta."

Bogart nodded and slid into the backseat. Morgan jumped into the front passenger seat and Fenner took command of the wheel. The massive car lumbered from the curb. Bogart's glance through the narrow oval rear window showed Romanoff watching from the brick entrance. He bowed slightly toward the car, then flitted back inside.

Bogart examined the car's interior. The door panels were unusually thick and the slight amber tint of the windows told him the car was bulletproof.

Morgan squirmed around, taking off his homburg and smoothing the crown, just as Bogart lit a cigarette.

"Gee, you do that, with the cigarette, and it's just like we was right back seeing *The Roaring Twenties*, you and Cagney together shooting the crap out of those cops. That's a very distinctive touch you got with cigarettes."

"Yeah, it's something I learned from a trained chimpanzee when I made my one and only jungle picture."

Morgan laughed. "Hey, didn't I tell you he's a kidder, Fenner?"

Fenner kept pushing the Packard along the streets of Beverly Hills, indifferent to Bogart's presence.

"Would you mind telling me what's going on?" asked Bogart.

"Yeah, we do mind," snarled Fenner.

"Hey, don't be so rude to Mr. Bogart." Morgan tipped back his homburg, reached into the gray pockets of the door and removed an embossed book, which he flipped open. "Look, Mr. Bogart, we'd love to have you sign the book. Fenner'n me can say we actually talked to you. Whatta ya say?"

Bogart signed the autograph book with Morgan's fountain pen. "You two guys have been following me, right?"

Morgan chuckled. "Sure."

"Why?"

"We got orders."

"Whose orders?"

"The boss."

Naturally, he should have known. *The boss.*

"We was looking after you, Mr. Bogart. We couldn't take any chances of losing you. I coulda done without Forest Lawn—funerals get me nervous. We even followed you to La Jawla. If we'da lost you, the boss woulda been very upset."

"Yeah, upset," snarled Fenner, passing a DeSoto cab.

"Say," asked Bogart, "did you fellas drop by my place last night and rearrange the furniture?"

"Gee, no, Mr. Bogart. One thing we ain't is yeggs." Morgan turned to look Bogart fully in the face. "After all, we got respect for you, Mr. Bogart. I mean, I really thought you was perfect in *Bullets or Ballots* and *Black Legion.* Ah, then you hadda go and be the good guy, like that dick in *The Maltese Falcon.* I liked it better when you was the hard guy in the rackets."

Bogart watched the traffic sliding by, headlights illuminating the limousine's interior. The Packard was traveling east on Sunset, toward the Hollywood Hills.

"Hey," asked Morgan, "how come you don't seem tough, like in the pitchers?"

"All that tough-guy stuff is for the cameras," replied Bogart. "I found out that if you think about something hard enough, that's all you need. If you feel tough, you'll look tough. Feeling is everything."

"Hey, yeah, I get it. What about dying? How do you make it look so real?"

"Dying? Dying is easy . . . in the movies. You have to know how to grunt and clutch your stomach."

"That makes a lot of sense," said Morgan. "I could

show some of those creeps how tough guys really act and talk."

"So you want to be an actor?"

Morgan nodded. "Hell, I know my stuff."

"Okay, Morgan, remember this. The audience is always ahead of you. If someone points a gun at your gut, the audience knows you're afraid; you don't have to make a face or pull back . . . Just believe you're the person you're playing and it'll come across as being authentic."

"Hey, thanks for the advice, Mr. Bogart. I'll remember it."

"You oughta shut up, Morgan," said Fenner. "You really talk too much, you know that, Morgan?"

"You oughta mind your manners around Mr. Bogart."

Bogart noticed they were passing along a high granite wall. Fenner drove into a road flanked by tall, gray stone pillars and a pair of massive gates, which opened as the Packard broke the electric eye.

The road was dark, overshadowed by tall trees. They passed a gate lodge with a sentry in front, holding a rifle at port arms. The Packard drove over an arched bridge that spanned a man-made waterfall. Ahead was the enormous silhouette of a large, fortresslike mansion.

Tall, narrow windows glowed throughout the mansion, and Bogart could see that they were barred. The corners of the structure were round bulges, like a medieval castle, rising to gabled turrets.

Fenner braked and stopped in front of the mansion.

Morgan looked up at the colonnaded loggia as a slash of light from the entrance vestibule lit up the columns. Then a dark shape came down the curving front steps carrying a briefcase. He paused briefly at one of the large flower pots, snapped off a carnation and slid it into his lapel. The light streaming from behind the man edged his hair in silver.

Morgan held the back door open as the man climbed into the car, unfolded the vicuña coat draped over his arm and scrutinized Bogart.

"I'm Arnold Grasselli," he said in a deep baritone with an accent that was unmistakably Chicagoan. Grasselli extended his hand. Bogart accepted it.

Now Bogart realized the mansion was Black Friars, and he knew that Grasselli was one of the underworld racket kings of Los Angeles.

Grasselli was a shade over six feet, in his mid-fifties, with gray hair. His clothing was marvelously tailored: a gray pinstripe suit with the carnation in the lapel. Grasselli regarded Bogart with deep black eyes which peered over a nose that looked as though it had been broken several times.

When Grasselli nodded, Fenner pointed the Packard down the curving drive.

Grasselli placed his hands together, fingers overlapping. His dark eyes never left Bogart. "I apologize for having to meet like this, but this was the most opportune time. Tomorrow would be too late, wouldn't it?"

"That depends on what time tomorrow. Morning or afternoon would be fine. Evening—that might be too late."

"Yes, I was hoping you'd be smart. You're very much like the characters you portray, Mr. Bogart." Grasselli smiled, his teeth white and gleaming against the tanned face. "I'm an admirer of yours. Perhaps because I see in you a man who has portrayed special kinds of men I've known. In the past, of course."

"Of course. I wouldn't want to think that you habitually hang around with the wrong crowd."

Grasselli laughed softly and ordered Fenner to take Beverly Drive, then Pico. Morgan pretended to stare straight ahead.

"I don't think you dragged me out of Romanoff's just to ask me for my autograph. Or did you?"

Grasselli chuckled again and, when Bogart came up with an empty cigarette pack, produced a gold case and offered one of his own cigarettes to Bogart. Bogart lit up, inhaled and settled back into the seat.

"I admire your talent; I gain great enjoyment from your films and I want to see you to continue to star in them. When Mike—Romanoff—came to see me the other day and told me about the affair that was occupying so much of your time, I decided to step in."

"You sound like you're worried about my health."

"Precisely."

"Guardian angel . . . that's a strange kind of role for these two friends of yours, isn't it?"

"Ever since the car tried to run you off the road, I've had you under their surveillance. The best protection in Los Angeles, wouldn't you agree?"

"I'd be crazy to disagree. No doubt you figure I'm out of my league."

Grasselli shook his head. "Mike has kept us informed. What *you* don't realize is that Brennan is not working alone. There is another element."

"I figured that," said Bogart. "There were too many questions that didn't make sense."

Grasselli gave Bogart an appreciative look. "There is another factor. The nature of our business requires a symbiotic relationship with the police department. Just as the police deem it necessary to have various stool pigeons, I realized long ago that it made good sense to do likewise. From our pipeline into the department, we've learned that the police consider the death of Lloyd Brennan to be murder."

There was a silence.

Bogart tugged throughtfully at his earlobe. No wonder he had noticed a twinkle in Fitzgerald's eye back at the Plantation. He gazèd out the window as the car carried its passengers farther and farther into deeply fog shrouded streets. They were headed west, Bogart judged. Ocean fog—wet and clammy.

"That's hot information to be getting from the police," Bogart said finally. "Why didn't Fitzgerald let me know?"

"As far as Fitzgerald's concerned, your only connection with the case is Dalt Brennan."

"What about Fabrini's murder?"

Grasselli shrugged. "Committed by the same person. A bit clumsy, not like the murders of Lloyd Brennan and Martha Pearce."

Fenner turned to Grasselli. "Fog's getting thick, boss." He slowed for a light at Barrington and turned on the windshield wipers.

Bogart watched the landscape, which changed gradually to empty fields. He realized they were getting closer to the coast. Isolated lamps wore a corona of light that glowed eerily in the fog.

Fenner slowed the Packard for a left turn onto Centinela Boulevard. Less than a hundred yards away, on the right, a flashing beacon slashed through the mist. A large wooden sign came into view:

CLOVER FIELD

HOME OF DOUGLAS AIRCRAFT

Past the sign, Fenner turned right and the road dipped downward, following the edges of a large, grassy field. Fenner followed the road for another quarter of a mile, then turned right again.

Grasselli picked up the briefcase from the floor, checked the brass clasp, then folded the vicuña overcoat on his arm.

The car stopped. Morgan opened the rear door and Grasselli stepped out onto the wet tarmac.

Bogart saw nothing but obediently followed the trio. Somewhere ahead an invisible aircraft sent out guttural warnings from its exhaust. Into Bogart's view came dots of runway lights. The slashing beacon came and went with regularity. Bogart felt the chill and the damp seeping through his trench coat. He pulled it tighter and jammed his hands deeper into the pockets.

They walked up a short flight of concrete steps, past empty gun emplacements, long abandoned since the fear of a Japanese sneak attack had become history.

Bogart stepped closer to Grasselli. "It makes sense now. Dalt didn't kill anybody, not Johnny Hawks, not Martha Pearce, not Paul Fabrini, and least of all his brother. He's been deliberately pushed over the edge. That means that someone else is behind the attempt to blow up the Academy Awards."

Bright lights on the edge of wing tips moved jerkily over the asphalt runway. Whirling mist spun off twin propeller discs. The DC-3 moved ponderously forward, its high nose coming toward them out of the fog. Slowly, with an increased roar of its engines, it turned sideways and became a dark-silver silhouette.

The plane stopped, its large tires glistening wetly under the engine nacelles. A door opened in the side and a figure waved.

Fenner and Morgan pushed a small metal step-ramp toward the door. Bogart and Grasselli followed behind.

"I can tell you another thing, Mr. Bogart," said Grasselli, pausing at the foot of the steps. "The Los Angeles Police think the deaths of Lloyd Brennan and Martha Pearce are connected."

"So," mused Bogart. "The key must be Dalt. Or Saints and Sinners."

Grasselli nodded, studying Bogart's face carefully. "Fitzgerald is giving the sanitarium the once-over. Accounts, incorporation papers, everything. Of course, that all takes time."

Bogart's face quickly changed. "Quesne! He's the link between Dalt and Saints and Sinners. I overlooked the obvious—collusion between Quesne and Pearce."

A figure moved in the DC-3 doorway and gestured at Grasselli. He mounted the bottom step, turned and shook hands with Bogart, shouting above the roar of the engine. "Wherever your lead takes you, Fenner and Morgan are at your complete disposal."

Bogart clutched his hat, hunching his back against the propeller blast. "I'll need your boys tonight," he yelled. "I'm busting into the warehouse where they keep the Oscars."

"Busting in?" repeated Grasselli. "Breaking and entering? Be careful of the company you keep, Mr. Bogart. It's starting to rub off." He hurried up the ramp and the door closed.

The DC-3 taxied up the runway. There was the powerful roar of motors at full revolutions. The plane trundled to the far edge of the field.

Bogart's brain whirled giddily with ideas. Quesne had directed Dalt to Saints and Sinners. Who had sent Dalt to Quesne? Geoffrey Carroll had claimed Dalt picked his own doctor . . . but he had only Geoffrey's word for that.

Geoffrey Carroll . . . was it possible he had killed Lloyd Brennan in a fit of jealous passion? Over another lover, perhaps? And had he been instrumental in pushing Dalt closer to madness? But to what end? Why would Carroll manipulate Dalt to carry out *Hollywood Armageddon?*

Was it possible that the other deaths had been the backwash of Lloyd's murder? Geoffrey Carroll cleaning up the loose ends? If so, that meant Dalt had been working entirely on his own. Simply a by-product Carroll hadn't counted on. Maybe . . .

The engines roared. A dim silver shape streaked past them. In another ten seconds the DC-3 and Grasselli were gone.

Bogart watched with his hands jammed into the pockets of his trench coat, his mind jammed into pockets of thought. What had Geoffrey stood to gain from Lloyd's death? The Topanga Beach house, for one. And all of Lloyd's literary properties. What about the inheritance from future royalties? Had Geoffrey withheld the choicest of Lloyd's material before shipping it to Raymond Chandler? Geoffrey could have easily salted the Communist literature into the boxes. Had he also salted the Columbia files?

Another confrontation with Dr. Quesne was in order. And a little talk with Geoffrey Carroll. Fenner and Morgan were going to have a busy time keeping tabs on him.

Finally they turned together and walked back toward the Packard, Bogart protectively wedged between the two big men. "Boys, I have a little job for you this evening."

Bogart draped an arm over Morgan's shoulder, ig-

noring the scowl on Fenner's face. As they were swallowed up by the fog, Bogart's voice became muted.

"Mr. Morgan, I think this is the beginning of a
beautiful relationship."

THIRTY-FIVE

"I don't like this," protested Fenner. "I don't like behaving like some two-bit second-story man."

"Shut up," said Morgan. "The boss says we help Bogart, we help Bogart."

It was an anonymous warehouse on one of the many side streets honeycombing the industrial area south of Hollywood and Vine, and it was suitably dark and deserted when Fenner and Morgan led Bogart around to the side.

Bogart crouched in the dim shadows, feeling naked and vulnerable. Morgan stooped to pick up a rock to smash in a small window over the employees' entrance. He turned to heave the rock but stopped mid-throw. "Hey, look at this."

"Yeah," said Fenner, "it's already busted." He reached through the opening and fumbled in the darkness. "And someone's already unfastened the latch."

Following Fenner's professional example, Bogart worked his way through the window, taking care not to slice his hands on the jagged edges. He saw dark stains on the ledge and paused. "Someone nicked himself coming through. This blood is still fresh."

Bogart cringed as his feet crunched on the shards scattered over the floor.

"Who do you suppose busted in ahead of us?" asked Morgan, dropping down next to Bogart.

"Keep your voice down," whispered Bogart.

They moved cautiously forward, staying only an arm's length apart. The unnerving silence enveloping the empty building seemed to be shattered by their every movement. After a moment Bogart's eyes adjusted to the darkness and he could discern high concrete walls, a ceiling crisscrossed with rusting water pipes and heaps of stacked bundles in the central storage area. Moonlight streaming through the high, barred windows illuminated the bundles and cast lengthy shadows that stretched across the cement floor and up the walls.

Aided by Morgan's baby flashlight, they weaved a path through the erratically stacked bundles. Morgan's beam raked across the top of one of them, revealing a four-color movie poster of Lizabeth Scott in *I Walk Alone*. Morgan whistled appreciatively.

Each of the stacks contained one-sheets for forthcoming motion pictures. Roy Rogers in *The Gay Ranchero*, Gary Cooper in *Unconquered*.

Lizabeth Scott groaned.

At least that's what Bogart thought until Morgan swung his light to the floor and centered the beam on the prostrate form of an old man in a security-guard uniform. Bogart dropped to his knees and examined the bloody spot on the unconscious man's forehead. "He's been sapped," said Bogart. "And he hasn't been out long."

"I gota feeling someone is still in here," whispered Fenner. "Hey, Morgan, you got a rod?"

"A rod? Are you kiddin'? I haven't packed a rod since we blew Chicago."

With greater caution they continued to explore the area around the bundles, but found only piles of lobby cards and production stills of Dennis O'Keefe in *T-Men*.

"Maybe," whispered Bogart, "we should be looking for some kind of office."

"Stick with me," Morgan whispered back. "I got a nose for this sort of thing."

As though following a scent, Morgan bloodhounded his way around *Black Bart* posters. Finally they came to a glass door with Manager stenciled on it in bold black letters.

Dutifully Morgan bent down to pick the lock, but the instant he put pressure on the knob, the door swung open with a squeak. "Someone already did the job for us," he told Bogart, flashing his light into the office and illuminating a photograph on the wall of Shirley Temple presenting Walt Disney with an Oscar.

The three of them stepped into the office quickly. Morgan swept his flashlight from wall to wall, object to object. "Whoever it was has already cleared out," said Morgan in a normal voice.

Bogart snapped on an overhead bulb covered with a green shade. For a moment the dangling string cast its shadow eerily across the room. Morgan whistled. Each wall was plastered from ceiling to floor with movie memorabilia. Photographs of stars receiving Academy Awards; dinner-party scenes; premieres at Grauman's Chinese Theatre. The far wall was devoted to one-sheets of the Best Pictures of the Year beginning with *Wings* in 1928 and carrying through to *The Best Years of Our Lives* in 1947.

But there was something wrong with the 1943 *Casablanca* poster in the center of the wall. Instead of being flat, the wall there protruded slightly. Bogart walked to it and touched Ingrid Bergman on the forehead. A panel already partially ajar swung the rest of the way open to reveal a six-foot-deep walk-in vault.

For a moment Bogart, Morgan and Fenner were blinded.

The vault's interior was painted a brilliant golden

color, and arranged on a bronzed table in the center of the room were several rows of Oscars. Three of them were lying on their sides, as though someone had knocked them over.

"Ever see anything like that in your miserable life, Fenner?" asked Morgan, snapping his fingers. "Think what those little pieces of metal're gonna mean to the winners."

"They don't look valuable to me." Fenner sounded cynical and looked cynical.

"I'll tell you how much they're worth," said Bogart. "Seventy-five bucks apiece."

"You're kidding, right, Mr. Bogart?" In the golden light Bogart could see Morgan's face dropping like box-office receipts.

Fenner sneered. "He's a kidder, remember, Morgan?"

"Take a look for yourself," said Bogart. "An expressionless golden boy with a heart of zinc and a body to match. Just a pinch of antimony and a trace of copper and eighteen-karat gold plating. A pawn shop wouldn't even give you the full seventy-five clams." He paused, enjoying the effect his words were having on Morgan. "Of course, I wouldn't want to destroy your ideals, boys. They *can* be worth millions to the man who owns one."

Morgan stepped to the dazzling table, reaching for the nearest Oscar. "I don't think anyone would mind if I just touched one of these—"

"I wouldn't touch that," said Bogart, "unless you'd like to see yourself spread all over this warehouse."

Morgan jerked his hand back. "Kidding again, right, Mr. Bogart?"

"Mr. Morgan, I've never been more serious in my

life. If I know *my* business, those things have been booby-trapped by whoever broke in ahead of us."

Fenner unconsciously maneuvered backward. "Hey, the boss didn't say anything about us getting ourselves blown up."

"Yeah, this is a wrinkle you didn't tell us about, Mr. Bogart."

"This town is full of wrinkles you never see," said Bogart. "One actress in particular. But then, I wouldn't ask you boys to do anything I wouldn't do." Bogart strolled casually to the table, stared at one of the Oscars for twenty seconds, then slowly reached out, gently placed his fingers around the body and lifted it up an inch at a time. He carried the statuette beneath the golden light and examined it. "Looks to me like the base plate screws into the main body. If I give it a slight twist . . ."

No one in the vault moved as Bogart began to inch the base plate counterclockwise. After a few gentle twists the base plate separated from the body of the Oscar. Bogart looked down into its hollow center and could see nothing. He rethreaded the two pieces and returned the Oscar to the table.

Without speaking, Morgan stepped up and selected one of the Oscars, duplicating Bogart's procedure—and care. He too found nothing. "Maybe you got a false alarm, Mr. Bogart," he said.

"Yeah," said Fenner, still scowling as he picked up one of the overturned Oscars and began twisting the base plate. "I think maybe you guys are—"

Bogart grasped Fenner's wrist so that the piece of plastic explosive lodged into the hollowed-out base wouldn't drop to the floor. "Just screw it together and put it back on the table," said Bogart firmly. His eyes wide, his lips parted in dismay, Fenner did as he was told.

Bogart respectfully picked up the second overturned Oscar and meticulously removed the base to find an identical piece of plastic explosive. He returned the Oscar to the table. "It's my guess," he said, "that only the overturned Oscars have been rigged."

"Yeah," agreed Morgan, "he musta done that so he could keep track. And he'd still be here rigging them, only we come along."

Bogart put a finger to his lips and motioned them out of the vault. Back in the office, Bogart pulled the string of the light and the room fell into darkness. Bogart had just reached the door when he heard a thud—one blunt object coming in contact with another. "Our pal is still out there," whispered Bogart. "Split up and see if you can nail him before he scrams out of here."

Back in the storage area Bogart found himself working his way along a row of cardboard boxes with *Angel of the Amazon* posters on them. The familiar face of Vera Ralston smiled enticingly at him.

Then her lips were drawing nearer to his and Bogart realized that someone on the other side of the aisle was pushing against the boxes. He sprinted away as the pile came toppling down. Vera's lips met only cold cement. He heard Morgan shouting and he could hear the echoing footsteps of someone running.

"He's breaking for the door." Fenner's voice came booming from the next aisle.

Bogart burst around the end of the aisle, crashing headlong into a running figure. They went down together and instantly came up together, ready to fight it out. Bogart lowered his fists. It was Fenner, angrily brushing dust off his sleeve. "Shit, he's getting away." Together they began to race for the door.

A feeble but threatening voice came from behind them. "Stop. Stop or I'll shoot."

"Christ," muttered Fenner, whirling. "It's the watchman. He ain't dozing no more."

Bogart and Fenner stopped and raised their hands.

The old man staggered out from behind a pile of bundles, holding a .38 revolver in one hand and clutching his head with the other. He took a fumbling step forward, then was buried in a pile of *Miracle of the Bells* bundles as they toppled onto him. Morgan hurried from the other side of the aisle and they all rushed out to the street.

They searched in both directions but saw nothing. "Looks like he got away clean," said Morgan. "Maybe if we cruise the neighbor—"

A dark-blue Buick came roaring out of an alleyway and sped past them. A Buick Roadmaster with a crumpled right fender.

"Give me the keys, quick," Bogart ordered. "I'm going to catch that sonofabitch myself."

"Christ." Fenner handed the key ring to Bogart, who leaped into the front seat and brought the Packard to instant life. Fenner and Morgan had barely jumped in when the powerful car leaped from the curb.

Bogart challenged the nearest intersection on two wheels. Morgan, in the front seat with Bogart, clutched the safety strap as the car accelerated. In the back seat Fenner clutched his strap just as avidly.

"That Buick's the same car that tried to run me off the road."

"So catch the bastard," said Fenner defiantly.

Bogart took another intersection with all wheels screaming in protest. "That was nice," said Morgan admiringly. "Just like the way you did it in *High Sierra*."

Bogart didn't tell Morgan that all the driving in *High Sierra* had been performed by one of Hollywood's finest stunt drivers. Bogart was intent on only one thing: catching the sonofabitch at the wheel of the sedan and getting the truth out of him. Beating it out, if necessary.

The Packard followed the dark-blue sedan down Fairfax, running a red light as it crossed Sunset, and sending several pedestrians scurrying at Hollywood Boulevard.

It was then that Bogart heard the police siren and saw a patrol car in swift pursuit.

"Don't look so worried," said Fenner. "You got three, maybe four blocks on that cop."

"Goddamn it," shouted Bogart, "I want that sedan. How'm I going to lose that cop?"

"You oughta know," said Morgan. "You've outrun a lot of cops, Mr. Bogart."

Swiftly Bogart negotiated some sharp curves leading into the Hollywood Hills. But so did the squad car, its siren grating on Bogart's nerves.

"Just like in *The Big Shot*, remember, Mr. Bogart? You and the girl, taking that mountain road with the motorcycle cop hot on your tail. And you kept going a hundred miles an hour."

Bogart didn't bother to tell Morgan that the camera had been undercranked and the car moving only twenty-five miles an hour.

The dark-blue sedan maintained its narrow lead, showing an expertness in taking the tortuous turns. It started up a winding two-lane road that led into the foothills overlooking Hollywood, the beams of the headlights caressing the curves.

Bogart pounded the steering wheel, frustrated that he could move no faster. He glanced back to see the headlights of the police car gaining. He stomped on the accelerator and overtook a slow-moving Oldsmobile Futuramic; Bogart worked his way back to the right, narrowly avoiding a crash with an oncoming Studebaker convertible.

The Buick reached the top of the grade and dropped out of sight as it began a plunging descent. Moments later Bogart reached the crest, the Packard sailing off the road and returning to the asphalt with a crash that sent Morgan's head to the ceiling. As the sedan wound along the circuitous road, passing under a street light, Bogart could see smoke curling off the tires. Morgan, rubbing his head, rolled down his window and leaned his elbow through the opening, whistling "The Best Things in Life Are Free." The Packard's speed increased on the incline; so did Fenner's grip on the safety strap.

As the Packard went into a sharp curve, Bogart eased his foot on the brake to reduce speed slightly. The car maintained its plunging descent. Bogart hit the brake harder. No response.

Bogart shot a glance at Morgan. "I think the brakes have given out." He pumped the pedal frantically. "Hell, I *know* they've given out."

Morgan knocked a speck of lint from the lapel of his suit. "All the quicker we'll catch that sedan and lose the flatfoot." He calmly unwrapped a stick of Juicy Fruit and shoved it into his mouth.

"Hey," said Fenner, coming forward from the backseat, "what if Bogart can't hold the road?"

"I never heard of a road or a dame he couldn't hold," said Morgan, gnashing his teeth.

Bogart's mouth was grimly set as the Packard whistled down the incline, barely hugging the road on the sharper bends.

For an instant, *déjà vu* swept over Bogart. During the filming of *They Drive By Night* in 1940, he had been riding in a truck when suddenly the brakes had gone out. George Raft had been at the wheel and, thanks to his cool head, he had brought the runaway to a stop by charging up an embankment.

It wasn't going to be that easy here. The hillside sloped into the road at steep angles.

His mind turning numb, Bogart watched the strip of white ribbon streak beneath the Packard's underbelly and prayed the road would soon level out.

If anything, the angle of descent increased.

The Packard began to sway. For greater maneuverability, Bogart crossed to the opposite side of the road at each sharp bend. Tires screeched on the curves; gravel spit from beneath the churning treads. The police car had dropped behind, and the Packard was gaining on the Buick. There was now less than a hundred yards between the cars.

Yards of gravel spewed into a culvert as the Packard barely clung to the asphalt during a hairpin contortion. Bogart could sense Fenner tensing behind him. Morgan remained strangely calm, chewing his gum energetically. Apparently he had full confidence in Bogart's driving.

Bogart swept both sides of the roadway, searching for a way of escape. Then to the left, halfway through a hair-raising, serpentine series of bends, he saw a wide dirt road that climbed into the foothills. He made his decision in a split second and cried, "Hang on tight," hunching closer to the wheel. It meant losing the sedan, but it might mean saving their necks.

As they came abreast of the turnoff, Bogart twisted the wheel sharply to the left. The rear of the Packard, tires squealing forlornly, swung almost completely about, so the hood was now pointed uphill and the car was sliding across the center line toward the hillside.

A Van Nuys laundry van came lumbering up the highway. Its driver saw the Packard rushing at him tail-first and froze at the wheel, waiting to die.

Not Bogart. He accelerated against the downward gravitational pull, stabilizing the wheel and preventing the car from fishtailing.

He prayed.

His eyes were wide open and yet he had the impression of a kaleidoscope of flashes—streaks of moving darkness, pools of white brilliance that were the headlights of the oncoming van. The world was whirling insanely in circles around him—it was a carrousel of fury and he was trapped in its catalytic core.

The Packard slid off the road. The trunk slammed against the hillside and the car came to a dead stop, shuddering one last time against the impact. The laundry van, its driver in a near state of shock, streaked safely past.

Bogart gunned the engine, dropped back into first and shot onto the road directly behind the van. He immediately swung onto the wide dirt road branching to the right.

Bogart swallowed the fear in his throat and kept his eyes on the road as the Packard, at high speed, clung to the uphill ruts, spewing gravel.

Bogart coasted behind a copse of sycamores and, with the hood pointed toward the top of the hill, shut

off the engine and headlights. The car rolled bliss-
fully to a stop. Bogart ripped on the emergency hand
brake when the Packard started to roll backward. The
hand brake held. Bogart sighed.

From below came the siren of the police car as it
proceeded past the turnoff and continued down into
the San Fernando Valley.

"I gotta phone here in the car," said Morgan, offering Bogart a cigarette. "I'll call some of the boys and
have 'em pick us up."

Bogart's hands were shaking slightly when he lit up.
He could still see the curves of the road whipping
past him; he still felt the falling sensation in the pit of
his stomach and the kaleidoscope of light, sound and
fury.

Fenner leaned over the front seat. For the first time
Bogart saw a smile on his face. He winked one eye
and said, "Nice driving, pal." He sat back and allowed
the sullenness to return to his face.

"Inspector?"

"Ah, Mr. Bogart. Should I consider this an honor?"

"Better get your bomb squad over to the warehouse
at Melrose and Fairfax where the academy stores the
awards. You'll find at least three of them rigged with
plastic explosives."

"Will I now? It would seem you and Mr. Cohn were
right all along. This should put everyone at rest, the
threat against the academy having been removed."

"It looks that way, but it doesn't explain why Dalt
was in Shrine Auditorium this afternoon."

"An astute observation. Shall I meet you—"

"I get nervous around Oscars, rigged or not. I've got
something else to do tonight."

"Ah, to be sure, a very busy man you are. May I ask what this nocturnal errand might be?"

"It's just a hunch I'm playing. And it takes me back to Saints and Sinners one more time."

THIRTY-SIX

Saints and Sinners remained shrouded in fog. The beam of the Cadillac's headlights whipped across the manicured grounds, across its mist-covered lakes and finally onto a copse of eucalyptus. A streak of white and black suddenly crossed in front of Bogart's car.

Bogart hit the brakes; the car lurched to a stop. A leering face was sizing him up from behind the trunk of a thick eucalyptus. A hand inched into view and beckoned at Bogart with a bent, gnarled finger. Mist curled behind the tree just as the figure stepped out into the beam of the headlights.

Bogart's heart leaped as the ghostlike figure charged the Cadillac. In the next instant his thumping heart relaxed; it was Jimmy Leonard, wearing the Chaplin costume and savoring that split second he had sent Bogart's heart racing.

"Charlie" danced a jig of pantomime, concluding it with a click of his heels. Charlie cocked his head acutely, resembling a dog that has heard a faraway train. Bogart stepped out onto the gravel roadway.

"Out a bit late, aren't you, Charlie?"

"Man's gotta rehearse with nature to find he's got a nature to rehearse with." Charlie chuckled at his own double-talk. "Studio grounds're open to me, anytime I need 'em."

"Seen the black car, Charlie?"

"I see a lotta jalopies. Some green, some red."

"I'm talking about the car that came to visit Dalt."

"Dalt? Dalt! He's an old friend. He musta got some bookings back East 'cause I haven't seen him for a . . .

a few days. Sometimes . . . sometimes that'll happen in show biz—you get busy, you don't have time to call. Car? Black car? Don't know what you're talking about."

"Sure you do, Charlie. Came up behind the sani—the studio. You were eavesdropping."

"*That* black car. You should specify which car, young man. Never hurts to be precise in this profession. Precision is what the public expects. Never saw their faces. Just Dalt talking."

"*Their* faces."

"New faces, that's what show biz is all about, young fella." Charlie chortled and fluttered like an agitated sparrow, a routine he concluded by taking off one of his sagging leather boots and pantomiming a bite into the sole. "Sure, two faces. Couldn't see either. Couldn't see either."

"There was a second man . . ."

"One thing about me, sonny, I can count. Played a count once who fell onto a conveyor belt. One and one is true. That's real counting. Everything counts in this business, young fella . . . only you ain't so young anymore, hey."

"You're telling me, Pop."

"Have I seen you somewhere before?"

"Only in the movies. Think about the car . . . the people . . . could you hear anything?"

"Comedy scenario plot, that's all. Comedy about Oscars. Slapstick business about a bomb. *Hollywood Armageddon* . . . needs a funnier title. That's the film I'm going to do, you know. Got a big part. Dalt promised me. Hey, did you say you're in pictures?"

"Charlie? Charlie, you get inside this instant."

It was the voice of Josephine Rossi, and she came storming across the lawn with an arrogant stride. She slowed when she recognized Bogart standing in the beam of the headlights. "Oh, Mr. Bogart, you startled me."

"Hello, Miss Rossi. Charlie and I were just having a chat."

"At this time of night?"

"Charlie's a busy man. You take an appointment when you can get it."

"Right now Charlie has an appointment inside. Movies, Charlie."

"Movies? Hot damn!" Charlie leaped into the air. He twirled his cane and danced around the eucalyptus.

> *Movies, movies, I love pitchers,*
> *Populated by star hitchers.*
> *Funny, funny, laugh, laugh,*
> *Charlie's the greatest with his walking staff.*

Josephine took him sternly by the hand and led him across the lawn toward the fog-shrouded sanitarium. Bogart followed their figures into the mist. Once again the house struck Bogart as an ominous, looming relic of a previous time.

Josephine beckoned him to follow her through the main entrance into a small auditorium. The middle of the room was filled with rows of folding chairs and in the back was a 16-millimeter projector pointed at a large, white screen.

"Every Friday night," explained Josephine, guiding Charlie into a chair, "we show films, at least to those who aren't bedridden."

"What kind of films?" asked Bogart.

"Oh, ones donated by studios and producers. Martha knew so many people in the business. It was their way of helping her through the difficult years. We have such a variety that each week we see something different."

"Cartoons," proclaimed Charlie, jumping from his seat. "Full-length features, short subjects, previews of coming attractions." Charlie lapsed again into a childish outburst and danced circles around Bogart. "I want the Dalt Brennan film," he chanted over and over. "Just before the final fade/Dalt will throw a big grenade."

"I never knew Dalt was an actor," said Bogart.

"Boom," cried Charlie, ducking toward the floor as he simulated explosions going off around him. "Just before the final fade/Dalt will throw a big grenade." Invisible objects leaped from his fingers as his arm unwound.

Josephine looked annoyed and explained, "When Mr. Brennan first came here, he donated an old training film. Made during the war, I recall."

"I'd like to take a look at it, if that's okay with you."

"I can't imagine why. It's a dreary little film. Not the sort of thing to show our guests. But I don't see why you shouldn't."

In a storage room off the main corridor, Bogart searched through stacks of films. Charlie stood behind him, continuing to throw invisible objects and ducking as they "exploded."

Bogart knew he had found what he was looking for when he saw the label on the can: *Anatomy of a Hand Grenade*. The can also carried the emblem of the U.S. Marine Corps.

Josephine began to voice objections when Bogart unthreaded a Mighty Mouse cartoon from the projector and loaded up the training film. Some of the patients had tired of waiting for the show to begin and were booing and stamping their feet. Josephine was distracted as she tried to quiet them; but the instant Bogart ordered Charlie to dim the overhead lights and he switched on the projector, the room became orderly.

The film was grainy and scratchy and full of splices which made the picture jump, but it quickly became clear to Bogart that this was a training film that had been produced at Camp Pendleton during the war years. It monotonously demonstrated the components of the hand grenade and its lethal use on the battlefield. The on-screen instructor was Dalt Brennan.

He was no actor, that was for sure.

In grenade-throwing exercises Brennan demonstrated that as one man threw, another armed with a submachine gun or B.A.R. should always back him up.

Next Brennan showed the procedure for booby-trapping grenades in abandoned buildings and ruins. He stressed the idea of having a second explosive planted on the premises, just in case the first failed or was discovered by the enemy.

"A backup system . . ."

Bogart lingered on the phrase. Had the rigging of the Oscars been part of a backup system? So everyone's defenses would be down by tomorrow night?

The credits began to roll. He was hardly paying attention, just waiting for the film to run out, when a single name caught his eye.

He had to look twice. He didn't want to believe it at first. But there it was.

A single name that began to shed light on certain events—and shroud others in greater mystery.

Produced by Quinn Tayne.

Bogart pondered several points, but kept returning

to one key fact. Why hadn't Tayne mentioned that he knew Brennan before 1947?

Tayne hadn't lied.

But he hadn't told the truth, either.

. . . Just before the final fade/Dalt will throw a big grenade . . .

THIRTY-SEVEN

Dalt Brennan, still wearing the uniform of a delivery man, kicked open a trap door in a supply room deep in the Catacombs of Shrine Auditorium. He shoved aside a rack of old Shriners' costumes that had concealed the small opening during the police search. He slid the rest of the way out, noiselessly closing the trap door behind him. Snapping on a flashlight, he proceeded through the supply room into a corridor.

Quickly he retraced the route he had taken when Bogart was in pursuit, passing through the boiler room and the dressing room and finally emerging into a wider corridor that connected with stairs leading to the main lobby.

The lobby was empty, the marble floor bathed in soft pools of moonlight which filtered through the panes of the entrance doors. He waited in the darkness at the head of the stairs. He was starting to cross the lobby when he heard voices from beyond the doors. The silhouettes of two men were briefly visible against the glass. One of the figures came to peer inside and Brennan pulled back into the shadows, snapping off his flashlight and holding his breath.

After a moment he could hear the guard moving away.

Brennan unlaced and removed his boots. Silently he made his way across the lobby, guided by the pools of moonlight.

Half a minute later he was in the projection booth on the main floor of the auditorium, selecting two 35-

millimeter film cans from those scattered throughout the cubicle.

He carried the containers down the center aisle, mounting the narrow stairway at the right-hand side of the stage.

He hurried to the center of the stage and bent down next to the giant birthday cake centerpiece.

He opened both containers, satisfied that nothing inside had been disturbed.

He glanced at his watch. It was shortly after midnight.

He had six hours until dawn.

More than enough time to do what he had to do.

Diligently he went to work.

THIRTY-EIGHT

Exhaustion washed over Bogart. He scanned the road automatically, dully realizing that it wouldn't take much to fall asleep. The Cadillac's headlights cut a harsh, winding path along Benedict Canyon Road. The lights picked out the telephone pole on the right—the pole he had so narrowly missed only four nights ago.

Someone wanted him out of the way. Tayne? The producer's credit line on the training film proved that he had known Dalt as far back as Camp Pendleton. And knew about Dalt's knowledge of explosives. Had Tayne kept in contact with Dalt all these years?

Was there an unseen link connecting the Pendleton training film and *Embarkation Point*? Fabrini had worked for Tayne from time to time. Was Tayne linked to *Embarkation Point* through Fabrini?

Bogart tugged slowly at his earlobe and pushed the questions to one side as he negotiated the turn onto the private road leading to Hedgerow Farm. He glanced into his mirror. Where were Fenner and Morgan? The two men were probably parked down the road, out of sight, obscured by the curves.

Bogart parked the car. As the motor died, he became aware of the lonely hillside, filled only with the sound of the harsh night winds that pulsed through the valley. Something pricked his intuition like a tingling electric shock.

Where was Harvey?

Bogart waited for the dog's greeting. There was no excited yelp, no sound of prancing feet.

Bogart crossed the lawn, keeping well to the side of the swimming pool. In the background, even over the blasts of wind, there was soft cackling from the chickens. He paused at the edge of the white picket fence; there was no sign of intruders.

He had never felt so tired. Sleep and fatigue dragged at him, making almost every movement an exercise in weariness. Bogart unlatched the door. The house was dark, illuminated only faintly by the late-rising moon.

"Harvey?" he called softly. There was no answer. Bogart's hair prickled at the base of his scalp. Where had he put the .45 automatic? He remembered: He had slid the gun into a drawer in the living room. He pressed the light switch.

The room remained dark.

A dark shape leaped instantly out of the shadows. Bogart had a fleeting impression of a goblin rising on tip-toe—a swishing sound, fast and deadly, came at him, and instinctively he ducked, throwing up his arm. A shattering, paralyzing pain came from his shoulder as something smashed against it.

He threw himself away from the human shape, collided with a chair. He stifled a cry of pain and sprawled over it noisily. The bulky shadow grunted as it lunged again.

Bogart jumped to a crouch, his breath coming fast, and threw himself desperately at the shadow. He lashed out with his fists and connected with the intruder's torso. Pain shot through his knuckles, but he threw choppy blows again and again; there was the pleasure of connecting with something solid and hearing the intruder gasp. The man was quick and muscular, and lashed out with a foot and twisted savagely away.

Then Bogart could see only darkness. His breath came in gusts behind his compressed lips; his eyes jumped from corner to corner. Then he heard the sudden swishing sound again, and ducked as an unseen object passed only an inch from his ear. Bogart grabbed for the man's wrist, then twisted hard, finding himself locked in an obscene embrace. Hands clutched at shoulders, fingers stabbed at eyes, and knees tried to gain an advantage.

They twisted and shoved, desperate gasps jerking from their mouths. They knocked over a table, shattering a lamp. The attacker flexed his shoulder to break Bogart's manic grip and took another vicious swipe. The blow landed on Bogart's collarbone, but he was moving fast and the bulk of the impact was weakened.

Confused, fearful, Bogart stepped back, colliding against a hand-carved coffee table. All arms and legs, he landed agonizingly on his back. He rolled, knowing he had only one chance . . . one chance before the dark figure bludgeoned him to death. He rolled toward the drawer with the gun.

The shadow engulfed him! Bogart lashed out in fear and panic. Adrenaline pumped new energy into his body, but it was only good for a few feeble jabs.

Another chair overturned, knocking the wind from Bogart and punching at his ribs with its backrest. The attacker breathed hard, hissing between his teeth. Bogart's breath came raggedly; sweat poured into his eyes. Lashing out with feet and fists, Bogart landed solid blows as they rolled on the floor. The andirons next to the fireplace toppled with a loud crash, one of them gashing Bogart's cheek.

Bogart slammed a hand upward, trying to get a clawing finger into the man's eyes. He wrenched with all his strength and kicked up with a knee into the intruder's crotch.

There was a sudden cry of anguish. Shuddering. Gasping for breath. But the dark shape was still agile. Bogart felt himself hurled away.

Instantly he grabbed at the overturned end table, ripped open the drawer, pulled out the gun—

The front door opened and slammed shut. Receding footsteps crunched on gravel.

Bogart stumbled through darkness to reach the door. Outside, many yards away, he saw a moving shadow. He dropped to one knee, raised the Colt with his right hand, steadied it with a trembling left and breathed once. He let out half the air and squeezed the trigger.

The running figure was nicely framed in the V-notched sights. The trigger pull halted halfway back.

Bogart cursed. *The safety was on.*

He flipped the .45 over and used his left thumb to slip down the catch. He quickly raised the gun to shoulder height.

The assailant was out of sight, a dark shadow absorbed into blackness. Bogart sighed and lowered the gun.

On wobbly legs he returned to the house. In the entranceway he ejected the clip and then jacked the one shell out of the breech. He stared at the hunk of heavy metal, threw it to the floor and kicked it into a corner.

Calling for Harvey, he crossed the dining room. In the gloom he found the boxer next to a large oval table. Bogart knelt down and felt the dog's neck and stomach. *Still breathing.* There was a lump near the left ear. He picked up the slack animal and carried him to the divan.

"Goddamn, you're a lucky dog, Harvey. Damn lucky little bastard he didn't kill you outright." Bogart stumbled through the dark areas of the house to the main fuse box.

The switch handle was down. Bogart pushed it back.

In the living room he set one of the fallen lamps back on its base, turned it on and slipped to his knees, resting an outflung hand on Harvey's haunches. The dog whimpered.

Bogart looked at the shambles. Home: a sanctuary, a man's castle, a place of refuge. Not a damn shooting gallery!

Blood ran down his cheek, staining his shirt collar. His hips and thighs felt like they had been run through a Mix-Master. Stabbing pressures against his ribs told Bogart they were probably cracked. His knuckles were raw and bloody; the nail on one of his little fingers was almost torn out.

Thoughts dragged feebly through his mind. His eyelids drooped and he forced himself to stay conscious just a bit longer. He had to call Fitzgerald . . . first thing . . . in the morning.

He slumped forward, his head resting on the divan. It would be Bogart's pillow for what little remained of the night.

DAY FIVE

Saturday, March 20, 1948

HAROLD R. STASSEN, REPUBLICAN WHITE HOUSE HOPE-
FUL, CALLS MOVE TO ABANDON PALESTINE PARTITION "A
DISGRACE" . . .

Variety MAGAZINE PREDICTS *Gentleman's Agreement*
AS BEST PICTURE; ELIA KAZAN AS BEST DIRECTOR . . .
ROSALIND RUSSELL TAGGED SHOO-IN FOR HER POWERFUL
PERFORMANCE IN O'NEILL'S *Mourning Becomes Elec-
tra* . . .

FUNERAL SERVICES HELD FOR MARTHA PEARCE, FORMER
SILENT SCREEN ACTRESS WHO COMMITTED SUICIDE LAST
WEDNESDAY.

PARAMOUNT PRODUCER JOHN MURREL ANNOUNCES
HIRING OF NICK COSTER TO COMPLETE "SINCE DEATH
WENT AWAY" SCREENPLAY ORIGINALLY BEGUN BY PAUL
FABRINI, WHO DIED UNDER MYSTERIOUS CIRCUMSTANCES
EARLIER THIS WEEK IN HOLLYWOOD.

TICKETS FOR ACADEMY AWARDS CEREMONIES TONIGHT
AT SHRINE AUDITORIUM NEAR SELL-OUT. MUTUAL & GIT-
TELSON TICKET AGENCIES REPORT ALL BUT 65 DUCATS
SOLD.

THIRTY-NINE

Brittle sunlight bit sharply into Bogart's eyelids. He blinked them open and sat up on the divan. He was instantly filled with some sense of expectancy, of foreboding.

Saturday.

Exactly twelve hours until the Academy Awards . . .

Bogart glanced down to see that Harvey was already awake, watching him hungrily and wagging his stubby tail. Bogart weaved an erratic path into the kitchen and splashed cold water on his face. It didn't do much to dispel his uneasiness. Sunlight reflected off the yellow drainboard in cheerful contrast to the weariness and fear weighing on him.

Harvey whined; Bogart scratched his head and opened a dogfood tin. While Harvey charged into his food bowl, Bogart rubbed his sore muscles and cursed Fenner and Morgan.

So they would be watchdogging him . . . yeah, sure. Where the hell had those two been last night, the one time he had *really* needed them? Suddenly he realized he was still dressed in yesterday's shirt and pants, and he yearned for a shower and a fresh change of clothing. A shave would feel—

The doorbell rang.

He slipped into the living room on stockinged feet and picked up the fallen .45. He found the ammo clip, inserted it and jacked the slide back. This time he made sure the safety was off.

He moved surreptitiously to the front door and

stood with his back against the wall. "Who is it?" he called out softly, innocently.

"Mr. Bogart? . . . Inspector Fitzgerald."

There was no mistaking the cheery voice. Bogart sighed and cracked open the door. Inspector Fitzgerald may have sounded cheery but there was no sign of joviality on his unusually dour face. He was wearing a heavy wool overcoat and fedora and seemed burdened by heavier weights as he crossed the threshold. Under his arm was a manila envelope. He pushed his glasses more firmly down onto his nose as he glanced at the furnishings.

Bogart closed and bolted the door. "It's a relief to see you, Inspector. I thought . . ."

Fitzgerald's eyes fell to Bogart's side, where the .45 hung loosely.

"Do you always answer the door well armed, Mr. Bogart?"

Bogart glanced sheepishly at the automatic.

"Would it have anything to do with those bruises on your face? Or why that lamp and table are overturned?" Fitzgerald arched an eyebrow and walked into the living room, examining it as he might a homicide scene.

Harvey pranced in from the kitchen, carrying a rubber bone in his mouth. He placed it dutifully at Fitzgerald's feet and sniffed at the detective's cuffs.

"All right," said Bogart, "I'll give it to you in a nutshell. I came home very late. When I got inside, someone jumped me. Tried to beat my brains out with a blackjack. I got my hands on this .45 and he took off. That's all there is to tell."

"That's quite a lot." Fitzgerald examined the overturned lamp, then took his pipe out, looking for approval from Bogart, who nodded impatiently. Fitzgerald poked the bowl into a pouch, filled it with loose shreds and lit it, never removing his eyes from Bogart. "Any idea of the culprit's identity?"

"If you're thinking it was Dalt Brennan, forget it. This man was strong. Big. He knew his stuff. And he'd been waiting. Conked old Harvey on the noggin to shut him up."

Fitzgerald sighed. "I was afraid you were going to get too deeply involved for your own good. On the noggin you say." He dropped to one knee and scratched Harvey's ears; the animal took an immediate liking to the inspector and lingered at his shoes, occasionally whining for attention.

"Sure now, I came here for two distinct reasons." Fitzgerald stood, facing Bogart. "First, we checked the academy warehouse thoroughly. The bomb squad found three of the statuettes with plastic explosive in their bases. There was more explosive material in a container left in the office. We also found some individual chemical detonators. We owe you our thanks, Mr. Bogart, assuming we decide not to cite you for breaking and entering. I hardly think Mr. Grasselli would approve of your *modus operandi.*"

Bogart's face revealed everything. He tried to cover up his embarrassment by lighting a cigarette, but he was all thumbs and could sense his face reddening. "Grasselli? I don't know who—"

"We picked up two of his associates late last night about a quarter of a mile from here. A patrol car found them observing your house suspiciously and took them into custody. For your own protection."

For his own protection . . .

"What'll happen to those two? They were doing a pretty good job of taking care of me. Until you butted in."

"I can't think of a worse punishment than breakfast in the jail house. Fenner and Morgan'll be released in a few hours," Fitzgerald said, leading Bogart down the hallway.

Harvey remained behind, too interested in chewing on his rubber bone.

"Tell me about your hunch—what you hoped to find at Saints and Sinners." Fitzgerald floated into Bogart's Mad Room and paced back and forth absorbing the atmosphere and details as little circlets of smoke drifted from his mouth whenever he removed the stem of the pipe. "Did you know you left your window unlatched, Mr. Bogart? No doubt that's how your unexpected caller got inside last night. . . . Go on, I'm listening."

Bogart told Fitzgerald about the training film. "I'm convinced that the explosives in the statuettes are a decoy, and that Dalt has hidden the real bomb in the auditorium. Otherwise why was he there?"

Fitzgerald stalked back to the door, opening it and examining its jamb, then turned sharply. "I believe as you do—that Dalt intends to carry out his attack tonight. But I'm afraid that it is still up to Mr. Hersholt to cancel the presentations. I'll be candid. This is the damnedest case, and I feel slightly helpless to stop whatever is happening."

"Now you know how I've felt. But you said you had two reasons for coming here."

Fitzgerald removed the envelope from under his arm, sliding out an eight-by-ten glossy photograph. He turned it to the light so that Bogart had a clear view of the grayish face. "Do you know this man?"

Bogart knew the man.

Dr. Quesne. Two hundred and seventy pounds, smiling jowls and all.

"What if I do?"

"It seems your name was written in prominent block letters on his desk calendar, underscored in red."

"Sounds like he's one of my biggest fans. But I wouldn't call Doctor Quesne a close associate. That would be a disservice to the medical profession."

"We know you visited him on Wednesday," said Fitzgerald, moving back into the living room.

"Quesne was the doctor who referred Dalt to Saints and Sinners. Right now I'd say he is an important link."

"*Was* an important link."

Bogart's head snapped up. Harvey whined. Fitzgerald brought a second photograph from the envelope.

Dr. Quesne was no longer smiling. Now he was stretched out naked on a coroner's slab with ugly miniature blossoms spread across his chest.

"Early last night Doctor Quesne was found with several bullets in his body, floating off the Santa Monica pier."

So, now Quesne was dead . . . the one strong link between Dalt and Saints and Sinners—silenced. Someone was still cleaning up loose ends.

"Who referred you to Doctor Quesne?" inquired Fitzgerald, sliding the photographs back into the envelope.

"Geoffrey Carroll. Which is something I wanted to bring up. I have a strong suspicion Geoffrey may be more involved than he seems."

"Really, now . . . About Mr. Carroll, I had similar suspicions."

"And?"

"They've taken me to some very colorful Hollywood places—movie studios, posh mansions, expensive restaurants, bars of unsavory character. But nothing connects Carroll with murder."

"One thing that connects up with Carroll is the suicide of Lloyd Brennan. Or should I say *murder*."

"I won't embarrass you by asking where you got such an idea. Did you simply deduce it? No matter . . . there's still nothing tangible in the Carroll connection. Geoffrey's alibi for the night of Lloyd's death is unshakable and his handling of Lloyd's estate gives no blatant indication of greed. On the contrary, some things have gone to charity."

"What has your check on Saints and Sinners revealed?"

"More privileged information, Mr. Bogart? Or perhaps you're a better fisherman than I thought." He dragged at the last few tobacco embers. "Sure now, we've been digging there, but I assure you, we can find no link between Carroll and Martha Pearce." The way he said it, there might have been other links, but he didn't elaborate.

"And Tayne? He knew Dalt and—"

"—Never mentioned it. I know, you told me. Why should he? Tayne must've produced a lot of training films, must've worked with lots of people. Forgetting one detail doesn't make him guilty."

"I hear feet dragging, Inspector."

"Yes, well, the law isn't always the easiest abstraction to work within. It isn't the cut-and-dried thing you often portray in your films." Fitzgerald went to the fireplace and knocked the dottle into a pile of cold ashes. "There were certain facts I should have told you, but at the time I thought it was for your own protection. It still pertains. So I'm asking you, Mr. Bogart, please don't involve yourself any further in the matter of Dalt Brennan. Leave this to the police."

"It's not that simple, Inspector. A long time ago I let Dalt down. Maybe it seemed right at the time, but it seems very wrong and very stupid now. And I intend to correct that."

Fitzgerald could stare just as defiantly as Bogart. Then a smile burst over the inspector's face. "Well now, I suppose I could take that as an effrontery to the law, but I rather admire your streak of stubbornness. It does my Irish heart good to see dandruff raised the way *you* raise it, Mr. Bogart. All right—ask your questions if you must. And should you learn anything, I'll expect a call. And should I find out anything, I'll be glad to relay it. You have my word on that."

As if to seal some new relationship, Fitzgerald thrust out his hand. The cherub smile, for the first time that morning, ran joyously across his face. "Of course, I might ask one of my boys to keep something of an eye on you. For your own protection."

"Of course," said Bogart. He saw Fitzgerald to his car, then returned to the house, where he started to fix ham and eggs. But butterflies kept bumping into each other in the pit of his stomach and he decided on a Scotch and soda instead. He settled wearily into the divan, deciding he had to get his thoughts straight before rushing away. First would come Carroll, then another visit to Shrine before the ceremonies. And another talk with Jean Hersholt would be in order.

Harvey pranced past him, bone in mouth. Suddenly it dropped to the carpet as Harvey's interest shifted. He began sniffing under one of the overturned divans. His mouth clutched some new morsel hidden there and he brought it across the room and carefully placed it at Bogart's feet, plopping down to chew on it.

Bogart set aside his Scotch and soda.

The object was something that didn't belong in the room. Something that filled Bogart with a sense of revulsion. He leaned down and picked it up.

It was a ten-inch length of heavy leather and rubber, with a thong at its thinner end. The opposite end was weighted with iron or steel. It was the blackjack carried by the assailant. Dropped during the scuffle and lost in the darkness.

Bogart balanced it in his hand, remembering precisely what it was.

A Russian blackjack.

And precisely where he had seen it before.

Lubianka Prison.

FORTY

Gravel crunched softly as the coupe reached the end of parallel limestone walls and passed between tall, imposing gates. Wrought-iron leopards, with eyes of bronze and spots of copper, seemed to spring to life on the vertical, twisted bars when the gates moved grudgingly in the wind. A well-trimmed lawn, interspersed with walkways of white crushed rock, rolled up to the edges of the French manor house.

There was no sign of life—anywhere. Bogart was touched by the deathly stillness of the house as he walked toward the main entrance. He tightened the belt of his trench coat and braced his hat as wind whipped the native California pines bordering the walkway. He checked the Colt .45 to see that the hammer was down and the safety off. He buried it deep in his pocket. It was a nasty day, cold and sharp despite the brilliant sunlight, and the March wind bit into his face.

Bogart rang the bell and waited two minutes. No answer. He rattled the knob. Locked. He walked the length of the porch. All the windows were locked as well. When the wind shook the multifaceted panes, his reflection jittered.

On the north side of the manor, Bogart strode beside an evergreen hedge until he came to a french window overlooking a croquet court.

Bogart picked up a small stone and nonchalantly broke a windowpane, then reached in and unlatched the doors.

Quinn Tayne could easily afford to replace thousand of windowpanes.

Bogart entered, pushing aside the gauzelike white drapes which billowed toward the center of the room like fingers pointing a direction. He relatched the doors and turned.

He was dazzled, almost blinded, by so much white.

Bogart was in a gigantic sitting room. On his right was an imported, French, ivory-colored fireplace, flanked with a collection of brass andirons. Each piece of furniture was upholstered in gold and white brocaded material.

A soft light enveloped the sitting room and reflected off the walls, which were wainscotted in creamy white marble. White tiles gleamed underfoot. A colonnaded entrance led to the rest of the house. Bogart went into the foyer, feeling the coldness generated by a floor of polished pale-gray marble. To one side was a grand curving staircase with lacquered ivory banisters. He passed through other spacious rooms, all done in white, cream and gold. Bogart had the distinct feeling he had stepped not into a home but a museum. Or a crypt.

The bleached decor was unchanged from room to room . . . there was nothing that gave evidence that a human being lived here. The emptiness continued to overwhelm him.

His heels clicking on the egg-white tile floor, he went from pure white to oyster white to cream white to frosty white, reaching a den that contained a desk and a white, French-style telephone. He paused to riffle through the desk and found nothing but a handful of unproduced screenplays. He came across stacks of studio and interoffice memos and four-page synopses of script ideas, all unrealized.

Bogart went up the curving staircase. Upstairs the sound of the wind was absorbed by the hand-tufted carpeting. He opened doors as he moved along the alabaster hall: solarium . . . women's powder room . . . recreation hall . . . library, empty of books . . . guest bedrooms.

At the end of the hall was an ornate white door with hinges that creaked. Bogart passed through an octagonal entrance foyer into a spacious bedroom with a Castilian canopy bed. A woman's room, he decided when he saw a vanity, covered with a faint film of dust, and rows of meticulously aligned perfume and lotion bottles. He scuffed his feet along the shaggy pile of the white Axminster rug and raised a soft cloud of dust.

Dominating the room was a life-size painting. The almond-shaped, green eyes of a lovely middle-aged woman gazed lovingly down at Bogart. Her slender body justified the design of a white satin gown, and there was a madonna-like quality about those eyes and the way she clutched a bouquet of white gardenias to her breast. The artist had captured a wistfulness around her sensuous mouth.

There was a gold name plate on the bottom of the frame . . . and Bogart knew who she was. Or rather he knew who she had been.

Mrs. Quinn Tayne.

The gold name plate read: Sylvia Fabrini Tayne.

Fabrini . . . ?

And Mrs. Tayne . . . Bogart remembered she had been the victim of a tragic automobile accident many years ago—1941? 1942?—the details were vague in Bogart's mind.

Bogart returned to the hall and followed an angling

corridor until it dead-ended at a single ashen-gray door. Bogart tried the knob. Now we're getting somewhere, he thought. Unlike every door he had opened so far, this one was locked.

Bogart stepped back and with all his force planted a kick just above the knob. There was the sound of wood breaking; splinters appeared around the lock. Bogart breathed heavily, stepped back and kicked one more time. The mortise surrendered with a shriek. The door swung open slowly.

Bogart felt for a light switch in the darkened interior and clicked it on.

The contrast was startling.

He stood in a luxuriously appointed screening room of rich, dark reds, wine maroons and deep purples. Pale-rouge lighting glowed from lamps concealed in scarlet ceiling valances. Bogart counted twenty plush, vermilion leather seats angled toward the screen, which was framed with a pleated and scalloped *couleur de rose* curtain. The garnet walls were lined with posters: *Blair at the Top; Blair's Big Score; London Calling, London Calling;* and even some of the very early Tayne productions: *The Boxer and the Kid; Runaway Rascals.* The posters spanned the early thirties to the present.

There was one poster, strangely out of place, for Tayne's production seal was not among the credits.

Embarkation Point.

Bogart tugged at his earlobe. Definitely not a Tayne Production . . . *or was it?*

In the rear projection booth Bogart found two Simplex projectors, a bench for rewinding and a panel that controlled lights and curtain.

Behind the last row of seats was a four-drawer filing cabinet, locked. Bogart was convinced it was out of place: first a locked screening room, now a locked file. He took out a pocket knife and inserted the small blade into the upper lock. He wriggled it, feeling the tumblers . . .

The blade snapped off, leaving a tiny, triangular point wedged in the lock. Cursing, Bogart used the knife's bottle opener to pry out the broken point.

There was a click.

He paused, then yanked hard on the top drawer. It slid out effortlessly.

He unearthed more scripts, dusty with age. He flipped through a chronological history of Tayne's past.

Then Bogart found it. *Hollywood Armageddon.* He clearly remembered the nondescript cover, now dog-eared and stained. *This* was the script he had delivered to Harry Cohn years ago. He was sure of it; hell, those circular rings were from Mayo's bourbon glass.

Other drawers contained piles of aging green and yellow memo carbons, all held together in packs by thick rubber bands. He riffled through them, reading Tayne's unending stream of consciousness and hearing the words being delivered in the odious tone he knew so well.

FROM: Quinn Tayne   July 8, 1941

TO: George Halley, production mgr.

. . . wish to thank everyone for the way my af-
fairs at the studio were handled following the death of my beloved Sylvia. Your condolences come at my darkest hour . . .

July 11, 1941

. . . George, regarding the costumes Marie Windsor is to wear in *Frontier Destiny*. Must they be so revealing? . . .

July 15, 1941

. . . first-class air tickets to Phoenix for location shooting of *Whirlwind Through Texas* are out of the question. Budgetary demands negate such squandering of my own money . . .

Bogart flipped through the years, watching Tayne's career prosper and skyrocket from independent nobody to second-string studio executive producer, and finally first string. And then a name caught Bogart's eye.

Dalt Brennan.

Sweet Jesus . . . it was a memo from Tayne to Clive Donahue, producer of *Embarkation Point*. Stamped *Confidential*. Dated June 10, 1946.

. . . now that we have concluded our private arrangements for *Embarkation Point*, I wish to stress two key points. Under no circumstances must my involvement be made public. I have a reputation to uphold at Columbia and any leak that I have put production capital into a nonstudio venture would lead to serious repercussions. For *both* of us!

The second point: I think it's time we seriously reevaluate the Dalt Brennan screenplay. While I agree that it is a brilliant piece of scenario writing, a bigger issue is now at stake. This is no longer the low-budget film originally visualized. We now have the added expense of Ty Power and Joan Crawford, and we must justify this burden to the budget by reconsidering the roles and asking ourselves: is some enhancement not in order?

There followed a short reply from Donahue:

I can see no reason why Ty and Joan cannot play the parts as conceived. I've talked with Ty and he feels the script is strong enough as is. He feels it will break the mold of romantic hero in which he has been cast for so many years . . .

Tayne's reply, two days later:

. . . if you will examine our agreement, you will recall that paragraph Six, subchapter D, entitles me to the right of script alterations should I deem them necessary. I've talked with Ty and while we agree on the excellence of Brennan's concept, he now realizes that a shift in image would be bad for him . . .

Tayne once again, June 19, 1946:

. . . I have taken the liberty, since you have been so busy with costuming and location scouting, to release Frank Taylor from the chore of rewriting. I have hired Paul Fabrini for all future rewrites. Paul is my brother-in-law and a long-time working associate whose superior work you will recall from *The Angel from Brooklyn, The Lonely Mountain,* and *So Proud is My Heart,* . . .

To Fabrini, the next day:

> . . . Paul, by and large, the revisions thus far have been excellent, but bear in mind that Brennan's original point of view is no longer applicable. Audiences will hardly accept Ty as a corporal or sergeant; I think he must be at least a Captain. And instead of coming from an Ohio farm, I think audiences would relate more to him if he were from a well-to-do family.
>
> As for Joan, I think we need to recast her characterization totally. Might I suggest . . .

To Donahue, in response to his outrage at the excessive number of script alterations:

> . . . Clive, I assure you that every change is necessary to showcase the stars. Might I remind you that Ty and Joan were entirely your idea. You must now reconcile yourself to the profound effect your decision has had. While the simplicity of Brennan's script was beautiful in its own special way, it is totally inappropriate for such high-powered players as Ty and Joan.

Again to Donahue, a week later:

> . . . please do not engage in any further conversations with Dalt Brennan about script changes. He has a history of making trouble for producers and has disrupted many films in production. My advice is not to allow him on the set. I wish there were a more pleasant solution to this problem but for the good of *Embarkation Point* I think . . .

And finally:

> . . . I must now insist that Dalt Brennan be
> barred from the set of *Embarkation Point.* Please
> see that this edict is rigorously enforced. His re-
> peated disturbances must not be allowed to in-
> trude on the fine performances of Ty and Joan. I
> realize you do not enjoy being the villain, but I
> must demand that Brennan, from this moment
> forth, be considered *persona non grata* . . .

Bogart glanced at the date: September 4, 1946. Just
about the time Dalt had come to the Garden of Allah
in the dead of night, awakened Bogart and Betty and
shot up their bungalow with his .45. It was all clear
now just what Tayne had succeeded in doing. Secretly
wresting power from Donahue . . . controlling the
financial and creative strings of production . . .
bringing in Fabrini to do a total rewrite . . . leaving
Dalt with a hatred for Hollywood that Tayne could
exploit to his own end.

Bogart shoved the relevant memos into his trench
coat along with the *Armageddon* screenplay. Four and
a half days of probing and living with uncertainty, fear
and risk had finally paid off.

Downstairs, in the ornate living room, he slid a cigarette into his mouth and immediately began to dial
Fitzgerald's direct line. He was just starting to fumble
for a match when a hand came from behind and
clamped down on the cradle. Bogart felt the barrel of
a gun pushed sadistically into his kidneys. There was
no mistaking the sensation; he had experienced it in
too many Warner Brothers thrillers.

"Well, well, the smart Mr. Bogart," said Valentine
Corliss, his black chauffeur's uniform in shocking con-

trast to the room's glaring white. "Put the phone down."

Bogart recradled the receiver and raised his hands slightly as Corliss patted him down. The cigarette dangled unlit between his lips. Corliss found Bogart's .45 and jammed it into his belt. "Naughty, naughty." He also found the memos and the screenplay . . . and the blackjack Bogart had carried in the depths of the trench coat.

Corliss tossed the blackjack in the air and caught it. "Very careless of me, leaving this behind."

Bogart turned slightly. "Say," he said, "you wouldn't happen to have a light, would you?"

FORTY-ONE

Violence was only a gesture away. Pickets of the North American Committee for Democratic Action had increased threefold as Bogart pulled up to the main gate of Columbia.

Bogart found the Cadillac surrounded. Men shouting obscenities pounded their fists on the car windows; two demonstrators leaped onto the rear bumper and bounced the car. Another man holding a baseball bat pounded the wood against the fender and hurled insults at Bogart.

Bogart clung to the wheel, his fear increasing as the muzzle of his own .45 automatic pressed against his ribs. "Keep both hands where I can see them," ordered Corliss.

More angry voices ordered them out of the car. Corliss had begun to sweat profusely.

Then the mass of humanity blocking the Cadillac lowered their placards to use them as clubs. A fat man clambered onto the hood and was about to swing a truncheon against the window when Bogart heard sirens.

Bogart saw a fleet of black-and-white police cars, several paddy wagons and a special riot squad disembarking from large trucks. The fat man jumped off the hood.

The protestors swarmed to meet violence with violence. At the same time, Columbia security guards charged through the gates and pounced on the rabblerousers from behind.

It was a coagulated mess, with men screaming and

fighting, and Bogart sat in the middle of it, silently drumming his fingers on the steering wheel.

"Just sit tight," ordered Corliss. "Just don't do anything stupid."

"There's enough people already doing that," replied Bogart. He wanted to light a cigarette but decided Corliss was too nervous. If he made a movement that was misinterpreted . . .

Only three feet from the Cadillac, truncheons and billy clubs descended. The car rocked as men fell against it, grappling. Placards smashed over bodies; the pieces of debris fell among the unconscious and the injured. Fists bludgeoned against faces; angry fingers clutched necks.

The riot squad was winning. Already unconscious protestors were being callously dragged to the waiting paddy wagons and hurled inside. Booted policemen trampled over the fallen and ground anti-Columbia placards to unrecognizable litter.

And then the battling mass of humanity in front of the Cadillac was cleared away and Bogart was motioned forward by the two Columbia guards at the main gate.

"Play it neat," warned Corliss, in control of matters again.

He pulled ahead, trying to smile, thinking he would be waved through, but one of the guards stepped in front of him, holding up one hand. Bogart rolled to a smooth stop.

He rolled down the window as the guard leaned against the side of the car. The guard's face was officious and almost seemed to scowl at Bogart, then at Corliss as his eyes swept the front seat. The automatic, hidden beneath Corliss's jacket spread across the seat, pressed tighter against Bogart's ribs.

Bogart smiled.

The guard stopped looking officious and smiled back.

Immediately Bogart could feel the tension against his ribs relax—but only a little.

"Sorry about this, Mr. Bogart. Hope you and the car're all right. If there's been any damage . . ."

"No, nothing to worry about, everything's fine."

"Don't think they'll be giving us any more trouble. Got just what they deserved. Goddamn Commies."

Bogart glanced back toward the street to see that most of the paddy wagons had been loaded. Bogart witnessed one policeman shove a man across the street and strike him repeatedly on the head.

As the Cadillac pulled onto the Columbia lot, the smile returned to Corliss's face.

FORTY-TWO

Lubianka Prison was dressed in gloom. Murkiness clung tenaciously to the walls of the interrogation room, while the main cell block housed a thousand pieces of jagged darkness. In the torture chamber an unnerving specter of darkness cascaded across the cold marble floor.

The central corridor, down which Bogart stiffly walked, was limned with a dankness that reminded him of the Shrine Catacombs. Corliss urgently nudged him with the automatic.

Quinn Tayne was patiently waiting at the foot of the corridor. The producer indicated no surprise at Bogart's presence, nor at the automatic.

"You look naked without your steno girl," lisped Bogart, tainting his words with sarcasm.

"It's her day off," replied Tayne very matter of factly.

"He was nosing around the projection room," explained Corliss somewhat defensively, as though disclaiming any responsibility. "He had the script, the memos . . . I told you years ago you shoulda got rid of that crap."

"You needn't go into all that," soothed Tayne, as though Corliss thoroughly bored him. "Bogie, your curiosity about Dalt Brennan has a way of leading you into trouble."

"It's gonna lead him into more than just trouble," blurted Corliss.

Apparently Tayne did not appreciate Corliss's tone of voice. "Really, Valentine, you shouldn't take these things to heart. A professional such as yourself should take the ups and downs in stride."

"The only thing Bright Boy here ever took in his stride," leered Bogart, "was dog crap on the sidewalk."

Corliss started to make a threatening move, but controlled himself. Bogart could feel beads of sweat pop out onto his forehead and neck.

"I rather like the corridor walls," Tayne was saying. "What do you think, Bogie?"

"Realistic as hell, Tayne. As realistic as the Russian blackjack Bright Boy left at my place last night."

"There was a certain amount of sloppiness to that," confessed Tayne, refusing to glance at Corliss, as if such a gesture might be in bad taste. "But as I said earlier, some things we must accept." Tayne placed his hands behind his back and strolled down the corridor. He gestured for Bogart to follow him and led the way into the headquarters office. "I'm concerned about the set design of this room. It needs a different mood."

"The way I figure it, this whole business started with the training film, when you and Dalt met at Camp Pendleton." Bogart crossed to the desk and leaned against it, assuming a relaxed pose. Corliss followed him rigidly, the automatic never leaving Bogart's body. "From the beginning," continued Bogart, "you realized how wild and unstable Dalt could be, and when you read *Hollywood Armageddon,* an idea formed."

"I'm fascinated," said Tayne. "Don't stop."

"Dalt's ability to handle explosives . . . the plot line of *Armageddon* . . . you saw a way of manipulating Dalt, but first you had to build a friendship. Dalt came to trust you. Maybe you were the one person in the world who seemed to want to help him."

"I think I know what's wrong," said Tayne. "The walls—they're muted. Yet the room needs an additional touch of dreariness. Valentine, make a note. We need a lichen effect, something to suggest dampness and molding decay. I think if we mix sawdust and a greenish paint and spray it on, we might have a more atmospheric touch. You were saying, Bogie . . ."

Bogart leaned further back against the desk, crossing his legs. "So, you planted a few seeds in Dalt's mind and gave them time to germinate. Meanwhile, you're planting another kind of seed in the minds of producers all over Hollywood: that Dalt's material is inferior and the man himself is bad to have around. So, for three years, nobody hires him."

"I never counted, actually."

"Then something almost went wrong. Clive Donahue. He read *Embarkation Point* and wanted to produce it. When you heard that, you knew you'd have to act fast, or Donahue would louse up your plan."

"You keep talking about a plan," said Tayne, yawning.

"I'll get to that. If the script was produced, Dalt might become recognized as a fine writer. And you'd lose your number-one clay pigeon."

"I think he oughta shut up," rasped Corliss.

"*You* shut up, Bright Boy."

"Mr. Tayne—"

"Let him finish, Valentine."

"Yeah, shut up and listen, Bright Boy. As I was saying, Tayne, you weaseled your way into the production of *Embarkation Point*. All you had to do was slip Donahue enough money so he could hire the stars he wanted. And that enabled you to manipulate Donahue. Such as hiring your brother-in-law, Paul Fabrini, to do enough rewriting so Dalt would receive no screen credit. And Fabrini went along with all that—except when it came to murder—and that was why he had to die. Isn't that right, Bright Boy?"

"Mr. Tayne, let me—"

"Don't interrupt," Tayne ordered.

"But you still needed one final touch, the clincher. That was Lloyd's murder, rigged by Bright Boy here to look like suicide. And then with Doctor Quesne serving as your flunky, Dalt was committed to Saints and Sinners so he would be cut off from everyone he knew. Martha is the one who gave you access to the grounds for the nightly visits to Dalt. Final briefing and indoctrination. To give him the last bit of rein he needed to make him think he was carrying out his own ingenious scheme. But then Johnny Hawks stumbled across the plan, and he had to be attended to by Bright Boy."

Corliss sneered; even Tayne allowed a slight smile to cross his otherwise reserved face.

"But killing Johnny was your first big mistake. You got Cohn into a lather, and then I didn't like a good friend like Johnny getting shot, so I stuck my nose where it didn't belong and that's when Bright Boy gave me that friendly nudge on Benedict Canyon Road. Then came Martha Pearce, who must've panicked when I came nosing around. Maybe she threatened to tell the cops what she knew. But she had to die too—another rigged suicide. Then Fabrini was going to tell me what he knew and he died."

Bogart kept his casual pose. "And there was Quesne, an impossible man to trust. He had to die too. And I kept asking questions, so you had to throw me off by planting those decoy explosives in the statuettes—and then I came across the grenade film, so you had to send Bright Boy again last night."

Tayne fidgeted slightly. "One thing bothers me, Bogie. Why would I go to such great lengths?"

"Ah, that finally brings us to the plan. *Your* plan. You want tonight's bombing to look like a Communist-inspired plot. That explains the misleading Commie literature we found among Dalt's and Lloyd's effects. Salted by Bright Boy here. I wouldn't even be surprised if you had something to do with rigging the little demonstration outside the studio, just to remind everyone of the Commie threat."

"Wild speculation," replied Tayne calmly.

"All right; agreed. Wild speculation. But let me run off at the mouth."

"Let's get back to the bomb," suggested Tayne. "I'm curious about the bomb."

"Let's get back to the bomb. It's a beaut. It blows Shrine Auditorium, and everyone in it, to hell. And HUAC has the Communist party as a scapegoat."

"How exactly is that achieved?"

"You rig it so Dalt takes the fall."

"Ah yes," said Tayne sarcastically, "I remember now. The 'salted' Communist literature among Dalt's effects."

"And Lloyd's, just to cinch matters. The bombing gives the film industry a rallying cry."

"I see. It wakes up all the 'dumb folk' to the dangers of communism in Hollywood."

"And it stifles the hue and cry of the liberals."

"And ultimately?"

"Still not hard to figure. Ultimately it's a stepping-stone to greater power."

"Power?"

"For you."

"Really . . ."

"The state capital . . . maybe Washington, D.C. You tell me."

Tayne's laughter was shrill and sardonic, and it gave Bogart a chill similar to the one he had experienced two nights before when he had found his home broken into.

Tayne chuckled conservatively. "Nothing so commendable, Bogie . . . or ridiculous. Political power? Let the others fight over that—let them flock around Capitol Hill and stake out their own empires to rule. I'll stay right here."

Empire . . . right here . . . in Hollywood . . . so that was it—not the power of politics but the power of film; control over the millions who bought tickets and watched films . . .

Bogart carried right on without pausing. "Let me guess why, Tayne. After tonight Hollywood will be an empire without a leader. Just like the city-states of the Roman Empire. What it will need, after Saturday night, is an emperor. A Julius Caesar."

Tayne remained silent, studying Bogart closely, for the first time perhaps giving the actor full credit. And for the first time Bogart was not underestimating Tayne.

Bogart remembered the devious tone of the memos, and tried to imagine the ruthlessness to which Tayne might plunge. The death of so many studio bosses, writers, stars and technicians in one flaming moment would paralyze the industry. It might take years for it to regain its strength. That meant time: time for one unscrupulous man to step in and seize command . . . reshape the movie colony into a cartel of studios under one central control.

Quinn Tayne's control.

Insane, inspired, insidious, ingenious. Tayne alone would be the Messiah-like figure to rise from the ashes of Shrine Auditorium to create order out of chaos. He would give catalytic meaning to those who had no direction, who were confused by the advent of the Cold War, who were profoundly disillusioned by a lack of peace in the wake of the armistice.

"I can almost imagine how you're going to go about it," continued Bogart. "Maybe you've been buying stock in the major studios. I wouldn't be surprised if you even had stock in the small independents— preposterous, I know—but let me keep guessing. Maybe you've got holdings throughout Hollywood— newspapers, magazines, radio stations, even that little bastard called television, which you can mold into your own personal propaganda weapon. You're really going to be ready for the new tomorrow."

"I think he oughta shut up, Mr. Tayne."

"I'm inclined to agree, Valentine." Tayne unfolded his arms and glared at Bogart. "You've talked long enough, Bogie, and frankly you're quite dull. I think it's time you set sail. I'm told you're quite fond of sailing."

"It beats trying to walk on the water."

"Valentine has made all the arrangements. You should enjoy the cruise, since it's aboard your own *Santana.*"

"Get moving," ordered Corliss impatiently.

Tayne brushed specks of lint from his suit. "I am sorry about one thing, Bogie. I really wish you could have seen *The Red Seduction.* I do think it's going to be the best film I've ever produced. The beginning of a new trend in filmmaking."

"Over my dead body," said Bogart.

"Precisely," promised Corliss.

FORTY-THREE

It was good to be alive. The sky was a dazzling azure blue broken only by fluffy, cotton-shaped escarpments of clouds and the blazing glare of the sun. Its warmth counterbalanced the chilly southeastern breeze that darkened the water. It was a beautiful day for sailing.

Cawing gulls churned overhead. The horizon was the rim of the world, and the land looked distant and unreal in the smoggy haze that clutched the southern California coastline. Reality was here and now, with the bow of the *Santana* splitting the gentle waves under its maximum diesel-driven speed of twelve knots.

Yeah, thought Bogart, it's great to be alive.

Valentine Corliss wiped a fine layer of foamy spray from his face and kept the automatic trained on Bogart.

The actor stood at the cockpit near the mizzenmast, the *chug-chug-chug* of the diesel engines an unpleasant throbbing to his ears. Without a crew to trim the sails, Corliss had ordered Bogart out of Newport Beach at full throttle. Now the *Santana*, a sleek, fifty-five-foot, double-masted yawl, was maintaining maximum speed. The sails remained furled and forgotten.

After smashing Bogart's ship-to-shore radio receiver and radio direction finder, Corliss had permitted Bogart to slide into his duffel coat and battered yachting cap. Now, at least, he felt slightly at home at the helm, even though he did not have his usual glass of Scotch secured in one of the holders especially built into the binnacle.

The sharp bow of the Santana tossed waves smoothly to port and starboard; occasionally the wind carried the spray into their faces. It was late afternoon now and the sunlight was reflected off the water like a thousand gems.

The Santana was no ordinary yawl. Among the fraternity of yachtsmen, she was considered one of the finest racing crafts afloat. She had placed second in the 1934 Santa Monica–Honolulu race, and since buying her from Dick Powell shortly after the war, Bogart had piloted her to other competitive victories. Bogart had sailed many voyages aboard her, and they had been special times enjoyed with special friends.

Now, very likely, he would die on her.

There was a ketch a half-mile to port; as long as she remained in view, Corliss would be foolish to try anything.

Bogart knew he needed a distraction.

It came almost immediately in the form of someone moving below deck, in the cabin. He heard coughing and the metallic ring of footsteps on the cabin ladder. Bogart glanced at Corliss, who had a superior smile on his face. He licked the wind-whipped spray from his lips and told Bogart, "Relax, Bright Boy. He's a friend of yours."

Dalt Brennan climbed onto the deck and stretched.

"He's been using the Santana to hide out," said Corliss. "We figured it to be the last place anyone would ever look."

"Distance," said Dalt, hearing only the sound of his own voice, "that's what we want to put between us and them."

"Them?" Bogart cocked his head.

"Sure, Humph, they're getting dressed right now—tuxedos, evening gowns, the works. And then they're

gonna be filing into Shrine. Like cattle to the slaughter. Sail, Humph. As far and as quickly as you can. I
bet we'll hear the blast clear out here."

The blast!

Bogart felt his blood congeal to ice and his hands
were frozen to the wheel as though they had been
lashed there. *Dalt had done it. Planted the explosives
in Shrine.*

"You better tell me about it," said Bogart, as soon as
he found his voice again.

"It's too late for anyone to stop it. Why bother?"

Corliss smiled, enjoying the cat-and-mouse game
Dalt had chosen to play.

"You were in Shrine last night," said Bogart.

"All night. I slept good."

"You planted the explosive."

"Explosives."

There was more than one, thought Bogart. Terrific.

"Where?"

"In the auditorium."

Just like *Hollywood Armageddon*, realized Bogart.
Lorre was right; Dalt was staying true to form.

"Where in the auditorium?"

"In the heart of everything."

"What?"

"Nine forty-five sharp . . . in the heart of everything." Dalt simply smiled when Bogart again asked
him where. It was the smile of a man who knew something the rest of the world didn't. It was a smile full of
vindictiveness and madness and revenge. It was bit-
tersweet and it must have tasted good on his lips.

Bogart glanced at his watch. Almost six-thirty.
Three hours and fifteen minutes until . . . and they
were a good hour out from Newport already.

"Why the gun, Corliss? How come you're holding it

on Humph?" Dalt took a step toward Corliss and then froze. For the automatic had swung to cover Dalt.

It was the mistake Bogart had hoped Corliss would make.

Talk fast, thought Bogart. Put on a performance like never before. Even if it's a performance that'll only be seen by two people. Hell, give 'em their money's worth.

"You want to know why the gun, Dalt? I'll tell you . . . because Tayne's been using you, setting you up. He and Bright Boy here were going to make it look like you were part of a Commie conspiracy—you and Lloyd. Brother and brother. You've been groomed for the big fall."

Dalt stepped past a gallow's frame, resting his arm on its top for support. "Set up? You're nuts, Humph. The script was my idea—Tayne was the only man who had the insight to understand. This is one time that someone else isn't going to take credit for my achievements."

"You talk about credit. Tayne's the one who manipulated Donahue to trick you out of credit for *Embarkation Point*."

Confusion spread across Dalt's face. He was wavering . . .

"And Lloyd . . . you don't think *he* was a suicide."

Dalt's eyes leaped from Bogart over to Corliss and down onto the automatic. "What do you mean? It *was* suicide."

"Not according to the cops. Inspector Fitzgerald says Lloyd was murdered. By the same man who murdered Martha Pearce. He has proof and is reopening the case."

Dalt's eyes burned into Corliss's. "I heard the radio . . . Martha committed suicide."

Bogart's eyes remained narrowed, his hands sweatily gripping the wheel. "No dice, Dalt. Fitzgerald has evidence to the contrary. They were both murdered by Bright Boy with the gun."

Corliss didn't confirm or deny. The only response was a smirk that promised death for both of them.

Bogart's voice rushed on. "And where do you suppose Bright Boy is taking us at gunpoint? For a pleasure cruise? For a weekend at Catalina?"

Dalt watched Corliss, sizing up the chauffeur in a new light. He began stalking back and forth across the deck, like a man trying to work off his doubts. But the doubts turned to anger. And anger to hatred.

The ketch to port was almost out of sight now. At the most, Bogart decided, he had two, maybe three minutes.

Talk, Bogart, talk . . .

"Maybe Bright Boy's taking us out to deep water, where it's convenient to drop a couple of bullet-riddled bodies overboard to the sharks. Think about it, Dalt; you've served your purpose. What good are you to Tayne now? You've just a loud-mouthed witness who'll talk his head off. He wants you dead so he can expose you first thing Monday morning as a martyr for the Communist Party—the Mad Bomber of Shrine. And Tayne becomes a hero all over the front page. The savior of Hollywood. And us—we're fish bait."

Dalt's wild pacing continued. Sweat broke out on Corliss; it was difficult for him to keep a close watch on Bogart while Dalt nervously paced the deck. Corliss glanced at the ketch, obviously eager for it to slip over the horizon.

"Dalt," ordered Bogart, "stand still for Chrissake or he'll shoot." The severity of Bogart's voice brought

Dalt to a stop. Some of the tension left Corliss and the devious smile returned to his face.

That's good, thought Bogart, just keep relaxing, Bright Boy. Keep thinking you got everything under control.

Corliss was unaware that Bogart was gradually angling the *Santana* abeam of the waves. As the yawl rolled in their troughs, he tightened his grip on the wheel and tensed his body. The ketch was only a dot on the edge of the world.

Casually Bogart asked, "Is that ketch out of sight yet?" His voice was so relaxed that automatically Corliss turned slightly to glance at the horizon.

That's when Bogart spun the wheel, whirled and dived at Valentine Corliss.

Again Bogart was hurtling clumsily through space, but this time he had the advantage of surprise. He had made no sound when he lunged, and Corliss was turning back when Bogart collided against him head-first. The impact carried Corliss back against the base of the mizzenmast. Corliss was erect but gasping and pale, the air knocked from his stomach. Bogart's arms remained tightly locked around Corliss's waist and he slammed his head into the chauffeur's midsection again. Corliss grunted and gasped a second time, his face a bleached white.

Bogart slipped on the deck as he attempted to stand upright. Awkwardly he clutched Corliss by the lapels, spun him around and delivered a right cross. It wasn't the best right cross ever delivered. It was far from the worst. Bogart simply gave it everything he had.

Corliss took Bogart's fist fully on the jaw and crashed into the wheel. Shaking his stinging knuckles, Bogart realized the .45 automatic was still in Corliss's right hand. He lashed out with his foot. The pistol leaped into the air and arced back to the deck, skidding across the teakwood like a shuffleboard puck. A hissing escaped Corliss's lips; hatred and panic flashed simultaneously in his steel-gray eyes.

Bogart punched again. Corliss crashed into the binnacle. Out of the corner of his eye, Bogart saw Dalt duck back into the cabin.

Bogart kept attacking. He threw a third flurry of punches.

With nobody at the wheel, the *Santana* was free to drift with the waves. The yawl turned slightly in the groundswell and Bogart was thrown off balance. He fell against the wheel, reaching for it to regain his stance. It took only seconds to face Corliss again, but those few seconds had been a lifetime for the chauffeur.

The fist that buried itself into Bogart's cheek was the fist of a furious man. Corliss followed through with a second powerhouse swing but Bogart, despite the stinging pain in his face, dropped to his knees with an agility that surprised even him. Corliss's fist grazed the top of his hair. Using his head as a battering ram for the second time, Bogart plunged headfirst, catching Corliss amidships.

Corliss caromed off the starboard lifelines and brought up his knee to plant it in Bogart's face. Bogart staggered backward, feeling as though he had been pounded by a sledgehammer. He thought his nose was broken—blood streamed from both nostrils—and there was ringing in his ears.

Corliss snarled and reached for a belaying pin wedged between two stanchions. Gripping the slender piece of wood at its thicker end, he took one step toward Bogart. But the *Santana* rolled violently and

Corliss was flung backward and over the starboard gunwale, his headlong plunge into the salt water punctuated by a short scream that was a mixture of defiance and surprise. Corliss reappeared on the surface almost immediately, dog-paddling and struggling to keep his head above the waves. Instinctively, Bogart reached for the orange life preserver hanging at the stern and flung it overboard.

Corliss was bobbing in the *Santana*'s wake by the time Bogart began to negotiate a turn. Bogart leaned against the wheel for support. Blood still flowed freely from his nose but his ears were no longer ringing.

Where the hell was Dalt? Bogart was too concerned about turning the *Santana* to answer his own question.

The southeaster had increased and was creating cat's-paws. Gulls still churned overhead, though their cawing was drowned by the whistling of the rising breeze. It was after seven o'clock and the early March sunset was already in progress. A stain of blood red clutched the horizon, topped by a gray-white cloud formation that reminded Bogart of an atomic explosion.

The *Santana* turned into the full force of the breeze. Bogart leaned to port, glimpsing the floating preserver and the bobbing head of Corliss. The sun surreptitiously slipped behind the massive cloud formation and the reddish cast intensified.

Bogart slowed the engines, head to the wind, and allowed the *Santana* to drift toward the orange life preserver. Bogart cut the diesels; the boat climbed and descended, the whitecaps of the swell slapping against the side.

He rushed to starboard and threw a heaving line to Corliss, who looped it around the preserver and signaled for Bogart to pull him in. It was a taxing effort to haul Corliss to the gunwale, and he felt an uneasiness about Dalt's whereabouts.

A desperate, clawing hand appeared under the lifelines and Bogart grasped it. He pulled Corliss upward, bringing the upper half of his torso onto the deck. Bogart found himself staring directly into his face, and he saw that Corliss was still clutching the belaying pin.

Corliss made a concentrated effort to pull himself further onto the deck, using Bogart as leverage. Corliss's face twisted in hatred was the last thing Bogart saw before he heard the first shot.

And the second.

And the third.

The bullets slapped savagely against Corliss, forming red blossoms that were neatly aligned across his chest. Corliss became a dead weight which slid back into the water, his eyes now lifeless. His head immediately sank beneath the waves and the floating strands of blond hair were the last things Bogart saw before the body sank out of sight.

FORTY-FOUR

Bogart wiped spatters of blood from his hands onto the deck. The boat lurched suddenly, as if in protest. The idling engine sounded erratic and the below-deck shudders reminded Bogart of the epileptic convulsions of a child.

He turned.

Dalt Brennan stood behind him, an M-1 rifle in his hands. Bogart took the smoking weapon and led Dalt to the cockpit. "You should've left Corliss to the cops, Dalt. We might have been able to straighten all this out. Now . . ." Bogart's voice had a disembodied timbre.

He leaned against the wheel, trying to shut off what he had just seen from his brain. Unconsciously, he allowed the *Santana* to drift to a southeasterly heading. The climbing wind would normally have cleared his head, but now it succeeded only in chilling him. He wiped more blood from his nose. His hands were shaking and he pulled the duffel coat tighter around himself. Almost seven-thirty. He felt he had recovered enough to man the helm again when he heard a welcome sound.

"Ahoy!"

The voice came from starboard. Not more than fifty yards away, drifting in the swell, was a hundred-and-twenty-foot schooner named *Zaca*. She was flying a house flag adorned with a crowing rooster.

It was Errol Flynn's subtle way of symbolically displaying his cocksmanship.

Flynn was astride the magnificent teakwood deck, wearing crimson bathing trunks and toasting Bogart with his martini glass. The other hand encircled the slender waist of a statuesque, bosomy blond in a two-piece bikini.

"You were ghosting, old man; I thought something might be wrong. It's unlike you not to hoist the sails. You're welcome to come aboard for libation and . . . well, whatever," offered Flynn.

Bogart shook his head and cupped his hands. "My radio's busted. Put a call in to the Coast Guard. Have them notify Inspector Fitzgerald of the LAPD that the bomb is set for nine forty-five. Got that?"

Flynn looked blankly at Bogart, then relayed the message to someone below deck.

Bogart continued to shout against the rising wind. "I'm short-handed here. You might give me some help back to port."

"Always obliged to assist a fellow seaman." Flynn gave his half-finished martini to the blond. "Keep this chilled until I get back, darling."

To the sound of creaking oarlocks and the splashing of oars, Flynn crossed the fifty yards alone in a din-ghy. He allowed the dinghy to drift and bump rudely against the *Santana*. Bogart secured the painter, then helped Flynn onto deck.

Flynn glanced at the M-1 Bogart still carried. "I say, sport, were you doing some shooting awhile ago? We heard shots."

"We were busting one very special clay pigeon," said Bogart. "You take the helm and get us back to Newport as quick as you can."

"Sounds like life or death, old sport."

Urgently, without further questions, Flynn signaled

the *Zaca* to follow and the two craft, remaining a hundred yards apart with running lights aglow, began the return voyage.

Still carrying the M-1, Bogart burst into the cabin. Dalt's features were flushed with anger as he rummaged mindlessly through a drawer of nautical charts. He ripped apart the Catalina Straits and flung the shreds to the deck. Bogart slumped into a lower berth and stared blankly at the pieces of paper fluttering around Dalt's boots. Dalt was suddenly aware of Bogart's sullen presence and he paused to study the somber, ashen face.

"Look," said Bogart in a near-whisper, his mind groping for words, "I've been trying to keep your neck out of a noose for the past four days. That's why I came after you in Shrine. I . . . you know, Dalt, I feel partially responsible for this mess."

"Everyone's sorry. *After* it's too late."

"It's not too late, Dalt. I've found the evidence that proves Tayne set you up. I've got the memos that outline, step by step, how he forced you out of *Embarkation Point*. It wasn't an industry against you, Dalt. It was *one* man."

"Don't give me that one-man theory. Tayne was using me? *I was using him!* He gave me the freedom I needed. He gave me the direction. And I accepted it all. You want to know why? Because *I* really wanted to do it. Do you really think *he* talked me into it?"

"So *you* used Tayne?" echoed Bogart. "What about your brother Lloyd? Is his murder something you can simply shrug off? And what about Martha Pearce?"

"I loved her. She was like a mother to me. Saints and Sinners was like going home again."

"Corliss killed her too. Is that something you can forget?"

Dalt's face reddened. He crumpled up another nautical chart and threw it down.

"Come back with me to Shrine, Dalt. I'll tell Fitzgerald the whole story. All you have to do is show us where the explosives are—"

"I warned you to stay away from Shrine, Humph. You're the *one* person I don't want there."

"Stop all this now and Quinn Tayne and Corliss will take the rap for Johnny Hawks, Lloyd and the others."

"Johnny Hawks?" Dalt's head popped up and for a moment he ignored the litter of maps on the desk. "Corliss didn't kill Johnny Hawks." His head popped down again and he continued to rummage without purpose. "Where're the southern California coast maps? We've got to plot a new course."

Bogart stared dumbfoundedly at the Garand still in his hands.

Corliss didn't kill Johnny Hawks.

He felt the blood rushing to his head; the Garand became a dead weight.

"Goddamn it," blurted Bogart, crossing the distance to Dalt in two giant strides, *"you shot Johnny!"*

A look of indifference cemented itself on Dalt's face.

Smoothly, Bogart elevated the M-1 barrel and pressed it against Dalt's jugular vein. As the rage stormed within him, he felt a sense of unreality, of detachment, as though he were watching all this unfold on a movie screen. He applied pressure to the Garand, feeling it bite deeper into Dalt's throat. He told himself repeatedly that he was Humphrey Bogart, but he remained a stranger to himself, ravaged by dark urges unleashed by his blinding hatred.

And a desire to kill.

Tears pushed from the lower corners of his eyes. He

took deep gulps of air, hearing alien sounds in his dry throat.

Dalt's mouth became slack and he jerked his head with a short, nervous snap. "Sweet Jesus, you're crying, Humph."

Bogart's rage was replaced by a feeling of emptiness. Inch by inch, he lowered the M-1 rifle away from Dalt's throat. He flung the weapon onto the bunk, rubbing his palms on his pants to cleanse them.

Neither spoke. For Bogart, there was nothing to say. There would never be anything to say again.

Carrying the M-1, Bogart climbed onto the deck, startled to find it completely dark except for the lights of the coastline. It was 8:15 sharp. One hour and thirty minutes until . . . he calculated they were still about twenty minutes from the *Santana's* berth in Newport Beach. From there it was a good hour's drive to Shrine. Steady, hard driving. That left him fifteen minutes—at the most—to find the explosives.

Flynn, sipping liberally from Bogart's Scotch reserves, agreed to dock the *Santana*, and at 8:23 the yawl slid against the jetty. Bogart returned to the cabin for Brennan. He had one ploy remaining: Take Brennan to Shrine with him. Once exposed to the danger of the blast, he just might crack.

The cabin was empty; the last of the nautical charts had been twisted and torn into confetti.

Bogart was beginning a hurried search of the boat when he realized she was sliding into the berth. He ran to the cockpit to see Dalt leaping to the pier even before Flynn had secured the first tie line.

Dalt leaped into the cab of a battered Dodge pickup as Bogart jumped to the dock. Bogart cursed himself. In his rage he had forgotten to remove any items from Dalt's pockets. Such as keys.

He fumbled in his own pocket for the key to the coupe as Dalt sped out of the parking lot, tires squealing as he swung onto Balboa Road.

Bogart dropped the keys in his haste and fell to his knees in the darkness to recover them. By the time he found them, jerked the door open and had the engine racing, he couldn't even see the taillights of the pickup.

FORTY-FIVE

". . . as we send our motion pictures out from Hollywood to the ends of the earth, the world on film also comes to us. Even though our hearts are physical like all other human hearts throughout the world, ours have added chemicals like cellulose acetate and silver and gelatine, all mixed up in them. On this our twentieth anniversary, we are getting out our special kind of family album . . . which will take us back to 1928. The pictures will make us smile, and bring tears to our eyes, and perhaps make us sigh a little at the memories stirred here tonight."

It was the corniest introduction to an Oscar show Bogart had yet heard, but the voice of Jean Hersholt rang with sincerity. Out there in Middle America, Bogart knew, there were people with smiles on their faces and tears in their eyes. And exhibitors drooling at the mouth.

It was the night of the Oscar. Fanfare and applause echoed through Shrine with exuberance, and that sound came over Bogart's car radio with spine-tingling clarity. Despite himself he felt a lump in his throat and realized he too was a sucker for Hollywood sentimentality.

The Coast Highway was a blur on Bogart's left as he maintained a constant seventy miles an hour, slowing only at Long Beach to maneuver perilously in front of slow-moving oil trucks onto Pico Boulevard. He slammed the accelerator and drove madly to the intersection that would put him onto the Harbor Parkway. Oncoming traffic was light for Saturday night, but the cars in his lane were getting more numerous the closer he got to Los Angeles.

One eye shot frequently to the mirror in search of squad cars; his luck held and his foot stayed on the gas pedal.

The Twentieth Annual Academy Award Presentations were underway.

A "Family Album" film was presented, with organ music by Wesley Tourtellotte and commentary by Carey Wilson, which sank into maudlin sentimentality as he described all the great actors and actresses who were now gone.

But Bogart was hardly listening. Automobiles conspired to block his way, making him pound the brakes and curse as he threaded tortuously from lane to lane. David Niven, one of Bogart's sailing companions, read the nominees for Best Original Screenplay. *A Cage of Nightingales . . . It Happened on Fifth Avenue . . . Kiss of Death . . .*

Bogart's mind was locked on another original story. And he was replaying it over and over in his mind.

Hollywood Armageddon.

Somewhere in its pages, he knew, was a dormant clue to what Dalt had meant by "in the heart of everything." Had Dalt meant in the exact center of the stage?

" . . . *And the winner is Valentine Davies for* Miracle on 34th Street."

Or had Dalt meant in the exact center of the auditorium itself?

"These original screenplay writers have a special gift; they must think two ways against the middle . . . they write on their typewriters but their minds must dwell scene by scene on some distant screen— and it's a long way from page one to the preview . . ."

Dalt had dwelt on his ideas . . . and now they were about to have their preview. Was it possible the explosives were rigged under the seats smack in the middle of Shrine? Under Harry Cohn's seat, perhaps?

"*Sidney Sheldon for* The Bachelor and the Bobby-soxer . . . *Abraham Polonsky for* Body and Soul . . . *Ruth Gordon and Garson Kanin for* A Double Life . . . *Charles Chaplin for* Monsieur Verdoux . . ."

Someone had once said that Harry Cohn's ass was wired to the rest of the world. Maybe his ass was wired to a stick of dynamite.

". . . *and the winner is . . . Sidney Sheldon, for* The Bachelor and the Bobbysoxer."

Bogart maneuvered briskly between a Hudson and some kids in a Model A. All that fine material that talented men had banged their brains out to get on paper, and someone got it for a piece of crap called *The Bachelor and the Bobbysoxer.*

They were wrong. Best Original Screenplay: *Hollywood Armageddon.*

His thoughts were fixed on Dalt Brennan as the radio droned meaninglessly. Larry Parks was talking about special-effects artists, and then about music. Original scores. Alfred Newman for *Captain from Castile* and Max Steiner for *Life with Father.* He perked up when the name Miklos Rosza burst over the radio. Good old Miklos Rosza had won for *A Double Life.* That made up for the academy not honoring him in 1943 for his great *Sahara* score.

And then pleasant, benevolent Donald Crisp chattered away about best supporting actresses: "*Perhaps the word supporting is well chosen, for it is the support of the actor to the star that inspires the great performance.*" He read the names like the honor roll of a royal blood line: Ethel Barrymore, Gloria Grahame, Celeste Holm, Marjorie Main, Ann Revere.

It was prattle to Bogart, for his mind was again mentally flipping the pages of *Hollywood Armageddon.*

He never even heard Celeste Holm accept her Oscar for her role in *Gentleman's Agreement.*

Whatever Bogart was searching for remained hidden, imprisoned among the mass of typewritten sheets. The radio—and the onrush of headlights—brought him back to the reality of Harbor Parkway.

Bogart sped around a slow-moving Pontiac, narrowly avoided a collision with a Chrysler. The Pontiac honked irritably at the Cadillac, but Bogart ignored the reprimand and maintained seventy miles an hour. He crushed a half-smoked cigarette in the ashtray and listened with indifference as Elia Kazan was named Best Director for *Gentleman's Agreement.*

Then Olivia DeHavilland's smooth, sophisticated voice was speaking of "old and new friends" in preparation for presenting the Best Actor award.

The Kaiser sedan ahead of him moved at a snail's pace. Oncoming traffic prevented Bogart from pulling around. He beeped his horn repeatedly, jabbed at his brakes to slow the Cadillac, but the Kaiser's driver could not be intimidated; he refused to pull over or increase speed.

It was almost nine-thirty.

Bogart hit the horn again and stayed on it, cursing through the open window.

Olivia DeHavilland had just named Ronald Colman, John Garfield, Gregory Peck, William Powell and Michael Redgrave as the nominees and was tearing open the Price-Waterhouse envelope when Bogart saw the USC campus on his left.

He maneuvered to the off lane and turned, cutting in front of a block of oncoming cars. He took the corner at Figueroa at high speed, the coupe leaning precariously on two wheels.

"And the winner is . . . Ronald Colman for A Double Life."

Shrine was now less than a minute away.

Life and time were running out . . .

FORTY-SIX

Bogart spilled out of the Cadillac while it was still lurching. The main entrance to Shrine Auditorium was aswarm with movie fans and there were three bleachers, flooded by spotlights, which contained another mass of curious autograph-seekers. As he began to elbow his way through, Bogart estimated that there were two thousand spectators between him and the door.

Common sense told him he should explain his problem to the security police, but that would take time. It was now 9:31. Bogart tucked his head tightly against his shoulder, dropped his face into low-flung shadows and merged with the anonymous masses.

He was congratulating himself on his nonidentity when a plump, middle-aged woman in a sickly green dress stuck her nose against his and shrieked his name. He froze in a spotlight of recognition, then plunged recklessly into the sea of torsos.

The wall he collided against was impenetrable. In unison everyone surged toward him. In seconds he was encircled and imprisoned and then physically attacked, not with malice but with love.

Hands tugged at his coat; fingers pawed at his legs; a thumb jabbed into his ear. The smell of sour perspiration mixed with the hot breath of his adulators. Hands sought to stroke his face, lips yearned to kiss him, fingers reached out gropingly to touch some part of his anatomy. He shoved in self-defense but felt smothered and suffocated by the noxious odor of so many bodies. More fingers pressed against his groin and thighs and his buttocks and his shoulders and his face and he thought he was going to be sick.

Nine thirty-three.

Then he heard the sound of whistles and the security police were pressing the crowd-turned-mob away from Bogart and clearing a path for him to the main entrance.

He literally ran inside.

" . . . *too little is known of their artistry, those masters of lighting who use broads, inkies, babies, gobos and cutters, scrims and reflectors to put the beauty on film for all to see. Nominated for the best achievement in cinematography in black-and-white films . . .*" The voice of Dick Powell echoed through the building over a central loudspeaker system.

Fitzgerald was waiting in the foyer, near Vomitory B, nervously smoking his pipe and just as nervously pacing the vastness of the lobby. Cohn was pacing with him, step for step, turn for turn. Lined up along the refreshment counter were members of the special LAPD bomb squad, equipped with metal detecting equipment and wearing bulletproof flak vests covered by canvas that made them resemble deep-sea divers marooned on land.

Cohn saw Bogart and whirled, the cigar cloud whirling with him. "Jesus Christ, where the hell've you been, Bogart? You scared the living shit out of everyone with that goddamn Coast Guard message. Just what the hell is happening?"

Fitzgerald was brimming with questions but he saw Bogart's strained face. "Get on with it, Mr. Bogart. It's your show now."

"We've got no time," voiced Bogart loudly over the din of applause that floated sonorously from the auditorium. "There're at least two explosives set to go at nine forty-five sharp."

"We know that, goddamn it, Bogart," snapped Cohn. "But where?"

"I'd have radioed if I knew where. All Dalt said was 'in the heart of everything.'"

"I'm sick and tired of your goddamn riddles and games, Bogart."

"Heart of everything," repeated Fitzgerald, rubbing the fresh stubble of beard on his chin. "How vague can it be?"

". . . *and the winner is* . . . Great Expectations, *Guy Green, J. Arthur Rank* . . ."

"All right," Fitzgerald said to Bogart, "you and I'll have a look in the auditorium."

"Why not pick pansies in the garden," barked Cohn incredulously. "You oughta get that bomb squad of yours moving, Fitzgerald."

"And trigger a panic? That's exactly what these boys would do the instant they stepped into that auditorium. The squad stands fast until I say otherwise."

"While you two're piddling around," roared Cohn, "I'm having a talk with Hersholt. That mealy-mouthed sonofabitch better listen to me if he wants my support for any more of this goddamn Oscar crap." Cohn stormed for Vomitory C. Fitzgerald chose B.

"The heart . . ." he muttered to himself, leading the way. "*Heart* of what?"

Once again Bogart was overwhelmed by the enormity of the auditorium. The stage was a splash of Technicolor and his eyes swept over it. Searched it.

Fredric March was being introduced by the evening's co-hosts, Dick Powell and Agnes Moorehead. Their voices buzzed on, but all Bogart was aware of was the stage.

There was the familiar replica of a multitiered birthday cake, with Oscars embedded into it like candles; a movie screen for the film excerpts; and the two six-foot-high Oscars (made of plaster of Paris and painted gold) on each side of the stage.

Fredric March, resplendent in tuxedo, was bathed in a spotlight as he prattled on about the nominees for the Best Actress award. As occasional bursts of applause swept the auditorium, Bogart shifted his gaze to the main floor.

He distinguished Darryl Zanuck sitting eagerly in a haze of cigar smoke: he could make out the head of Celeste Holm adorned by pink carnations fastened to a black velvet ribbon. There was a special kind of rotundity only ten rows down which he knew to be Peter Lorre, and he saw the unmistakable, lovable girth of Sydney Greenstreet. Further off, identities blurred, and he was looking at an ocean of dazzling jewels and flashy, stylish clothing.

Black lace with white ermine; violet satin with chinchilla cape; pale-blue angel cloth gowns with rhinestones and pearls; ankle length ballerina skirts; flame-colored taffeta; tight bodices and low-cut bodices.

Fitzgerald moved along the center aisle as unobtrusively as possible, searching the floor of each row.

"If you note a special glow on his metallic hide," March was saying, pointing to one of the six-foot Oscar replicas, *"it's because his opportunity to play Romeo to some lovely Juliet is coming up right now. Isn't it, Oscar?"*

A greatly amplified voice reverberated from some hidden echo chamber. *"Yes."*

The audience didn't know whether to laugh or snort derisively. March, meanwhile, was reacting to the echoing voice as though startled, but it would never win him an Academy Award, Bogart decided.

"*Your Juliet will be either Joan Crawford for* Possessed, *Susan Hayward for* Smash-Up—Story of a Woman, *Dorothy McGuire for* Gentleman's Agreement, *Rosalind Russell for* Mourning Becomes Electra, *or Loretta Young for* The Farmer's Daughter."

As March tore open the envelope handed to him by Warde Ogden, the Price-Waterhouse representative, Bogart observed that Rosalind Russell, who was considered the most likely to win, was half out of her seat. He saw Susan Hayward nervously fidgeting. She was wearing the tiered white lace dress cut dangerously low and touched off by the exuberant Geoffrey Carroll hairstyling.

"*The winner is . . . Loretta Young.*"

A gasp sounded from the audience. Rosalind fell back into her seat, crushed by steamrollers. Just as stunned, Loretta, the "dark horse," came out of her saddle, only feet from where Bogart stood. She hurried past him, stumbling on her full-length green taffeta gown; the diamond necklace bobbed rhythmically on her throat.

He wandered along the aisle, studying faces as he went. Lilli Palmer in white lace strapless gown, flanked by Rex Harrison; Claude Jarman, Jr., in urgent need of a haircut; Marjorie Main, Richard Widmark, Dinah Shore and George Montgomery; Cornel Wilde; Mary Pickford and Buddy Rogers; the Zanucks; Joan Crawford, Ethel Barrymore, Edmund Gwenn, John Garfield.

Bogart paused at Lorre's row and hissed. Lorre was too engrossed in the stage activities to hear. Walter Pidgeon was in the outer seat and he gave Bogart a peculiar look.

"Hey, Doc," said Bogart; he had intended only to whisper, but it came out a shout that was heard to the far end of the aisle. Mrs. Lorre leered at Bogart as Lorre bounded up and, like a faithful hound, followed Bogart back up the aisle.

"Where have you been all day? I tried to reach you everywhere. Why do you torment me this way? You ask me to help and then at the eleventh hour you desert me in darkness. You know how I despise darkness."

"Welcome to the age of enlightenment," said Bogart. "There're at least two bombs planted in this auditorium."

"Where?"

Bogart shrugged. "We're got only six minutes, Doc."

Lorre gulped. "Not enough time to empty the auditorium. What do you propose?"

"A lot of prayer. . . . Duck to the other side of the aisle and get Fitzgerald over here."

The house lights dimmed again; it was time for the Best Picture of the Year award—the final presentation of the evening.

Oscar's almost over, thought Bogart. Yeah, really over.

"*. . . we want to pay tribute to the thousands who never win an award,*" Fredric March was saying. "*. . . they are the extras . . . among them are stars of yesterday . . .*"

As Bogart waited for Fitzgerald, he again scrutinized the surface of the stage. He tried to absorb every detail, sweeping his eyes across every object, big or small.

Hollywood Armageddon.

He was mentally flipping through its pages again. Close-up. Tight shot. The Academy Award. The

statuette bursts into flames and the screen dissolves to
blackness. Golden statuette. Black statuette. Hatred,
revenge, holocaust, fire.

Oscar equals death.

Something new obtruded on Bogart's thoughts.
What he had told Morgan when they broke into the
warehouse: "An expressionless golden boy with a
heart of zinc and a body to match. . . ."

Heart of zinc.

*"The award we are about to give is a tribute to each
and every one of Hollywood's extras—because the Best
Picture of this or any year could never be made without their special contributions . . ."*

Heart . . . was that the heart Dalt had been referring to? Had he meant that in a literal, not a figura-
tive, sense?

Bogart's eyes again swept the stage. His attention
riveted on the six-foot-tall Oscar replicas.

Beneath that painted gold was a heart.

The explosive?

Had Dalt remained faithful to his screenplay by rigging the giant versions of Oscar?

The house went completely dark as a film clip of
Gregory Peck in *Gentleman's Agreement* flickered on
the screen. Peck was standing at the desk of an exclusive hotel, asking the clerk if the hotel was "restricted." The manager hedged, unsure of how to handle such a delicate situation.

How to explain to Fitzgerald? No time to explain.
Just get those Oscars off the stage!

Then the inspector and Lorre were at his side and
he was pointing at the replicas. "The bombs are
in those giant statues," he said in a near-whisper.

"Impossible," blurted Fitzgerald. "We checked those
replicas thoroughly yesterday."

"Brennan hid overnight in the auditorium and planted the things *this morning.*"

"Jesus!" Fitzgerald turned and started instantly for the nearest vomitory. "I'm getting the bomb squad."

The auditorium darkened for a clip from *The Bishop's Wife,* with David Niven and Cary Grant.

"Just casually stroll down the aisle with me, but don't take your time," ordered Bogart, pulling Lorre with him.

They reached the lip of the orchestra pit housing conductor Ray Heindorf and his seventy-five musicians just as an excerpt from David Lean's *Great Expectations* flashed onto the screen. Bogart and Lorre mounted the stairs and ducked behind the side curtains. At an acute angle, Bogart could see a scene of Pip the English youth scurrying across a windswept graveyard. A bony hand reached out to clutch the runaway lad.

And Bogart felt bony fingers on his shoulder and he turned to stare blankly into the cheerful face of Agnes Moorehead. "Bogie, darling, whatever are you doing backstage? You really should be wearing a tie and jacket instead of those awful sea clothes, but I suppose nothing is sacred anymore, is it? And Peter, dear, what a surprise. Are you tonight's gruesome twosome, or do I have a wrong number?"

"Terrific for an academy horror act," blurted Dick Powell, who dissolved out of the backstage shadows. "But I wish they'd told us you had an act. You're not scheduled on the program. I—" Powell's mouth sagged noticeably when Bogart rushed past him.

It was Edmund Gwenn who now filled the screen, dressed as a department store Santa Claus in a clip from *Miracle on 34th Street.* Pointing to the Oscar replica on the far side of the stage, Bogart told Lorre, "Just grab that thing and jackass it off the stage."

Before Lorre could protest, Bogart shoved him through the curtain and blindly followed. The darkness was sudden and Bogart stumbled, frantically trying to remember the position of the replica. Reflected light from the movie screen guided him to the Oscar. Without hesitating he threw his arms around the replica and rushed behind the curtain just as he heard Gwenn utter, "Has Santa got a surprise for you."

Has Dalt Brennan got a surprise for you!

Roddy McDowall was poking his head from behind a counterweight and watching curiously as Bogart emerged backstage. Mike Romanoff was stationed at a table laden with champagne bottles, polishing crystal glasses, when he saw Bogart and crossed to join him. "I say, you didn't come back last night after meeting Grasselli. You didn't call, so I assumed all our fears about the academy were . . ." He studied the replica in Bogart's arms, saw the fear on Bogart's face and turned white. "That isn't . . . ?"

Bogart nodded just as Fitzgerald and the bomb squad, moving like men underwater, arrived. The squad leader, a young man with curly blond hair and a splash of freckles across his cheeks and nose, took the replica from Bogart.

Powell and Moorehead pressed in for a closer look, sensing a drama about to unfold. "Please, stay back as far as possible," requested Fitzgerald. "Give Sergeant Phillips all the room he needs."

Phillips laid the replica on the floor and probed its sides for telltale seams or ridges. A squad member with a metal-detecting device nodded that he was getting a reading. The squad leader swallowed. "The only way in," Phillips said with the casualness of a dentist discovering a cavity, "is through the bottom." Bogart watched in horrified fascination as a protective layer of felt was peeled from the bottom. Romanoff, his face yet a shade whiter, still stood next to Bogart, his weight pressed against Bogart's shoulder. Fitzgerald lit his pipe with the slow assuredness of a man who had all the time in the world.

Phillips moved his hands inside the Oscar, paused, then moved slowly upward, withdrawing a packet of explosive material.

Thank God . . . 9:42 . . . three minutes to disarm . . . Bogart whirled in confusion. *Lorre* . . .

There was a prolonged silence on the other side of the curtain, as though the ceremonies had come to a standstill.

Where the hell was Lorre with the second Oscar replica?

FORTY-SEVEN

Rudely bathed in the beam of an accusing spotlight, Lorre was frozen in the center of the stage, clutching the second replica to his breast, his face full of guilt and embarrassment. The audience's tittering turned to guffaws and the guffaws to belly laughs and soon the entire gallery was howling.

Fredric March had a reputation for ad libbing, and that talent, Bogart was pleased to see, sprang into evidence. "*At this time the academy would like to make a special presentation to Mr. Peter Lorre, for his many sinister contributions to motion pictures. And the academy has further decided to honor Mr. Lorre with an Oscar the size of his own screen greatness.*"

The subsequent laughter and applause were overwhelming. Lorre, weakly managing a lampoon of a smile, rushed from the stage.

Lorre gladly relegated his Oscar to a junior member of the bomb squad and leaned heavily against Bogart's shoulder. "You have subjected me to the ultimate indignity," he scolded Bogart. Then his eyes widened from ovals to circles as he watched the next step in the disarming process.

Phillips, hunched over the first replica, was shaking his head. The packet he had removed carried neither the detonator nor the clock. An assistant pointed to the stopwatch slung on a lanyard around his neck. Phillips, a soft sheen of perspiration forming on his forehead, acknowledged the seconds ticking away. He returned to the cavity, his arm disappearing up to the elbow.

"Rest assured," Fitzgerald told Bogart and Lorre, "Phillips has had extensive training disarming bombs in Europe. As you can see for yourself, he hasn't made a mistake yet."

Yet . . .

The team working on Lorre's Oscar quickly duplicated the squad leader's actions step and step, and soon was ready to imitate his next movement.

The auditorium darkened suddenly. My God, thought Bogart, another film clip.

"Jesus," whispered Phillips, freezing in place, not daring to move his fingers. "I need light." Half a dozen hands fumbled in the darkness, and almost simultaneously as many lights snapped on and drenched the replica in a glaring sea of light. Strangely, while they should have been running for their lives, Powell, Moorehead and the others were locked into position, afraid to move.

Then Bogart heard the persuasive sound-track voice of Robert Young. He remembered the scene from *Crossfire:* Yeah, this was the bit about racial prejudice. There was talk about Monte the killer and how he was tainted by hate. His prejudice was like a gun. If he carried it, it might go off. And kill someone.

They were all going to be killed, thought Bogart, tensing with rage. Why were the disarmers working so damn slowly? Fitzgerald sensed Bogart's fear and edged toward him. "Phillips is searching for the timing device. Once that's cut, the exposive'll be deactivated. No sense messing with anything else."

The squad leader continued to probe deftly, though with agonizing slowness.

It was 9:44. One minute to go.

"Mr. Bogart!" A familiar accented voice blasted

through the semidarkness. Phillips jumped slightly, then resumed his probe.

Bogart didn't have to turn to know that it was Jean Hersholt. "I really must demand an apology from you and Mr. Lorre for these outrages. I—" His voice trailed off as the young squad leader removed a packet of colored wires from the stomach of the Oscar. A clock and a dry-cell battery dangled from the wires. Hersholt lapsed into silent embarrassment and shock. Fitzgerald placed a reassuring hand on Hersholt's shoulder.

Phillips hovered above the packet with a pair of pliers. He traced the wires back and forth under the approving eyes of his assistants. The men crouching over the second replica had also found the corresponding packet and were meticulously imitating the squad leader's motions.

Snip!

At the same instant the pliers bit through one of the wires, the house lights were restored. Another *snip* and the packet was separated from the battery and clock. Neutralized.

Fifteen seconds before 9:45 . . .

Gently Phillips, his brow covered with streams of perspiration, pulled out the now useless detonator. "Okay," he said to the second team leader, "earn your money."

". . . *and there you have it, ladies and gentlemen, the five contenders for the Best Picture of the Year.*"

Closing his ears to the applause and the anticipatory murmur that followed, the second team leader duplicated the procedures.

Snip!

Bogart swallowed and squeezed his eyes closed.

Snip!

He was afraid to look at his watch because he knew the time had to be up. The only thing he heard was Fitzgerald's soothing voice. "You can relax, Mr. Bogart. It would take a brutal impact to set those charges off now."

Bogart opened his eyes and felt alive and human again.

"May I have the envelope, please . . . ?"

Phillips hefted the packet under Fitzgerald's nose, gave Bogart a wink and picked carefully at the oblong side of the explosive until he had peeled back a layer of material laid over a cone-shaped cavity. He turned it upside down. Hundreds of little iron pellets fell out and rolled across the stage. They bounced and rattled against Bogart's feet and tapped playfully at Hersholt's shoes.

"And the winner is . . . Gentleman's Agreement. Twentieth-Century Fox. And accepting the award is producer Darryl F. Zanuck."

"If those things had exploded . . ." began Hersholt, but he was incapable of finishing his thought.

"Hey, easy," soothed Phillips, clutching Hersholt's arm. Bogart escorted the academy president to a nearby wooden chair. Loretta Young appeared immediately with a cup of water. "What you need, Jean," said Romanoff, "is a touch of champagne."

The applause died away finally. The booming voice of Darryl Zanuck reverberated through the auditorium. *"I feel thankful we won this year, as* Gentleman's Agreement *deserved it. This makes up for the shortsightedness of academy members when my film* Wilson *didn't win Best Picture Award the year it was nominated."*

Applause, but reserved. Even in Hollywood too much show of ego could be a turnoff.

Bogart should have been sighing with relief, or shaking the hand of the squad leader, or patting Fitzgerald on the back or himself on the back or just passing out—God knows, he was tired enough—but instead there was just one thought on his mind: The conservatives weren't going to like *Gentleman's Agreement* copping the big award.

He started to laugh at the irony of it all, and finally had to shove a handkerchief into his mouth to keep his laughter from interrupting Fredric March's closing remarks.

And then the Twentieth Annual Oscar show was finished.

And Bogart kept on laughing.

FORTY-EIGHT

Shrine emptied swiftly. The losers scuttled away to sulk or lick their wounds or drown their disappointment in intemperate party-going. The recipients triumphantly gathered backstage for a brief session with photographers and members of the Hollywood press corps.

Bogart remained on the periphery, shaking hands with several of the winners and bringing Lorre up to date. Romanoff personally poured the champagne and suggested to each Oscar holder individually that he or she forsake the Mocambo party and drop into his nitery instead.

Soon there was only the cleanup crew and lingering members of the LAPD bomb squad, which tenderly saw to the removal of the unexploded components. As Romanoff supervised the removal of the unopened champagne, Bogart informed him of everything that had happened.

"I suspect," said Romanoff, "that you're becoming as fine a storyteller as myself, and I suspect that the caper is wrapped."

"*Caper?*" repeated Lorre, having regained his composure after several glasses of Romanoff's champagne. "Are you finally condescending to the jargon of a sleazy private detective, good prince?"

"The caper," said Fitzgerald softly, pausing to puff on his pipe, "is not quite finished. There's still Mr. Quinn Tayne and his chauffeur. I've put in a call and they should be receiving official visitors shortly."

Bogart was so startled he couldn't speak for a few

seconds. "You knew it was Tayne and Valentine Corliss?"

Fitzgerald told him he had only put it together that afternoon.

Bogart launched into a brief description of his visit to Tayne's home, then described the voyage on the *Santana* and the death of Valentine Corliss.

"Where's Dalt now?" asked Fitzgerald.

Bogart shrugged. "He knows about Lloyd. He might have gone after Tayne."

"About your friend Dalt . . ." said Fitzgerald, his voice hesitating.

"If you're going to tell me he killed Johnny Hawks, I've already figured it out."

"Dalt shot Johnny?" Lorre almost choked on his own words. "I don't think I'm going to feel well for a while."

"Ballistics determined it was an M-1 rifle that killed Johnny," said Fitzgerald. "And Geoffrey Carroll, during one of our talks, distinctly remembered Dalt having an M-1 at the house. Then I went back to Topanga Beach, where Dalt used to practice at an old, deserted rifle range. It took considerable digging to find some old .30-caliber slugs, but a few of them finally matched up with the slugs we found in Johnny."

"What exactly put you onto Tayne?" asked Bogart.

"When we investigated the records at Saints and Sinners. Seems that a film corporation was funding Martha Pearce. On a silent-partner basis. Tayne was president of the board, and Paul Fabrini was the secretary."

"Did you find that Fabrini was—"

"Yes, the brother of Tayne's late wife."

"I shall die," said Lorre, "if I do not immediately

join my long-suffering wife who is awaiting me in the lobby."

"You've become nothing more than a bleeding domestic," said Romanoff accusingly.

"I have no intention of remaining in suburbia. I shall dump her off in the driveway and meet you in less than an hour." Lorre shook hands with Fitzgerald and scampered away.

Fitzgerald pocketed his pipe. His eyes twinkled and his manner took on an elfin quality. "There's one thing I'd like to be asking you, Mr. Bogart. It seems my wife . . . long-suffering in her own way . . . well, I've told her about meeting you and she expressed a little interest in dropping by Warner Brothers."

"A *little* interest, Inspector? Well, I suppose a *little* interest is better than *no* interest. Love to have her. Especially you."

"Me?"

"There's no place on earth more unromantic than a movie studio, Inspector. You should be right at home."

As Bogart started up Vomitory B, he threw his arm around Romanoff and, for the first time in five days, had the urge to whistle.

Romanoff smiled.

It was a fitting exit from Shrine.

Bogart was whistling Max Steiner's theme music from *Treasure of the Sierra Madre.*

FORTY-NINE

Snarling leopards lunged at the night sky, their brass eyes gleaming. The gate to the Tayne estate rocked in the wind, slamming frequently against the stone wall behind it, as Bogart swung onto the oval drive. He parked fifty yards back from the mansion, further progress being impeded by an ambulance and several police cars, their red lights slowly winking in protest.

The brief bursts of red illuminated an old Dodge pickup—the one Dalt had driven so recklessly from Newport Beach.

The door to the coupe was almost yanked from his grasp by a gust of wind as Bogart lumbered out of the car. Hunching his shoulders and pulling the brim of his hat down, he moved against the wind, shivering. It was a bone-marrow cold that whipped at him and set his teeth chattering.

Bogart felt a different kind of coldness when he saw two men emerge from the house, burdened by a white-covered object on the stretcher between them. He watched as the object was loaded into the coroner's wagon. He took out a cigarette, shoved it between his lips, then ground it into the gravel.

A policeman came down the steps, saw Bogart and veered in his direction just as the coroner's wagon passed, its red light flashing.

The cop shone his flashlight into Bogart's face. "Sorry, bud, but I'll have to ask you to leave. This is police business."

"It's okay, officer. I'm Humphrey Bogart. I—"

"Oh, right, Mr. Bogart. Don't worry, it's all right. I saw you at the Saints and Sinners sanitarium the other night."

"What's happened?" asked Bogart, nodding his head toward the ambulance as it wound down the drive.

The cop shook his head. "I ain't been upstairs, Mr. Bogart. All I know is, some of the guys got a call from Inspector Fitzgerald to pick up Mr. Tayne and . . ." he referred to his notebook, ". . . a Valentine Corliss. Only they got here a couple minutes too late. The first guys on the scene swear they heard the shot as they drove up . . . In this wind, I dunno. Apparently two guys had been arguing in the upstairs projection room. One man dead. The other gave himself up. The detectives are up there right now, piecing the whole thing together. If you want, maybe I find out for you the whole deal."

Bogart's eyes dropped to the gravel, to his crushed cigarette.

Dalt dead . . . Tayne in custody? Tayne dead . . . Dalt in custody? Either way it didn't seem to matter because Dalt was already gone from his life. What the hell difference did it make now?

He turned his glance back to the policeman. "Don't bother," he said calmly, "it doesn't matter. Maybe I'll read about it in the newspapers tomorrow. See you around, friend."

Bogart drove back along the gravel lane, glancing into the rearview mirror to see the mansion's facade still illuminated by the twirling lights. The coupe passed through the wrought-iron gates and again the wind battered at the leopards and they seemed to claw desperately at Bogart, as if to prevent him from leaving.

Then Bogart turned onto the street and the house was only a memory.

FIFTY

"You ever notice, Doc, about people who drink?" asked Bogart, gazing into a half-empty glass of Scotch and soda.

"No," said Lorre.

"They live longer."

"Why?"

"How should I know? They just live longer."

"Thank you for clearing up one of life's mysteries."

"Doc, I don't trust anyone who doesn't drink."

Lorre quickly took a sip of his bourbon.

Bogart watched the milling wall-to-wall crowd, while desperate waiters bulldozed from the booths and tables to the kitchen and back. Table-hoppers corkscrewed and twisted from one packed table to another. The babble of voices hung like a visible layer beneath the haze of nicotine smoke.

Romanoff's was alive and thriving.

Lorre seemed indifferent to the chaos of humanity as a gray stream of smoke trickled through his pendulous lips. "That's right, dear Bogie. Don't trust any of them. That's being smart."

Romanoff slid next to Bogart, noting the number of empty glasses.

Bogart raised a questioning eyebrow at Romanoff's frown. "I've got a reputation to uphold, Prince."

"Have you ever considered giving up drinking?"

"Once," said Bogart, looking up through his V-shaped brows. "It was the worst afternoon of my life."

Lorre snickered as Romanoff leaned in to Bogart.

"Academically speaking, I believe the awards committee owes you a debt of gratitude."

Bogart looked at Romanoff balefully. "Look, Prince, I don't give a damn about the academy. The only reason I'm in this industry is to make enough money to tell any sonofabitch in the world to go to hell."

"Spare us the rest of your cynicism," said Lorre, his eyes watering from an overabundance of smoke. "We've all heard about your Fuck You Fund." He raised his glass and clinked it against Bogart's. "Let us forget the academy and the industry. Here's to the three of us." Romanoff grabbed a Scotch and water from a tray as one of his waiters squeezed by. The three of them clinked glasses.

Bogart lowered his voice conspiratorially. "You know what we do, all of us actors and actresses in all the world? Not just now, but all the way back, to Edmund Keane, hell, clear back to Shakespeare? We act out bedtime stories for the world and we get paid for it."

Lorre half-smiled and placed his cigarette holder between his lips. "There's some truth to that. Not an abundance of truth, but some."

Bogart peered around at the diners and drinkers, elbow to elbow, greeting friends and dodging enemies.

The goldfish bowl of Hollywood.

"A nightclub's a place not to have good manners," said Bogart. "Maybe that's why I go to them."

Jamieson appeared at the table. "M'sieur Romanoff." He pointed discreetly. "Mr. Cohn and a large party are waiting. He insists . . . the best table for his guests."

Romanoff raised his hand. "Mr. Cohn is not the

best producer in town. He'll wait for what is available—"

"Move outta the way, Frenchie," demanded Cohn loudly.

Bogart looked up. "What happened to *you*, Harry? Looks like you ran into a Mugger's Ball."

Cohn's tuxedo was rumpled, the stitching in one shoulder torn and gray padding shredding out. The satin lapels were almost torn off, the French cuffs open and flapping. He snorted disgustedly and fingered a bruised cheek. "I got lost in those damn Catacombs. Took a wrong turn looking for Jean Hersholt. Wandered all over the place. Then I ran into a couple of snot-nosed cops. Jesus, the dumb bastards had never even heard of me. I tried to tell them about Hersholt, about the bombs, but they figured I was the bomber. They roughed me up. One of them don't look so good himself. Goddamn it."

Bogart shrugged while Lorre chuckled almost inaudibly.

Cohn planted his palms down on Bogart's table and leaned in. "Okay, so I got slugged, but you gotta admit I called the tune on the bombs. Admit it. I was fuckin' right, Bogie. If I hadn't got you all steamed up looking for Brennan, Hollywood would be in mass mourning."

Romanoff looked pained. "You can be heard clear across the room, Harry, chap. Can you modulate your tone to the low roar of a DC-6?"

Bogart studied Cohn coolly. "It's what they say about you, Harry. You're all hearts and flowers."

"You don't think I got sentiment? I got sentiment. Remember that little contract player, the one who impersonated the nurse? Well, I'm not throwing her ass out of the studio like I should. I'm giving her a break."

Bogart frowned. "Norma Jean? I bet you're giving her a break."

"I'm giving her a raise. Max Arnow, he figures we gotta change her name, give her a big buildup as a dynamite sex symbol. Bill her as a featured player in a couple of biggies. We got plans for that doll, Bogart. She can't act, but hell, with that body, tits and ass like that, who needs to act. Max has decided to name her Marilyn. Marilyn Monroe. Alliterative as hell. Rolls off the tongue."

"I can see why your mind is on your tongue, Harry. Only save it. You're not touching that girl."

"Who said anything about touching her, for Chrissake."

"Don't bullshit me, Harry. The kind of plans you have for Norma Jean aren't just for the sake of motion picture art. I got hot news for you. You're gonna keep your hands off."

Cohn slowly raised himself to glare at Bogart. "Yeah? What's she to you?"

"Let me put it this way, Harry. You leave Norma Jean alone if you want Santana Productions on the Columbia lot. It's that simple."

"Fucking blackmailer, that's what you are, Bogart."

Bogart studied the inner conflict of lust and greed fighting in Cohn's expression.

"Shit, Bogart, you drive the hardest bargain of any man I know. And I've slugged it out with the best." Finally he relaxed and smiled, a hint of admiration crossing his face. "I want your pictures, Bogart."

"You don't want them. You *need* them," said Bogart.

"Come and see me Monday morning. We'll settle the deal."

Cohn turned abruptly and threaded his way through the crowd to rejoin his guests.

Romanoff chuckled. "Even Cohn cannot take away what you did, Bogie, old fellow. A good thing, a splendid thing."

"Yes," said Lorre. "Very much the sort of thing we do on screen, but all in one piece, not broken up in short takes. Even Cohn must have felt the uniqueness of it."

Bogart looked at his two friends. "You get caught up in something and you keep going. If I had thought about dying, I wouldn't have done it. If you're alive, you're alive. Otherwise to hell with it."

Lorre raised his glass. "Again very true, but most of us don't have the wit to realize it. We are in death, when we are in life."

Bogart refilled his glass. "When I go, Prince, assuming you're still around, I want you to be my chief usher. Think of it as a very exclusive dining establishment. You lead each mourner to his assigned pew, just like you lead them to your goddamn tables. Treat 'em the same snobbish way and seat the important ones in the rear of the chapel. The big studio heads you keep outside with the chauffeurs. Those lizard eyes of yours better watch out for protocol. That's one time I don't want you fouling up the catering."

Bogart finished his Scotch. "Now enough talk about death," he snapped, "and give me another coffin nail."

EPILOGUE

Bogart stood on the second floor of the Knickerbocker Hotel with a parcel and a film can under his arm. D.W. Griffith answered his knock almost immediately; Bogart was pleased to see that the face glaring back into his was relatively sober.

"No, I don't want a drink," said Bogart automatically, "and you don't need one either." He walked to the window and opened it; the fresh air dispelled the noxious odors.

Bogart turned. "I'm returning your print of *Birth of a Nation* and I'm bringing *you* something for a change. Enjoy it."

Curiously, Griffith took the parcel and placed it on a littered table. Slowly, deliberately, he took off the wrapping.

Inside was a film can.

It was labeled *Casablanca*.

Inside the can was a complete 16-millimeter print.

"Where the hell did you steal this?"

"Don't ask," said Bogart. "What's important, it's now yours."

Griffith kept his head turned away from Bogart. "This calls for a celebration," Griffith said finally, crossing to a table covered with gin bottles. Griffith poured himself a stiff one. Bogart sighed and stared idly out the window.

"You oughta go easy, you worthless drunk," said Bogart.

"It's my town," replied Griffith caustically. "If I

wanna drink, I have that right. I'm dying. This whole town is dying."

"You're getting maudlin on me again, Griff. You oughta shut up when you get maudlin."

Griffith drank almost all the gin in his glass in one swallow. "I mean, Bogie, it's *dying*. Sure, it looks prosperous and thriving but there's a cancerous growth beneath the surface, eating away at the foundations, eating away at the people who make it happen. Eventually it's going to consume everything and everyone."

"Sure," returned Bogart, "but it's gonna be reborn again, and not the way you think. This town's got a future because there's always going to be a need for films. How they get made, that's what'll change. Before too many years it won't be the studios controlling this industry—it'll be the independent producers, because they're going to be making cheaper films. And when the Feds get through busting up the monopolistic hold the studios have on theaters, the indies are the boys who're gonna supply most of the product. And Hollywood will prosper like never before. You're looking at a rosy business that's gonna get rosier, Griff."

"At least *you'll* live to see it."

"I'll live to enjoy some of it. A guy like me always has one up on the rest of the world. I'll live as long as I'm supposed to live; then some new faces will take over and they'll forget me after a while. That's the way it should be."

"Everything passes," said Griffith, "sure, but what's recorded on film, that's for eternity."

"Can the crap, Griff," ordered Bogart, walking to the stack of film prints. "If it's okay with you I'm taking *Intolerance*, even if you do think it's a piece of shit." Bogart started for the door, then paused. "See

you next Tuesday, you goddamn rummy." He closed
the door with a slam.

Griffith drifted toward the semiopen window and
closed it, shutting out the street noises. He clutched a
newly opened gin bottle, took a healthy belt straight
from the mouth and turned toward the window.

Through the streaked glass he could see the steep
slopes of Mount Lee and the word HOLLYWOOD on the
hillside, bathed in early morning sunlight.

Griffith raised the bottle when he saw Bogart
climbing into his Cadillac. He blinked away the fuzz
in his eyes, and for the first time in weeks felt a degree of warmth, of closeness.

Hollywood, the dying town, was sprawled beneath
his window, unknowingly consigned to its fate.

He proposed a toast before he took another long,
healthy drink from the bottle.

Here's looking at you, kid.

Dell Bestsellers

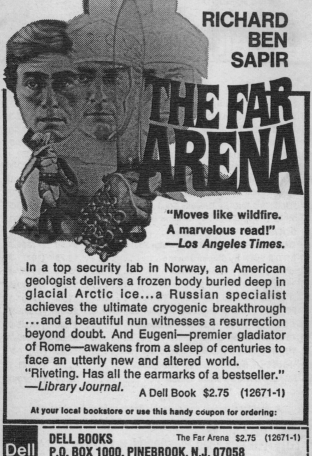